Boudicca

Boudicca

and the Women at War

John Daniels

Copyright © 2001 by John Daniels.

Library of Congress Number: 2001116572
ISBN #:   Softcover   0-7388-6748-9

All rights reserved. No part of this book may be reproduced or transmitted in any form or by any means, electronic or mechanical, including photocopying, recording, or by any information storage and retrieval system, without permission in writing from the copyright owner.

This is a work of fiction. Names, characters, places and incidents either are the product of the author's imagination or are used fictitiously, and any resemblance to any actual persons, living or dead, events, or locales is entirely coincidental.

This book was printed in the United States of America.
To order additional copies of this book, contact:
Xlibris Corporation
1-888-7-XLIBRIS
www.Xlibris.com
Orders@Xlibris.com

Contents

Preface
    Historical context. 13
Chronology 17

PART I
47—50 a.d.

Chapter 1
    Colchester 24
Chapter 2
    Reconciliation 33
Chapter 3
    The Nazarene Army 53
Chapter 4
    Morfudd 58
Chapter 5
    Atak Reports 74
Chapter 6
    Consummation 82
Chapter 7
    Scapula Moves 89
Chapter 8
    Trapped 104
Chapter 9
    Bodin Takes Over 109
Chapter 10

Sabinus Repays a Debt 128
Chapter 11
　　Scapula Reports 130

PART II
50—54 a.d.

Chapter 1
　　The Parisi 136
Chapter 2
　　Caratacus Puts His Finger on It 147
Chapter 3
　　Caratacus Takes a Journey 158
Chapter 4
　　Basil Goes Recruiting 162
Chapter 5
　　Owain in Rome 173
Chapter 6
　　Dedreth and Marius 196
Chapter 7
　　Paul 218
Chapter 8
　　The Twentieth Legion 239
Chapter 9
　　Owain Comes Home 255
Chapter 10
　　Scapula Reports 261
Chapter 11
　　Coilus 264
Chapter 12
　　The Loan 272
Chapter 13
　　Church Business 283
Chapter 14
　　Fidchell and Other Games 294

Chapter 15
 Catus Has a Visitor 304
Chapter 16
 Tetra Has a Visitor 312
Chapter 17
 Atak's Last Visit 322
Chapter 18
 Brennius Fights 341
Chapter 19
 Ingenius Brings News 356

Part III
58—61 A.D.
(Three years later)

Chapter 1
 Owain Corresponds 370
Chapter 2
 Veranius Makes a Proposition 374
Chapter 3
 Arviragus 387
Chapter 4
 Caradawg 403
Chapter 5
 Tutor 409
Chapter 6
 Caratacus Returns 422
Chapter 7
 Prasu Takes a Journey 434
Chapter 8
 Boudicca Takes a Journey 448
Chapter 9
 Prisoners 462
Chapter 10
 The Trigger 473
Chapter 11

    The Rising 487
Chapter 12
    Interlude 497
Chapter 13
    Victoria 503
Chapter 14
    The Swath 517
Chapter 15
    One Church 528
Chapter 16
    Mancetter (Manduessedum:
    Place of Chariots) 538
Chapter 17
    After the Battle 549

Afterword 554
Notes 556
Bibliography 558
Maps 562

Dedicated to Charli

She was very tall, the glance of her eye most fierce; her voice harsh. A great mass of the reddest hair fell down to her hips. Around her neck was a large golden necklace, and she always wore a tunic of many colors over which she fastened a thick cloak with a brooch. Her appearance was terrifying.

Dio Cassius

Preface

Historical context.

Midway through the first century, Rome was absolute master of Europe and the Middle East. Its legions were magnificent machines of destruction against whose walls of shields Rome's victims beat their swords in vain. To overcome his reputation as a nonentity, the newly installed Emperor Claudius needed a quick and glorious victory. During the previous century, Julius Caesar had conquered Gaul (modern France and Belgium) in seven years. Britain was much smaller and inhabited by a disorganized rabble of competing nations, so it should be an easier victim. In 43 a.d., four battle-hardened legions and their auxiliaries crossed the Channel. Forty-four years later, long after the Boudiccan revolt that forms the centerpiece of this book, the Romans were still struggling to establish a defensible northern frontier along the Forth-Clyde line. Anglesey (Mona) did not fall until 78 a.d. Britain (i.e., the two thirds of it that was conquered) was not fully incorporated into the Empire until Hadrian's rule in 120 a.d.

Why should the often-demonstrated and much vaunted military and administrative efficiency of Rome require seventy-seven years to bring two thirds of a small island into its empire? The Celtic Britons were tough, intelligent and stubborn warriors— but then so were the Gauls and many other peoples conquered by Rome. In terms of lasting impact on the character and history of Britain, the subsequent invasions by the Angles, Saxons, Danes and Normans were far more effective. Apart from a few good roads and urban centers, the most lasting byproduct of the Roman occupation was Welsh Christianity.

One suspected cause for what can only be classed as a Roman colonial failure could indeed be laid at Christianity's doorstep. During this mid first century period, the Romans were not the only ones invading other countries. The disciples of Jesus of Nazareth, undergoing a transition from Jews to Nazarenes to Christians, were not yet embroiled in the great priestly controversies that splintered Christianity into hundreds of competing sects and separated it from its roots. Along with their own students, they embarked on missionary journeys that spread like shock waves across Europe, Africa and Asia, healing the sick and preaching the gospel of peace, gaining converts not only among nations governed by Rome but among Romans themselves.

The trail left by Paul and his disciples is clearly visible; that left by other followers of Jesus less so. There is sketchy evidence, supported mostly by a vigorous mythology, of Philip's mission in Gaul, of Zachaeus' domicile in the caves above Rocamadour and of Simon Peter and Joseph of Arimathea's presence in Britain. The Venerable Bede tells us of a robust Celtic Christianity that existed in Britain long before Pope Gregory dispatched Augustine to convert the 'barbarous, fierce and pagan' Britons in 582 a.d. Almost three hundred years before Augustine arrived, Britain's premier saint had been martyred and his name given to the new city, St Albans, that had grown up near the one destroyed by Boudicca. Because of the close familial relations between the Celtic people of Gaul and Britain at the time of the Roman invasion, it is not stretching credibility too far to assume that the spiritual fire spreading throughout Gaul would find ready fuel in Britain. Did the peace-spreading missionaries and the competing religious organizations springing up in their wake adversely affect Roman performance?

At the time this book begins (47 a.d.), the Romans have established a thinly defended frontier stretching roughly from Exeter to Lincoln. Aulus Plautius Silvanus, who led the invasion and served as Britain's first Governor, has just been recalled and Ostorius Scapula has arrived to take his place. Peter and Philip have returned to their own missions and left primitive British Christianity in the hands of Joseph of Arimathea and his disciples, prominent among whom is Elsa, the loved (but mostly unheeded) friend of Boudicca. Alarmed by the sudden conversion of many warriors into peace-loving Nazarenes, the Council of Kings and Druids have declared the Arimathean Nazarenes to be disloyal heretics and set up in its place a 'true' Nazarene religion that will encourage its followers to fight Rome.

Boudicca, the daughter (in this book) of the great British king Caratacus is, like many women of her time, a trained warrior, unable to fight openly because she is married to a king who supports the Roman occupation. Her life has suddenly grown brighter because her father plans to welcome the new governor by taking a few bites out of his legions and has hinted that there might be a role for her in the campaign. She is going to meet him at the Colchester home of her bitter rival Queen Cartimandua, an unscrupulous northern queen of great beauty and sex appeal who views Roman governors as potential means for satisfying her own ambitions.

Does the book present a credible picture of the Britons of that time? Against the popular impression of woad-painted savages being brushed aside by a vastly superior civilization it is useful to compare a few other pictures and assumptions that can be drawn from history:

In the years prior to Boudicca's last battle in 61 a.d., two of the four legions deployed in Britain were defeated by the Britons: significant military accomplishments requiring more than average tactical skills. (Not something to be achieved by undisciplined mobs) The 2nd Legion's refusal to join Paulinus in the final battle with Boudicca indicates a high level of respect for the Britons' military abilities.

Chariot warfare was considered obsolete by the time of the Roman invasion, but its use fit the Celtic psyche. Obsolete or not, to build and deploy the numbers used by the Britons required significant manufacturing as well as military skills. It also required a network of roads that were in existence long before and after the Romans built their own far superior roads. The primeval east-west Icknield Way, for example, was untouched by the Romans and made it easy for the later Anglo-Saxon invasions to reach the upper Thames.

The British King Caratacus most likely addressed the Roman Senate in Greek, the language commonly used on formal occasions throughout the empire. Facility in Greek and Latin as well as in Koine, a popular *lingua franca*, must have been a logical byproduct of the centuries of trade between Britain and the Mediterranean countries that preceded the invasion.

Julius Caesar spoke of the Druids, not as witch doctors but as astronomers, politicians, judges, philosophers and mathematicians. They eschewed writing because they believed, as did many contemporary intellectuals (e.g. Seneca), that writing atrophied the memory. The trained human memory was the primary medium for storing and conveying information among educated Britons of Boudicca's time, as it was also with many of their European and Asian peers. Their common language for public and private documentation was Greek.

As no novel about the Celts of that period would be complete without an opportunity for the Hibernian Red Branch Knights to demonstrate their skills or without a duel fought in the nearest ford, these are dutifully provided.

Chronology

DATE	EVENT
55 b.c.	Julius Caesar invades Britain
54 b.c.	Julius Caesar invades Britain again
5 b.c.	Birth of Jesus of Nazareth
5 a.d.	Rome acknowledges Cunobelinus as King of Britain
40	Emperor Caligula (Gaius) attacks Neptune in Boulogne
41	Caligula murdered
41-54	Emperor Claudius reigns
43	Roman invasion of Britain
43-47	Plautius term as 1st Governor of Britain

45	MaiDun (Maiden Castle) destroyed by Vespasian
45	Apostle Paul begins missionary journeys
46	First Jerusalem Council
46	Claudian temple erected in Colchester
47	2nd Legion garrisoned at Exeter
47	Brigantes under Cartimandua become a Client Kingdom
47	Plautius given ovation in Rome
47-52	Ostorius Scapula s term as 2nd Governor
48	Claudius wife Messalina murdered
48	Cogidubnus becomes Client King of Regni
49	Scapula s invasion of Wales stopped by Brigante disturbance
49	Cartimandua uses treaty to claim Roman help with disturbance
49	Claudius marries his niece Agrippina
49	First Iceni revolt against Scapula
49	Jerusalem Council battle over circumcision

49-50	Apostle Paul in Corinth with Aquila and Priscilla
50	Caratacus battles 20th and 14th legions in Western mountains (Wales)
50	Caratacus betrayed by Cartimandua and taken to Rome
50	Claudius adopts Nero, Agrippina s son
50	Venutius declared loyal to Rome
51	20th Legion defeated by Britons to avenge Caratacus capture
51	Caratacus addresses Claudius and the Senate and is pardoned for attacking the Roman invaders
51	Nero assumes *toga virilis* (adult status)
52	Scapula dies in Britain
52-57	Didius Gallus term as 3rd Governor of Britain
52	Venutius invades Brigantes
54	Claudius poisoned by Agrippina and Nero
54-68	Nero reigns as Roman Emperor
54-59	*Quinquennium Neronis*: the five relatively peaceful years of Nero s minority under the guidance of Seneca
55-56	Civil war in Brigante

55	Nero murders Claudius son Britannicus
55	Nero's advisers counsel caution in Britain
56	Cartimandua quarrels with Venutius, falls in love with Velocatus
56	9th Legion sent to aid Cartimandua
56	Nero advised to abandon Britain
57	Nero decides to invade Wales
57-58	Veranius Quintus term as 4th Governor
57	Veranius vows to complete conquest in 3 years
58	Veranius dies in Britain
58	Nero murders his mother Agrippina
58-61	Suetonius Paulinus term as 5th Governor
59	Nero poisons his aunt and shaves off his beard
60	Paul brought to trial before Festus
60-61	Decianus Catus, Procurator, robs British nobles
60-61	King Prasutagus of Iceni dies, his kingdom is eliminated and population brutalized
60-61	Seneca's loans called creating great financial hardship
60-61	Boudicca is flogged and her daughters raped

60-61	Boudicca instigates revolt, defeats 9th Legion
60-61	Colchester, London and Verulamium (St Albans) destroyed
61	Decianus Catus flees Britain
61	Battle at Mancetter, British defeated
61	Paulinus recalled
61-71	Petronius Turpilianus (peace-maker) term as 6th Governor
62	Galgacus succeeds Boudicca as Arviragus
65	Seneca commits suicide
66	Jewish revolt
77	Agricola Governor of Britain
78	Mona (Anglesey) conquered
120	Britain (south of Forth-Clyde line) incorporated into Roman Empire
122	Hadrian builds wall between northern Britain and Scotland

PART I

47—50 a.d.

Chapter 1

Colchester

Boudicca, High Queen of Iceni, was twenty-five and the mother of two daughters when she first saw the Romans' new city of Colchester. Rain had fallen during the night and as the mist thinned the distant walls and roofs that spread like a disease across the face of the holy hill ahead of her stood out brilliantly in the early morning sun. She hissed with anger at this desecration of a site at which Britons had worshipped for generations and reined in abruptly. Her little band of riders clustered awkwardly around her and she felt a jolt, heard the thump of a falling body and a gurgling cry of pain. Rhys the Druid Ovate, as bad a rider as only a Druid could be, must have fallen when his mare walked blindly into the back of Boudicca's horse. Atak, her huge middle aged leather suited German adviser, who was an ex-Roman auxiliary cavalry prefect, came to her side with an alarmed look on his face, pulling on his beard as he always did when anything upset him. She gave him a frosty glare then turned her gaze back on the city.

Mounted on a great Iceni black that her husband King Prasutagus (whom everyone called Fat Prasu) had given her as a wedding present, she was covered in dust that had been streaked by rain. Her long braided red hair had been fastened behind with a golden clasp. Freckles spread across her upper cheeks and nose making a strange contrast with ice blue eyes that could remain immobile at will and sear with sudden displeasure. A plain bronze and leather helmet and a small round shield hung from one side of her saddle, and a great tartan cape that held her clean clothes, formed her bedroll and protected her from the weather was fastened behind. A long sword, its hilt bound with copper and gold so she would not have to break her taboos by touching its iron shaft, was at her left side. She wore a leather jacket over her linen shirt and tartan trews, woven with the colors of a high royal, tucked into tooled leather boots. The only sign of her rank other than her long hair and her trews and the way she bore herself was the filigreed gold torque around her neck. At the rear of her column a standard bearer held the hated white and purple banner proclaiming Fat Prasu's status as Client King of Rome as far from her sight as possible.

Absent-mindedly she rubbed her shoulder while she let hatred of Rome seethe within her like the fumes of a mind-numbing brew. She spat on the ground and cursed the city that Claudius had ordered to be built as Britain's new capital. Some day she would burn it, and that day could not come soon enough.

"It's the taboo," said Rhys, nodding at her shoulder. He had climbed back on his mare and edged up beside her, an insufferable smirk on his flabby face. When she had tried to kill Claudius on his way back from Colchester to Rome, an iron-headed barbed lance thrown by one of his Praetorians had pinned her to the floor of her racing chariot. "You cannot touch iron and not pay the price. Next time, Duw will send down hemorrhoids, boils and warts."

She scowled at him. "You've said that to me a thousand times. You would have me lay with a lance in me and not pull it out?"

Rhys wagged his jowls. "A taboo's a taboo," he said.

What a pompous ass, she thought. Atak had twisted the barbed head out and in shock she had grabbed it. Rhys had grimly enjoyed her suffering, saying that because she had gripped iron her shoulder would always ache when it rained. It rained a lot in Britain. For a queen to kill Claudius with her own hands would have broken an even bigger taboo. What would Rhys have brought down on her for that? She kicked the black into urgent motion so that its rump hit Rhys' spavined mare, almost unseating him again, and rode on toward the city, her ragged band hurrying to catch up.

They rode past the defensive dykes that had been so quickly trodden down by the Romans as Atak had predicted, past the old and battered round huts surrounding the ruined palace at Gosbecks and on up the hill to where the new city was taking shape. Many of the buildings were no doubt the shops and warehouses that Ingenius had told her about. When the shops were finished and filled with goods, Britons could come to buy or barter for their needs instead of traipsing all over the countryside looking for buyers and sellers. Ingenius was one of the first Britons to have a shop from which to sell the jewelry he was so clever at making. He had been born a cripple and that had made him an outcast among the health worshiping Britons, but Elsa the Nazarene had healed his twisted leg. He had fallen in love with Elsa and married her, promising to become a Nazarene and seek the Kingdom with her. Instead, he had learned how rich a clever Briton could become by serving Rome. He had put himself under the protection of the bat eyed Catus Decianus, a disgusting little clerk who cheated his fellow Romans as much as he did the Britons and made no secret of his intent to be Procurator of Britain some day. Ingenius had been a good Briton until corrupted by Catus, but the news she was going to give him would rattle his teeth and shake his complacency. She loved Elsa and did not enjoy seeing her shoved aside to please a Rummy clerk.

A broad paved street ran parallel to the river. Below, boats plied back and forth carrying supplies between anchored ships and shore. Tents and buildings of timber, brick and wattle in various stages of construction lined both sides of the street. She had to weave her way among stacks of barrels and amphorae waiting to be carried into the shops. Horse drawn carts lurched along the newly paved street or down track ways leading to the river. Romans, free Britons, slaves and camp followers rode or walked in every direction.

As they plodded slowly down the street an officious looking blue jawed Roman, dressed in a plain toga but obviously a retired legionary, stepped in front of them, arms raised and eyes fixed on the golden hilt of her sword. She reined in and stopped abruptly, held out a hand to keep back Atak and the guards.

"You speakee Koine[1]?" said the Roman.

"You certainly do," she said.

"You will removee weapons immediately," said the Roman, gesturing toward their long swords and daggers. "Givum to me. Britons not to carry arms on Roman territory."

She stared down at him, eyes narrowed. She felt an insane urge to ride down this vermin that insulted a British royal with his pidgin Koine but tightened her lips and restrained herself. She could not afford the delay it would cause to punish this oaf. "I am Boudicca, Queen wife to High King Prasutagus of Iceni, Client of Rome," she said, her Latin crisp and clean. "If you will open your eyes you will see that we are protected by his banner. Our right to arms and free passage is governed by treaty. You are breaking Roman law by hindering our movement on this road."

"I am breaking Roman law? I am a Roman."

"Then obey your laws and move aside, Roman." She urged her horse forward and the legionary jumped back, cursing under his breath.

"I will see if you have a treaty or not," he roared after them. "I will see who is breaking Roman law."

"Look at that," she said to Atak as they rode on. She angrily pointed toward a mound being leveled by British slaves. A newly scraped track way led around it on its way from the street to the river and on top of the mound a foundation was being prepared for a large building. The area was marked off with ribands and garlands. "Duw has been worshipped there for a thousand years."

"It's going to be a temple," said Atak.

"I wouldn't wager on it." She dug in her heels and her horse leaped forward so that Atak and the knights had to gallop to catch up, leaving Rhys and his mare far behind.

She stopped at a shop in front of which lay piles of rusted iron and ingots of bronze. This had to be Ingenius' shop. She dismounted and threw her reins to one of the guards. "You will say nothing to him about Elsa," she said to Atak. Atak had married Elsa's mother Tetra and she didn't want him blurting out the news she wanted to convey. Atak nodded dumbly and followed her into the building.

It was dark and hot inside, full of smoke and lurid light from a forge against the wall opposite. Britons stripped to the waist and glistening with sweat worked at benches or on the floor, and the air pulsated with the noise of hammers and saws and clanging metal. Many of the Britons stopped work and gaped at them until a familiar figure showed in the gloom and bent a knee. It was the young black haired Ingenius, stripped to the waist and smelling of sweat. Streaks of soot from the forge covered his face and chest, but his brown eyes sparkled at her. He looked healthy and happy, but that would change when she told him her news. "Get up," she said. "Where's Cruker?" Cruker was her chunky little man at arms, on loan to Ingenius.

"Gone to get lead from the wharf," said Ingenius, kissing her hand. "He'll be back soon." He turned from her with a wide grin and punched Atak in the midriff. "Come and see what we're doing," he said, and led them back toward a low heavy table near the forge.

Several long round wooden forms were fastened to supports rising from the table and as they watched, two men slipped a long sheet of lead on to the table and worked it around one of the forms. They used ropes and mallets to straighten out bulges in the lead. When they were through, the lead had been shaped into a pipe, with one edge overlapping the other.

"Now they have to solder it so it won't leak," said Ingenius, as two workers brought a heavy smoking bucket suspended from a wooden beam and laid it on the floor next to the table. The men dipped ladles into the bucket and carefully poured the molten contents into the gap between the two overlapping ends of the lead pipe. "Joseph of Arimathea is in the tin trade," said one of the men in a singsong voice as they did this, and she turned sharply at the mention of the familiar name. Joseph had been with Simon Peter when Peter healed her grandfather of a stroke five years ago. He had since become Cyndaf[2] of the Nazarene sect declared heretic and illegal by the High Council of Kings and Druids.

"Why is he talking of Joseph?" she asked Ingenius.

"They're Saracens," he said. "They worked in Joseph's tin mines and Cruker brought them here to help us. They always say that when they pour metal so they don't move the pipe before the solder sets. They're pouring tin mixed with lead and these are water pipes for the governor's palace. When they're hooked together with these round bands, water can flow along them and they won't leak."

"How do you get them to go around corners?" asked Atak.

"The Rummies make knees out of sandstone," said Ingenius, "but I'm going to make mine out of iron."

Not interested in water pipes she drifted away from the table. "What are these?" she asked, angry again. She kicked a heavy mass of slave chains piled on the floor.

"For prisoners," said Ingenius. He looked embarrassed. "Catus said they will go to Gaul and not be used for Britons."

"They will be used for Britons," she said, trembling with rage.

"I know they will," said Ingenius. "But let me show you something." He picked up a length of the chain by one end. "The fifth link from either end is brittle. You can break it with a rock. We're getting the word out so our people know."

He dropped the chain at Boudicca's feet. "If we don't make the chains," he said. "Someone else will. And theirs won't break." He reached for a hammer and struck the fifth link of the chain a sharp blow. The link shattered but she didn't feel mollified.

"What about the jewelry? I thought you came here to do that, not build chains for Britons."

"I still am," said Ingenius. He led them to a row of tables against the front wall of the shop. There were alabaster windows above the tables to give light, and men sat and worked with the delicate tools of their craft. The tables were littered with finely worked ornaments of bronze, silver and gold in various stages of completion. She picked up a few to examine them and then lost interest. Right now she was more interested in the straightness of a sword than the curve of an amulet.

"I have bad news for you," she said briskly. Ingenius looked at her but said nothing. "Elsa has left you. She has gone back to Joseph of Arimathea and his heretic Nazarenes." It was cruel but letting himself be used by Romans such as Catus irritated her. As a High Queen, governed by the policies of Kings and Druids, she could have no overt truck with heretic Nazarenes. But she loved Elsa and could never forget that she had brought her firstborn baby back to life and healed Boudicca herself of a terrible hemorrhage.

Ingenius' shoulders sagged and he leaned back against one of the benches, chin on his chest. She could see his eyes were wet and felt a pang that she quickly obliterated. A little reminder that he was Briton first and artist second and that he had hurt someone she loved would help to keep his mind focused. While they stood in stony silence, a group of men came in pushing small carts in which were stacked metal ingots. She smiled when she saw the stocky figure of Cruker. Cruker came over, bending a knee in salute and grinning at Atak.

"I want you to leave this," she said to Ingenius, her voice kinder, "and come with us. Cruker will look after things while you're gone."

"Where?" said Ingenius, not raising his head.

"To meet my father."

Ingenius brightened and looked up at her.

"He's at Cartimandua's summer palace," she said. "He is

planning an attack." And he had better have a place in it for me.

"King Caratacus here in Colchester? The Rummies will kill him if they find out. Does he know the new governor arrived a week ago?"

Aulus Plautius Silvanus, commander of the Roman invasion forces and the first governor of the area that had so far been conquered had been recalled. His replacement could not step foot on British soil until Plautius and his staff had left, so there had been a lull in the fighting that had gone on continuously since the invasion four years ago. The lull would now be over.

"Caratacus wants to give him a welcome," said Atak. "But not here."

"Prince Venutius is here also," said Boudicca. "His army is to join my father's, and before that his brother Caswal is to be married." And if I have anything to do with it, she thought grimly, Venutius and I will be together when we attack. Venutius, impoverished second son of the vanquished king of Kent, was her true husband, banished four years ago because he could not accept her marriage to Prasu.

Her betrothal to the much older Prasu had been arranged to keep him in the British Alliance. But before her marriage could take place, she and Venutius, whose job it was to train her in warfare, had fallen in love during a raid on Gaul. She had kept her virginity, but after her marriage and before the Romans came, word had been brought that Prasu had signed a treaty with Rome. In her anger she made love with Venutius, but her family made her go back to Prasu so she could find out what the Romans planned to do. Pregnant, she didn't know until her daughter was born whether Prasu or Venutius was the father. The doubt had been removed when she saw the eyes of him she loved in Goneril, her baby. But she had been forced to banish Venutius and he had become a successful general of five thousand under Prince Salog of the Belgies.

As far as she was concerned, her duty to Britain had been

done. The Romans never told Prasu a thing. He could continue to crawl into bed with Habren her lady in waiting and play his games of Fidchell with her. Goneril and Gwenda, her daughter by Prasu, were doing well in the care of Habren and their Druid teachers. She loved them both dearly and felt guilty that she could not be with them always and watch them develop. But she was trained as a warrior not as a mother. Her hatred of Rome was far stronger than her love for home and children. There would be time for such things when the Rummies had been driven out of Britain. She would go to war and if Fat Prasu could not stomach the risk of disclosure he could divorce her.

It is time I fought for Britain with my true husband, she told herself. If he still will have me.

Chapter 2

Reconciliation

Cartimandua, High Queen of the Brigantes[3], was Boudicca's cousin. Her kingdoms in the far north were governed by underkings owing allegiance to her and by treaty were currently beyond the reach of Rome. Her summer palace sat near the river's edge, only a short distance away from the street of shops. It was common knowledge that the palace was a love offering from Governor Plautius to keep her close to him. "Now I hear she's after the new governor," said Ingenius.

When they had cleaned themselves and changed clothes, Boudicca, Atak and Ingenius set off walking there, Rhys tagging along behind. At the palace, the first thing she noticed as the gate opened was a group of legionaries in highly polished armor taking their ease in a garden at the side. Atak nudged her. "Guards," he said. "I wonder if the governor's here."

The steward was a heavy set Nubian with a pock marked face, tired brown eyes, a wide black mustache with graying ends like frayed rope, sagging shoulders and a glistening bald head. He wore a long robe, white with blue vertical stripes, and black leather boots. His pole of office was also white with blue stripes that spiraled down the pole. When the steward put the pole down he twisted it with his long pink tipped fingers, and the spiraling blue stripes seemed to dig a hole in the ground.

"I am Boudicca, Queen of Iceni," she said. "I am expected."

The steward picked up his pole and turned around. "Folly me." He led the way down a short path through a formal garden, ending at the double doors of the palace, which was large and rectangular in the Roman style. Its wattle walls were whitewashed and the exposed timbers painted blue. The area before the doors had been covered with red brick. Large white urns with trimmed bushes in them were arranged at each corner. A servant opened the doors when the steward tapped his pole and they went inside, first into a small atrium, out of which rose a staircase, and then into the large hall.

Even though it was an autumn day, the outside air damp and cool, there were no fires burning. Several braziers were placed around the floor but none were lit. Without the fires that filled most British houses with a haze that made the eyes burn, the air inside Cartimandua's palace was cool clear and damp, and Boudicca could see every detail of the hall. Instead of being the usual packed dirt with flagstoned areas near the fire pits, the floor was tiled, a large circular mosaic in the center.

"There's a hypocaust under the floor to heat the building," whispered Ingenius. "But it doesn't work."

Brightly colored hangings festooned the high walls and there were more windows than would be found in a British house. The windows were tall and wide and covered with thin sheets of translucent alabaster. Couches and tables were arranged in various groupings, and large vases filled with flowers were grouped artistically in corners of the room. Except for six warriors standing motionless against the walls, the hall was empty.

"Where is everyone?" she said.

The steward shrugged. "Queen come," he said. "You sit. Bring drink. Back soon." He disappeared through one of the doors let into the wall furthest from them. She could hear his pole hit the mortar between each tile as he let it drag along behind him.

"My father should be here by now," she said, as they sat down. "So should Venutius and his brother."

A door opened near the one through which the steward had passed. A short man with black hair, low forehead, black eyes and protuberant teeth stood partly concealed behind it so that only his head was visible. When the man saw that she observed him, he drew back and the door closed.

Ingenius got up to examine the mosaic floor, his footsteps echoing eerily. He was on his knees examining the design when yet another door flew open. A man rushed in, his face livid with anger. He stopped, his strangely glassy eyes fixed on them, arms outstretched and hands open as if ready to grab something. But for a short under-tunic he was naked. "Where is she?" he said.

He was a big man of middle age, not tall but broad and heavily built. His chest and stomach heaved, and the muscles stood out in his arms and thighs. His entire visible body seemed to be covered with black curly hair. The face was broad and strong, cheeks pulled back in a grimace of displeasure, and the hair of his head was thick, black and curly, flecked with little wisps of gray. "Where is she?" he said again, head moving in small jerks to take in the hall.

"Where is whom?" said Boudicca, rising, her voice icy.

The man flung his right arm out as if to ward off a blow then disappeared, slamming the door after him. Almost immediately, the steward reappeared followed by a servant carrying a tray.

"Who was that man?" she said.

"What man?" the steward said. "Drink. Eat cake. Queen come."

She touched neither the cakes nor the wine and sat in frosty silence as Atak tucked in. Without warning, Ingenius suddenly kicked one of the couches across the tiled floor. He did the same with another couch, almost hitting one of the warriors, who moved a few paces to his left. Then Ingenius sat down on a couch and put his head between his hands. You might well grieve for what you have lost, she thought. As time passed, her anger at Cartimandua's insolence rose to a boil. "We will wait no longer," she said, finally. "My father must not be here." She stood up, but as she did heard the noise of many people approaching. She sat down again and the steward came in and banged his pole.

"Queen come," said the steward. He stood to one side and with a rustle of gold embroidered blue silk and a flash of countless brilliants, Cartimandua swept into the hall and bore down on them. Several Roman officers and civilians, and a short British king with big teeth followed her. In the forefront, close enough to touch Cartimandua, strode a burly man wearing a chlamys and the long paludamentum of a general, a burnished helmet grasped in his left hand. Boudicca recognized in him the angry man who had earlier burst in on them in his under-shift. She also sensed the man's station.

"You must forgive my rudeness," said Cartimandua, kissing Boudicca's hand as they bowed to each other and smiling graciously on the three men. "I have been discussing my treaty with Rome instead of greeting my guests." Boudicca had never seen skin so creamy white as Cartimandua's, nor a figure so beautifully shaped, nor eyes that promised so much and gave so little. Her hair was a deep brown through which veins of copper gleamed and it was braided into a long coil that swept like a docile serpent down her back and around her waist.

"Allow me to present his Excellency Publius Ostorius Scapula, newly appointed *legatus Augusti pro praetore* by Caesar Tiberius Claudius Drusus," said Cartimandua. "Governor, this is my cousin Boudicca, High Queen of Iceni, Client of Rome and, like me, of the royal family of the great Cunobelinus."

The governor had not taken his eyes off Cartimandua since they had come into the hall, his lust for the northern queen so apparent that Boudicca recoiled from him with contempt. "I have already seen the governor," she said, and Scapula's head jerked back as if he had been struck. He made a stiff bow as the short British king shouldered his way past Scapula to stand in front of Cartimandua. Boudicca suddenly realized the short king was the man who had peeked around the door when they first came in.

"Let me also present King Ofar Bigtooth," said Cartimandua.

King Ofar reminded Boudicca of a shorter King Lud, the former husband of Cartimandua. Like Lud, whom Boudicca heard had been killed by one of his own under-kings, he was coarse featured, black haired and shabby of dress. His teeth and gums seemed too big to be concealed by his lips, giving him a perpetual snarl. Even while being introduced he did not take his eyes off Scapula.

After the rest of Scapula's party had been introduced a legate whispered something in Scapula's ear then bowed to Cartimandua. "The governor must return to his palace," he said. "He is sorry that the hypocaust put into your palace doesn't work. Most likely rodents have blocked the pipes. He wonders if perhaps you would ask your King Ofar to crawl through them. He's about the right size and would doubtless scare them away. The governor thanks you for your hospitality and hopes that he may return it when his engagements are less pressing."

Cartimandua called her steward and the atrium filled with light as the doors opened. The new governor stood immobile, staring at Cartimandua and the bristling figure of King Ofar. Then with a curse, Scapula strode to the atrium. When he reached it, he hesitated for a moment then walked out without looking back. King Ofar, hand on his sword hilt, followed the Romans outside.

"What a fool," said Cartimandua. "But like Plautius he will be my lap dog before another week has passed. And now, my cousin queen, your father is here, and your lover and his brother."

"My what?" said Boudicca, her face red. What could Cartimandua know of Venutius, whom she had not seen for so long?

"Tush, my dear," said Cartimandua. "The world knows you are lovers. Go rescue our guests from their hiding places," she said to the steward.

"I will trouble you not to use such expressions," said Boudicca.

"I do understand," said Cartimandua, her gaze on Atak. "I would not have your red beard jealous."

"I am not jealous," said Atak.

"Then you must serve me," said Cartimandua. "I need men not easily made jealous."

Atak pulled on his beard.

"Be quiet, Atak," said Boudicca. "My cousin plays games. I am not Scapula to be made sport of," she said to Cartimandua. "Nor will you confuse Atak with your wiles."

Cartimandua smiled. "If Venutius is not your lover," she said. "You will not object if I make him mine. He is a most handsome man."

Boudicca flushed and her eyes narrowed but she said nothing. There had always been hostility between the two of them, especially since Cartimandua had convinced Kings and Council that the Romans would stop their advance if only her father Caratacus were removed from his post as Arviragus (Commander in Chief) of Britain. They had not stopped their advance. Cartimandua had simply done Rome a service by neutralizing Britain's best general.

While Boudicca brooded a door opened admitting her father, High King Caratacus, followed by her brother King Eudal Marius who had been elected to his father's post as Arviragus, her cousin Elidurus King of the Trinoes, Venutius' brother Caswal, and a young woman who must be Aled, Caswal's betrothed. The girl was good looking but seemed shy and withdrawn. She couldn't be more than sixteen. But where was Venutius?

As Eudal Marius walked toward her she could see he had changed. The arrogance that characterized him before he was made Arviragus had vanished and a long succession of defeats had embittered him. His face looked sallow and his eyes darkly sad so that she felt a twinge of compassion. But still, she told herself, had she been Arviragus she would not have made the mistakes he made. Like most British generals he thought battles could be won by throwing enough warriors at the enemy. He had not spent time, as she had during her forced tenure with Prasu, poring over scrolls depicting the great campaigns of the past, looking for ways in which the Rummies' vast supremacy could be nibbled away until the odds were more even. Her father had grasped this and had learned how to play on Rummie nerves from a distance, threatening attacks that didn't materialize and taking sudden bites out of their cohorts before vanishing into the swamps and forests. But her father was no longer Arviragus, and without experience in the field, no one was about to offer the post to her. She must get experience. Some day she must be Arviragus.

Her father was dressed in tartan trews and a white shirt open at the neck to reveal the curly blond hairs on his chest and the twisted gold torque around his neck. He came straight for Atak, shoulder length blond hair swinging as he walked and bright blue eyes sparkling. "Whisht," he said, pounding Atak on the shoulder and waving her into silence. Rhys, sticking out his belly and smoothing his green robe, must speak first. The Druid always spoke first, even one as dull and pompous as Rhys.

Rhys stretched out his arms and gathered to himself Caswal on his right and Aled on his left. "By the gracious consent of Cartimandua, High Queen of the Brigantes," said Rhys, "who herself rules her nations by the grace of Duw-Bran, Mighty Thunderer and Lord able to destroy all his creation and burn it eternally in flaming oil, we are gathered here today to witness the tying of the holy contract of marriage between Prince Caswal, brother to Prince Venutius, mighty defender of Britain, and his betrothed, the Princess Aled, daughter of Rusticus, High King of the Belgies and sister to Prince Salog of Sarum."

"It is not yet noon," said Cartimandua, looking down her nose at Rhys. "We will have the wedding then because that is when the feast will begin."

Rhys bowed, crestfallen, and sat on a couch. Boudicca would have asked her father about Venutius but Cartimandua was too close.

"And isn't the widow Angarad anxious to see you again," said Caratacus to Atak.

"She's here?" said Atak. He grabbed his beard and felt the

blood leave his face. He had encountered the fearsome widow Angarad while up in the western mountains helping to build forts with Caratacus. As big as himself, covered in dried blood from a cow she had just slaughtered and still carrying the animal's intestines around her shoulders, she had almost cracked open his skull with her iron chin and then raped him.

For answer, Caratacus roared with laughter and seized Cartimandua around the waist with both hands. With a quick motion, Cartimandua wrapped the long coil of her hair around Caratacus' neck and pulled him to her. Caratacus stopped laughing, and his hands dropped from her waist to her tightly covered bottom. "By Beli Mawr," he said, breathing hard, his face almost touching hers, "I would forget that I'm a married man old enough to be your father and that you are the spawn of my own dead brother." She pulled tighter on her hair and kissed him full on the lips. Then she flipped the hair over his head as she pushed him away and struck him across the face with its braided end. Caratacus fell back with a curse. It serves you right, thought Boudicca.

"The kiss is for my uncle," said Cartimandua. "The whipping is for the man you are and the thoughts you were having."

"I would it were the other way around," said Caratacus. "But I know I cannot compete with the likes of Scapula."

Cartimandua lunged at him like a snake, hair pulled back to whip him again, but Atak seized her arm and stopped her. She glared at Atak, frozen in a posture of absolute grace, then nestled back against his chest while she looked up at him with eyes as gentle as a doe's.

Mother Nerthus, thought Atak, as a dark corona narrowed his vision to a bright circle. He stood naked in a pool of warm water, a soft skinned Cartimandua as naked as he clasped within his arms. She smiled up at him, lips softly and moistly apart, drawing the essence out of him like a flood as he moved to take her. From a great distance a voice, a sharp well-known voice, a displeased and angry voice, said: "Atak!" Suddenly, Cartimandua was gone, the pool had disappeared and only the dark corona remained. "Atak!" the voice said again.

A cold despair flooded through him because he had lost what he so urgently craved at the moment he thought he had gained it, and he stared blindly around the hall. "Where is she?" he said. His voice sounded like someone else's, and then he slowly realized he still held Cartimandua. As he pushed her slowly from him Cartimandua put two fingers on his lips. Then she left him and he sat down abruptly on a couch as Venutius entered through the atrium.

Boudicca's heart pounded as Venutius came toward her and her anger at Atak dissolved. She could not blame poor Atak for getting himself so obviously aroused by that temptress. Her father had been no better. Venutius looked five years older than she knew him to be, but the aging had improved him. His movements were slower but more assured and the old uncertainty had gone. He seemed taller and more erect, harder, more of a man. His chin was adorned with a short beard as blond as his hair, and she felt the energy flow from him to her as his diamond blue eyes met hers. "It is good to see you again," she said. Her voice sounded unnatural and restrained because it had been so long and she had sent him away.

He took her hands in his. She turned their hands over, and there on his finger was the ring she had left in his tent after the massacre at MaiDun[4]. He had been away with his army and had never acknowledged receiving it. "Yes," he said. "I wear it always."

"I'm glad." She looked up at him and tried to tell him with her face that she still loved him.

"I heard you have another daughter now."

"Yes, Gwenda. She is very much like Prasu."

"And Goneril?"

"Goneril is like her father also."

"But not like Prasu."

"Not like Prasu. She will be a warrior like her father."

He squeezed her hands so tightly she almost cried out. "I would like to see her."

He had been banished before Goneril was born and had never seen her. "You shall."

"What color is her hair?"

"It is like mine. But she does not have my eyes. They were the first thing I noticed in her. They were the first things I loved in her."

They stood there mute as the bond grew back between them, knitting their severed hearts together. "So Caswal is to marry?" she said.

He reddened. "There is no settlement for him." Of course there wouldn't be. As the youngest son of a defeated king there would be nothing left to give him.

"Then how?"

"I would ask your father to foster him."

"It's a little late for that." He nodded, sheepish. Why don't you ask me for help, you silly man?

Her father's voice rang out with an oath and they both turned toward him. He was talking to Cartimandua, Eudal Marius at his side. "What else did he tell you?" said Caratacus.

"There will be ten thousand ex-legionaries settled in Colchester and Verulam[5] by this time next year," said Cartimandua. "They will relieve the legions so they can root out the arch devil Caratacus. His legions will be up to strength in three months. Each of them will have a doubled first cohort like Vespasian's."

"Then he will strike by Beltane," said Caratacus. "If we let him." He pulled the still glassy-eyed Atak from his couch and steered him toward Boudicca and Venutius.

"You heard Cartie," said Caratacus, looking from one to the other. "Scapula will be up to strength in three months. We must move quickly." Venutius stared at Caratacus as if trying to remember who he was. "We must leave," said Caratacus, "as soon as the wedding feast is over."

"Do you believe her?" said Boudicca.

"I don't have to believe her," said Caratacus. "It makes sense and that is always believable. And you, my good friend," he said, turning to Venutius. "We have had our disputations in the past, but tis in my heart to admit you've become a good general. Never let it be said that Caratacus is parsimonious about giving credit where it is due. You should be Arviragus of Britain instead of Eudal Marius, and that is something that should be said by me who is the boy's own father."

Venutius took a deep breath and edged away from Boudicca. "I would be the last to deny," he said, "that such titles are for High Kings. And I am far from being even an under-king."

"We must find a new Arviragus," said Caratacus. "Sad it is for me to say but the kings have turned away from Marius."

"What about King Guderius?" said Atak.

"He won't take it. Neither will Linus."

"Why don't you become Arviragus and carry Pendragon again?"

Caratacus shook his head sadly. "It is taboo for me to pick up again that which I have cast from me. We must find someone to carry it who knows what to do with it and won't dishonor it."

"Why tell all this to me?" said Venutius, his voice bitter. "I can never be Arviragus."

"You could if you were a High King," said Caratacus, looking at Boudicca. "I would you were High King of Iceni instead of fat Prasu. And I know that in such an opinion I am not alone." Boudicca bit her lip as Cartimandua and Ofar came to her father's side.

"If Venutius were King of Iceni instead of fat Prasu," said Cartimandua, going up to Venutius, "then my cousin would be his queen and I would not be able to do this." She put a hand either side of Venutius' head and pulled it to her, kissing him full on the lips. He made as if to draw back from her, but she persisted and his hands went around her and pressed her to him. Furious, Boudicca raised a hand to strike, but Caratacus caught it.

"Nay, lass," he said. She let her father hold her and stroke her hair, but her body was stiff with anger. Cartimandua pushed Venutius' head away momentarily to look at Boudicca. Venutius put a hand behind Cartimandua's neck and grabbed her braided coil of hair. So fierce was his kiss that she bent back from the force of it. Boudicca winced and closed her eyes but could not keep them closed. Clamped between Venutius' arms and body, Cartimandua appeared to be trapped until Venutius let her go with a curse and put his hand to his face where it was suddenly bloody. I'm glad she bit you, she thought. Now hit the bitch.

"By Duw," said Venutius. He pulled his hand away and looked at the blood on it and then at Cartimandua crouched like a cat facing him, his blood on her lips. Ofar moved between them, but because he was so short he did not block their view. Then Venutius went berserk. "You will tease no more," he roared, and hurled himself at her, knocking Ofar out of the way as he did so. Quicker than Venutius, Cartimandua rolled onto the floor to avoid his grasp, picked herself up and ran for the atrium.

The warriors standing by the wall drew their swords. Venutius ran after her and Ofar, his sword drawn, ran after Venutius. The steward banged his pole on the floor, keeping time with Cartimandua's footsteps as she ran up the wooden stairs leading from the atrium to the rooms above. Boudicca heard shrill cries as servants got knocked out of the way, and then the thunder of Venutius' footsteps running up the stairs, Ofar and the warriors' right behind him. By Duw, she thought, he is going to rape her. She sat down on a couch and looked bitterly at the floor. A harsh cry and the sound of a blow came from above. There was the crash of a door slamming and the noise of iron bolts driven home. Heavy footsteps ran across the floor above then another door slammed. There was a scream.

"Well," said Caratacus, sitting down beside Boudicca. He kissed her forehead. "If Cartie's going to be busy we can at least get on with the wedding."

She gritted her teeth and glared at her father. "I hope you have planned something for me to do," she said. "I have played mother and wife long enough. I was not trained to lie abed and play Fidchell all day with Fat Prasu. I have done what I was made to do and what a waste of time that has been."

"Aye, it seems that way," said Caratacus, "but it was a gamble we had to take."

She grunted, thinking of Venutius up there with that woman. But for Fat Prasu, Venutius would be her husband, hers alone.

"If you can tear yourself away from your fat husband for a while," said Caratacus, "I do have a job for you."

"What?" she said, interest reviving.

"I have an army for you. You can help us welcome Scapula. But Prasu must not hear of it."

At last, after all this time she was to be given a command? She gripped Caratacus' forearm with both hands.

"Tis not much of an army," said Caratacus, "but the Council has great hopes you can make it into something."

"What is it?" she asked eagerly. "Trinoes? Catuves? Our own Silures?"

"They're Nazarenes."

"Nazarenes?" Her eyebrows shot up as her heart sank. "Nazarenes don't fight. They want us to turn the other cheek and love the Rummies."

"These will fight. At least, Owain Longhead says they will. They're Cartimandua's Nazarenes."

Owain Longhead was her own brother in law, husband to her sister Gwendolyn and an ambitious Druid Pencerdd[6], a member of the High Council of Kings and Druids. Owain intended to be Archdruid someday and had been trying to find some way to get control of the Nazarenes. Attracted by the healings and teachings of Philip of Gaul and Joseph of Arimathea, Britons were abandoning the Druid god Duw in favor of the Nazarene's God and were laying down their arms in droves to pray for peace. Owain was sure there must be some way to divert all that wasted energy into defeating Rome, and another Nazarene missionary called Basil had convinced him it could be done by setting up a competing group under his control. All that had to be done then was to convince Britons that these were the true Nazarenes and that true Nazarenes hated Rome. This army must be Basil's idea. "How can we trust an army that she raised?" she said. "Especially a Nazarene army?"

"They belong to Owain now and his Bishop Basil. Owain feels if we can get em to fight, Basil can convince more Nazarenes to join his group. Britons love a fight."

"How many are they?"

"Owain says he'll have a thousand. They're assembling near Verulam. Brennius and Iorwerth will be there to help you. I want you to stay close to your uncle Guderius and send em in to burn Verulam once he's cleared the 20th legion out of the way."

"When is the attack?"

"As near Samain as we can get."

"Do I attack the 20th too?"

"No. Guderius will do that."

"Then my army is fit only to burn houses and kill civilians?"

"We don't know what it's fit for till it has fought. After Verulam we'll see what else we have for it. And for you."

In other words, she thought grimly, if these Nazarenes don't fight I'll be exiled back to Prasu. It didn't sound promising and she didn't trust Cartimandua but anything was better than playing queen to Prasu.

There was another heavy crash above them and Caratacus looked up at the ceiling. "We must get us a new Arviragus," he said. "Venutius is the man were he but a High King."

"Why don't they make Cartie Arviragus?" she said bitterly. "She is a High Queen and has the money and the armies."

"She's a witch. None but a fool or a eunuch would trust her. She tells us some of what the Rummies are doing and then tells them what we're doing. She has an insatiable appetite for teasing men and playing with their minds until they become slavering slobbering sots. But, my darling, she could be the means of making Venutius Arviragus."

She glared at him. "You would have her marry Venutius? You would wish that on him?"

"She will suck him dry but he will be a High King. Sure as fate the Brigante kings will turn against him and he'll come back to us with Ofar there snapping at his heels. With a little luck he'll bring a quarter of her armies and as much gold as he can carry. By Beli Mawr, with her armies on one side and mine on t'other, Venutius as Arviragus and her driving Scapula out of his mind, we can throw these Rummies off this land for good."

Boudicca closed her eyes and hissed between her teeth. She would sacrifice anything to help Venutius. But marry him to Cartimandua? It was too painful to think about. But at least she would have an army and could fight with him.

It was noon. Servants hurried into the hall carrying bowls of water, several cloths, a rug, a small brazier from which a light haze of smoke arose, a table, wine, glasses, a basket of food and a large sprig of mistletoe.

"We are ready to begin the wedding," said Rhys. "Let us pray to the three faces of Duw, that in his mercy he will not lay all of us low with demons and divers diseases." He bent his head and prayed, but Boudicca could not keep herself from wondering what was happening upstairs. She came to with a jolt when Rhys clapped his hands. "Prince Caswal will kneel before Duw," he said, and Caswal knelt but looked around nervously.

"And now the Princess Aled," said Rhys. A servant placed the bowl of water before her and she washed Caswal's hands. When she was done, Caswal performed the same service for her, and then a servant dried their hands.

"Clasp the hands you have washed pure together," said Rhys, "as your hearts must be washed pure and clasped. Do you, Aled, Princess of Sarum, swear before Duw that you have chosen this man of your own free will and consent?"

"Yes," said Aled.

"You realize that Duw may strike you down dead if you lie?"

"Yes."

"And cover you with boils and diseases?"

"Yes."

"And did you bring a symbol of your unmarried state to burn before Duw and this company?"

Aled blushed, nodded her head and pulled something out from beneath her tunic. It was probably the little hat she had worn to signify her status as maiden, thought Boudicca.

"Then cast it into the fire."

Aled dropped the material into the brazier. It crinkled and smoldered but didn't burst into flame. Rhys bent down to blow on it and it gave off dense clouds of smoke.

"By Crom Cruach and his twelve sons," said Caratacus, nudging Boudicca. "This wench will not part easily with her maidenhead."

Rhys lifted his blackened face from the smoking brazier and wiped the tears from his eyes. "Do you, Caswal, Prince of Kent, swear before Duw that you have chosen this woman of your own free will and consent?"

"Yes," said Caswal.

"And you realize that Duw may send upon you nine times nine plagues and cause your organs to burst in nine places if you lie?"

"Yes."

"And have you some symbol of your unmarried state to cast into the fire before Duw and this company? Something that will burn?"

"Yes," said Caswal, and gingerly placed a piece of broken wood on top of Aled's still smoking offering.

"Looks like a piece of his hurly stick," said Caratacus, nudging Boudicca again. Irritated, she moved away from him. "From what I hear, he will play just as well without it as he ever did with it. Tis not the greatest champion of war games that is about to bed our little filly."

"Now," said Rhys. "You will join hands over the fire and together touch the ashes of your childhood nine times."

Rhys looked around the room, a look of thunder on his face. "Who will guarantee the virginity of Aled, Princess of Sarum, before the three faces of Duw?" he said, and the little princess cringed in embarrassment. Rhys waved his hand magnanimously to indicate that no answer was needed. "Queen Cartimandua has verified her virginity," he said. He patted the princess on the head. "And have you brought evidence of your dowry?"

Aled burst into tears.

"It's all right," said Rhys. "Queen Cartimandua has inspected the dowry of Princess Aled. It is upstairs." Rhys coughed, and his watery eyes momentarily turned upwards. "It is not possible to view it at present."

Boudicca glared at him. What a pompous ass. Everyone knew what Venutius and Cartimandua were doing. Oh Venutius, how could you?

Rhys patted Aled on the head and turned to Caswal. "Have you brought the settlement?"

"Prince Venutius," said Caswal, his voice hardly audible, "has it."

Rhys drew himself up and frowned. "What?" he said. "I didn't hear."

"Prince Venutius has it."

"I have not seen it," said Rhys. "Remember that the three faces of Duw are watching all we do and say. He will cover with hemorrhoids, warts and foul sores any who break their oaths. Who can guarantee the settlement?"

"I cannot guarantee it," said King Elidurus. "The Rummies have taken even our seed. May it grow nothing but swamp grass for em."

"I will guarantee it, man," said Caratacus. "Get on with the flaming wedding."

Rhys cleared his throat. Before he could speak, Boudicca heard footsteps going across the floor above. The footsteps were slow, and she couldn't resist staring at the ceiling and following them with her eyes as if watching the owners of the feet themselves.

The footsteps reached the other side of the room and she could hear bolts being slowly withdrawn.

Rhys bent over the table at his side and poured wine into two glasses. He handed one to Aled and one to Caswal. "You will drink this wine," he said, "as a symbol of the joining together of your blood in the children that Duw may give you if you are obedient." As the young couple dutifully drank the wine, the last of the bolts was withdrawn and the door above creaked as it opened.

"Now," said Rhys, a wary eye on the atrium, "in the name of Duw and in the presence of these witnesses, I hold above your heads the holy mistletoe." He held up the mistletoe. "You may kiss each other," he said, "beneath this holy plant but you must not consummate the marriage until after the feast. If either one of you breaks this holy contract of marriage, Duw-Bran will pour down fire and brimstone on your head and cover you both with warts."

The kiss was short and nervous. Rhys lowered the mistletoe and reached into a basket that sat on the table. His eyes on the atrium, he pulled out two handfuls of dried corn and flung them toward the bride and groom, missing them completely. "I pronounce that you are man and wife. May you have many children."

As Caswal and Aled kissed each other again, Cartimandua and Venutius appeared in the atrium. For a few moments, the hall was deathly still. No one moved and it seemed to Boudicca that no one breathed. Venutius looked subdued and unsure of himself, while Cartimandua looked as queenly and dignified as if she had just returned from a stroll in her gardens. Whatever happened upstairs, thought Boudicca, hasn't changed her but it's changed Venutius. He won't even look at me.

Cartimandua broke the spell. She walked rapidly over to Caswal and Aled and kissed them, while Venutius walked slowly over to stand on the other side of Caratacus and Atak. His eyes were glassy and his face made her think he walked in his sleep. "The wedding is over?" he asked, his voice dull.

"Aye," said Caratacus. "How was it with Cartie?"

"I don't know," said Venutius.

"How can you not know, man? Did you bed her?"

"I don't know," said Venutius, a bewildered expression on his face.

Caratacus looked at Boudicca, eyebrows almost touching his hair. What could Venutius mean by that? she wondered. What else could they have been doing? She ached to tell Venutius of her Nazarene army and ask his opinion of it, but now a new wall had been erected between them. Once again they were to be strangers. Caratacus would find some way to get Cartimandua and Venutius married so Venutius could be Arviragus. It would please her to see him get Pendragon, the great white and green pennant emblazoned with a red dragon that identified an Arviragus of Britain, but at what a cost!

Cartimandua reached down into Rhys' basket and scattered more dried corn over the newlyweds. Cartie didn't act like a woman just raped. What had she done to Venutius? The northern queen clapped her hands and the steward banged his pole. "Let us begin our wedding feast," said Cartimandua, "and give honor to the new family begun today."

Much later, the newly weds having left the feast, Boudicca thought about her army as she watched the outlines of the hall slowly disappear in the blue smoke given off by the braziers that had finally been lit. She found herself looking once again at Venutius, chewing absently on his meat. The still glassy-eyed Atak sat to Venutius' right, and next to Atak sat a morose Ingenius, no doubt brooding about Elsa. King Elidurus was at Venutius' left wolfing down food as if his stomach were a bottomless pit. Rhys had left for Caer Leon to care for her sick sister, Gwendolyn, Owain's wife. Suddenly, Venutius jumped up as if startled and dropped his meat. Elidurus bent down and picked it up. There was dead silence as everyone stared at Venutius. He crouched, arms outstretched, the fingers of his hands splayed wide as if to catch something. His head turned from side to side in little jerks as if seeking someone. "Where is she?" he said, his voice thick. By Duw, thought Boudicca, that's what Scapula and Atak said. And they had looked just as stupid.

Cartimandua placed her hand on Venutius' wrist. Venutius jumped as if startled from sleep then slowly sat down. Elidurus offered Venutius the meat he had dropped and when Venutius refused it ate it himself. Venutius cast a furtive look first at Cartimandua and next at Boudicca. His face was expressionless, his eyes glassy. What had Cartimandua done to him? Was it so little time ago that she had felt his love returning and had been so ready to fight at his side and be his willing bed partner? And now they were to marry him off to that bitch?

Chapter 3

The Nazarene Army

Boudicca's uncle, High King Guderius of the Catuves, shook his head when he saw Boudicca's Nazarene army. He was older than Caratacus and his heavy face characteristically reflected gloom. To Boudicca's anxious eyes his face was now gloom superimposed upon gloom. "We can't do anything with this lot," he said.

His own army, twenty thousand in all, waited near the Thames beyond the Roman frontier. He had come down at Caratacus' bidding to examine hers. Subidasto, an underking of Prasu's, had also ridden down through the unoccupied nations to join her bringing with him fifty Iceni horsemen. Subidasto was Prasu's principal Fidchell opponent, but he hated the Romans and had often helped her do things to hurt them in the past. Caratacus had commandeered Atak to help him attack outposts of the 14th legion. Guderius was to entice the 20th away and take a few bites out of it while Boudicca burned the new town being built at Verulam.

"What do you think, Subidasto?" Boudicca asked as her mind echoed Guderius' words. How could she do anything with this lot? And if she failed it would be long before she was given another role in this war.

Subidasto looked gloomy too. "They're a rag tag lot," he agreed. "Half have no weapons and the half that do are too old and decrepit to use em. They all look diseased. But twould be a shame not to burn Verulam while the 20th is away chasing King Guderius. Thanks be to Andraste I brought fifty good horse with me."

"Thanks be to Andraste and the three faces of Duw," she said absently, wondering how she was going to get Verulam burned. Vallo, a Druid Ovate well seasoned in the cure of wounded soldiers, had ridden down with Subidasto also. He was at her right side and they would likely need him. Thank Andraste too that she had brought twelve good men of her own.

They were all on horseback, standing on a ridge at the edge of the swamp near Verulam and looking down through the drizzle on five hundred or so unkempt men and women. The swamp gave off the vilest stink she had ever encountered and she held her tartan cape against her nose to deaden it. The little Nazarene army had been gathered together after its journey from Brigante by Iorwerth, an elderly dispossessed Trinoe noble, and her cross-eyed eighteen-year old nephew Prince Brennius, heir to what was left of cousin Elidurus' half occupied Trinoe kingdom.

Subidasto's horsemen also stood along the ridge and held their noses against the stink while they looked at the army below with disgust. Many of the supposed warriors were horribly disfigured by disease. Some sat in the swamp moaning piteously and quite a few stretched out motionless on their backs as if already dead. She felt her anger rise at Owain Longhead and his bishop for sending these poor people out with such futile hopes. Cartimandua must have known they were for her army, she thought bitterly, and handpicked them herself. Was her hope for success just as futile as theirs? As she watched, appalled at the sight of her first command, Brennius and Iorwerth came galloping toward them, mud flying from the hooves of their horses.

"I can't look Brennius in the eye," muttered Guderius.

"Neither can I," said Vallo. "My eyes are crossing already."

"How many of em can fight?" said Subidasto, as Brennius and Iorwerth reined in. Iorwerth glowered.

"And aren't they a fine looking lot," said Brennius. "We will take Verulam in no time at all and then we can burn Colchester."

"How many can fight?" said Subidasto again, looking at Iorwerth. Iorwerth scowled but still said nothing.

"Why, I would say a good four ninths of em," said Brennius.

"And the rest?"

"I would say they'll be ready when they've eaten. Lord Owain and Bishop Basil said they're all raring to go."

"Go where?" muttered Guderius.

"They've had no food for three days," said Iorwerth. "Doesn't that stupid Council know that warriors must eat to fight?"

"They'll have to raid the farms to get food."

"If we put em up against the farmers," said Iorwerth, "the farmers will kill more than the Rummies."

"How many diseased?" said Subidasto, looking skyward to avoid Brennius' crossed eyes.

"Why, I would say no more than six or seven ninths. They can still swing a club."

"Against a Rummy lance?" said Guderius.

"They'll fight," said Brennius. "Bishop Basil promised they would all be healed if they bought a candle and fought."

"How many captains are there?" said Subidasto.

"It's not captains they need," said Iorwerth. "It's food and medicine."

She jerked her horse around. This could not go on or the battle was lost before it began. "They're a sorry lot all right," she said. "But Subidasto is right. We must do something to help my father and do it well. Then we can leave this stinking swamp."

"What do ye propose to do?" said Subidasto.

Not trusting Brennius she turned to the scowling Iorwerth. "How many are able to fight?"

"Maybe fifty," said Iorwerth, holding his nose.

"If you give me two days," said Brennius, "I'll bring a hundred of my invincible troops in from Trinoe."

She looked at Iorwerth dubiously.

"They'll be my men," said Iorwerth. "I'll send word with him."

"You have two days," said Guderius. "We attack in three."

"That will give us maybe a hundred and sixty and my cavalry," said Subidasto. "The Rummies won't take everyone with them when the attack starts. We're going to kill the rest and burn their town with that many? We'll lose that many getting in."

"I'll send you two hundred," said Guderius. "I can ill afford them."

"We won't lose any getting in," she said, suddenly making her mind up what to do. "We'll hide our weapons and mix in with the diseased. Put the worst looking ones in front."

"Mix with those diseased?" said Iorwerth.

"Wrap a wet cloth around your head. Tis no worse than facing a wall of Rummy shields."

Vallo touched her arm. "The best defense against the disease," he said, "is to rub mud from the swamp over your bodies. It has therapeutic qualities."

She clapped her hands together and beamed. "The stink from that alone will make the Rummies back off. They'll think we're all rotten with disease."

"You think the Rummies will let us just walk in?"

"We're not walking in we're walking through. They're building their town across our main road to Llan Dun[7] where we need to go to get healed. If we look and smell diseased enough the guards will back off. We'll go into the fort after King Guderius has drawn off the 20th and take care of any leftovers. Then we'll go into Verulam and burn it. My father wants a good example set so Owain and Basil can raise a real army from the Nazarenes."

Iorwerth looked at the Nazarenes, glowered and spat on the ground. "I will not spread that shit on my body," he said.

"I will spread it on mine," she said. "And you will spread it on yours. We will do whatever it takes to show Rome it is not the master of Britons." She looked steadily at the grouchy old nobleman and he lowered his eyes.

"What about the horses?" said Subidasto.

"Brennius can have them held here until the fires go up."

"What if the fires don't go up?" snarled Iorwerth.

"If the fires don't go up, my good friend," said Boudicca, "we won't need the horses. We'll be dead."

There was a long pause. Brennius unsheathed his sword and examined it. "Tis but a poor excuse for a weapon," he said. "Twas my father's and he got a kink in it fighting at the Thames."

She unfastened her sword belt and handed it to him. "Take mine. Give yours to one of your men."

Chapter 4

Morfudd

Owain Longhead, wearing the crimson robe, hat and gold chain that identified him as a member of the High Council of Kings and Druids, stood at his tent door on the island of Mona[a] and watched Basil and the two blue robed bards struggle up the hill toward him. They were on a path that zigged and zagged, and it would be a long time before they reached his tent. The buildings of the Druid College down below were covered in snow and knitted together by skeins of tracks carved out of the prevailing whiteness by hundreds of Druid footsteps. Icicles hung from their roofs and dripped black holes in the snow beneath. The skies were lead gray and a cold damp wind laden with flurries of snow and sleet rattled the leather sides of the tents.

Basil, the Nazarene preacher who had replaced the apostle Philip and who had been engaged by the Druids to stop the exodus of peace seeking Nazarene converts from Britain's armies, carried a bulky package under one arm and held down his flapping robe with the other. His companions carried nothing. As Owain watched, Basil slipped and almost fell. The two Druids stood back in alarm from the portly Hebrew so they would not be pulled down with him if he crashed to the ground but Basil recovered and struggled grimly on, clutching his package and skirt. Owain shivered and pulled his robe closer about him. A drop of ice cold moisture collected on the end of his long beaked nose and he wiped it off with the back of his hand as he reentered the warm tent and sat down at his table.

There were several scrolls on it waiting to be read, and Morfudd, a Druid Ovate who was his assistant, sat nearby at another smaller table. Impressed by her beauty and sharp intellect, he had asked the Council to assign her to him. Now, as she scratched away laboriously at a scroll with her bone pen, he was doubly glad that he had done so. It gave him a warm feeling to have her close by and so fully under his control. His wife the Princess Gwendolyn, the voluptuous but hysterical daughter of Caratacus and Genvissa, had gone back to her mother at Caer Leon, leaving him without any feminine companionship. Not that Gwendolyn provided much, he mused. Not only was Gwendolyn dense as bedrock, she persisted in prattling inanely on and on even when they were making love. It took his mind off what he was doing and very often he couldn't complete the act. No wonder Queen Genvissa had so slyly encouraged their marriage by appearing to resist it. Who else would have married her?

Morfudd's presence had gradually become important to him. His duties would be dull indeed if she was not here to share them under his guidance. He sighed. Morfudd's pen made so much noise as it moved across the scroll that he felt obliged to clear his throat. She stopped writing and looked at him with those calm blue-gray eyes that were so like Dedreth's, the heretic Nazarene girl he had once loved to no avail. He opened a scroll as an excuse not to be stared down by that steady gaze and cleared his throat again. "I thought so," he said, staring at the uniform lines of Greek script. "Your pen has split. Some of your lines are double."

"Can you read what I've written?"

"Yes," he said. "But it's not as neat as it could be. And there are little splatters that might be misinterpreted."

She shrugged and began to write again. He got up and went

over to her side. "Let me see it," he said, and she handed him the pen. It was a small diameter piece of animal bone as long as his hand. The marrow had been extracted from it and it had been shaped into a point at one end. The craftsman who made it had carefully cut a narrow slit in the point so the ink would find lodgment in it. Below the place where the craftsman's cut stopped there were teeth marks. In spite of the many warnings he had given her she must have chewed on the pen. The bone had split for some distance down the shaft. Whenever the writer made a sideways stroke it was apparent that the split pen would vibrate rapidly, accounting both for the noise and the imprecise calligraphy.

He was about to explain this to her and reiterate his warning not to chew on the pen when for some unaccountable reason he found himself looking not at the pen but at the flaxen hair that fell down her well formed back in three braids, each of which ended near the curve of her hips and the swell of her bottom in a small copper ball, and at the creamy white and subtle rosiness of her cheek, beyond which, if he bent his head slightly to the right, he could see the long curly lash of her right eye, and at the delicate tracery of her ear, across which lay a stray gossamer strand of golden hair that wound its sinuous way down her long white neck to disappear within the loose folds of her robe, there to bury itself within the depths of that delectable valley separating the breasts whose upper contours swelled gently with each breath. She turned to look up at him, eyes wide, bright and inquisitive, and the movement intensified the beauty of her and the intelligence of her and the fresh smell of her. He stepped back startled and collided with the small brazier that kept the tent warm. "I must get you a new pen," he said.

She reached up to take the pen from him and his free hand lightly brushed the soft down of her arm as it came to rest around her wrist. He didn't let go of the pen right away, and for a few moments their hands and eyes were softly joined together. With a smile she gently extracted herself from his grasp, the movement of her hands so graceful it seemed as if she caressed him. A strange unaccountable longing filled his heart and he was irritated when the servant opened the tent flap and announced Basil. Basil came in with the two blue robed Druid bards and stood with mouth open, blowing like a winded horse.

"Shall I leave?" asked Morfudd. He shook his head and motioned to her to go on writing.

After Basil had bowed, speechless from the climb, he sat down heavily on the stool by Owain's table and dropped the package he had been carrying on the floor. His cheeks, florid from the cold, flapped loosely as the breath went in and out of him in great gasps. He clapped his hands together several times and then blew on them. Little beads of moisture and snow stuck to his whiskers, cap and cloak. His protuberant brown eyes rolled from side to side and then fixed their surprised gaze on Morfudd, scratching away with her broken pen. The two Druids bowed respectfully to Owain and stood behind Basil. Neither the climb nor the cold had affected them. They glanced nervously at Morfudd and probably wondered how they should behave toward a green robed Ovate priestess, their superior in rank. He felt pleased that Morfudd ignored them, and returned their bows with a solemn bend of his head, conscious of the dignity of his position. "Bring wine and cakes," he said to the servant.

Basil stood up when the servant entered with the tray and took a cup from it. He went over to the low cupboard behind Owain's table, on which rested Owain's pitcher of drinking water and a bowl. Basil poured water into the bowl and washed first the cup and then his hands. Owain watched in amazement as Basil scrubbed away for what seemed an interminable period. After he had wiped his hands and the cup on Owain's clean cloth, he bustled back around the table still carrying the cloth and cleaned off an area of Owain's table before setting the cup down on it.

"I can't get used to this wretched climate," said Basil. "You will excuse me, my lord, but it is much milder where I come from." He emptied his cup and held it out to the servant for a refill. "Forgive me," he said, glancing back at the two Druids. "Are you acquainted with my assistants Logan Bullhead and Spuden the Sagacious? Your College of Druids has graciously permitted them to assist me in the work of organizing the Nazarenes."

Owain nodded again and smiled briefly at the two bards. Spuden returned his smile but Logan's face remained wooden. Owain sat down behind his table and folded his hands, conscious of the Druids' eyes resting on his coveted crimson robe. How unattainable such a robe must seem at this early stage of their career! "And how is the work progressing?" he asked.

Basil sighed. "With the help of the Father and my lords of the Council," he said, "we have now built seven synagogues. In every city and town we have visited, people hear the name Nazarene and surround us as soon as we begin to preach the good news."

"Then things are going well," said Owain.

"There are some problems, my lord," said Basil. He waved his hand as if to indicate the problems were minor in nature, then drained his cup and looked furtively at Owain while the servant refilled it. "The Lord Jesus warned that many would come seeking only the loaves and fishes." He paused, as if expecting Owain to say something, but Owain simply stared at him. Why did the man talk in riddles? "In other words," said Basil, "they bring us their sick and expect us to heal them for nothing. If we healed them for nothing, they would go away afterwards and we would never see them again. If we allowed this to continue we could never build an organization."

"That's true," said Owain. "Organization is the key to success in any venture. Without organization we have nothing." The noise of the scratching pen stopped and he glanced at Morfudd. She held the pen to the side of her nose and looked curiously at Basil. Then she shrugged and continued writing. The pen had left a smudge of ink on her nose. He felt an insane urge to go to her and wipe it off.

"Simon Peter and Philip, of course, encouraged this," Basil went on. "Joseph of Arimathea and his misguided followers heal any who come to them and demand nothing in return. They baptize, which is now illegal, without making any provision to organize synagogues so their converts can be properly taught and supervised. Worse than that, they tell people to call no man father but to pray directly to God. How could we ever organize if this were allowed to continue?"

"You have made all these points before," said Owain. "You have the full weight of the Council behind you to make sure such conditions do not continue. We have declared Joseph and those who follow him heretic to the true Nazarene religion and traitorous to the British nations. We have declared all heretic baptisms null and void and sufficient gold and craftsmen have been made available to build the synagogues you asked for. You need heal no one unless they have first agreed to join a synagogue, and you will be given first degree Druids to assure the converts are properly educated. With Queen Cartimandua's help we have even created a new army for Nazarenes to fight in. It seems to me that the framework of your organization is fully in place and that it simply remains for you to fit the people into it."

Basil pulled his stool closer to Owain's table and leaned forward. Owain got the uneasy feeling that Basil wanted to worm more concessions from the Council and made up his mind not to give an inch more. "My lord," said Basil. "It is true that I have made these points before, and that the Council has graciously approved measures to correct them. But none of us realized the depth to which the poison of Joseph's heresy has sunk into the people's mind. While we are gaining many converts, few of those already baptized by Joseph's disciples are joining our synagogues, and our own male converts disappear when we mention circumcision."

Owain nodded sagely. "Britons have an aversion to mutilation," he said. "You will have to work harder to overcome it. If we are to keep the support of the Jerusalem Council, we must present circumcision as an order from Duw to those males who wish to become Nazarenes."

"It would help," said Basil, "if you and the other male Council members were to be publicly circumcised as an example to encourage our Nazarene converts."

In the dead silence that followed, Owain became aware again that the scratchy pen had stopped writing. His cheeks grew hot. Morfudd must be picturing to herself what he would look like on public display getting circumcised.

"I am fully qualified to do it," said Basil.

Owain couldn't repress a shudder. "Unfortunately," he said, "Britain is bound by Molmutian law. A holder of kingly or priestly office must be free of any mental or bodily impairment. Any Council member, King or Druid who submitted to circumcision would have to give up his post."

Basil smiled sympathetically, and Owain got the feeling the man had anticipated the response he would get. "Perhaps it would be better," said Basil, "if we created an organization separate from your Council."

Owain felt his hackles rise. "You would separate Druids from religion?"

"Only until such time as your laws are revised to permit circumcision. In Alexandria, for example, religion is organized separately from the civil government. Each synagogue provides an elder to a central committee presided over by a president. I would propose that the Druids you appoint be detached from the Druid organization so they can be circumcised, and that we call them elders. When your laws have been changed the elders can go back into the Druid organization."

"And you, of course, would be the president."

"At the Council's pleasure, my lord. I would be simply a bridge between Nazarene and Druid."

"And how would this new organization be able to overcome the obstacles that prevent the old from succeeding?"

Basil clasped his hands together and took a deep breath.

Here it comes, thought Owain. "If you will forgive my bluntness," said Basil, "the present organization savors too much of Druidism. To the ignorant soldier and his wife initially attracted to Christ, it looks as if they are being asked to support Druidism under a new name. God is still called the Three Faces of Duw, or Duw-Bran or Duw-Ceridwen or Duw-Mabon or just Duw. To them Duw is a complicated Druid god they've never understood, and the new priests look just like Druids. What we need is an entirely new identity. Our religion must look as if it is completely independent of Druidism, although we, of course, will know that it isn't. It needs to drop this three-headed Duw as the name for God and it needs to speak of the Jerusalem Council as head of the organization. This way, if any problems occur, the Jerusalem Council will be responsible not the Druids."

Owain scowled. "It is apparent you do not grasp the Druid concept of Duw," he said. "Duw is not three headed. He is three-faced, three natures in one, not three heads on one body."

Basil waved an airy hand in dismissal. "It's too complicated. What we need is one God, elders instead of priests, and the elders need new robes entirely different from those identified with Druids. Let me show you." He reached into to his package and pulled out a long robe of Egyptian linen, beautifully crafted and worked throughout with gold and silver braid and studded with precious jewels. He stood up to display its full length and Owain gasped. "It has eight colors," he said, angrily counting them with his finger. "An Arviragus or an Archdruid can only wear seven, and we have none in this land higher than an Arviragus or an Archdruid."

"There is one higher, my lord" said Basil, pointing toward the sky. "The Father Himself is higher, and this is His robe to be worn by the President, who is the servant of the servants who represent Him on earth."

Momentarily nonplused by the man's audacity, Owain glanced at Morfudd. She laid down her pen and came lithely around Owain's table to examine the robe, the copper belt around her waist accentuating the catlike sinuosity of her body. Basil let her take it from him and she stroked it gently with her long pale hand while she examined the fabric. Owain wondered what it would feel like to be stroked so gently by Morfudd's hand. Then with a short laugh she handed the robe back to Basil.

"It's meaningless," she said, smiling at Owain. "If it had a multiple of three colors, or five, or the seven reserved to High Kings, it would have been an affront. But eight is a meaningless number." Of course, thought Owain. The number had no significance.

"The only ones it will offend," said Morfudd, going back to her table, "are the Romans. The purple is reserved to Caesar and the Senate, and they will frown upon its use by British priests."

"Let me see," said Owain, and Basil laid the robe across the table. A broad purple band passed around the neck of the garment, along each edge and around the hem. Of the seven other colors the most prominent was yellow. To Owain's taste the robe was gaudy. "Is it your intention to dress all of the elders in this?" he said.

"Oh no," said Basil. "As President, I will be the only one to wear that garment. With it, I will wear a purple cloak. The elders will wear robes with the same colors, only the hem color will be pink rather than purple."

"And of course you will wear a golden crown?" said Morfudd. "With eight carbuncles and sixteen white ostrich feathers?"

"No," said Basil, and Owain realized that Morfudd's sarcasm had gone over his head. Basil reached down into his parcel and came up again with a large purple hat. "The elders will wear similar hats but they will be white."

Owain felt his hackles rise again. "You know that white is a color reserved to full Druids?" he said. "Blue for Bards, green for Ovates and white for Pencerdds? We can not risk confusion between a Druid doctor and an elder."

"There should be no confusion, my lord," said Basil. "No Druid wears an eight color robe and a white hat."

"That's true," said Morfudd. "No Druid would wear such things."

"But our Pencerdds wear white hats and our Council members wear white plumes in their caps. If they are Pencerdds, they also wear a white enameled clasp to indicate their status." Owain touched his own clasp to make his point, looking at the two bards as he did so. "If a Council member is an Ovate, as a few of them still are, he wears a green enameled clasp. The uninitiated might fancy that an elder wearing a white hat is a Druid Pencerdd rather than, as he is most likely to be, a bard."

"I'm not sure that blue hats would match the robes," said Basil. "But if you insist, I will obtain blue hats."

"That would be preferable," said Owain. "Sometimes we find ourselves forced to do that which we had rather not do, and to do not that which we would rather do."

"What?" said Basil, but Owain looked at the tent wall.

"Do I understand what you are promising?" Morfudd asked Basil. "A new name for Duw and new uniforms for our priests will cause Britons to flock to your synagogues, get themselves circumcised, join our armies and fight against Rome?"

"I would it were that simple," said Basil, with hearty laughter that continued too long to fool Owain. Basil used his laughter to play for time while he thought up an answer to Morfudd's question. "We will, of course, need new doctrine," said Basil, shaking his head and coughing to clear away the last of the laughter. "Our organization needs to identify the arch enemy Rome as anti-Christus and Britons must be told to serve in the Father's army if they want His kingdom instead of Rome's. We must tell them our elders are the only legitimate means for communicating with the Father and the gates to the Otherworld—the Kingdom—will be forever closed if they do not obey them. They must be told that the time for free healing is past and that they must now buy candles if they want our elders to pray for them."

"Well," said Morfudd. "That should certainly convince them." Basil nodded eagerly, as if glad to find Morfudd in agreement.

Owain frowned at her. He could not allow her sarcasm to go unchecked even though Basil did not seem to grasp it. "I cannot say that any of this will come to pass," he said to Basil. "I have been authorized by the Council to oversee the organization of the Nazarenes and have great latitude in bringing this about. What you have proposed, however, is a radical departure from what has been previously envisioned. I must meet with the Archdruid and discuss it with him before I can allow you to proceed."

"Of course," said Basil. He folded up his gown and put it back into the package with his purple hat.

The man looks too self satisfied, thought Owain. If we don't give him what he wants, he will blame us for his failure. And if we do give him what he wants we've lost control of the Nazarenes. He rose and bowed to Basil, nodding to the two bards as they prepared to leave. "You will escort these gentlemen back to the College," he said to the servant. There was a rattling of scrolls and he turned to look at Morfudd with another frown.

"If you were to be offered a post as Nazarene elders," said Morfudd to the two bards, "would you accept circumcision and thus separate yourselves from the Druid organization with all its rights and privileges?"

Owain was shocked and gave her a stern glare. But then he felt impelled to look at the bards, who had said nothing during the entire interview. Their faces reddened. "Well?" said Owain.

"No," said Logan, glancing at Spuden.

"I would bear the circumcision," said Spuden, "if I were to be well compensated for the pain and stigma, and if I were assured my rights would be restored. But I would rather wear the blue robe of the least senior Druid than a robe and hat such as the one we've just seen."

"Thank you," said Owain, bowing again as the three men and the servant left the tent. He turned to look at Morfudd, who had returned to her writing. "That was an impertinent question," he said. "And one you should not have asked."

"On the contrary," said Morfudd, not looking at him. "It was quite pertinent. The entire effort to organize the Nazarenes can founder on this one sharp rock." She laid her pen down and looked at him. "Why not avoid the circumcision problem by appointing women priests to head the synagogues?"

"The Jerusalem Council would never approve. Even though many of the Nazarene missionaries are women, the female sex, as you must know, has no standing in the Jewish community. At some point they will undoubtedly bar Nazarene women from performing priestly functions."

"That may be their view," she said. "But this isn't Judea. British women of the Blaenorion[9] will not accept loss of standing in order to join the Nazarenes."

"You certainly wouldn't," said Owain, smiling. "But right now, we need the support of the Jerusalem Council more than we need to let women play an equal role in their religion. Having only men priests is an expediency that can be corrected later when we have our own Nazarene organization on a firm footing."

"Wouldn't it be simpler in the meantime," she said, "to recruit Jews to head the synagogues?"

"It would," he agreed. "We don't, however, entirely trust Basil. Doubts have been raised about his own Jewishness, and whether bona fide Jews or Nazarenes would associate with him in this venture. Besides, if we did bring in Jews to head the synagogues, we would lose control of his organization. With our own Druids in there we can at least recover it if he takes it in the wrong direction. His effrontery in selecting a white hat for our bards is an indicator of how far he could digress if not carefully watched. But your point is well made. We may have trouble convincing our Druids to get circumcised and wear a meaningless robe with those silly hats."

Morfudd got up from her table and came over to him. She reached out and adjusted the clasp that held his cloak together then looked up at him, still holding the clasp. A faint waft of perfume came from her, so delicate it was impossible to tell if it was her natural smell. It was a sweet, fresh smell. Unable to stop himself, he put a hand on each of her forearms and pressed them to his chest. His breath came faster.

"You've already thought of and through all my suggestions," she murmured, her eyes cast demurely downwards. "That is why you are the teacher and I the student. It is only because of your guidance that I won my way to being an Ovate. I do so admire my teacher, and I can see why the Council gives him all of its most difficult problems to solve."

"But it has also given me you to help," he said. "You ask the questions I would be afraid to ask and bring out the answers we need to hear."

"My questions sometimes shock you."

He nodded, and put one of her hands to his lips. The movement brought her closer to him and her stomach lightly brushed against his. The woman scent of her seemed overpowering and he gave a little involuntary gasp.

"What have you heard of your wife, the Princess Gwendolyn?" she asked, and he abruptly lowered her hand.

"She is still at Caer Leon with her mother," he said, his senses in a turmoil. "Rhys sent word she has fits of hysteria almost daily and they are getting worse. He has tried all nine herbal cures and none work. He thinks it is Duw-Bran's curse on her for some sin and that it is only his prayers that have saved her from something worse."

"Rhys is not one of our brighter Ovates."

"I don't know of any Ovate as bright as you. But he is particularly dull."

She smiled her appreciation. "What about the Nazarenes?"

He closed his eyes and was silent, until her arm came out from his loosened grasp and her hand put his to her mouth. She lowered it gently so that it came softly to rest against the valley separating her breasts as her stomach pressed lightly against his. He closed his eyes tightly and hoped the perspiration forming on his brow wouldn't run down his face. "The only Nazarenes who could help her," he said, his voice hoarse, "appear to be the ones we've declared heretic. It's the price we've had to pay for our Nazarene army."

The pressure of her against him increased perceptibly, and she gave him a sympathetic look, her eyes moist and her soft lips partly open. "If she cannot be cured, what will you do?"

"I don't know," he said, injecting as much gloom into his voice as he decently could. He ached to put his arms around her soft scented body and pull her to him, and something told him she would not resist. Beads of perspiration ran down his forehead and trickled down his nose as he visualized what would then happen. But his Druid training nagged at him. If he made such a move he would have taken the initiative. He would have sinned against Duw, defiled his marriage contract and corrupted his student. And if he buried himself in that tempting softness Morfudd would expect marriage and that could be complicated.

After all, he had married into the first family in the land and couldn't afford to offend it. If he took the initiative and Morfudd exercised her right to an immediate marriage in recompense, he would have to divorce Gwendolyn and give Gwendolyn's dowry back to Caratacus. Worse even than that, he might thereby lose the support he would need from the family if ever the post of Archdruid came within reach. If, however, Morfudd took the initiative she could not in good conscience demand an immediate marriage and he could enjoy the relationship he so urgently desired with her while he waited to see whether Gwendolyn continued to grow worse. If she did worsen, and it seemed likely that she would, the family might release him from his obligations and still look favorably on his ambitions. If they did that, he would then be free to marry Morfudd. Right now, urgent as was his need, he must restrain his natural impulses and wait to see if Morfudd would initiate something. He wished she would initiate something. Morfudd must surely sense that was what he wished.

But Morfudd simply kept his hand against her breasts and her stomach against his while she looked at him with that steady gaze that made him uncomfortable. She made no further move, and the back of his neck prickled as he wondered what he ought to do next.

Suddenly, there was a commotion outside the tent and a servant flung back the leather flap. Startled, Owain pushed himself away from Morfudd. "A courier, my lord," said the servant. With a surge of relief mixed with disappointed lust, Owain rushed to the door, Morfudd right behind him. A horseman charged up the slope and skidded to a halt in the little clearing before the tents. It was Atak, Boudicca's German counselor.

"A great victory!" shouted Atak in his atrocious Celtic, jumping off the horse and handing the reins to a servant. "King Caratacus has won a great victory against the Rummies!"

"That's wonderful news," said Owain, the sweat on his brow suddenly cold in the outside air. Leaving Morfudd standing in the tent doorway he ran to Atak, grabbed his arm in welcome and guided him toward the Archdruid's tent as the horn sounded, calling the Council members together. He would be the first to enter with Atak and thus share in the reflected glow of the victory. At the same time, however, he could not suppress a feeling of bitterness toward Caratacus. He had not seen fit to consult the Council before attacking the Romans, and even though he was no longer Arviragus and thus not obligated to heed the Council's advice, his action smacked of caprice. The current Arviragus was worthless but that did not justify independent action by the only leader the Romans feared. Caratacus had sent a message saying he was about to attack, but it had asked for no advice and did not indicate where the attack was to take place. How could Britain ever be unified if the Council were not allowed to perform its primary function?

And how could he Owain be expected to perform his own functions without the support of such a woman as Morfudd? Caratacus must surely understand that he Owain had been tricked into marrying his mad daughter the Princess Gwendolyn, and that he Caratacus was therefore obligated to help Owain cut the coil that held him in bondage. But Caratacus had never brought up the subject and it was unlikely that he ever would. Partly regretting that he had not had the courage to take advantage of Morfudd's obvious willingness to give herself to him, he ducked into the Council's tent still holding on to Atak's arm, bitterness drawing a deep frown across his forehead.

Chapter 5

Atak Reports

To Atak, Owain looked out of sorts. Maybe he needed a woman. Boudicca had said that Owain's wife had become unhinged by her marriage and it might be a long time before she was well again. He was glad he had picked a healthy woman for himself. Tetra was a Nazarene, an ex-disciple of Philip and the mother of Elsa. She wept a lot but there was nothing wrong with their sex life.

As he ducked into the Archdruid's tent and pried his arm loose from Owain's grip, he wondered how best to say what he had to say. The Council had been told that Caratacus had crossed the Severn on Samain night to meet Guderius' army near Verulam. Now, Caratacus had sent Atak to report on the results. "Make it sound good," Caratacus had said. "Their noses will be out of joint."

The red robed Druids wandered in to squat in a semi circle and Atak was shocked when he saw Archdruid Belinus. The old man had become frail. It won't be long, thought Atak, before he leaves for the Otherworld. The last time Atak had seen the Archdruid was just before the invasion when, as High King Cunobelinus, he was still Arviragus of Britain. Cunobelinus had fallen ill and was at death's door when Simon Peter healed him during his visit to Britain. Shortly after that he had given up command of the armies and the Romans assumed he had died, but Kings and Council had made him Archdruid Belinus. He had asked Simon Peter to send someone to teach the Druids about Christus and Simon Peter had sent Philip. It had been a big mistake. Warriors had become Nazarenes by the hundreds, laid down their weapons and now spent their time praying for peace. Atak had seen entire armies disintegrate overnight. Things had become so bad that the High Council had banished Philip and brought in Basil to stop the hemorrhaging.

The Archdruid greeted Atak then squatted before the Council. "So my son King Caratacus has won a great victory," he said. "Please tell the Council what happened."

"King Caratacus," said Atak, "sends his greetings to the Council. At the head of his armies, thirty thousand men in all, he crossed the Severn on Samain night. He destroyed many camps and fortlets belonging to the 14th legion, burned stocks of food and put several hundred Romans to the sword while many others fled. While he was doing this, King Guderius and his Catuve army attacked north of Verulam and destroyed a garrison and much food stocks, and freed many slaves.

"As we thought, the 20th legion sent cohorts to intercept King Caratacus and King Guderius. This left the 20th's base at Verulam undermanned. The new Nazarene army led by Queen Boudicca attacked the city at Verulam. The legionaries guarding the fort fled when her army approached and the city and fort were put to the torch and many colonists slaughtered. King Guderius cut some pieces out of the 20th and then went to ground in the marshes, while King Caratacus fought off the 14th and took refuge in the Ordoe mountains. All in all, less than two thousand Britons were lost. The Rummy frontier is now in disarray and the legion commanders are facing the anger of the new governor."

The Council cheered when Atak had finished. The Archdruid stood, leaning on the tent wall for support, and the Council grew quiet. "I can rest in peace," he said, "now that I know my son Caratacus has vindicated himself and proved that he is Britain's bravest and cleverest warrior king. He should have sought our advice first, but then it was we who dishonored him by taking away Pendragon and he is a proud man."

A young member stood up to speak. "My Lords," he said. "May I propose that this Council request King Caratacus to again become Arviragus of Britain?"

As the Council cheered, Owain stood, a black frown on his face. "I must remind my young friend Lord Bodin," he said, "that we already have an Arviragus."

"I propose we declare the present Arviragus incompetent," said a voice. "While his father makes fools of the Rummies, he's still trying to find someone who will trust him with an army."

"They tell me his lands have not produced but two thirds of what they should produce," said Bodin, and Atak saw Owain frown again. These two must be enemies. "The bees cannot make honey and the water is drying up in Llyn Brenig. The bulls are acting like eunuchs and the widow Angarad has had to be called in." Atak shuddered at the familiar name. He could still feel the dent in his skull that Angarad had placed there with her chin.

"Does anyone speak for the Arviragus?" said the Archdruid.

"No!"

"Then King Eudal Cyllinus Marius is declared incompetent. Who will tell him?"

"Young Bodin the Fox suggested it. Let him be the one."

"I will gladly go," said Bodin.

"And who will ask King Caratacus to be Arviragus?"

"His taboos will not let him take up what he has cast away," said the Archdruid. "But this Council owes it to him to make the request and I would ask Lord Atak to convey this to him."

Atak stood and bowed to the Archdruid. "I too fear that King Caratacus cannot accept," he said. "But I will ask him."

Owain pulled Atak to one side as the Council broke up. "Tell me truly," he said. "How was the Nazarene army?"

"What Nazarene army?" said Atak. "Those people you sent were diseased and useless. They only joined because Basil said they would be healed if they bought a candle and fought. Without Subidasto's fifty men and two hundred from Guderius she would have had no army."

"She burned Verulam with two hundred and fifty men?"

"She got in by taking the diseased with her and covering them with bog slime. The Rummies ran to get away from the stink. She said they weren't even Nazarenes."

Owain gripped his arm. "This mustn't get out," he said, "but she's right. They are a nucleus around which to form a proper army once Basil has convinced the Nazarenes to fight."

"Tetra says Nazarenes will never fight."

"She means the heretics like Elsa. The true Nazarenes are the ones who accept Basil's teaching and join our Nazarene army."

"Why don't you just stick with non-Nazarenes?"

"Because, my dear man, the heretics are decimating our armies. Their healings attract thousands. It's a tremendous unifying force and we have to find some way to use it in our cause." He stopped and glowered as Bodin, the young Council member, passed by them. "I must warn you," he went on, "to convince your wife to support Basil. That man who just passed us is arguing for drastic action against the heretics."

"She says Basil is a thief. He stole a bag of gold from her in Gaul. It was my gold."

Owain shook his head as if none of that mattered. "Bodin wants control of the Nazarenes. He wants the Council to kill those who set up the Nazarene College as an example. Your wife would be in danger and most certainly her daughter Elsa."

Atak clutched Owain's robe. "You tell Bodin," said Atak, "that if anyone touches Tetra or Elsa he won't live to dwell on it. And his death won't be quick."

"Then you had better kill him first," said Owain. "Elsa is the one he most wants to kill."

***

Owain hurried back to his tent, eager to tell Morfudd the news. It was already dark from the lowering clouds and the dying wind whipped the snow around him in erratic gusts. He must find some way to have Morfudd without raising the specter of divorce. She would feel so warm and comforting in his arms and it had been so long since even the unsatisfying Gwendolyn had been within them. He sighed as his pace quickened. He needed this relationship with Morfudd. Without it, life would be too lonely and monotonous to bear.

He flung the leather flap aside and felt the warmth of the tent envelop him as the flap closed. Morfudd was not at her table. She must have gone to the latrine tent. He went to his table and sat down. Right in front of him was a small scroll. He picked it up and unrolled it. It was in Morfudd's scratchy Greek handwriting.

> My Lord Owain Longhead of Caer Went (Why is she being so formal, he wondered?)
>
> It became clear to me, after you left to attend the High Council, that I must withdraw from this most cherished appointment as your assistant. Much as I yearn for a continuance of the intellectual and physical stimulation I have always derived from my long association with you, the emotional cost of repressing the natural effect of such stimulation is greater than I can bear. I am, after all, a woman: and the emotions of a woman are not as easily concealed as those of a man. While I cannot help admiring your great intellect and feeling the womanly warmth such admiration inspires, I cannot overlook the fact that you are the captive of an unfortunate marriage. While I esteem the bravery with which you face life deprived of those emotional and physical comforts that a wife should provide, my esteem, rather than bringing

comfort to you is instead a source of danger. So long as your marriage continues, my emotions are illegal, and if you ever reciprocated them in a weak moment, as I believe almost happened today, could sully your honor and reputation. While your marriage is a marriage in name only, it is nevertheless a legal and holy relationship that must be honored so long as it exists. It is therefore, with great reluctance but with a conviction of the rightness of my decision in the eyes of Duw and our fellow Druids, that I surrender my post.

Your obedient servant in Duw,
Morfudd.

"Yes, yes!" said Owain, laying the scroll down and even in his shock at her resignation agreeing with Morfudd's clear perception of his own rightful needs. Then "No, no!" he said, as he realized that Morfudd might at that moment be leaving the college. He plunged out of the tent and stood momentarily blinded by the dark gray and misty whiteness that blotted everything from view. The wind had stopped and the snow fell in thick gentle silent swirls, caressing his face and hands with momentary kisses of cool wetness.

Why did he always have so much trouble with women? The ones he loved abandoned him, and the one he had never learned to love was a millstone around his neck. Morfudd was the ideal wife for him, possessed of beauty, intellect and a true appreciation of the untapped need for love and devotion within him. He gasped as he thought again of her loveliness and of the delights implied by her letter should she replace Gwendolyn as his wife. A dark shape loomed through the snow and his heart leaped, thinking it was Morfudd, but it was Bodin. Bodin looked at him strangely. His emotions must be showing, and he struggled to get his face under control. "What do you want?" he said.

"I came to see Morfudd," said Bodin.

"Why? What business can you have with her?"

"What is that to you?" said Bodin. "I asked her to do something for me and I have come to see if she has done it."

Owain was so angry that he trembled. He wanted to tell Bodin that as the most junior member of the Council he should be seen and not heard. But something about this upstart overawed him and immobilized his defenses. "You must not give her things to do," he said. "She is assigned to help me."

"You don't own her," sneered Bodin. "She tells me she has lots of free time. She has special knowledge that is of great assistance to me and has gladly offered to help."

"Then I am withdrawing her offer," said Owain. "You must not visit this tent again."

For a moment Bodin hesitated and Owain feared he would force his way into the tent and find Morfudd gone. But the new Council member must have realized that he couldn't conquer Owain, possessed as Owain was of more seniority and marital ties to the first family in the land. Bodin sniffed contemptuously, turned on his heel and disappeared into the snow.

Owain tried to calm himself down. What had Bodin asked Morfudd to do? He should have asked, but Bodin most likely would not have told him. And why had Morfudd agreed to help Bodin without asking him Owain first? The only special knowledge she possessed was her grasp of the Hebrew language gained during a two-year sojourn in Judea. Why would Bodin be interested in Hebrew? With a sudden pang he remembered that Bodin was unmarried. He was also much closer to Morfudd's age. Was the man attempting to worm his way into Morfudd's heart? Was his request for help a mere device just to get closer to her? Suppose Morfudd married him? Life without Morfudd would be a terrible blank, but the thought of her married to this supercilious upstart of a new council member was too much to bear. With an anguished cry, he set off down the hill. Her letter had made it clear she would do nothing without marriage. Then his marriage must cease to exist so he could marry Morfudd. He would bare his soul to Caratacus and ask to be relieved of his mad, useless wife. He must find Morfudd and tell her the good news.

"Morfudd!" he shouted, as he ran slipping and sliding down the hill. The snow ingested his voice into its silence, and soon he ceased to shout.

Chapter 6

Consummation

Eighteen months later

The marriage between Venutius and Cartimandua was to take place in Cartimandua's palace at Barwick. Not only were Boudicca and Prasu there but Governor Scapula himself, escorted by a cohort from the 9th Legion and several Roman dignitaries. Caratacus came disguised as a bard.

Prasu, eager as he was to see the British nations unite under Roman rule, expressed doubts about the marriage. "Venutius has acknowledged Cartimandua's treaties with Rome," he said, as he and Boudicca ate their morning meal with Habren, Goneril and Gwenda in Cartimandua's drafty hall. "But there are rumors that those foolish Britons who still insist on fighting Rome want him to be Arviragus as soon as he becomes a High King. If Venutius became Arviragus she would have to divorce him and if she divorced him then of course he would no longer be a High King and could not be Arviragus. I hope he sees the logic of not accepting."

Boudicca ached to tell him the Britons would more likely kill Cartimandua so Venutius' status as High King would not be threatened but she restrained herself. Much as it grieved her to see Venutius marry that witch, she wanted to see him as Arviragus and would say nothing that might threaten it. Venutius' marriage would be as much a charade as her own. Besides, Venutius wanted to see her as soon as the wedding was over. She leaned forward and took the tray of food away from Gwenda, then picked up the little girl, kissed her tenderly and placed her in Prasu's arms. Gwenda was his favorite, and he would quickly forget about Venutius if he played with her. Goneril, the love child of Venutius and she, was her own favorite.

Goneril was six years old and already an expert with the hurly stick. She took it for granted that all the children in the palace should defer to her. Gwenda, mild and placid, yielded easily, much like her father. The sweetest and prettiest of the two, her quick cornflower blue eyes forever peered brightly through a tangled mass of long blonde-white hair as if looking for something to laugh at. Goneril of the diamond eyes and brilliant red hair ran in front of the pack, ready to challenge or explore. Gwenda ran just as hard, but always to follow Goneril. Goneril ran silently with narrowed eyes and pursed lips. Gwenda ran noisily with eyes bulging and mouth stretched wide with joy. If Goneril weren't here, Gwenda would run after someone else but would never lead the way. Goneril was the daughter of her true marriage.

The contracts had been signed and the wedding feast begun. Now, as Cartimandua walked back into the palace with Scapula, Boudicca caught Venutius' eye again. He moved his head almost imperceptibly, but she read his meaning. Slipping away from Prasu, who was hurrying to catch up with Scapula, she passed through the crowd to the stables, mounted her horse and rode through the forest to the river where Venutius had said he would meet her.

The trees thinned out and the ground became a grassy bank sloping down to the languidly moving water. She dismounted and let her horse graze, sitting with her back to a tree so that she could bask in the sun and let her eyes rest on the beauty surrounding her. Other than the quiet rippling of the water, only the sleepy noise of insects and birds broke the peace. The afternoon sun shimmered in the heat rising from the ground and painted a fractured image of itself in the nacreous river. If she had not been so excited about meeting Venutius on his wedding day she would have gone to sleep.

She heard his horse approaching but would not get up. She would sit here and he would sit beside her while they drank in the beauty of his new realm. A shadow fell across her and there he was. She looked up at him towering above her in his regal wedding finery and the forgotten visceral thrill went through her. Had it really been so many years?

He dropped to his knees at her side, his face close to hers.

"And now I must call you Sire," she said.

He raised her hand to his lips. She saw her ring on his finger and suddenly felt secure in his love. "We are equal at last," he said. "I am a High King and you are no longer far above me. You are married for Britain's sake and so am I."

"We are by no means equal. Your bedmate is the most beautiful woman in Britain. My bedmate grows fatter and lazier every day."

"My bedmate is a witch I fear to sleep with. She has wrung every iota of concession out of the Council and has so tied her kings that I am High King in name only. I have no power."

"If you have enough to make you Arviragus it is all we need."

"She has tied Scapula in even worse knots. What she got out of him would cost him his life if Rome knew. He's out of his mind with lust for her but she is too clever for him."

"And whom do you lust after?"

He was on her in a moment, and she found herself flat on the grass. "Stop. Stop," she cried, so urgently that he froze.

"What is it?"

She began to giggle uncontrollably. "Our clothes," she said, pushing him away. "We cannot go back with grass stains all over your royal knees and my backside."

She pulled the clothes from herself as quickly as he did and they were together naked, the heat rising within barely cooled by the damp grass without. Their bodies became streaked with green and dotted with unfelt bits of leaf and twig as they eagerly writhed together seeking the long remembered sensation of lips and hands against loved flesh. "Oh my darling man," she gasped. "How I have ached for you. It has been so long this is like a wedding night for me."

It was over all too quickly, but never mind, she told herself as she luxuriated in the feel of him. This is my wedding night, and now we are both equal we can be true man and wife. And the more I take from him the less there will be for that bitch. I hope he cannot do anything at all when she takes him to bed.

"I had made up my mind to do this," said Venutius, his head sideways on her breast. "I would consummate my marriage in no other way. From now on you are my true wife."

"I will go with you wherever you go. Prasu has Habren and the girls. I have you. And now I want you again."

***

Some weeks later

It was pitch black when Boudicca rode into Colchester, Venutius at her side, his handsome powerfully built man at arms Velocatus and the few survivors of their little group behind. The place teemed with retired legionaries and they rode carefully and quietly, keeping to the dirt tracks behind the houses and shops. She stopped behind Ingenius' shop. It was dimly lit inside and through a small grill in the door she could see Ingenius working near a large steaming vat. She tapped on the door.

He squinted at the grill as if to see his visitors and raised his heavy ladle as though it were a weapon. "Who is it?" he said. When he saw who it was, he put the ladle down. The door opened and the smell of boiling tallow came out.

"It stinks in here," she said as he went down on one knee.

"I'm making candles," said Ingenius. "Catus has me doing it for Queen Cartimandua's Bishop Basil."

She stood looking down wearily at Ingenius. She felt anything but queenly in her dusty tartan trousers, shirt, cloak and leather boots. Her long braided hair was full of dust and her face dirty. "We must sleep," she said. "We hurt the Rummies again, but we've ridden all last night and today and we're exhausted."

"How many of you are there?"

"Nine," said Boudicca. "King Venutius is with me."

"Your men can sleep in the storehouse, Sire," Ingenius said to Venutius, who looked as tired and dirty as she did. "There is water and fodder for the horses, and the Rummies never go behind the shops at night. I can find room for you both above." He led the way to a ladder that went up to a loft. He had made the loft into his own quarters now that he was no longer married to Elsa. Boudicca flopped on Ingenius' cot just as she was, barely aware of Venutius on the floor beside her before she fell asleep.

Ingenius came up at noon carrying two buckets of water for them to wash in followed by Cruker carrying loaves of bread and a roast of meat. Boudicca and Venutius sat on Ingenius' bed as Velocatus and the warriors squatted against the opposite wall. Their faces brightened when they saw the food and soon they were all eating and drinking.

"Where did you come from?" asked Ingenius.

"The Rummies are building a new road from Lincoln to Leicester," she said. How was she going to tell him about Elsa? "They're putting fortlets all along it and we just wiped out two of them." She gulped down the last of her wine and stood, looking down at Venutius. These puny little attacks that Venutius loved would have to cease. They must focus their resources on something worthwhile if they were really to hurt the Rummies. She was beginning to feel that Venutius, much as she loved him, did not have a big enough grasp to be Arviragus. Council and Kings had not yet met to confirm his election and he took the delay as an affront. "We lost too many men doing it," she said. "We must plan our attacks better."

Venutius looked black. "You can't kill Rummies without losing men," he said.

"I want to kill Rummies as much as you do," she said, "but we'll need every man we can get to defeat a legion and we need to focus on that."

Venutius snarled. "Get those Nazarenes to quit enticing our men away," he said, "then we'll have enough soldiers."

She saw she would make no headway with Venutius and turned to Ingenius. "We came to see you for two reasons," she said. "The first is that we need weapons. We want you to make some for us."

"The Rummies dole iron out to me," said Ingenius. "They keep track of what I use."

"Then you must waste more. With what you waste you can make weapons for us and send them to Basil inside the candle barrels."

Ingenius' jaw dropped. "This is Rummy headquarters," he said. "We'd never get away with it."

She smiled triumphantly. "Cartie's treaty gives her unlimited rights to supplies," she said. "Shipments to Basil will be neither stopped nor searched."

"How does she manage to play both sides?"

"Look," said Venutius, waving away the question. He brought out the head of a Roman lance and handed it to Ingenius. Made of iron and weighted with lead, the point was twisted so it would dig into a shield or a man's body and be difficult to withdraw. She shuddered, remembering the feel of such a one inside her shoulder. "We want you to make a few hundred like this that will go through a Rummy shield. Ours are too light. They bounce off their armor."

Ingenius nodded and sat down to examine it.

"When can we have some?" she asked.

"I'll put a hundred in the next shipment. Next month."

She sat down on the bed next to him and put her hand on his arm. "Elsa is in the Rummy fort at Longthorpe. She was in a village near one of the fortlets we wiped out and the Rummies took all the villagers. They will send her to Rome as a slave."

Ingenius dropped the lance head and stood. His face was white and tears were in his eyes. He must still love her. "When?" he said.

"I don't know," she said.

Ingenius dried his tears. "I'll go to Catus," he said. "He will give me a warrant to get into Longthorpe. Sabinus is there. He is my friend and will help me get Elsa out. Especially if I tell him you wish it."

Boudicca reddened and cast a quick look at Venutius. Julius Sabinus was a tribune, stocky but handsome, her own age and one of the few Romans she had been able to tolerate. He had spent much time at Prasu's palace and had made his interest in her obvious. She had never encouraged him but his courtesy and good humor never slackened. Much as she loved Venutius she couldn't ignore the fact he was jealous as well as hot headed. If he got wind of Sabinus' interest he would not rest until the tribune had been killed. "She won't come back to you, you know," she said.

"I know," said Ingenius. "It's my fault she left me. But I love her dearly all the same."

"As soon as it's dark," she said, "we're off to Thetford. I must see my daughters and put in an appearance as Prasu's queen or the Rummies will get suspicious. You can ride with us then go on to Sabinus." She paused and looked again at Venutius. "Remember me to him, and while you're at Longthorpe keep your eyes and ears open. Find out what you can about Scapula's plans."

Chapter 7

Scapula Moves

Armed with a warrant from Catus, Ingenius dismounted outside the Roman fort at Longthorpe. It was early morning and raining lightly, so he held the bag of scrolls Catus had given him to carry to Quintus Marcellinus under his cloak. He left his horse tied outside, and the centurion in charge of the guard let him in after reading Catus' warrant and searching him for weapons.

A legion laid a heavy burden on the supporting countryside. It demanded utensils, food and other stores not only for its current needs but also for long-term storage. In addition to its own support, the legion was responsible for activities requiring the forced labor of thousands of Britons. The ancient network of British roads and bridges had to be improved or new ones surveyed and built, and huge quantities of stone, metal scraps and gravel needed to complete them had to be quarried, shaped and transported. Canals had to be dug and boats built to transport cargoes. Granaries had to be constructed, harvests allocated to fill them and fortlets built to protect them. Grain, horses, dogs and cattle for export had to be rounded up and got down to the ships. The taxes levied on all landowners and tenants had to be collected either in kind, which required assessment and storage, or in coin which varied by nation and had to be valued in accordance with prevailing exchange rates. All of this required an army of clerks and accountants, most of whom were Britons.

While he waited he looked anxiously around the fort, wondering where Elsa might be. A long row of low wooden buildings must be the barracks, and the large high building besides which many horse drawn carts stood must be the granary. Other buildings like the one he waited to enter seemed too open and too full of activity to be prisons. And the large neatly raked square he had passed was empty. The prisoners must be outside the fort in a stockade. Sabinus would know where.

When he handed Catus' scrolls to the British scribe interviewing those in line, the Briton glanced quickly at them then beckoned Ingenius to follow him. The Briton, his baldhead surrounded by an untidy fringe of sandy hair, was dressed in a short gray robe and sandals. He led the way to a room at the end of the building and knocked on the door. At an answer from within, the Briton opened the door and Ingenius found himself face to face with Quintus Marcellinus. The Roman sat behind a table covered with scrolls and had been looking out of the small window when the door opened. He was thin for a Roman, his hair and beard black and his skin sallow as if from spending too much time indoors. He looked at Ingenius through half closed lids then held his hand out to take the scrolls.

Marcellinus glanced at them casually then let them roll up and looked again at Ingenius. "You are here to see Titus Julius Sabinus?" he asked.

Ingenius nodded. "Sabinus is my friend," he said.

"Sabinus is not your friend," said Marcellinus. "Sabinus has stepped down." Ingenius recoiled in shock. "Well, if he hasn't yet, he soon will."

"What has happened?" said Ingenius. Unbidden, he sat down on a bench near the door.

"He was wounded when your Britons attacked one of our forts. The legatus is with him now and has ordered me to execute six British nobles when Sabinus is gone. I tell you this because you will be one of the six. Sabinus was the most loved of our tribunes, a man marked for great advancement. The Britons butchered him beyond reason."

Ingenius stood, surprised even in his grief for Sabinus that Marcellinus' threat affected him so little. "Let me see him," he said.

"You will see nothing and no-one," said Marcellinus, turning to stare again out of the window, "save the man who will carry out your execution."

"If you will read the scroll," said Ingenius, "you will see that I am under the protection of Catus Decianus."

Marcellinus picked up the scrolls and stared at the innermost one for a long time then let it roll itself up again.

"Please let me see Sabinus," said Ingenius. "He is my friend and he would wish to see me."

"Take him," said Marcellinus, and Ingenius followed the Briton out of the room.

"You're lucky," said the Briton. "I saw what Catus wrote, but Marcellinus was too upset to read it. The legatus, he's hopping mad about the raid. Seems as if they took the heads off two of em. If you can get word back, tell them not to take Rummy heads. It makes them mad and then they kill a lot of poor villagers who had nothing to do with any of it. And that isn't fit. It isn't right."

"I'll pass the word," said Ingenius.

"It just isn't the fitness of things," said the Briton. "By the way, my name's Sadoke. And this here is the officers' quarters." Sadoke stopped before a door guarded by two legionaries. "Quintus Marcellinus sent him," Sadoke said to the legionaries, who jerked their heads as permission to enter.

There were several cots in the sparsely furnished room, and around one a group of Romans gathered. Several turned to face Ingenius as he approached. The faces were not friendly, and one or two of them were stained with tears.

"I am a friend of Sabinus," he said. He tried to look at the figure lying on the bed, but an angry senior tribune he recognized as Rutilus blocked his view. He had not seen Rutilus since he met him at Prasu's palace in Thetford two or three years before.

"What are you doing here?" said Rutilus, his mouth working with anger. "You Britons are savages. By Jupiter you will pay for this." He shoved Ingenius, and Ingenius fell back.

"Wait," said one of the men around the cot. "He wants to see him."

Rutilus stood aside, eyes glaring, and Ingenius went to the cot. He was shocked at Sabinus' appearance and knelt by the bed, tears running down his cheeks. Even though the young tribune's wounds had been cleaned and wrapped it was evident he had suffered terrible cuts and must have lost much blood. His breathing was faint, and Ingenius barely heard his own name.

"I'm sorry, Sabinus," he said, afraid to touch the wounded Roman. "I am so sorry." Then it came to him what to do. He stood up and faced Rutilus. "You must believe me and do what I say," he said to Rutilus. "Sabinus' life can be saved."

Rutilus didn't answer but another tribune grabbed his arm. "What?" the tribune said. "What must we do?"

"There is a woman among the prisoners," he said. "Her name is Elsa. She will heal Sabinus." The tribune hesitated. "Come, man," said Ingenius, starting for the door. "Do not waste time."

The tribune rushed to overtake him and led the way out of the building, mud splashing up from their feet as they ran, Rutilus hard behind. They left the fort and ran to its south side where Ingenius saw a stockade filled with wet British women, children and animals. There was no shelter. Anger welled up in him as he thought of Elsa trapped here, treated as an animal. The guards opened the gate at the tribune's order and Ingenius rushed inside. He looked around frantically until a woman grabbed his arm.

"I'm looking for Elsa," he said, tears streaming down his face. The woman didn't seem to comprehend. "Brigit," said Ingenius.

The woman's face lit up. "Over there," she said. There was a crowd against the fence and he forced his way through. Elsa stood looking up at a frightened boy being held up from the other side, and the crowd had made a circle around her. "She healed him," someone said, and then Elsa looked around and saw Ingenius. Her wet clothes were torn and dirty, her hair bedraggled, her face weary, but her wide eyes looked at him with that same calm poise that had always humbled him. He clasped her to him.

"Thank you, thank you," said the boy's mother, and he could hear the noises of a crowd murmuring in awe beyond the wall. "Glory be to Duw and to Brigit for my son."

"My darling," he said. "My darling Elsa." He kissed her and held her to him, and she kissed him and patted his cheek.

"Don't cry," she said. "I am doing God's work and that is the happiest work of all. I have been able to help so many here. And many are converted to become true Nazarenes. Even those who think I'm a goddess and call me Brigit." She looked at the two tribunes.

"Is this the woman?" said Rutilus. It was obvious the tribune didn't recognize her, bedraggled as she was, although he must have seen her often at Prasu's palace.

"She is my wife," he said.

Rutilus snorted. "I thought as much. This is just another British trick. Well both of you will die for this."

"Wait Rutilus," said the other tribune. "Let's see what she says."

Ingenius clasped Elsa's hand. "Sabinus," he said. "You remember Sabinus."

"Yes," said Elsa, still gazing at the two tribunes.

"He's been badly wounded. He's dying. Can you save him?"

She turned her eyes on him, and he cast his eyes down. "Do you still believe in Christ?" she asked.

"I don't know what I believe since you left me," he said. "I know there is something to believe in, but I don't know how to do it."

"You have grown more honest," said Elsa, stroking his cheek. "Go back to Sabinus. You will find him well."

He looked at her, unbelieving.

"Do as I say," she said, smiling at him.

"But what about you? I can't leave you here."

"I will always be where God wants me to be, Ingenius. Now go with these good tribunes."

He let go of her, unsure of himself.

"Well?" said Rutilus. "Is she going to heal him?"

"Sabinus is healed," he said. He didn't know why, but the certainty that Elsa had healed Sabinus flooded his being. While he stood gazing at Elsa, a woman pushed past him and fell at Elsa's feet. Elsa reached out to touch the woman's face as if no longer conscious of his presence. He turned and walked blindly toward the gate, the tribunes following him.

"You will wait here," said Rutilus, when they reached the guardhouse.

"Sit over there," said a centurion, pointing to a stool against a wall, and Ingenius sat there until it was past noon. He wondered if Sabinus had really been healed. At noon, a legionary appeared with a bucket of hot food and doled some out to the centurion and his guardsmen, but offered none to Ingenius. Then shortly after, two brisk legionaries showed up to collect him. They moved him quickly out of the guardhouse and down a broad graveled path to a low building before which stood the legion standards. A guard opened the door as they approached and he found himself steered through an anteroom toward another door that remained closed until a legionary asked permission to enter. Then the door was opened from within.

Ingenius was ushered in at a fast pace by the two legionaries, who saluted and then retired to stand by the door. The man sitting behind the large table was balding, his remaining hair black laced with silver, forming a neatly trimmed fringe around his head. The eyes were brown, birdlike and piercing, the chin strong and clean-shaven. He was dressed in a simple toga edged with the broad purple of a senator, and he sat erect and vigilant, his elbows on a large map that covered most of the table and his hands pressed together so that the fingers supported his chin. This must be Caesius Nasica, *legatus legionis* of the Ninth Hispana. Two legates stood woodenly behind the table, one on either side of Nasica, and it looked as if they had all been examining the map. The legion commander stared at Ingenius, lips pursed, for several moments before speaking. Without looking directly at it, Ingenius tried to comprehend the nature of the map. There was a large island close to the mainland in the corner furthest away from Nasica. A jar of ink lay on the map and a stylus. They had been drawing lines and entering numbers.

"You are the husband of this woman who healed my tribune, Titus Julius Sabinus?" said Nasica.

Ingenius' heart lifted. So Sabinus had been healed. "I am Ingenius, son of Lord Degveth of the Silures," he said. "I was the husband of Elsa but our marriage is ended."

"You have put her away from you?"

"I have not put her away, your Excellency," said Ingenius. "She left me to follow Christ." He glanced down at the map when he sensed Nasica's eyes had strayed from his face and thought the island must be Mona. Several lines had been drawn across the map.

"I have heard of this Christus. His followers have caused problems in Rome. What is your relationship with Catus Decianus?"

By the look on the commander's face, Ingenius knew he held Catus in contempt. "I own a workshop in Colchester," he said. "Catus Decianus arranges for me to get raw materials and orders for goods which he has shipped abroad for trade."

Nasica sniffed. "And I suppose you are getting rich from Roman trade?" he said. Ingenius cast his eyes down as if unwilling to answer. The line that crossed the map and ended in what looked like the estuary of the holy Dee must come from this fort. Other lines came up from the south at different angles and stopped when they joined another line that must follow the Dee into the mountains. Figures had been written on the map where the lines intersected, but he couldn't make out what they might mean. There were lines heading down toward the Severn estuary. He forced himself to look away from the map and saw that one of the legates was watching him with a cold stare.

"The woman has been removed from the stockade," said Nasica, "and cleaned up. She has been attracting people with all kinds of diseases and I have given orders that she is to remain inside the fort until the crowds have gone and we can let her go free. I don't understand her religion, but I cannot argue with such results as we have witnessed. Tell me, how does she perform these wonders? Are they magic?"

"It is not magic, your Excellency," said Ingenius. "What it is I can't explain. But it is not magic."

Nasica looked at him for a long time without saying anything, and he felt worthy of the contempt he saw in the faces of the commander and his legates. How could he have lived with Elsa and not come to understand more about this great power she wielded? Like a child he had run after the toys brandished by Catus and away from his most precious asset. His promises to Catus and his partner the great Seneca had been far more important to him than his promises to Elsa. No wonder she had left him. He couldn't prevent the tears from filling his eyes as he thought of what he had so casually let go, and what he could not ever regain.

"You may go," said Nasica, at last. "You will be out of this fort by morning. Quintus Marcellinus will give you papers to take to Catus Decianus."

Ingenius bowed and turned toward the door, hardly able to see for the tears. The legionaries opened it, the centurion escorted him through the anteroom, and he found himself outside, a hard burning sensation in his throat.

When he turned a corner to walk down the graveled road that led to the officers' quarters, he saw a crowd of legionaries and some centurions outside Sabinus' building. The centurions made no effort to keep order. He reached the fringe and tried to get through but found it impossible. The men began to shout: "Sabinus. Sabinus." The door opened, and Sabinus stood on the threshold, other figures dimly seen behind him. He was fully dressed in armor, and held his helmet to his chest with his right hand. The crowd gasped in awe. Ingenius himself could not restrain a gasp. There was no sign of injury on the tribune.

"Where is the woman?" shouted someone in the crowd. Sabinus turned and Elsa came to his side. The crowd grew still, the only sound the breathing of men seized by the wonder of Sabinus' healing. Elsa wore a long white pleated stola that covered her from her waist to her feet, and a white mantle that draped her hair and fell gracefully around her shoulders to below her waist. Sabinus or one of his friends must have purchased the clothes to send back to their women folks in Rome and given them instead to Elsa. Her hands were clasped in front of her, and she stood erect and confident by Sabinus' side. Ingenius felt the lump in his throat grow hot and hard again as he saw the great beauty of her and remembered the feel of her close to him and the look of the gentle eyes that had been for him alone. She looked fresh, clean and graceful, her lips parted in a quiet serene smile as she gazed at the men facing her. Many of them kneeled before her, but she opened her arms and bade them rise.

"You must not kneel to me," she said. "I am a child of God as are all of you. I am a follower of Lord Jesus, the Christ. He came to show us that God is love and that the power of God's love destroys the evils that would imprison us, as we learn to humble ourselves, have no gods but his God, and love our neighbors as ourselves. We must love all without discrimination, just as we would have them love us."

"Show us," said many voices. "Teach us of Christus."

Sabinus raised his hand, and the noise died down. "Caesius Nasica has granted Elsa her freedom," he said, "in gratitude for my healing. I too am grateful for my healing, although I cannot yet comprehend it, and for our general's action in rewarding Elsa's goodness. If she wishes to teach us of Christus, I for one would be anxious to learn. But I remind you that, while she has been given her freedom, we haven't. Many of us march tomorrow, and it will be months before we return."

A centurion pushed his way forward and knelt before Elsa. Even though she gestured for him to get up, he wouldn't. "Come with us, Elsa," he said. "We will make a chair for you and carry you, and you will have your own tent. Come with us and teach us."

"You would have her march with us, her enemies, against her friends?"

"She has no enemies," said the centurion. "And if she has no enemies she has no friends. You heard her say all men are the same."

"What about us who stay? Why shouldn't she teach us?"

Sabinus raised his hand again, and the centurion got up as the hubbub died down. "A legion on the march is no place for a woman," said Sabinus. "And we should not ask it of her. We must free Elsa as our general commanded. Perhaps when we return she may come to teach us."

"What about Gallus and Rufus? They are close to stepping down. Will Elsa come and heal them?"

Elsa stepped forward. "I will try," she said. "Take me to them."

The crowd surged off in the direction of the legionaries' barracks, Elsa in the midst of it. Ingenius found himself alone with Sabinus. "I cannot believe my eyes," he said, touching the tribune's cheek. "Even though she healed me of a crippled leg."

"I knew that all was over," said Sabinus, taking Ingenius' hand. "I could feel life draining away. Then suddenly my strength returned and I was normal. The people around me fell away in horror. I was horrified. How can flesh torn such as mine be suddenly whole with not a mark on it? Look at my eye," he said. "It was out of its socket. Elsa says it isn't magic, but I don't know what else to call it. Magic or not, I'm grateful to be alive. There is nothing I would not do for her to show my gratitude."

Ingenius turned away, and Sabinus put a hand on his shoulder. "I know you love her very much," he said.

"I loved myself too much," said Ingenius, "to have any left for her. I am not worthy of her and she has cast me off."

"I wouldn't give up hope, my friend," said Sabinus. "I have only met one woman whose strength and courage is that of a man. There will come a time when Elsa will need the strength you can give her, and by that time you will have learned to be worthy of her. And you too have earned my undying gratitude. Some day there will be an opportunity for me to pay my debt to both of you."

"I came to ask you to help set her free," said Ingenius, blinking away his tears. "She has done that herself. She has little need of my strength. But I will treasure your friendship."

Sabinus' face reddened and Ingenius wondered what troubled him. "How is Queen Boudicca?" said Sabinus, and Ingenius remembered how he had held Boudicca's hands so long when he sat before the firepit with her at Prasu's palace. Was she the woman whose strength was that of a man? Was Sabinus in love with her? "She is quite well," he said. "I will tell her you asked about her."

***

It rained steadily. Ingenius shivered in the clammy air and pulled his cloak closer about him. His horse munched on the wet grass behind him, blowing from time to time as the grass tickled his nose. It was well into the forenoon, but the skies were lead gray and there was no sign of a break in the clouds. He had left the fort before dawn and ridden south toward Colchester. Once away from any chance encounters, he had headed west across country and then north until he reached the hard packed dirt road that led to Leicester. If the Ninth legion was heading west to join up with the Fourteenth, as he had surmised from the map, this was the way they would come.

Concealed among the trees and on a slight rise, he could see enough of the road beneath to observe whatever passed. If the legion left shortly after dawn it should be close by this time. He led his horse further into the woods so that any noise it might make would not attract attention, tied it to a tree and went back to his position near the road. Sure enough, before long he heard the sounds of approaching soldiers and his heart beat faster. He must get an accurate count so he could report back to Boudicca and Venutius.

He broke off a small dead branch and made a notch in it with his hunting knife for every century of eighty men that passed him. He made a notch with a diagonal cut across it for every squadron of cavalry. When the last baggage cart and cavalry squadron had passed, he counted his notches. Forty-eight centuries had passed him and ten squadrons of cavalry: almost four thousand heavy infantry and three hundred auxiliary cavalry. This was a formidable force: more than three quarters of what must be available to Nasica. The Roman general must only have two cohorts of infantry left and no more than twenty squadrons of cavalry to defend Longthorpe and Lincoln. If Scapula had ordered the Fourteenth out in the same strength, he was taking a great risk. The occupied nations would be open to attack.

It was late at night when he arrived at Prasu's palace at Thetford and no lights showed in any of the buildings. The gatekeeper let him in but insisted on waking Einon the steward. Einon, wakened out of a deep sleep, was crotchety, but he pulled on his ceremonial robe, picked up his ceremonial pole and ploughed toward the royal sleeping quarters through imaginary head seas, his knees rising high at every step and his body rolling from side to side like a ship in heavy weather. The servants were aroused, and soon Boudicca herself appeared. She sent Einon off to bring Venutius, while Ingenius wolfed down food and drink brought from the kitchen. As he ate he told her about Elsa and Sabinus' healing. "Sabinus asked about you," he said, looking directly at her. She reddened but seemed more interested in what he had found out about the legion's movements.

"Get me the map," said Boudicca to Einon, when Ingenius explained what he had seen. Venutius had arrived by this time and Ingenius traced with his fingers where he thought the lines were that he'd seen on Nasica's map.

"Then they know where my father is," said Boudicca. "We got word the Fourteenth also left but two cohorts behind and it's three days ahead of the Ninth. Four days ago the Twentieth left Gloucester marching north. The Twentieth and Fourteenth must plan to surround my father in the Ordoe mountains. The Ninth is in reserve."

"Then Caratacus should pass to the north and attack Lincoln while the Rummies go up the Dee," said Venutius. "Scapula's left himself wide open. We must get a rider to your father."

"Better than that," said Boudicca. "My father has fifty thousand men and hundreds of chariots. Cartimandua has more than twice that. Fifty thousand from her would give us almost eight Britons to each Rummy. If we were men enough we could break the two legions up from both sides of the Dee and destroy em."

"By Duw," said Venutius, standing up. His face reddened and Ingenius thought for a moment he was about to strike Boudicca. "You will not cast our manhood in doubt. If your father will attack I will bring in the Brigantes."

"My father will attack," said Boudicca. "But can you trust Cartie's men?"

"I have kings enough with me," said Venutius. "Scapula is with Cartie in Barwick and the kings don't like it."

"I trust you," said Boudicca. "But my father will need to know that Cartie's kings stand with you before he decides to attack."

"He will know," growled Venutius. "I will send word to him

in six days. Get a rider to him and tell him that." He turned abruptly and left them without a farewell.

"He's an irascible man," said Boudicca, "but for the chance to destroy two legions it were better he went away angry. Now I must get a rider to my father and you must leave to make more of the weapons we need. Before we go, I must show you my darling daughters. You have not seen them in over a year."

He followed her out of the hall into a passageway and stopped as she almost collided with King Prasu. He carried a candle and a servant was with him. The king's gray hair had thinned into mere wisps and he looked much older. Ingenius bent a knee. "What is it?" asked Prasu. He looked plaintively at Ingenius and bowed to him as Boudicca brushed by.

"Go back to bed," said Boudicca. "I am going to show Goneril and Gwenda to Ingenius."

"Oh," said Prasu, and waddled slowly off with the servant, the candle leaving behind a long thin trail of evil smelling smoke..

The two little girls were asleep in their cots, faces barely visible among the sheepskins. Boudicca bent over and kissed each on the forehead. "So Sabinus was healed of his wounds," she said. "I'm glad to hear it. For a Rummy, he's a good man."

"He thinks much of you."

"Aye. But I want him and all Rummies off our land." She came to him and gripped his arm. "By Duw, Scapula has left himself wide open. When my father and Venutius attack, my Nazarenes will raise this kingdom and destroy Colchester."

"I thought the Nazarenes were useless?"

"The first lot were. This is a new army that Owain raised. Subidasto has been training it here in the Iceni swamps and he thinks it can fight. By Duw, Scapula has broken our treaty and ordered our weapons confiscated. We will not give them up and we are ready to fight. The Catuves and the Trinoes will join us. When we've destroyed Colchester, we'll help finish off Scapula's legions."

"What will King Prasu do if you raise the Iceni?"

"King Prasu will play Fidchell. It's what he is best at." She stood by Ingenius' side while they looked at the angelic faces in silence. Then she patted his cheek and went off to find a rider.

He remained, still looking at the little girls, half blinded by tears. Elsa and he should have had children. She would not have left had she something like this to care for.

Chapter 8

Trapped

Two weeks later

To Boudicca, the ambush looked good. During the night several trees along the road to Colchester had been partially cut ready to be pushed over. Just ahead of where the trees would fall and block the road, a trail led off through the swamp to rejoin the road much further down. It was a logical short cut for a cavalry troop to take.

Two days before, Brennius and Iorwerth had taken five hundred of the least able bodied in Boudicca's new Nazarene army into the woods near Colchester. At dawn they were to lead them into the city, now almost undefended since Scapula had sent most of his forces west. At the same time, Guderius was to attack the Roman camp at Longthorpe with ten thousand men. Brennius and Iorwerth were to start riots along the waterfront, raise the Catuves and burn down all the buildings they could. Faced with such an uprising, the legionaries in Colchester would send a courier for the cavalry, and the cavalry was what Boudicca intended to destroy. Without the rapid assistance that cavalry could give, Colchester would be doomed.

"When we drop the trees," said Subidasto, "we'll keep two hundred of your Nazarenes behind em to yell and shout like there's five hundred. The cavalry will have to get to Colchester with no delay so they'll take the trail. And that's where we'll get em."

They rode down the trail to a point where it narrowed as the flat terrain on their left rose into a small hillock covered with trees and brush. On their right, great pools of stagnant water dotted with clumps of swamp grass and reeds came up to the path. There would be little maneuvering room here for cavalry under attack. Trees had been cut, stripped of branches and hidden in the undergrowth. At the signal they would be thrust among the cavalry, breaking it up and forcing it into the swamp while the Nazarenes handpicked by Subidasto attacked with lances and arrows.

"It is a good job," she said approvingly.

The first hint of trouble came when the expected rider from Colchester galloped by. He had barely passed the place where the trees had been cut when one of them slowly crashed across the road behind him. "He didn't look back," said Boudicca. "Do you think he heard it?"

"No," said Subidasto. "His mind was on getting where he's going." He waved to the men behind. "Drop em," he said. "They'll be here before noon." The trees began to fall and the Nazarenes hurried to take their places. Boudicca and Subidasto rode down the trail just beyond the ambush site and stopped among the trees to wait. Steam rose from the bog and drifted across the trail. It mixed with the drizzle so that it was difficult to see for more than a few horse lengths. The air felt cold and clammy and Boudicca shivered.

Noon passed and there was no sign of the cavalry. If the man that passed them was the messenger it should have been here long before this. Had the rider heard the tree fall and warned the Romans to go some other way? Or had Brennius botched the rising and no one had sent for the cavalry? The drizzle had now turned into a steady rain.

"Worst part is always the wait," said Subidasto. He must see that she was fretting.

"Aye," she said.

At last, one of the scouts they had sent out to watch for the Rummies appeared. "They're coming," he said. "There's three or four centuries of infantry and two squadrons of cavalry."

"Infantry?" said Subidasto, gnashing his teeth.

"Quick marching. They're almost to the trees."

"What should we do?" said Subidasto. "Trees won't stop infantry. We should send some of these to help."

"No," she said. "They wouldn't get there in time and wouldn't be much help if they did. The cavalry will come this way. We'll wait for them." Her hands trembled in anticipation and she tried to still them by breaking off a branch and ripping off the twigs and leaves.

"They're coming," said Subidasto, and she saw the first horsemen looming through the rain at a steady trot. When the column was across their front, Subidasto gave the signal and they both rode forward. A heavy set woman picked up her war trumpet and let loose a blast that brought the Romans bolt upright in their saddles. The tree trunks were thrust through the ranks of the horsemen, breaking up their formation and sending many into the swamp. Lances and arrows hissed softly over Boudicca's head and buried themselves in men and beasts. The Rummies reeled in shock.

She waved her arm to bring the Nazarenes forward. "Finish them," she shouted. A few moved forward but most hung back. Angry, she raised her sword then moved her horse forward to face the cavalry, now starting to regroup. "Finish them," she shouted again.

Many of the horsemen were in the water but were not hampered by it. Subidasto had assumed the ground would be soft but it was hard enough to bear horses. The surviving cavalrymen got themselves together and prepared to charge back across the trail.

Suddenly her Nazarenes were in full retreat, slashing their way through the undergrowth in panic, Subidasto on his horse roaring at them to stop and face the enemy. He turned, saw that she was alone and urged his horse toward her as the cavalry charged. She jerked her horse to one side and, though it was taboo for a queen to draw blood with a weapon, drove her sword down on the neck of one of them as he passed then felt a searing pain in her side as another went between she and Subidasto. The taboo, she thought, I broke the taboo. The sword fell from her useless hand. Then the Romans were past, up the hill and on to the Nazarenes. They screamed in fear as the cavalrymen reached them and armored infantry appeared on the hilltop.

She put her hand to her side and felt the streaming blood. In a daze, almost doubled over with pain, she tried to turn her horse but couldn't. Subidasto, bleeding from a cut in his upper arm, reached down and grabbed her reins. "Come on," he said.

Subidasto got the two of them onto the trail and picked their way among trees, fallen horses and Rummies. He got both the horses to canter and she held on grimly, the pain a white fog that blinded her. They rode until it seemed they would never stop, and then Subidasto slowed. He led them off the trail and she was barely conscious of winding through trees. Then he was beside her horse and she slipped from it to the ground, his gentle arms breaking her fall.

Dully, she felt him pull her shirt back to examine the wound. The pain was intense but not as severe as the pain she felt at their failure. Never again would she lead Nazarenes. The heretics would have refused to fight, but these Nazarenes formed up and then fled. Atak had been right when he said they were useless.

"Tis not as bad as it must feel," said Subidasto, and she was surprised how comforted she felt by his words. She had half expected to die for breaking her taboo. "Tis a bad cut but the blade didn't go in far. It hit your hip bone." He took off his shirt, cursing as he felt his own wound, and tore it into strips. "Ye'll forgive me," he said, "if I lower your trews. It's right over your hip."

Bound tightly and comforted by his assurances that the wound was not fatal, the pain seemed less alarming and she felt better. Before long she slept.

Subidasto's hand on her arm woke her. "Shhh," he said, holding a finger to his lips. The afternoon light was fading, Boudicca was wet through, cold, and her throbbing side was stiff. Noises came toward them and the sound of Roman voices. She looked up at the tree above. Maybe they were hidden. But then a centurion stood before her, sword in hand.

"Get up," said the centurion, and other legionaries crowded behind him gawking at them. One had their horses.

"She's hurt," said Subidasto. "She can't move."

"Who are you?"

"I am King Subidasto."

"And the woman?"

"She is one of my noble's wives. He was killed."

"Do we put them down?" said a legionary.

"No," said the centurion. "For these we can get a ransom."

Rough hands picked her up and she almost shrieked from the pain, biting her lips until she tasted blood. Every step felt as if a knife twisted inside her and she lost consciousness. When she came to she lay at the bottom of a cart, shaking from side to side as it trundled over the rough trail. The journey seemed to last forever, but finally, gates creaked open, heads peered down at her from over the side of the cart and she was again lifted and carried into a wooden building. She heard a door open and she was in a small storeroom, casks and utensils scattered about the floor. One of the legionaries carrying her kicked a space clear and they laid her down none too gently on the dirt floor.

"Where is King Subidasto?" she gasped as the legionaries turned to leave. One of them drew his finger across his throat and grinned at her. The door closed behind them and she could hear bolts being driven home. What were they going to do to her and Subidasto? Thank Duw he had presence of mind enough not to identify her. Then the pain went through her side like a red-hot sword and she fainted.

Chapter 9

Bodin Takes Over

Owain shivered and hugged his cloak tight about him, glad he had listened to Morfudd's advice and put on the extra tunic. She sat on the ground next to him, part of a great circle of wind whipped snow covered figures, the kings and captains and Druids of Caratacus' armies, huddled hip to hip around the huge bonfire that burned in the middle of the mountain fort. Servants moved among the seated figures pouring wine and mead from large amphorae. Morfudd's right leg was against his left leg and her right leg was against the left leg of a fierce bushy bearded captain grown maudlin from the drink. Morfudd's leg was soft and gave off heat. The captain's leg was hard and just as cold as his own. Morfudd's leg moved often, so he had to keep adjusting his to stay in contact, each adjustment sending an icy blast up his tunic. The captain's leg never moved, even when the man wept, which was frequently.

"I'm freezing," said Morfudd. "Could I have more wine?" He waved and a man filled their cups. It was a cold night and he thought longingly of his warm tent on Mona. He wished he were there with Morfudd. Feeling amorous he put his free arm around her waist and she gave him one of her enigmatic sideways looks. He took his arm away. It had been almost two years now since he had asked Caratacus to relieve him of the burden of his marriage.

Caratacus had said Rhys thought he had found a cure and asked Owain to wait two more years to see if it would work. Owain had felt obliged to agree even though experience told him no cure of Rhys' ever worked.

Morfudd had agreed to remain as his assistant and not take any more assignments from Bodin. Owain had made it as clear as he could that his wife was not likely to get well and his great desire was to be rid of her just as soon as possible. No matter how often he made this clear, however, she made it equally clear that nothing dramatic was about to happen until his old marriage was over. This was unsatisfying, and the more his intellect told him there was nothing he could do but wait, the more his emotions told him he couldn't wait, and the more his fears told him he might lose her by waiting. Even though she accepted no assignments from Bodin that he knew of, he had observed them together on occasion and jealousy had become his constant companion. He had insisted that she accompany him on this journey into Caratacus' mountains because he wasn't willing to leave her exposed to Bodin's advances while he was about the Council's business. He sighed and pushed himself a little closer to her. She moved her leg again, letting in a cold blast, and the captain to his right began to sob.

An ancient bard with a long white beard and a voice lost often in the wind stood by the fire and regaled them with the timeworn story of King Cassivellaunus' seven day entertainment of the Caesar Julius on the Bryn Gwyn.[10] Owain paid little attention to the story but listened to detect any inaccuracies that might have crept into the bard's memory. Although he could almost touch the writhing flames of the fire, its heat barely seemed to reach his front and did nothing at all for the rest of him, chilled to freezing by the constant shifting of Morfudd's leg. Like all the others, he had downed several cups of wine mixed with honey. His head spun and his stomach burned, but the rest of him felt like a block of ice. His fingers were so cold he couldn't let go of the wine cup. Caratacus sat to his right, several men away, his face and beard brightly illuminated by the flames. His son Eudal Marius, much happier now that he was no longer Arviragus, sat to the right of Caratacus. Owain wondered how Caratacus could look so cheerful and alert on such a night.

The bard stopped speaking in the middle of a sentence, although he was not at the end of his story. The cold-stupefied audience sat still, expecting the bard to go on. But the bard's attention was fixed on something else and gradually, heads began to turn away from the fire and the bard and out toward the perimeter of the fort. With a sudden curse, several men staggered to their feet and drew their swords. Caratacus got to his feet, as did the maudlin captain to Owain's right. Reluctantly, Owain detached himself from the warm softness of Morfudd and stood. He gazed where the others gazed and stiffened in shock.

Faintly illumined by the firelight, a ring of ghostly men surrounded the crowd of kings and captains. Judging by the distance between each one, Owain calculated there must be fifty of them. Each stranger wore a heavy cloak dusted with snow and was armed with a long sword, but the swords were sheathed. Each man, his arms folded, looked impassively to his front and made no response to the cries of alarm.

Caratacus pushed his way through the crowd and approached one of the strangers. Before he reached him, Owain, moving to join Caratacus, saw another figure materialize out of the darkness and stride toward the fire, two attendants behind him. The man was a giant and walked as a king. His long broad cloak swept back behind him with the wind of his passing and the massive gold torque at his throat and the silver hilted sword at his side glinted in the firelight. Even in the dim light and with the dusting of snow on it, Owain could see that the man's long flowing hair was gold and fine as silk. Owain caught up with Caratacus as he stopped to face the strange royal. A soft hand touched Owain's arm and he knew that Morfudd was at his side.

"I am honored by your visit," said Caratacus, bowing, "though it is dismayed I am that you found it so easy to pass through my warriors."

The strange king threw back his head and laughed. Then he bowed to Caratacus. "Be not dismayed nor angry at the warriors charged with guarding you," he said, his voice powerful but mellow. "Not even an Ulsterman let alone a Briton would see a Knight of the Red Branch that decided not to be seen nor heard. Am I addressing the mighty High King Caratacus, Arviragus of Britain and Lord of these lands?"

"You see Pendragon over there," said Caratacus, nodding toward the huge red and white and green pennant barely illuminated by the flames. "Pendragon follows me around by wish of the High Council, but it does not belong to me. I am but Caratacus, High King of the Silures, Ordoes and Demetes."

"Then who is Arviragus?" asked the strange king.

"There is no Arviragus," said Caratacus, "until Venutius, High King of the South Brigantes, wins the war he's fighting against his wife and the Rummy legions that came to fight me and ended up fighting him instead. And now may I be told the names and titles of he who wears the cloak of Manannan to get through my warriors?"

"'Tis not the cloak of Manannan we wore," said the strange king, "nor that of any other god. My knights must leap over branches as high as their foreheads and duck beneath those at their knees without disturbing a bird or a leaf. Their step must be so light they break neither twig nor withered branch underfoot, and should their foot take up a thorn while running they must pluck it without pause. They must be so fleet that, given the start of a single tree in the thickest wood, they must escape unwounded from any pursuer. Their breath must be so gentle that neither a hair in their nostrils nor a shimmer of their cloak must betray the fact they are alive and not dead. They must stand so still the birds light on them as if they were trees or rocks scattered on the mountains of Mourne."

"'Tis wonderful that they run and leap and breathe and stand in the way you describe," said Caratacus. "And tis certainly a pretty picture they make standing around my fire. But are they useful, now? Can they fight as well as stand still?"

"To become a Red Branch Knight," said the strange king, "they had to stand in a hole up to their knees and ward off the javelins of nine warriors standing nine ridges away. Any one of them is the master of three British knights and the equal of four."

The men standing around the two kings guffawed and turned to look at the Red Branch Knights, still standing in a circle, arms folded. One of the British captains unsheathed his sword and waved it in the air.

"Whether each one of em is equal to four of ours," Caratacus said, "can only be determined by test. And now that you have called in question the valor and competency of my men such a test we must have. But you have not told me your name and titles."

"It would break my taboos to tell you who and what I am. Where is my all-knowing Druid, Mag Mac Ilmanach?"

An old man appeared at the strange king's side. At first, all Owain could see of him was a disembodied white beard, white hair and bright eyes shining in the firelight. Then it gradually became apparent that the Druid wore a mantle of dark feathers that made his body appear invisible, and carried a gold branch with silver bells that tinkled whenever he took his hand off them. Owain looked at Morfudd and smiled. No British Druid would wear such a cloak or carry such an ornament. This was a Hibernian Druid of the old school, whose knowledge, though undoubtedly extensive, was probably limited to the lore of his ancient land. The Hibernian kings and nobles were relatively unsophisticated and easily impressed by feathers, bells and archaic lore. British kings would never stand for such nonsense. The Druid faced Caratacus and shook his golden branch so that the bells tinkled wildly.

"Hear this geas[11]," said Mag Mac Ilmanach to Caratacus. "Thou shalt not seek the name of this king until he has left these shores or bad cess will fall upon your kingdoms."

"I might not even seek it after that," said Caratacus, "unless he does something of more interest than telling me his knights stand up to their knees in holes while javelins are thrown at em. Over here, we find better things for our knights to do."

"Ah, and it's blathering you think I am?" said the strange king. "Well I will not be arguing with you either over the weird customs of the Britons. I have come to you as one cousin king to another to offer you a hand with your adversaries the Rummies. All I ask in return is a little favor that will cost you nothing. Because you are a cousin king you may call me Silent, for that is what I usually am."

"What about the test?" said Caratacus. "You must prove to us your assertion that one of your knights is the equal of four of mine. We cannot talk about trading favors until this question is settled. Bring out your champion and let's try him on for size."

"If you wish to test the truth of my assertion," said Silent, "then bring out your four best knights and I will have them face RoBachrach, the smallest and weakest of my Red Knights."

A small wiry knight with heavy red whiskers, whose head could be no higher than Owain's chest, appeared from behind the strange king and bowed to Caratacus.

"Should we dig a hole for him to stand in?" said Caratacus, "or is he already standing in one?" Owain was about to laugh with the others when Morfudd pulled on his sleeve. "Don't let them fight four to one," she whispered. "It's a game these Hibernians love to play and RoBachrach will win."

"One against four of ours?" said Owain. "And he a shrimp? Morfudd, it's not possible."

"The little ones are very quick on their feet," said Morfudd. "And the four that face them invariably take up the same positions, east, west, north and south. More often than not they end up killing each other, especially if they're as drunk as our men. Have them fight twelve to three and put the twelve in two ranks. It's the same ratio but it changes the pattern they're used to. It'll throw them off balance."

It sounded so logical that Owain clutched Caratacus' arm and told him Morfudd's suggestion. He didn't, however, tell him it was Morfudd's idea. "By Duw, I like it," said Caratacus, slapping his thigh. "Bring out three of your knights," he said to the strange king, "and we'll match em against twelve of ours. Tis the same ratio."

King Silent hesitated. "Twill make the fight last too long," he said. "I had in mind something a little quicker so we could get down to business."

"I will guarantee its quickness," said Caratacus. "My knights will clear this up before you can say Conaire Mor, Great King of Leinster.[12]"

Immediately, Mag Mac Ilmanach raised his right leg off the ground and his right arm that held the golden branch with the tinkling bells high in the air. He shook the branch vigorously. A long wail came from his throat and a series of imprecations in a tongue that Owain identified as an archaic Hibernian dialect. After doing this for a short time, Mag Mac Ilmanach lowered his leg and arm and spoke hoarsely to the strange king.

"Alas," said Silent. "By mentioning the name of a king who's name cannot be mentioned, you have broken a geas. My knights are now prohibited from fighting until the sun has risen three times."

There was a howl of rage from the captains standing around the two kings. Owain grimaced. A fight at odds of four to one would have provided great entertainment for the chilled warriors and now they were disappointed at losing their treat. Caratacus held up his arms and the noise died down. "Perhaps twould be best," said Caratacus, "if your Druid would tell mine what your geas are. That way we might find some way to talk without upsetting the scheme of things. While he's doing that, sit you down by the fire and drink some wine. Then you can tell me about the favor you want to do for me."

"And the one I would have you do for me," said Silent, making his way toward the fire. He squatted and Caratacus crouched beside him. Cups were thrust into the hands of the two kings and wine poured into them from a heavy amphora. Owain crouched down also at Caratacus' side and Mag Mac Ilmanach crouched at Owain's side but said not a word. Morfudd, not of the inner circle, did not crouch but stayed within earshot of Owain.

"What favor would you have us do for you?" asked Silent, dropping his cup and then rubbing his hands together in the heat from the fire.

"That would depend," said Caratacus, "on the favor you want from me. If tis a large favor, then I might ask a large favor of you."

Silent rubbed his hands some more then turned his back to the fire. "The favor I would ask of you," he said, "is so little a favor that you will not think it worth your while to ask anything in return. But because you are a cousin king, and because you are beset by these pestilential Rummies, I would like to do you a favor out of the goodness of my heart." He looked sideways at Caratacus, who still faced the fire, and Caratacus winked at Owain but said nothing.

"The favor I would ask of you," said Silent, "is the borrowing of the widow Angarad."

Mag Mac Ilmanach made a strange sound like the snuffling of a duck sifting the marsh grasses for insects. Owain glanced at the Druid in some alarm but the old Hibernian merely stared at the fire and went on making the noise. Caratacus made no reply to Silent's request.

"The reason we have for the wanting of her," Silent said, "is to look at our bull. Oh, tis no ordinary bull, mind you. Tis a great war we fought among ourselves to win this bull, and the sire he is to be of the grandest line of cattle that ever was sired. The sire, that is to say, if we can get him interested in his work. Tis a great curse that has been put upon him, and Mag Mac Ilmanach here spends most of his day cursing the curse that was put upon our bull, that he be such a great bull to look at and yet not be interested in his work."

Mag Mac Ilmanach made a sound like a monkey chattering.

"There he goes again," said Silent. "You see our problem then. Mag Mac Ilmanach has tried every curse on curses that is known in Hibernia and nothing seems to work. The only hope we have, after killing the half of Hibernia to get this bull, is to get the widow Angarad, whose fame is spread over the whole civilized world for her way with such animals, to put her hands on him as only she can and get him back to work before we become the subject of satire and the laughing stock of all Hibernia."

Caratacus held his cup out for more wine and took a long drink before answering. "If it's the widow Angarad you're after," he said, "you're more than welcome to the borrowing of her if you can find her. Tis a bad time to come looking after her, however. When it's cold like this, the widow finds a cave and snuggles up with the bears until the fine weather reappears. She tends to be irritable if you wake her before she's ready. And she will not take kindly to being sailed across the stormy seas. But if you can find her you're more than welcome to borrow her just so you get her back here before Beltane."

Mag Mac Ilmanach struggled to his feet and shook his golden branch with the silver tinkling bells. He made a series of angry birdlike noises, sounding to Owain like a freshly flushed covey of quail.

"Did I break another geas?" said Caratacus.

"No," said Silent. "He's still trying to curse the curse that's on our bull. This has been going on for three months now and that's why it has come to mind that we must try something else. Of course you will give me the loan of a couple of your knights to help us find the widow?"

Caratacus signaled a warrior to come fill the cups. "Tis glad I am," he said, "that our Druids are not as noisy as yours." The two kings took a long drink. Caratacus spat in the fire. "It has come to my mind," he said, winking at Owain again, "what the favor is you can do for me for the borrowing of the widow Angarad."

"And the loan," said Silent, turning his face back to the fire, "of two of your knights to help us root her out."

"You must take four of my knights," said Caratacus. His voice was slurred and Owain wondered if too much wine had been poured down the High King's gullet. "According to your reckoning, two of my knights would only be half a knight of yours and I cannot give you half a knight. You must take four and then you will have one."

"Four it is then."

"Before I tell you what the favor is, I must have my own Druid lay a geas on you. Owain, lay something on him."

Without knowing what Caratacus had in mind, Owain wasn't sure what would be appropriate. But then Mag Mac Ilmanach began to hiss like a gaggle of geese and it came to him what to say. "Hear this geas," he said to the strange king, then raised his right arm. "Thou shalt accomplish that which it is given thee to do," he said, "or thy bull will forever think he is a eunuch."

Silent leaped to his feet, eyes glaring wildly. "Another curse on our bull," he said. "You hear that, Mag Mac Ilmanach? Another curse on our bull." Mag Mac Ilmanach stopped hissing. He held out his cup and a soldier filled it with wine. Silent crouched down and looked sullenly at Caratacus. "And what is this favor you would ask?"

Caratacus held out his cup, a contented smirk on his face. "When you first came among us," he said, "I told you the Rummies had gone off to fight King Venutius of the Brigantes. Now Venutius and me had agreed that when Scapula came after me with his legions, I would entice him up the Dee into the land of my good friends the Deceanglies, guardians as they are of our holy mother river Dee. With the marshes in front of em, and my armies behind em, Venutius was to attack em from the east with fifty thousand Brigantes. He was to crush em against the sharp teeth of my chariots.

"But when the time for the attack came, most of the kings he thought would go with him chose to stay with Cartimandua. The kings that were for him thought it more important to get rid of Cartimandua than fight Scapula. To put it in a nutshell, the Brigantes were in a flaming uproar, and Cartimandua summoned the great Scapula himself to help her sort out the mess. Scapula took his legions off to Brigante and bad cess to him for leaving us sitting here with nothing to fight."

The fire had died down a little and the circle around it drew back a little to let the soldiers come in with more great logs to feed its appetite. So far as Owain could tell, not one of the Red Knights had moved a muscle since he first noticed them.

"So Scapula is now in Brigante?" said Silent.

"He is indeed," said Caratacus. "He took the Twentieth and the Ninth legions with him to put down Venutius, but my own daughter started a rising thinking Venutius and me were fighting Scapula. He sent the Twentieth back to put down the rising and the Fourteenth to Wroxeter so they can come looking for me in the spring, assuming I'll sit here and wait for em. And there, my cousin king, is where you can do me the favor."

"And the four knights will be ready to leave at daybreak?"

"As soon as you agree to do my favor."

"And what is the favor?"

"It is that you would send your stealthy men, they who are unmatched at being unnoticed, into the Rummy camp at Wroxeter and bring me back their sacred eagle and legion standards."

Silent got up and stood looking down at Caratacus, one hand on his hip and the other holding his cup. "By Taranis himself," he said, holding his cup out to be refilled, "your favor is no light thing. They guard their aquila day and night with their best guards. If we take it from them they will pull out their hair, tear their clothes, foam at the mouth and go berserk. Their commander will be sent home in deep disgrace and utter condemnation to kill his wife and children and open his veins in a warm Rummy bath. Caesar himself will find his life in danger if the honor of one of his legions is stained with such a stain."

"The mind quickly takes that in," said Caratacus. "I would

have you not only take their sacred eagle and standards but leave a trail that even a Rummy can follow as you come back into my mountains. I have a little arrangement just below that will give my men a good crack at berserk Rummies with foaming mouths. Before you came, I was sitting here praying to Duw and anyone else who'd give an ear about how to get the Fourteenth to leave their warm tents and come up here in the dead of winter, and you have given me my answer. Tis Duw Himself must have sent you."

"Then by Duw we will do it," said Silent. "Give us three days and we'll put the aquila in your royal hands."

Caratacus stood up and called for more wine. The fire roared as the new fuel took hold, and Owain stood up and backed away from the flames as the two kings clashed their swords and drank together. "In three days," said Caratacus, "we will have the widow Angarad here drunk or sober, with or without the bears, and you can take her to your ship as soon as the aquila's in these hands that itch to hold it."

Owain felt Morfudd's hand on his arm and pressed it to his side as the kings crouched down again and the bard recommenced his account of Julius Caesar's entertainment right in the middle of the sentence he had been uttering when the Red Knights loomed into view. "That king is right," she said. "The Romans will go berserk if he steals their aquila. Remember how upset Claudius was when they stole his elephant."

***

It was noon on the third day since the Red Branch Knights departed on their errand. The widow Angarad had been tied up and brought to the fort. She lay on her back in a tent close to Mag Mac Ilmanach's and the noise of her cursing overshadowed his. Four captains had been assigned to feed her with wine and honey and keep her entertained but the attention did little to soften her indignation. Morfudd was in her tent memorizing Hebrew scrolls so Owain and she could deal better with Basil, who often justified his strange actions by quoting Hebrew Scripture.

Owain knelt in Caratacus' tent and watched Caratacus draw lines on the floor with his sword point to show Marius and the other kings what he planned to do when the Fourteenth legion came looking for its aquila. The plan used Caratacus' proven tactics of enticing the Rummies into situations they couldn't resist so he could take a few bites out of them and disappear before they could bring him to battle. A great wall of stones had been built across the old track way that crossed the Severn marshes from the east. Where it wended its way into the mountains, the track way was dominated by sheer hills. Crossing the marshes and the raging Severn would wear the Fourteenth down, so that the wall, defended by lances thrown from the hills and trees above, would be a formidable obstacle. It would take time for the legion to break through, and during that time Caratacus' warriors could severely damage the Romans without harm to themselves. Once the barrier was broken his warriors would withdraw into the mountains carrying the aquila. The legion would follow and would be nibbled at until it grew tired. At the appropriate moment the aquila would be thrown down upon it so the legion would go home to its camp.

His admiration of the plan was broken by a commotion outside. He struggled to his feet and staggered out of the tent, knees stiff from the kneeling and the cold. When he saw Bodin the Fox walking briskly up with a courier his mouth drooped. What could Bodin be doing here? The Council must have sent him but for what?

"The Council has sent instructions for you and Morfudd," said Bodin, nodding slightly in greeting as he brushed by Owain. His tone of voice implied that the Council was dissatisfied with Owain's work. "I will tell you what they are as soon as King Caratacus has received the bad news." The courier had already been admitted to Caratacus' tent, and now Bodin pushed his way in and crouched down alongside the kings. How dare the man take such liberties? Owain thought. Bodin had no right to squat with the kings. He, Owain, was the Council's emissary and the only one entitled to squat. He bit his lip in anger when he saw that no one questioned Bodin's right to join the assembly, and crouched down near the door where he could keep an eye on his adversary. The courier's news was bad.

"Your daughter Queen Boudicca is a prisoner," said the courier to Caratacus. "She's wounded and in a Rummy cavalry camp near Colchester."

"Bad?" said Caratacus.

"Cavalry cut in the side. She can't move."

"Where is her army?" asked Caratacus.

"It went to pieces when the Rummy cavalry charged."

"Then by Beli Mawr she must be got out," said Caratacus. "How much of her army is left? And what happened to Subidasto and Guderius?"

"King Subidasto was taken with Queen Boudicca. King Guderius put up a good fight but colonists from Colchester trapped some of his men in Tas. King Antedios came out against Guderius and was killed. His wife Queen Antea was saved and taken back by the Rummies, she being a Rummy herself. The Nazarenes, what's left of them, have gone home."

"I never met a Nazarene yet who could fight," said Caratacus. "Marius, you must take a thousand horsemen and get her out. While you're there see what can be done for Subidasto. Go now."

"Wait," said the courier, as Marius leaped to his feet.

"Well?" said Caratacus.

"The Council received word that King Venutius has made peace with Queen Cartimandua and Scapula. He's now to be High King only of half South Brigante and had to promise not to fight Rome. He has sent scouts to guide you to the Derwent. From there, he says, you can attack Lincoln. The Council feels that if you threaten Lincoln, Scapula will pull back. Otherwise, the Council fears he may attack Mona and get the gold stocks."

"We can't get out through the Severn," said Caratacus, rubbing his chin. "If our Hibernian friends have done their job right, the Fourteenth are heading across it right now and I will not meet them head to head." He glared at the courier. "Is there any flaming thing else you have not told me?" he asked.

"Yes, Sire. Your wife the Queen Genvissa and your daughters the Princesses Eurgen and Gwendolyn have been captured by the 20th legion."

"How in the name of Crom Cruach did that happen?"

"The Princess Gwendolyn ran away from Rhys and her mother and sister were trying to find her. They ran into a foraging party."

"Do the Rummies know who they are?"

"Yes Sire. Rhys the Druid told them thinking they would be freed."

"I always knew he had sawdust for brains. Is there anything else?"

"No, Sire," said the courier.

"I also have brought instructions from the Council, Sire," said Bodin, standing up. "But they affect only the Nazarene question and I will give them to Owain Longhead."

Caratacus waved his hand in dismissal and Owain felt glad that no greater attention had been given to Bodin's announcement. Give instructions to Owain Longhead indeed! Anyone might think that it was Bodin himself who was to give him instructions. He didn't feel he would be able to listen to Bodin with that degree of calmness required of a Pencerdd and Council member. He would get agitated in front of Morfudd and make a fool of himself. Morfudd must not be present when Bodin relayed the Council's message.

"Here's what we'll do," said Caratacus, breaking Owain's train of thought. "Marius and Atak will leave right away to get Boudicca out. Take your men round by Caer Sws so you'll miss the Fourteenth. Bledud, your men stay by the wall until the Rummies show up. Do as much damage as you can but get out and follow us as soon as the Rummies break through. The rest of us will break camp tonight and go out by the Dee to join Venutius."

"What about the aquila?" said Bledud.

"Drop it on em or they'll follow us all the way to the Derwent."

"What about your wife the Queen?"

"We'll see about that when we find out where she is."

As the war council broke up, Owain took Bodin by the arm and steered him out of the tent. "Come with me," he said, "and tell me exactly what the Council has told you to tell me." But before they could set off, Caratacus called him back.

"I would like you with us," said Caratacus. "This arrangement between Cartie and Venutius won't last long. I'd like you to try again to make Cartie join the Alliance. If anyone can pull it off it's you. Tell her Venutius can be Arviragus and what a feather twould be in her cap to own an Arviragus of Britain."

"Thank you, Sire," said Owain. "I will." He beamed with pleasure at the compliment.

"Have that other fellow tell the Council that you're going."

Outside the tent again, still beaming with pleasure, Owain looked around for Bodin and scowled. The young council member and Morfudd stood near the entrance to her tent having an animated conversation. As he approached she laughed at something Bodin said and then they saw him.

"Bodin has been telling me of Basil's problems," said Morfudd, a wide smile lighting up her face.

"Basil's problems are our problems," growled Owain. "If he fails, we have failed." Morfudd's smile faded and he realized how pompous he must have sounded. He made a great effort to throw off the gloom that the sight of them talking and laughing together had cast over him and smiled painfully. "I suppose his eight colored robe is attracting too many flies?" he said, and was pleased when Morfudd laughed again. Bodin might be younger but Owain felt he could hold his own against him in a battle of wits.

"Why don't you join us while Bodin gives me the Council's message?" he said. "You may think of some good questions to send back with him."

"I've already told her to join us," said Bodin, and Owain felt his anger rise again. "Let's go into Morfudd's tent," said Bodin. "I'm sure it smells better than yours."

Morfudd's tent was smaller than Owain's and in the midst of his rising anger he had to admit that because it smelled like Morfudd it smelled better. Her cot was against the far wall. One end of it and the small table in front of it were covered with stacks of scrolls. Bodin sat on the cot and swept the table clean, piling the scrolls that had been on it on top of those on the cot. Then he pulled the table closer to himself and leaned his elbows on it. "Sit down," he said, as if this were his tent. Owain glanced angrily at Morfudd, but unmoved by Bodin's effrontery she pulled out a stool for Owain and a box for herself.

"I'll get right to the point," said Bodin. "The Nazarene situation is unsatisfactory. The Council is shocked at how little progress has been made."

Owain frowned. "We have a Nazarene army under Queen Boudicca," he said. "And I understood from Basil that his organization is growing rapidly."

"We just heard how effective Queen Boudicca's army is," sneered Bodin. "It's a rag tag of the old and diseased. In the meantime, our other armies are losing three men to the heretics to every one recruited by Basil. The Council is so concerned they sent me to talk to Basil."

Owain felt the hair rise at the back of his neck. So that was it. This upstart was trying to use Owain's preoccupation with the problems of Caratacus and Venutius to wrest control of the Nazarenes from him. He scowled, but smiled stiffly when he saw Morfudd looking at him. "And what did Basil say?"

"It doesn't matter what he said. Basil is a fool. The real problem is the heretics. Our own organization can't succeed while they continue to subvert people with their healings. The heretics must be eliminated."

"You would kill them?" said Morfudd. "There are high Druids among them." She looked genuinely shocked, and Owain exulted. This must show her what went on inside this upstart's mind.

"Kill them or exile them," said Bodin. "Preferably the former. If we are to succeed against Rome we must be as ruthless as Rome. It is time for strong measures and strong leaders. Arimathea's so-called Nazarene College and its followers must be destroyed."

Owain sniffed disgustedly. "You will not convince the Council to take such measures," he said.

"The Council is already convinced," said Bodin. "I made a point of convincing it."

Owain sat silent, nonplused by Bodin's effrontery. This man was far more dangerous than he had thought. He must find some way to warn the Council of the consequences that might ensue should this madman's suggestions be carried out. To kill the Nazarene College with its high-ranking Druid members and charismatic healers could start a civil war. Now he regretted Caratacus' invitation. It would take him away from where he most needed to be. In the meantime, however, he must conceal his anger and find out as much as he could of Bodin's plans so he could develop a counter strategy. "Killing off the Nazarene College will not solve our problem," he said. "Without healers how are you going to attract those who want to be Nazarenes and convince them to fight?"

"Fear," said Bodin. "They'll be told they will be stricken down by Duw if they don't obey our priests. Without our priests' sanction the Otherworld will be forever closed to them. When they see that Duw has burned a few heretics and roughed up the others, they'll be ready to hate and kill Romans. Fill them with fear and they'll flock to us. Fear will take the place of healings and be more effective. It always has been."

Owain stood up and smoothed his robe with unfeeling hands. He looked at Morfudd, who stared at Bodin as if fascinated by him. Then he looked at Bodin, who gazed at him with a half sneer on his face. He made a great effort to control his temper and spoke deliberately, regretting the faint tremor he could detect in his voice. "That is the most cynical dissertation on religion

I've ever been forced to hear," he said. "You are a disgrace to the title of Druid."

"Nevertheless," said Bodin, his eyes narrowed to slits. "The Council has instructed me to tell you my plan, which I have just done, and to see that it gets accomplished. It has directed me to tell you that you are to remain with King Caratacus until you can assure the inclusion of Brigante in the Alliance. As you will no longer be needing Morfudd, the Council requests you to release her at once so she can help me."

"And if I do not release her?"

Bodin shrugged. "I was merely being kind," he said, "She has already been assigned to me and is no longer your assistant."

Baffled, Owain turned to Morfudd. "Is this what you wish?" he said.

She stared at the young Druid with wide eyes. "I must do as the Council directs," she said, without looking at him.

The bile rose in his throat and he almost gagged. Without a further word he turned on his heel and went blindly out of the tent. Little drops of cold rain felt like needles puncturing his skin as he hurried onward, his mind blank with shock and anger. Before he reached his tent a cheer went up from the crowd of soldiers standing near Caratacus' tent. The Red Branch Knights had returned, and someone held up and waved the standards and aquila of the Fourteenth legion. He paused for a moment, too dazed to comprehend, then plunged into his tent, knocked his servant away with a snarl and threw himself face down on the cot.

Chapter 10

Sabinus Repays a Debt

Boudicca lay on a heap of straw. Euletha, the camp follower assigned by the Romans to look after her had placed skins over her, but she never felt warm or dry or clean. Euletha had recognized her but had sworn not to tell. She also told Boudicca that Subidasto had promised to get a huge ransom for her. Without that promise she would have been killed. Killed? Killing seemed an abstraction.

A physician visited her once and caused her untold agony taking the remnants of Subidasto's shirt from her wound. He had rebound her waist and given her something foul to drink, but her side was swollen and inflamed and she couldn't move without pain. She had no idea how many days she had lain there, drifting in and out of consciousness. Little light reached the storeroom and she only knew it was daytime when Euletha came in to clean her, give her food and drink and take away the fouled straw.

Her arms seemed strangely thin and she had barely strength to lift them. Did Venutius know she had been captured? Had Prasu been approached about a ransom? Would he put his own life in jeopardy by offering a ransom for his traitorous wife? At times she was tempted to tell the Rummies who she was if only to get the ordeal over. But then they might execute Subidasto and

Prasu, and maybe Goneril and Gwenda. She gritted her teeth and hung on, not sure whether she was conscious or dreaming.

***

The door opened and Euletha came in. A Roman stood in the doorway looking at her. Not the physician again, she hoped in horror. He bent down by her bed and put a hand on her arm. She could barely see his face in the dim light. "I will get you out of here," he said. It was the tribune Sabinus. Had Ingenius sent him? Or was she dreaming? "We must find Elsa," said Sabinus. "She will heal you."

He went away and she wondered if he would come back. She hoped he would and then wondered why she should wish for a Roman to come to her. She drifted off to sleep but was partly conscious of being lifted on to a wooden plank and covered with skins, then of being carried out into fresh cold air and placed on the straw covered floor of a cart. She wakened more fully and saw Sabinus looking down on her as the cart rumbled forward. It chattered and swayed and the movement sent shocks of pain through her until she slept.

The cart stopped. Those were British voices. A face peered over the edge of the cart. A familiar face. "Cruker," she said.

Cruker touched her shoulder and she saw that he wept. "We'll get you home as fast as this four legger can do it," he said.

Another face appeared by Cruker's. It was Sabinus again. Why did all these men weep so? "I must leave now," said Sabinus. "Ingenius is at Thetford preparing for your arrival. He has sent for Elsa. I will visit soon if I may." He turned to leave, but came back. "They don't know who you are," he said. "You have been ransomed and will be safe."

Safe, she mused as the cart rumbled on again. What about Subidasto? Would Prasu ransom him or let the Rummies kill him? She and Subidasto had committed high treason against Rome. Would Prasu take them back or turn them over to the Rummies?

Chapter 11

Scapula Reports

To Tiberius Claudius Drusus Caesar Augustus Britannicus

Written from the fort of Queen Cartimandua, in the heart of the Brigante nation, the northernmost penetration of the Empire's forces.

Hail Caesar!

You must have already received word of the great victories I have won, but I felt it necessary to write to you and set at rest any false rumors that might have reached your ears. Cowards loyal to Plautius have spread them and they are all false. I have not yet been able to identify who they are (although I have my suspicions) but I know you will support me when I take ruthless punitive measures. The slow death is too good for them.

Although I resisted postponing the campaign against Caratacus until the chaos left behind by Plautius had been rectified, I quickly came to see how great was your wisdom. The insolent attack on our territories shortly after I arrived, during which our new town at Verulamium was destroyed by a mob of diseased cripples, showed our legions were poorly led, dangerously demoralized and under strength. The attack proved there was no line of fortifications worth the name. I paced off the distances between our key forts myself and found that some were over a day's march apart while others were less. Most were not even the regulation shape—one was shaped like a polygon! Despite the constant bickering and grumbling, I insisted the forts and their supporting roads be moved and rebuilt to conform to administrative regulations. After only three years of rebuilding and retraining, I have brought the legions up to the standards necessary to assure overwhelming victories for Roman arms.

The barbarians have been taught who is master. Their arms were confiscated and they lost a lot more of their lands and goods and slaves. In addition to all this, which as you can imagine has placed a great physical and mental strain upon me, I also succeeded in negotiating a much better treaty with our client Queen Cartimandua of the Brigantes. This treaty is much more in Rome's favor and I am sure that with your support the Senate will approve it. Even though there have been problems with the Brigantes it is to our advantage to keep this rich and powerful queen on our side. I find her easy to manage now she has learned that I am not one to trifle with.

Last year, after almost superhuman efforts, I was ready to launch my campaign against Caratacus and was delighted when I received your authorization to proceed and ordered the legions to attack. The charge that I seriously weakened our defenses to chase Caratacus is completely unfounded. There were uprisings of course, but then there always are, and the detachments left behind were able to handle them without exorbitant losses. After several days march I assembled the legions at Viroconium[13] and made a tremendously inspiring speech to our men such that the hills echoed with their cheering. After that they couldn't wait to get their hands on Caratacus and his painted warriors!

Before the legions had marched two days, however, I received a dispatch from Queen Cartimandua informing me that a huge force of more than 300,000 barbarians under her rebellious king consort Venutius was about to divide her nation then attack Ratae[14] and Verulamium! Her own loyal forces were insufficient to put down the insurrection and she asked for immediate help.

I struck off at once to the north with my legions and established my headquarters here at the Queen's oppidum, a bleak place swept by wind and rain. It is not as comfortable as the governor's palace in Camulodunum[15], but then Caesar's governors must undergo any hardship to serve the empire!

It didn't take long for me to grasp what the rebels were about and develop a strategy for bringing them to heel. I ordered the 9th to establish a defensive line west of the Humber to keep Venutius' army in the north and provided Queen Cartimandua with German auxiliaries to scour her territory and root out the rebel kings. With several of these in my hands and his brother's family held hostage by Queen Cartimandua, I was able to force Venutius to the negotiating table and bring the civil war to a conclusion. Having been taught a sharp lesson he was reconciled to his wife and submitted to Rome as she directed. At her request, I permitted him to rule over part of southern Brigante under his wife. We can now count upon him as a loyal friend of Rome and he will not trouble us again!

While all this was going on, however, the barbarians attacked my palace at Camulodunum. In the action that followed, my son Marcus Ostorius led dismounted cavalry against a British fort and saved the life of Antea (Seneca's daughter) who married Antedios of Iceni Minor. Antedios was killed in the attack so that is one less British king we have to worry about! I know that you will accord Marcus high honors for his bravery.

The best news, that of my decisive victory against Caratacus, I have saved till last! Gnaeus Hosidius Geta received a report that Caratacus had built a wall blocking the entrance to his camp. The 14th crossed the Severn, raging as it was with winter floods, and attacked the wall. Even though many casualties were suffered from arrows and missiles fired by barbarians on the hills above, bit by bit the wall was pulled down until the 14th could get through in force. Once through, the barbarians must have suffered casualties so terrible that they broke and ran, disappearing into the mountain passes. Caratacus' army is thus no more!

The only bitter taste in this great achievement is the carping rumor being spread that Caratacus stole the standards and the sacred aquila from the 14th, and that they were thrown down on top of the 14th after the wall was breached! Could anything more preposterous be imagined! To accomplish such a deed, Caratacus' men would have had to penetrate to the very center of a busy Roman camp, enter the principia, guarded as it is day and night by Geta's own guard, break into the sacellum, and then leave the camp carrying the legion's most precious possessions! This rumor alone should forever destroy the credibility of the vipers spreading it.

Caratacus himself, deprived now of an army to fight with, seems to have retreated into his mountains to lick his wounds, but Queen Cartimandua has promised to send scouts to locate him. When we find him he will be sent to Rome in chains so that you can show our people the effectiveness of our campaign in Britannia!

Salutations from your right arm in the north!

Long live Caesar!

Publius Ostorius Scapula

Legatus Augusti Pro Praetore.

PART II:

50—54 a.d.

Chapter 1

The Parisi

It was late in the evening when Einon the steward pounded on the floor with his stick and announced the visitor. Boudicca sat before the firepit in the large smoky hall at Thetford with Goneril, Gwenda, Prasu and Tetra, Atak's Nazarene wife. Tetra had been a disciple of Philip of Gaul and like Elsa her daughter was a heretic Nazarene, tolerated because of Atak. "This here is Lord Owing," said Einon. "Come to see the Lady Tetrium." He disappeared into the haze as the crimson-robed Owain walked forward to join them holding his bedraggled crimson hat. His boots and the bottom of his robe were wet and stained with mud from his journey.

Boudicca rose with Tetra and took her brother-in-law's hands as he bowed to her. "Let us offer you refreshment," she said, and waved to one of the nearby servants. It seemed to her that Owain had aged. He was bald around the crown of his head and the hair on its sides, still bedraggled from the rain, was tinged with gray. The cheeks under his eyes were dark and lined, and his mouth drooped when he swallowed as if he were fighting some great sadness. My mad sister Gwendolyn, she thought. He's grieving for her.

Owain sat down next to Tetra and they all looked at Prasu, who had barely acknowledged Owain's arrival. "Please make my home your own," said Prasu. His eyes bespoke little interest in the new arrival and they drifted back to the fire while his face settled into its habitual gloom. Boudicca shook her head grimly. He had been sullen and depressed and she herself had been in a black mood ever since she came back wounded from her failed revolt, disgraced in her own eyes by the collapse of her army and her own capture. Ingenius had not been able to find Elsa and her painful wound had healed slowly under the Druid's care.

She had also discovered that Sabinus had paid her ransom so Prasu would not know that she had been captured. It was humiliating to think that a Roman had saved her from the consequences of her defeat, even one she had grown fond of. Subidasto had been identified as leader of the revolt and executed. Because of Subidasto's treason and rumors about Boudicca's part in the revolt, suspicion had fallen on Prasu himself. His Roman guests had left the palace so he felt he was punished unfairly. Subidasto's death had also deprived him of his only pleasure: the games of Fidchell that had so engrossed the two of them. All that seemed to cheer him now were his daughters, especially Gwenda.

Servants brought in food and wine, and there was little conversation while Owain ate. When he had finished, he sat back. "You have heard," he said to Boudicca, "that Scapula has moved your mother Queen Genvissa and your sisters to Longthorpe?"

"Yes," she said. "Atak and King Caratacus are in Brigante to see what can be done to rescue them."

"I have just come from there," said Owain, turning to Tetra. "Lord Atak sends you his love." He looked again at Prasu but the old king's attention was fixed on the fire so the Druid turned his heavy lidded eyes back on Boudicca. "Scapula has the Ninth legion camped at the Humber. If Cartimandua breaks her treaty with Rome he can slice her nation in two. King Caratacus and King Venutius have told her they will not move against the Ninth unless she joins the alliance and recognizes King Venutius as

Arviragus. She has finally agreed. Kings and Council will meet next week at Almondbury."

He lapsed into silence and Boudicca sensed that something troubled him. It felt cold and she signaled a servant to put more wood on the fire. Lamps were placed around the floor so their feeble flickering light mixed with the last of the twilight. Disturbed by the commotion, Prasu recoiled with surprise but his gaze went back to the fire as raindrops hissed into it and smoke billowed out.

"I have come to ask for Lady Tetra's help," said Owain.

"My help?" said Tetra. She put her hands to her mouth in alarm.

Boudicca rose. "I must see that King Prasu gets to his bedchamber." She called a manservant, who eased Prasu out of his chair and got him waddling, Goneril and Gwenda trailing behind. Owain and Tetra rose but she waved to them to sit down as she followed Prasu. I wonder why he needs her help? she thought. His sham Nazarenes must be in trouble if he had to turn to Tetra. Tetra had never shown much resourcefulness and she had often wondered what Atak saw in her.

Tetra's heart beat faster when the high-ranking Druid clasped his hands on top of his knees and looked at her. He seemed embarrassed. She had met him only a few times in the company of Atak or Boudicca and he had paid to her only the minimum attention required by courtesy. She had always thought him too interested in manipulating kings to have much concern for the wife of a foreigner such as Atak. And he must know she was a real Nazarene, sympathetic to the College he and his Council had declared heretic. Why he had come to see her?

"The High Council has acted unwisely," he said. His voice was low and humble. "I must bear my share of the blame and I feel obliged to help undo what we have done."

"You mean about calling the Nazarenes heretics?" she said, suddenly angry. For all she knew, Elsa's life was in danger because of the Council's unwisdom. But she tried to suppress her indignation.

"The Council did what it thought was best at the time," he said. "Many of us, myself included, believed Philip and Joseph were quite right and that we should lay down our arms and pray for peace. We didn't wholly trust Basil's claims to be able to get Nazarenes to fight against Romans. Back then, however, it seemed as if the Romans would quickly overrun us. It took them only a few years to conquer Gaul, and we feared our time was too short and our faith too weak to trust all to Philip's God. Basil's plan offered a compromise acceptable to more of us. But now it is seven years since the Romans landed and they control less than a third of Britain. Even that is in constant turmoil and we hear that many of their soldiers have deserted like ours to become Nazarenes. Three years have passed since we decided to follow Basil's counsel, and all he has produced are storehouses full of candles, empty synagogues and a useless army. In the meantime, more and more of our warriors are refusing to fight."

"Has it occurred to your Council," said Tetra, still angry, "that the reason both you and the Romans are finding it hard to make war is because of the prayers of the Nazarenes?"

"It has occurred to some of us," said Owain, but she wondered if it really had occurred to him. "The Council, however, does not easily change its mind. Most members still feel we should continue with Basil."

"Pah!" she said in disgust. "Basil only wants to get rich and doesn't care how."

"I know. But he has been supplanted by one who is much more evil. His name is Lord Bodin."

"I have not heard of him."

"You will." Owain's voice was grim. "Basil is a weak man who tried to get converts through fraud and bribery. Bodin is a strong man who will get them through fear. If he gains many converts and they agree to fight, the Council will not challenge his approach."

Tetra felt a sudden chill at Owain's words. "Nazarenes will

not fight. They will only join those who can prove they are following the Master by healing," she said.

"Those who are already Nazarenes will not join Bodin," agreed Owain. "But we fear those who are not will unless we provide an alternative. Bodin says Britons who don't obey his priests will find the power of Duw called down against them. They will be denied entrance into the Otherworld—into heaven."

Tetra couldn't prevent a hiss of contempt. "The power of God cannot be called down to hurt people," she said.

Owain nodded solemnly. "But it can be made to appear that it does," he said. "Joseph's Nazarenes will be eliminated so they can no longer attract converts."

Tetra put her hand to her mouth. "You mean they will be killed?"

"Yes," said Owain. "I do mean that. Your daughter Elsa will be in grave danger if Bodin gets his way. We have to make sure he doesn't. That is why I have come to ask for your help."

"What can I do?" she asked.

"Those of us in the Council who are against what Bodin is trying to do," he said, sipping his wine delicately, "feel that we must set up a separate organization. One that comes closer to the ideals set by Philip and Joseph."

"Closer? Why not the same?"

"I have no doubt it will be the same in time. But the Council cannot suddenly announce that what it had proclaimed heretic is now legitimate. Nor can it suddenly declare that Bodin's organization, set up under the guidance of the Council, is now illegitimate. A transitional organization must be set up so that when Bodin fails we will have an organization ready to assimilate his converts." He tapped her on the knee. "We cannot afford to lose any converts."

Tetra felt dizzy. Why did the Britons make everything so complicated? "Why doesn't the Council simply tell everyone to lay down their arms and pray to God?"

"I would life were that simple," said Owain. "But without an organization we wouldn't know how many Nazarenes there were and we couldn't tell them how or when to pray. Suppose they prayed for the wrong things! Unity must be just as important in praying as in anything else."

"Nazarenes are united by love," said Tetra, "not by priests telling them what to do. You will never know how many Nazarenes are praying because the Master told them not to pray in public like hypocrites but to pray in private. Only God will know when their prayers are enough to bring in the reign of peace, but if everyone laid down their arms and trusted God it would happen quickly. Philip said so."

Owain placed his wine cup on the floor and looked at her solemnly. "That is what Philip said," he agreed, "and I believe it. But we must remember that we're trying to convince the Council not the Nazarenes. To most of the Council it doesn't make sense to simply trust an unknown number of people to pray without guidance whenever they feel like it. If the Council doesn't see an organization within which people can be directed to pray for the same things in the same way and at the same time it will turn to Bodin simply because he has one that will. Perhaps later on, when the true Nazarenes have joined it and the war is over and the reign of peace is closer we can dispense with this organization, but right now it is absolutely essential. The Nazarenes in Judea and Asia Minor are forming organizations. Surely, if they have found it to be necessary it must be as necessary for us?"

"Philip always said the quickest way to kill the Christ spirit is to let the priests form an organization around it," she said. "But I know it's difficult to do the things the Master said all by yourself. You have to trust that everyone else who is following Christ is doing the same thing too, but sometimes you wonder if they really are. You can't help thinking that perhaps you are the only one really following Christ."

Owain reached out and laid his hand on top of hers. She was surprised how soft and warm his hand was. "That's why organizations are essential," he said. "We can share ideas, compare our progress and get help when we need it. To work alone is dangerous. Without guidance from those qualified to lead, an individual can stray and not be aware of it. The most important thing we must do if we are to serve God is to submerge ourselves in the unity of God's purpose. And that requires us to organize."

"I can see that," said Tetra, and she felt she really could. It made sense and she wondered why Philip and Joseph had been so against organizations. Perhaps she had misunderstood what they meant. "If the Nazarenes in Judea are doing it, I suppose it must be all right. But how can I help you with your organization?"

"We want you to be the head of it."

She put her hands to her mouth and stared at him. The head of a Nazarene organization? The idea frightened her. Then, in her mind's eye, she saw Elsa, sure of herself and her calling, deciding to leave Ingenius for Christ. She must hold her mother in contempt for not being strong enough to divorce Atak and leave all for Christ too. But what if Tetra was to become High Priestess of the Druid's Nazarenes? How would Elsa regard her mother then? And what if Tetra succeeded in making them into true Nazarenes?

"In Asia Minor and Judea," said Owain, "the Nazarenes are so enthused about Christus that they are giving all their goods and money to men they call bishops. The bishops have deacons who help them collect the money and put it into the hands of moneychangers to get interest for it. They use the interest to feed the poor and widowed just like the Jews have always done and to build what they are now calling churches instead of synagogues. The bishops are organizing themselves into metropolitan areas and electing head bishops who are becoming quite powerful. The people are doing whatever the bishops tell them to do. We would like you to become bishop of the anti-Bodin Nazarenes."

"Bishop?" she said suppressing her excitement. "But why me?"

Owain opened his arms, the palms of his hands upwards, as if the answer was self-evident. "You came here with Philip as his disciple," he said. "You spent many months teaching in the Druid College at Mona. You are mature and carry yourself with the dignity fitting to such an office. You are the mother of Elsa, who is famous as a healer among the Nazarene College, and therefore would be viewed sympathetically by them. You are married to Lord Atak, a principal adviser to King Caratacus and Queen Boudicca, and therefore your loyalty to our cause is beyond question. We can think of no-one as qualified as you to hold such a post."

"Where would I have to be?"

"In Mona, close to the Druid College. A fitting residence would be provided for you and Lord Atak."

Tetra drew herself up and folded her hands in her lap, gripped them tightly to subdue their trembling, conscious now of the importance of dignified behavior. "What would I have to do?" she asked.

"As I mentioned earlier, " said Owain, " there is to be a meeting next week. Many of the Council members who have agreed on the need for a new organization will be there, and I would like you to meet them and let them know that we can count on you to be our bishop."

When Boudicca returned, Tetra seemed dazed. "I have asked Lady Tetra to become Bishop of our new Nazarene church," said Owain, rubbing his hands together. "And she has graciously accepted."

"I thought Basil was your bishop," said Boudicca. She had heard rumors of the battle between Bodin and Owain, but wanted to hear what Owain said.

"Basil is to become Queen Cartimandua's bishop and organize the Nazarenes in Brigante. Lady Tetra will become bishop of the Nazarenes in our nations."

So Bodin had stolen the Nazarenes away from Owain and the incompetent Basil was banished to Brigante. Now Owain had set up a new church to compete with Bodin's and Tetra was to be the figurehead. Boudicca tried not to grimace. Tetra had never impressed her as a likely leader. Her response to every crisis was a flood of tears. What had possessed Owain? Dismissing the problem as being none of her concern, she decided that she would go with them to Almondbury. She had had enough of laying low now that she had recovered from her wound. Prasu didn't need her and neither did her daughters, looked after as they were by Habren and the servants. She had been imprisoned here long enough. She would see Venutius made Arviragus and he would give her an army, a real army. She directed a servant to get Einon, then smiled at Owain.

"You must be tired from your journey," she said. "In the morning, when you have rested, we will all go to Almondbury."

***

The journey took them across marshes, through dense forest that covered the lowlands and hills and on up the valley of the Derwent, where they threaded their way among hill forts and the large camps of Caratacus' and Venutius' warriors. Even though it was midsummer there were times when the rain fell heavily and the wind gusted and Boudicca felt as cold and damp as if it were November. Leaving the Derwent and the forests behind, they rode until they came to the rolling bright green moors and rocky outcroppings that typified Brigante. Owain had brought six of his guards with him, and Boudicca had brought six of hers, Owain having said that Cartimandua would permit no more than that.

At last they entered a wood and came to a river. After sending a man ahead to find a ford Owain assured her that one more day would bring them to Almondbury. "We should be there before the sun sets," he promised, as the horses picked their way among the stones along the riverbank. Before they had gone much further there was a clatter of racing hooves behind her and they stopped to look back. It was the man posted as rearguard.

"There's a rider coming from the east," said the man. "Rummies are chasing him. Looks like he might be hurt."

"Romans? How far behind him and how many?"

"A mile or more. About thirty of em."

"Into the woods, then," said Owain. Boudicca's heart beat faster as they hurried through the trees and up a hill until they were out of sight of the river below. In a small clearing on a low rise, they came to a halt and dismounted, hands on the horses' noses to keep them quiet.

Owain had stayed near the river with the rearguard man, and first she heard the rattle of the approaching Briton's hooves and then a shout. The clatter died away and she could hear only the soft urgent noises made by the horses and their riders as they climbed panting up the hill to join them. The strange Briton entered the clearing, Owain hard on his heels, then rolled off his horse and collapsed on the ground.

He lay face down, the visible side of his face a deathly chalk white, and the back of his shirt soaked in blood. His breath came in short gasps and his eyes were glazed. Boudicca ran to him, kneeling on one side of him, Tetra on the other. "It's Lord Tasget," said Boudicca, raising the man's head and wiping the sweat from his forehead with her tunic. "He's a Parisi from King Divicorix' court. Get water for him." The Parisi nation was on the coast to the east of Brigante and like Brigante outside the Roman frontier. Tasget was unconscious, and she could see a great wound in his side from which the blood oozed. She knew how it must hurt. He was middle-aged but lean and wiry. His hair had been black but now it looked like gray iron. He was dressed well and armed with a jeweled hunting knife. She took the water from one of the men and poured a little into Tasget's mouth.

"He's dying," Owain said.

Boudicca got up as Owain left the clearing to watch the Romans. The noise was loud as they passed and entered the ford, and Owain came back trembling in anger.

"By the Three Faces of Duw," he said. "Brigantes were leading them. What's Cartimandua up to?" He stood by her side looking down at Tasget. Tasget moved and opened his mouth. He tried to lift himself up to speak. Boudicca and Owain dropped to their knees to hear as Tetra restrained Tasget from rising further.

"What is it?" said Boudicca, putting a hand on Tasget's shoulder.

"Divi," said Tasget, choking on the blood and phlegm in his mouth.

"King Divicorix?" said Owain, and Tasget nodded weakly. Tetra put a little water to his mouth and he spit it out.

"Carat . . . Carti," he said.

"Queen Cartimandua?"

Tasget nodded again, and hatred filled his face. "Traitor," he gasped. "Traitor."

"Queen Cartimandua is a traitor?" said Owain, his face impassive. "What has she done?"

"Carat . . . Carti . . . " said Tasget. "Tell Divi . . . " His eyes bulged, then he fell back dead.

The men dug a grave, laid the body inside, replaced the earth and scattered leaves over it. "This man was on his way to warn Divicorix" said Owain. "Cartimandua must have arranged something with the Romans. Her treaty with Scapula forbids Roman troops from entering her territories, but those were her men leading them."

"We must get to my father at once," said Boudicca. "Tasget was trying to say his name so maybe he knows what evil she's up to." But what could it be? Cartimandua had agreed to join the alliance and Venutius was to be made Arviragus. Why had she invited a Rummy cavalry troop in? What was she after?

When it seemed certain the Romans would not return, Owain led them down the hill and across the ford. He sent a man far ahead to scout while they plodded slowly on.

Chapter 2

Caratacus Puts His Finger on It

Cartimandua's palace at Almondbury was already full of kings, princes and Druids here to witness Cartimandua's entry into the Alliance, so Boudicca decided to take one of the tents erected in the grassy square. She had barely thrown her clothes to a servant to put away when Atak and Owain came in. Owain had told Atak about the dead Parisi. "What do you make of it?" she said to Atak. "What's she up to?" But before Atak could say anything, she waved him into silence. "First," she said to Owain, "did the Council members tell you where things stand?"

"Cartimandua's joining the alliance," he said. "She's giving us a hundred thousand warriors. We're to have a ceremony tomorrow to seal the bargain."

"That's good," said Atak. "A hundred thousand will make a big difference."

"Part of her price," said Owain, grimly, "was an agreement from Divicorix and his kings that she will name his successor when he dies. She's always wanted the Parisi lands and the Humber under her control. But Divicorix is not old. He may outlast her."

"There are other ways of dying than by old age," said Boudicca. "The question now," she looked at Atak, "is what is she after? And where are the Rummies she's brought in?"

"We must send out scouts to find them," said Atak. "And we must give Divicorix more warriors when he leaves. She might have these Rummies ambush him now that she can name his successor."

"That's it!" she said. "That way, her hands will be clean. Let's go see my father."

Caratacus had a cubicle in the palace, closed off by drapes and guarded by two of his own warriors. The room was well lit by stone lamps. Her father sat drinking wine at a table, and Venutius and his brother Caswal sat across from him. An amphora and several cups stood on the table. Caswal leaped up and Caratacus pushed back his chair when Boudicca entered. Caratacus lurched a little as if from the wine and his eyes were bleary. Venutius staggered to his feet arms outstretched and she was in them in front of everyone. She no longer cared who knew of her love. "Are you both sober enough to talk?" she said.

"We're sober enough," said Caratacus.

They sat around the table, Boudicca between Venutius and Caswal, while she told her father and Venutius about Tasget's message and the Roman cavalry squadron. "They're here to kill Divicorix so she can take over the Parisi," she said. "This talk of joining the alliance is just to lull us to sleep."

Caratacus belched and slapped his hand on the table. "Don't jump at the first bait she dangles," he said. "Look for the biggest thing she can get her hands on and work down from there."

"Tell us what she can get her hands on," said Venutius. He shoved the amphora toward Caratacus.

"She and me have done a lot of talking," said Caratacus. He leaned back and scratched his belly, a pleased look on his face. "She's a surprisingly rational woman when there's no-one around to get her conniving among em."

"I know you've tried to bed her," said Venutius, without rancor.

"My own niece?" said Caratacus, equally without rancor. "Let's put the pieces on the table. If she's after what we're after we must help her. If she's not after what we're after then we must nudge her in the right direction."

"Or stop her," said Boudicca.

"You'll never stop her. And I don't know if that's the best thing. She has Scapula so rattled he don't know his butt from his ear hole." Caratacus took a long drink then wiped his mouth with the back of his hand.

"Put the pieces on the table," said Venutius.

"The first piece," said Caratacus, "is the Rummies. What's the best she can do with a squadron of Rummies?"

"Give em Divicorix," said Boudicca.

"She can also give em our new Arviragus."

Venutius stared straight ahead, a puzzled frown on his face.

Atak whistled. "That would be a prize for Scapula," he said. "To snatch an Arviragus and send him off to Rome. But would she do that to her own husband?"

Caratacus gave Atak an overstretched smile that said Cartimandua would do that and worse. Venutius pushed his chair back and stood up. "By Duw," he said to Caratacus, "your mind is more twisted than Cartie's. Why would she have me made Arviragus if she's out to get rid of me? Why didn't she just have me killed if she wants me out of her way?"

"You're worth nothing dead," said Caratacus. "You're worth a lot more as a live Arviragus. And that brings us to the second piece." He leaned back in his chair and glared around with bleary eyes. They're both drunk, thought Boudicca. Our first night together and Venutius will go to sleep.

"She wants to marry Scapula," said Caratacus. "That's why she don't want you dead. You're the bait that will get Scapula for her. With him under her thumb, she'll control all Britain. She'll give you to Scapula so he can drag an Arviragus around Rome in a cage. For that he would put his own wife away and marry the three Morrigans. Cartie worked this out with him and Scapula fed this to Tasget so he'd work us all up like screeching geese."

Venutius jumped up with a curse and drew his sword. "Then

by Duw she shall die," he said and lurched toward the door. Boudicca was on her feet and with strength that surprised her spun him around so quickly that he dropped his sword.

"Quick!" she shouted at Atak. Atak jumped up, grabbed Venutius and pinned his arms.

"Let him go," said Caswal, his high-pitched voice cracking.

Boudicca brushed past Caswal and wheeled on her father, lips trembling with anger. "You don't know any of this," she said. "Cartie's after Divicorix and if we don't help him he'll be dead, and then the Parisies will belong to Cartie."

Caratacus narrowed his eyes and shrugged. "Believe what you like," he said. "They're going to belong to Cartie anyway when she marries Scapula. We have less than fifty men between us. We'll be hard put to stop Cartie from doing anything she sets her mind to."

"If she marries Scapula and combines her forces with his," said Owain, "the war will be lost and we can't take that risk. As soon as King Venutius is confirmed as Arviragus, we must get him out of here. If the cavalry is really after King Divicorix, Queen Boudicca and the rest of our men can still escort him to safety. That way, we will have covered both contingencies."

Boudicca nodded agreement. She turned away from her father and went over to Venutius. "Shall I tell Atak to let you go?" she asked. "Are you calm now?" Venutius nodded sullenly and Atak released him. Venutius picked up his sword and for a moment she thought he was going to swing at Atak but he sheathed the weapon, motioning to Caswal to sit by him at the table. She sat down next to Venutius. "Do you really believe she'd marry Scapula?" she said to her father. She felt cooler now that Venutius had calmed down.

Caratacus nodded. He seemed a little more sober. "Don't assume the war would be lost. She would lead Scapula around by his testicles and the Britons would be united under a British queen with four Rummy legions at her command. It would be years before that addlepated Claudius found out what was going on. By then, she'd be ready to take on the empire. The biggest mistake we can make is to underestimate the depth of her scheming."

"The question is:" said Owain, tapping his chin with his fingers, "Would she be the wife of a Roman governor or would the governor be the husband of a British queen?"

"Nobody governs Cartie," said Venutius. He sounded proud of his evil wife.

"Then if she can rule the Romans in Britain, perhaps we should help her," said Owain.

"By help her, you mean give me to the Rummies," said Venutius.

Owain shook his head vigorously. "No, no," he said. "No, no."

"We're not going to help her become queen of all Britain," said Boudicca. "She would be worse than Rome. Venutius, you must disappear as soon as you're sworn in. You too, Caswal. Take Aled and go with your brother so Cartie can't take you hostage again. Now how can we make sure she doesn't marry Scapula?"

"You can't," said Caratacus.

"Then Cruker must kill him when he comes up here."

Venutius snorted. "Cruker's not the man. Use Velocatus."

"Velocatus it is then," she said. Velocatus was twice the size of Cruker and famous for his great strength.

"Is that it, then?" said Caratacus.

"Yes," said Venutius. "She's not going to trade me."

"There will be consequences if we kill a Roman governor," said Owain. "We should think further on it."

"If Velocatus uses a little skill," said Boudicca, "they won't know how he died or who killed him."

Owain shrugged. "I must go to Mona with the other Council members," he said. "Lady Tetra has agreed to assist us. Perhaps Lord Atak will accompany us." Atak nodded.

"I must get to the Derwent soon," said Caratacus. "We have to get Genvissa and Eurgen away from Scapula. And Gwendolyn, Owain."

Owain nodded but didn't seem any more excited than Caratacus at the prospect of his hysterical wife being rescued.

Venutius poured more wine into his cup. "Come with us," he said.

"No," said Caratacus. "The armies will want to kiss your Pendragon and get you drunk. Besides, I want to blather some more with your wife. Just the two of us together and a jug of wine and she might let me in on a few things."

"Like her bed," said Venutius. "Well, you're welcome to it." He looked at Boudicca, and she felt her cheeks redden.

***

Tetra squatted in the Druids' tent and shivered. The early morning drizzle filled the steamy air with the noise of a thousand drips. It was cold and damp and the small charcoal brazier did little to help. The Druid High Council members who had been delegated to install King Venutius as Arviragus and bind Cartimandua into the alliance squatted in a half-circle. They stared at her and Owain, their eyes as cold and cheerless as the wind outside, and looked hostile when Owain said Queen Cartimandua had decided not to join the alliance just yet and that their warrior servants had been requisitioned by Queen Boudicca to protect King Divicorix. They began to chatter ominously, but Owain raised his voice and went on talking and the chatter faded away.

Owain reminded the members that he was the Druid most qualified to guide the Council in the religious aspects of its search for unity among the British nations. It surprised her to hear him speak of the evil Lord Bodin as if he were merely assisting Owain. In recounting her own qualifications, he laid more stress on the fact she was Atak's wife and a member of Boudicca's household than on the fact she was a disciple of Philip and the mother of Elsa. The gist of Owain's speech, it seemed to her, was that to appoint her as Bishop would be a logical step in conforming the

British Druid-Nazarene church to organizational developments in Greece, Egypt and Judea.

Nothing was said about the need to get back as quickly as possible to the true teaching of the Lord Jesus or about the likelihood that civil war might break out should the real Nazarenes be persecuted. When Owain finished speaking and the glassy eyed Druids agreed that she should be made Bishop of the new Church, she didn't know whether to be pleased or mortified. What did Owain think she had agreed to? Whatever he thought, she was going to mold the church as she felt Philip would have molded it. She would tell this to Owain as soon as they got out of this tent. She prepared to rise, but the Council was not yet finished with Owain.

"I don't see that you had the right to give our guards to Queen Boudicca," said one of them, an old man with wispy white hair, watery eyes and a red nose.

"I didn't assume the right," said Owain. "I merely agreed that King Divicorix should have as much protection as we can afford. Even with all our guards, my own included, there will be barely enough to defend him should this Roman cavalry squadron attack. Of course, the Council can withhold its guards. Those six men, however, are likely to be the difference between success and defeat."

"Why are you so sure they're after Divicorix?" said another member.

"More likely they're after Caratacus," said some one else.

"The Parisi noble who died," said Owain, "warned us that they were after King Divicorix."

"Why did Cartimandua insult us by inviting us here and then telling us she won't join the Alliance without the full Council?"

"I don't know," said Owain, "but at least she's agreed to let us swear in the Arviragus."

There was more muttering and mumbling but it was brought to a halt by the sound of the Hirlas horn.

"It's time for the ceremony," said Owain. He grabbed Tetra's arm and propelled her out of the tent into the drizzle. "I'm afraid I didn't make your new role sound too exciting," he said, as they hurried toward the grassy sward in the center of the fort. "But I've learned that the best way to bring about necessary change is to convince my fellow Druids that their decisions change nothing. Once we have your organization in place our task will be to show that anything proposed by Bodin would change what they have already decided upon. If we can show that, and I flatter myself that my skill in handling the Council is superior to Bodin's, all his scheming will come to naught. But in the meantime, speed is important."

Not used to being hurried along like this, Tetra found herself panting as she struggled to keep up. The drizzle grew heavier and wetter, and her clothes stuck to her. "We must set up the church as Philip would have done," she gasped.

"Yes yes," said Owain, "but here we are, and now I must leave you." The drizzle had turned to rain by this time making it difficult to see, but the great bulk of Atak set him apart from the throng. She hurried toward him with a heavy heart as Owain disappeared among the tents.

Atak threw his cloak over her and she snuggled up against him, glad to be held close and yet disquieted within. Owain's speech and attitude had so deflated her expectations that she felt like resigning her new appointment. Only the thought of the respect she would gain from Elsa and the other Nazarenes made her decide to go forward. But she resolved again that if she could not build the Church as she felt Philip would have built it, she would resign. Atak must have sensed the battle going on within her. He looked down at her and gave her a squeeze. She raised her face for a kiss and felt better.

Boudicca stood by Atak, Tetra on his other side, and looked around the crowded square. The Druid Council members entered and formed a half circle behind the blue robed regalia bearers. Caratacus and Divicorix entered next with Cartimandua between them. All were dressed splendidly in brightly colored silk robes and all were lavishly bejeweled.

Caratacus seemed his usual self but Divicorix peered around nervously. Someone must have told him about Tasget. Cartimandua, the most regal of the three high royals, walked erectly, head in the air as if conscious that all eyes were on her. Her copper hair, blackened by the rain and shaken by the wind, was coiled high above her head. A man dressed in a gaudy multicolored robe walked with her holding on grimly to a purple hat that threatened to blow off. "It's Basil," hissed Tetra. So that was Owain's Bishop Basil from whom Bodin had stolen Owain's church. So now there were four Nazarene churches: Bodin's, Basil's, Joseph's and Tetra's. Boudicca shrugged. She had lost interest in Nazarenes. Only Elsa seemed to know what to do.

The high royals took up their places, and their kings and nobles, all soaking wet but colorfully and beautifully dressed, stood behind them. When all was ready, a regalia bearer raised the Hirlas horn to his lips and blew a watery blast. The crowd to his right parted, and Owain as deputy Archdruid, wearing a special hat with white ostrich feathers, entered the circle. The statuesque Velocatus, Venutius' man at arms, followed him bearing the furled Pendragon. The rain poured and the wind gusted so that trees and tents rattled and robes flapped as Owain and Velocatus took up their positions.

Boudicca's heart beat faster as Venutius, dressed in the full regalia of a High King, strode briskly into the circle and stood before Owain. She had never seen him look so handsome. Owain began to speak, but before long her father interrupted him with some caustic remark. Venutius went down on one knee and a regalia bearer handed him the ceremonial sword to kiss.

As soon as Venutius had kissed it, Owain motioned to Velocatus to lower Pendragon's pole so the banner could be unfastened. Pendragon uncurled itself partially to flap and crack in the wind, and the crowd murmured in awe. Velocatus held it out and Venutius kissed it then drew his sword and turned to face the crowd.

"Black wind or no," he roared, sword held high, "I will defend Britain against the foul Rummies." He sheathed his sword and was about to turn away when Cartimandua said something in her sharp clear voice. Venutius scowled and glared at Basil, who raised both hands over Venutius' head.

Venutius sulkily went down on one knee before Basil, who bent forward to place both hands on Venutius' head. Boudicca could hear Basil mumble a prayer over Venutius, but the prayer came to an abrupt end when Basil's large purple hat blew off. Venutius stood and unsheathed his sword. He waved it over his head as Basil backed away. "I will defend Britain," said Venutius, "in the name of the true Nazarene church." He sheathed his sword and walked out of the circle followed by Velocatus carrying Pendragon. The crowd cheered as it ran for cover.

The wind now blew with such force that Boudicca and Tetra had to cling to Atak as he pulled them inside the doorway of the wooden palace. Great sheets of rain crashed against the walls and water quickly covered the floor behind the doorway. Cartimandua rushed in holding her hair, which had uncoiled itself like a soggy serpent around her shoulders. Her attendants rushed along with her and they disappeared among the crowd. Caratacus seemed to enjoy the storm as he entered the hall. He stopped when he saw them.

"And isn't our new Arviragus off to a fine start with Manannan's black wind at his back," he said. He smiled at Tetra and then at Boudicca, the rain running off his hair and down his face and beard.

"Venutius will be a good Arviragus," said Atak, "but he has a hot head."

"I would rather a hot head than a cold one," said Boudicca, glowering at Atak. "Cold ones back off when things go badly."

"I tell you true," said Caratacus, laying a hand on Atak's chest. "I'm tired of fighting. I yearn to sit by the fire with my ladylove, drink warm wine and eat chestnuts. Venutius is welcome to wrestle with the flaming kings and druids."

A young boy forced his way through and tugged at Caratacus' robe. "She says to come right away," said the boy.

"Oh she does, does she?" said Caratacus. "You tell her I'll be there soon." The boy pulled on his unruly hair and sped away.

"Any word on the Rummy squadron?" said Atak.

"Not a peep."

Atak pulled on his beard and looked thoughtful. "There'll be no-one here to cover us when all our men have gone with Divicorix."

Caratacus snorted. "The Rummies won't show up here," he said. "They're after Venutius." He stalked off.

"And I must find Divicorix," said Boudicca, kissing Atak and Tetra. She had not been surprised when Owain told her Cartimandua wouldn't join the alliance. Cartie had no intention of joining it. She had got them up here to cover the assassination of Divicorix, but that wasn't going to happen.

Boudicca found Divicorix at the stables in his traveling clothes, nervous and distraught. The journey to his kingdom was wet and windy but completely uneventful. No Rummies appeared. So it wasn't Divicorix they were after, she thought, alarm building in her breast. Maybe her father had been right and it was Venutius. As soon as she could she headed south with her six guards.

Chapter 3

Caratacus Takes a Journey

Atak rode with Tetra at the end of the long line of Druids. Finding that Boudicca had commandeered most of the visitors' guards, Cartimandua had provided them with an escort of Brigante warriors to see them safely home.

About noon on the second day out they came to a crossroads and Samnus, the surly captain of the Brigante guards, led them off to the right through a deep gorge. In the middle of the gorge, the road climbed steeply until it emerged onto hills covered with rock outcroppings. The dirt road itself was strewn with boulders and small rocks, and the going was slow and painful. One of the scouts came back to say there was a spring of water on a hill to their right. They left the road and climbed laboriously up the hill until they came to a small depression surrounded by a ring of tall rocks. The spring and a pool of cool water were in the middle of the depression. Gratefully, Atak and Tetra dismounted. Samnus made obeisance to the god of the spring and led their horses to drink.

Atak's legs were stiff and he stretched several times then went outside the circle of rocks to sit down on a boulder warm from the afternoon sun. From there he could see the moors roll endlessly on, their smooth contours broken only by rock outcroppings or clumps of trees. Fast moving fleecy white clouds filled the sky, each of which had its own distinctive patches of yellow and gray.

The clouds threw enormous black shadows that moved over the bright green and gray moors like great fish gobbling up patches of sunlight. One of the shadows gobbled up the road they had traveled down. Back in the direction from which they had come he saw movement in an area that had just been shaded. It was too dark at that distance to make out, but he thought it was a line of horsemen. Tetra brought him a cup of fresh water and sat down on the rock beside him while he watched the sunshine approach the horsemen. When it reached them and glinted off armor he stiffened.

"It's the Rummy squadron," he said and went to warn Owain and Samnus. They came back with him and he sat down again by Tetra.

"Are they coming after us?" she asked, fearfully.

"No," he said, to quieten her fears.

Owain squatted by Atak's side as a shadow covered the horsemen. Then Atak turned to Samnus. "You'd better keep everyone out of sight," he said. Samnus grunted and went back to the pool. The horsemen were so close now that they were distinct even in the shade. As the light swept over them again he caught his breath.

"What is it?" whispered Tetra.

"That man in the middle," he said. "He's in chains. Can you see who he is?"

"By Duw," said Owain. "It's Caratacus."

"That's what I thought," said Atak.

"This is what I feared might happen," said Owain. "Cartimandua arranged it. She needed a great prize to get Scapula to marry her and Caratacus is a much greater prize than Venutius. Caratacus is famous in Rome but few Romans have heard of Venutius."

Atak glowered. "Then why didn't you say so?"

"It would have been no use," said Owain. "Caratacus wanted

to seduce Cartimandua. He was so blinded by desire he walked right into her trap."

Looking back, Atak had to agree. He had seen the lust in Caratacus' eyes. He grunted. "And you let her trap him?"

"Not completely," said Owain. He looked at both of them with a patronizing smile. "I sent a letter with one of King Venutius' men asking King Bledud to come north with sufficient force to overcome the Roman squadron just in case. It's obviously heading back to Longthorpe and they should meet some time tomorrow."

Atak stole a quick glance at Owain. The Druid had explained everything to his own satisfaction and it would be someone else's job to rescue Caratacus. By this time, the Roman squadron and its prisoner had disappeared behind the hill and Atak stood up. "I'm going to follow them," he said.

Tetra put her hands on his arms. "Please don't," she said. "King Bledud will rescue King Caratacus."

"He might not get the word," said Atak. He climbed on his horse but she looked so sad and tearful he dismounted again. "I'll go with you to Mona," he said. He kissed her and she smiled happily.

"We must move on," said Owain, and they picked their way carefully down the hill to rejoin the road. Owain rode with Atak and Tetra at the rear of the line.

They hadn't been on the road long before they breasted a hill and ahead of them was a small clump of oaks. As they drew near, Atak heard a murmur from the front of the line and some of the men urged their horses forward until they stopped among the oaks. He rode in among them to see what they stared at. Too late, he tried to stop Tetra. She gasped in horror and turned her face away. A man had been pinned to one of the oaks with a lance. His face told of a slow agonizing death. There were other bodies, some of them small and dwarflike.

"It's the Merrimar Gunes," said one of the men. "They must have attacked our Arviragus."

There was no sign of Venutius so he must have escaped or

been captured. Atak tried to back Tetra's horse away but found their way blocked by Owain's horse. The Druid's face was bloodless and his lips trembled.

"What is it?" he asked.

"That's the man I gave King Bledud's letter to," said Owain. "What happened to King Venutius?"

"He got away," said someone.

"Or he's dead," said someone else.

Atak forced his horse out. "I'm after Caratacus," he said.

"Atak!" cried Tetra. "They will kill you."

He reached over and kissed her. "They won't," he said.

"Then I will come with you."

"No," said Owain, grabbing her reins. "Atak is too old and wise a soldier to do anything foolish and you could not help him. You must start work on the church."

"Yes," said Atak. "Work on your church. Pray for us." He whipped his horse around and galloped off down the hill. Tetra's tears had made him sad but already he was glad to be away from women and Druids both. Getting Caratacus away from the Rummies and finding Venutius was something he could bite into.

Chapter 4

Basil Goes Recruiting

Some months later

Tristram snorted and Dedreth, foster sister to Boudicca and a heretic Nazarene, reined him in. They had just crested a hill and emerged from the forest. Three figures on horseback, mere specks at this distance, rode toward her, coming from the east. She edged Tristram back into the trees and waited, stroking the horse to keep him quiet. Below them stretched the familiar estuary with its little islands and the great Tor of Ynis Witcin (Glastonbury Tor), near the foot of which was her village and the synagogue that Boudicca's grandfather Cunobelinus had built for Simon Peter. Other villages within the land that Cunobelinus had granted to Joseph of Arimathea straggled along the banks of the estuary and sent spirals of blue smoke into the clear spring air. Ahead of them, only a few isolated clumps of trees broke the long stretches of gorse and yellow woad. The path they were on disappeared around a bend but reappeared much farther on, wending its way eastward over the rolling hills.

The trail that led down to Joseph's village joined the road they were on and the horsemen would soon reach it. They rode at not much more than a walk, and as they got closer she could see that one wore a multicolored but dusty robe and a large purple hat. He was too plump to be a warrior. The other horsemen were dressed in similar garments but their hats were blue. Bulky rolls behind all of them spoke of a long journey. They reached the trail and stopped, looking down it toward the village. If they passed the trail, she decided, she would wait and then make a dash across the gorse to the village. But instead of passing it, the horsemen turned into the trail.

"I wonder who they are," she said to Tristram. They looked harmless but she had better find out who they were and what they wanted. She made sure her own roll of clothes was secure then urged Tristram forward, the bracken and twigs crackling beneath his hooves. He snorted with delight as they burst through the last of the trees and galloped onto the long sloping field of gorse. The travelers must have been alarmed by this sudden appearance of a charging horsewoman and stopped to watch her approach. Tristram skittered to a halt, raising a cloud of dust that caused the plump man to raise his hands in protest.

"I am Dedreth of Carys," she said. "From the village ahead of you. Might I ask your names and business?"

The plump man drew himself up and puffed out his chest. "I am Basil, Lord Bishop of the Brigante Nazarene Church and servant of Cartimandua, High Queen of the Brigantes," he said. He reached behind him and took a candle out of his roll. "Here," he said, offering it to her. "I have blessed it myself. If ever you feel sick, light this and the Lord Jesus will make you well. We usually sell them for a silver piece but you can have that one as a gift."

"Ah," she said. Without taking her eyes off Basil she jammed the candle under her robe. "You are not a Briton."

"No," said Basil. "I am from Judea. I was one of the chief disciples of the Lord Jesus. These are elders of my church, Logan Bullhead and Spuden Sagacious. They are both Britons, lately of the order of Druids."

The two men bowed to her.

"We are looking for Elsa, the girl who heals," said Basil. "She is sometimes called Brigit by the people. We have been told she lives in your village."

Elsa wasn't in the village, but she didn't feel like telling that to Basil. She would take this motley crew to Joseph and he would know what to do with them. "What is it you wish with her?" she asked.

"Then she does live here?" said Basil, a satisfied look on his face.

She nodded curtly.

"He wants her to join our church," said Logan Bullhead.

She decided she felt more at ease with the ex-Druids. "We have many ex-Druids among us," she said. "Do you know a bard named Goronwy?" The Druids shook their heads. "What rank were you?" she asked Logan, to be polite.

"We were both bards," said Logan, "until we were circumcised. We can't rejoin the Druids until the law is changed. And we don't see any sign of them doing that."

"And we were not compensated," said Spuden.

"Sometimes," said Basil, "we are forced to have done to us that which we would rather not have done to us, and to not have done to us that which we had rather have done to us." Dedreth pricked up her ears. She had heard that phrase before. It sounded like something Owain, the Druid to whom she had once been betrothed, would say.

"You will not wish to rejoin your Druids when you see how large and safe our church will become," said Basil. "The Druids are being eliminated by the Romans. The Romans respect our church. Their governor, Ostorius Scapula himself, has said this to Queen Cartimandua. They are very religious themselves."

The two men shrugged.

"Are you acquainted with Lord Owain of the Council?" asked Dedreth. She still felt guilty about jilting poor Owain, even though it was so many years ago.

"Oh yes," said Logan. "He encouraged us to get circumcised. He didn't have it done himself, though."

"I suggested he have it done," said Basil. "It might have helped him in Rome, to say he was a Jew and not a Druid."

Dedreth's eyebrows shot up. "Lord Owain is in Rome?"

"King Caratacus was taken there with his family," said Spuden. "Lord Owain has a ransom note that Claudius signed when he was captured by Caratacus, and the Council sent him to Rome to negotiate Caratacus' release."

"He will not be successful," said Basil, raising his nose. "The Romans hate Druids."

"They hate Jews more," said Logan. "Claudius expelled a bunch from Rome."

Basil drew himself up and looked offended.

"So King Caratacus was captured?" asked Dedreth. "We hear nothing since the Druids left Ynis and the glass and tin trade stopped."

"Queen Cartimandua betrayed him," said Spuden.

"That is not true," said Basil. "He was captured by a Roman cavalry squadron."

"She also tried to do away with her husband, King Venutius," said Spuden. "They say it was the Gunes of Merimar but she paid them to do it. They killed some of his men and beat him with clubs. He almost died. Queen Boudicca was so upset she became ill."

She had not seen Boudicca for so long. "She is all right now?"

Spuden shrugged. "She's at Thetford with her husband."

I must go to her, she thought. I will go tomorrow. Tristram pawed the ground, anxious to be off. "I will take you to our village," she said. "We can offer you a night's lodging to help you on your journey."

"But this is our destination," said Basil. "We came here to see Elsa. I can offer her a high position in my church, perhaps even as a Deaconess, but she will have to drop the name Brigit.

I have the full authority of High Queen Cartimandua to organize our church in any way I think proper. We are getting many converts from Lord Bodin's church because he has made them afraid of not getting into the Otherworld. Our church, of course, can guarantee entrance into the Otherworld. Now that we have found this girl Elsa, I will spend some time in your village to see if there are others, perhaps even including yourself, who will also make suitable members for our church."

"That is very good of you," said Dedreth, gritting her teeth. "I'm sure Joseph of Arimathea will be glad to welcome an old acquaintance."

"Prince Joseph is here?" said Basil. He looked alarmed. "I thought he had gone back to Judea."

"No," she said. "He has given up his tin trade and decided to make his home in Britain. He has been elected Cyndaf (Chief) of the Nazarene College, which is in our village. His wife and sons Josephes and Galaad and his daughter Anna are also with us. Now follow me, and I will lead you to them."

The fields near the estuary were bright with blooming woad and many laborers tended them. Cattle grazed in a common area near the ancient round wattle huts lived in by members of the Nazarene College and those who worked the farm. Joseph himself lived in a house built on the edge of the village. The tide was low and she waved a greeting at old Lord Dardad who had once sat on the High Council of Kings and Druids as she led the three horsemen across the causeway that disappeared when the tide came in. They dismounted in front of Joseph's house, and Joseph and his sons Josephes and Galaad appeared at the door as a servant collected the horses and led them away. Josephes, tall like his father, vigorous, impatient and dark skinned, was dressed in traveling clothes.

"Boudicca has been sick," was the first thing she said, and Joseph looked grave. "Her father was betrayed by Cartimandua and Owain has gone to Rome to plead his case. I must go to her tomorrow."

"You must rest from your journey first," he said. "Josephes is just about to leave to take your place."

"Caratacus was not betrayed by Queen Cartimandua," said Basil.

Joseph looked on impassively as she introduced Basil and the two ex-Druids. He ushered them all in to the house's dark and smoke filled hall. Several ex-Druids were inside but left through a rear door as they entered and Joseph called for refreshments. There were no seats so they remained standing. Joseph was courteous to Basil. "I don't recall having seen you among the disciples," he said. "Perhaps I missed you in the throng."

"I was one of the seventy," said Basil. He stood right in front of Joseph. "The Lord sent out the twelve to preach the good news about the Kingdom," he said, "and they came back empty handed. So he sent out seventy of us and told us not to go house to house but to stay in one place. I stayed in the house of a candle maker for months and made hundreds of candles for him until he finally agreed to become a Nazarene, then I heard that the Lord had been crucified. It was quite a shock to me, when I returned to Jerusalem, to find that the twelve, who had been so unsuccessful, were now acting as if they alone were the ones who had been picked to spread the word."

"They were," said Josephes.

"Then why did he send out the seventy?" said Basil, stabbing Josephes in the chest with his stubby forefinger. "And if the twelve were so good, why did one of them turn him over to the Romans? There was no Judas among the seventy."

"There was no Simon Peter either," said Galaad.

"Simon Peter is nobody," said Basil, and Dedreth felt her hackles rise. "Paul is the one they're calling Apostle these days. And he wasn't one of the twelve either. Paul is getting thousands of converts. I've written a letter inviting him to preach here. He will most likely bring thousands into our church."

"Does Paul sell candles too?" she asked, but was interrupted before Basil could reply. A servant appeared with a tray from which they each took a cup of cool wine. Basil downed his in one gulp and held out his cup for more. "You cannot know Simon Peter and speak of him with such contempt," said Dedreth. Joseph laid a restraining hand on her arm but she ignored it. "I have traveled with Simon Peter and witnessed his great works. I will not hear him slandered."

Basil opened his mouth but said nothing.

"I should like to meet Paul if he comes," said Joseph, and his mildness made her angry. There were times, she thought, when even Joseph shouldn't be such a peacemaker.

Basil raised his arms in a conciliatory gesture, almost as if he were blessing the entire village. "That can be arranged," he said, "if you were to join our church."

"But I have a church," said Joseph. "It fills heaven and earth and is neither built by men nor manipulated by them. What would be gained by joining your church?"

"It is well that you have a church that no-one can see," sniffed Basil, "but it is not so well for others. All true believers should be in one fold and led by men who can be seen and heard, and it should provide instruction and guidance for the ignorant, who must be taught about God. There must be organization, doctrine and ritual, or they won't know what to believe in or how to go about believing in it. Without the kind of church we provide the ignorant will quickly go back to idolatry and all that the Lord came to show us will be lost."

"But what the Lord came to show us," said Joseph, "is that organizations don't lead to God. They lead only to competition for control of the state and Temple, and to battles for the chief seats in the synagogue. To follow an organization is to become the tool of ambitious priests. Tell me truthfully, is your church designed to serve God or Basil?"

Basil drew himself up and stuck out his chest. "I can see that you would not blend in with our organization and therefore I withdraw my offer. But you will permit me to speak to the girl

Elsa, whom I understand lives here. She at least might see the wisdom of belonging to a properly organized church."

"Why should she wish to join your church?" said Josephes. Dedreth got the feeling that Josephes' contempt for Basil was the equal of her own. "She is already closer to Christ than I suspect you will ever be."

This time Joseph placed a restraining hand on his son's arm. "Of course you may speak to Elsa," said Joseph. "She is not here, but my son Josephes will take you to her. She is with his wife and my daughter Anna in a place where there are many sick. Perhaps, when you get there, you can help them. We find that doing such work brings converts to Christ more than we can number."

Basil looked around as if to make sure his two ex-Druids were paying attention. "What is the nature of the sickness, that so many are taken with it?" he asked.

"It's some kind of plague," said Joseph. "The only good thing about it is that it keeps the Romans away. Dedreth has just returned from there." Basil backed away hastily. "Perhaps she can describe it for you."

"Those who recover," said Dedreth, "tell us it's like receiving a blow at the back of the neck. They're prostrated by it and lose consciousness. They babble in strange tongues and swell in various places."

"But aren't you afraid of getting it too?" said Basil, rubbing the back of his neck.

"You are always safe when doing God's work," said Dedreth. "You are in no danger if your heart is pure. Isn't this what the Lord Jesus came to show us? God gave us dominion over the entire earth, and as we purify our hearts we image God's power. Nothing can hurt us if we are good."

Basil turned again to the two ex-Druids, his hand still caressing the back of his neck. "I must stay here and talk more with Joseph and the Lady Dedreth," he said. "We cannot afford to let dissension drive apart God's people." He turned back to

Joseph. "If you will forgive my hasty words a few moments ago," he said, "I would like to talk more on the subject of church. It is too important to dismiss so hastily, and we Nazarenes must stick together." Joseph nodded gravely, and Basil turned back to the Druids. "Go with Joseph's son to Elsa and see if you can get her to come back here. She may talk more freely if we are all together."

"You are not coming with us?" said Logan.

"No. As I said, I must talk more with Joseph and the Lady Dedreth."

"We are not going there by ourselves."

"But you must," fumed Basil. "We must talk to Elsa."

"If it's that important," said Logan, "come with us."

Basil glared at his two elders, but neither of them backed down. "Very well," he said. "We will all go in the morning if Prince Joseph will have one of his servants guide us."

"A servant will show you to the guest quarters," said Joseph. "After you have washed and changed, you must join us for our evening meal. We can talk more then, if you still wish it."

"Of course I still wish it," said Basil. He and his two elders went out docilely enough behind the servant.

"I have a feeling," said Joseph, putting his arm around Dedreth, "that they will be gone before the evening meal is ready. I had better tell Samuel to leave their horses where they can be easily found."

"I hope they go," she said. "Spuden and Logan are funny, but Basil is a horrible man. He gave me a candle. If we are visited by evil we are to light it and the Lord Jesus will come and save us."

"I'm glad you didn't tell me about that before," said Joseph. "I would have lit it right away. Let us see Josephes on his way and then walk down to the synagogue. The fresh air will feel good." Galaad declined to go with them and after Josephes had mounted his horse and left she and Joseph set off together. The synagogue was not far away and they walked along the edge of the mud uncovered by the fallen tide.

It was good working with Joseph and the others, she thought. There were times, however, when her body clamored for a mate, and the black sparkling eyes and auburn beard of Selyf, the Duroe knight who had championed her so long ago against Boudicca's brother King Marius, would appear in her dreams. Selyf had probably married by this time, and even if he hadn't he was not right for her. He had no interest in seeking the Kingdom. She had thought that something might grow between she and Galaad, but Galaad was too spiritual. She drew a sharp involuntary breath at a sudden vision of Selyf naked in the grass beside her and Joseph looked at her. He knows, she thought. He knows what I'm thinking. I must go to Boudicca.

By this time they had reached the mound and the little roofless building dedicated to Jesus' mother that Tewdos and his men had erected so long ago under Atak's watchful eye. In her mind she could see Simon Peter dropping to his knees and praying, while Tewdos gathered the stones that would demarcate the outlines of the synagogue and Atak fussed over the camp's defenses. It had been before the Romans invaded. While they were building the synagogue Owain had them all kidnapped and sent away in a ship because he was afraid that Marius, angry at being forced to fight a duel with Selyf because of her, would attack their camp and take her prisoner. Poor Atak had tried to fight off the kidnappers and had been badly wounded, but Simon Peter had healed him. Their ship had been blown off course and they had spent many happy weeks on the Isle of Peace (Isle of Man). From there they had sailed to the Whithorn peninsula, where Peter had healed many and left a stone inscribed in commemoration of his visit.

She followed Joseph through the garden until they stood before the wattled walls of the synagogue and Joseph touched with his boot the corner stone that Simon Peter had laid. "You know," he said, "it is much easier to fight a war with oneself about things than about thoughts. And the most difficult thoughts to overcome are passionate thoughts."

"What must I do?" she said.

"You must marry. Jesus' mother was married at fifteen and happily so until her Joseph departed. The important thing about following the Christ is that we divest ourselves little by little of those carnal thoughts and impulses that blind us to God's Kingdom. Jesus was no ascetic. He loved good company and a good meal and warned us we can enter the Kingdom in no other way than by following in his footsteps. First he healed, then he overcame death for others and himself, then he rose above our comprehension so he could no longer be seen. You cannot begin where he left off. Your hunger for a mate is quite normal. It is dangerous to repress it if the repression fills your mind with thoughts you are not yet equipped to defeat. The body will take care of itself in good time, but for now, if it is hungry you must feed it. You must marry someone whose progress you can help and who will help you in yours."

"But who is that?" she cried, resting her face on his chest. "Galaad is not interested in marriage and I know no-one else who seeks the Kingdom."

"God knows," said Joseph. He stroked her hair, and she felt her tears soak into his robe. "We have to humble our own sense of what is right for us and discover what God has created us to do and to be. There is nothing lacking within us because we're God's image. As we find out what we are, we find everything that we need to be at hand. The Kingdom of God is always at hand. It's within us."

Chapter 5

Owain in Rome

There was a crash right behind him and Owain leapt to one side, cannoned off the rough hot brick wall and almost fell. One of the guards put out a hand to steady him and he recovered his balance, brushing the brick dust and dirt from his crimson robe. It had frayed where the brick scraped it and he felt angry. Urine had spattered his robe and legs and he cringed with revulsion. He tried to walk faster but the centurion and the two guards in front blocked the narrow street. They walked in a slow measured pace entirely unmoved by the detritus showered on them from above and behind and by the swarms of flies and biting insects that dogged every step. The air was so hot and motionless he found it difficult to breathe. He looked around listlessly and behind the two guards who followed him was a crowd of dirty urchins and beggars. The riff-raff hurled obscenities, picked up things from the filthy street and threw them at the guards. Nothing in Owain's entire experience had equipped him to visualize what a city such as Rome must look, feel, sound or smell like.

The guards had brought himself, Caratacus' old steward Fergus and their small baggage to the outskirts of the city in a horse drawn wagon but the wagon and Fergus had been left at a guardhouse. The centurion said over a million people lived in

Rome and it would be easier to reach their destination if they walked. It had been late yesterday that he left the ship at Ostia and he had not yet been offered food or drink. He felt thirsty, weak and nauseous. His face, neck and hands itched in a thousand places from insect bites, his ears were numbed by noise, his mind was deadened by bewildering scenes and his lungs were raw from hot fetid smells. Much more of this, he thought, and I will go berserk.

They were forced to stop at a cross-street, the guards jammed against him so closely that their hot armor dug into him painfully. The stifling air settled on him like a pall and he felt himself sag, held up only by the pressure of the guards against him. He would have swooned but a sudden increase in the noise around him brought him to. A tide of frightened people swept down the street they were about to cross and he could hear screams and shouts echoing among the buildings. Frightened too, he wondered what was happening.

"It must be a fire," said the centurion. "Either that or another building fell down."

Unreassured by the centurion's analysis, Owain looked anxiously upward at the buildings towering crazily above him. They went up many stories in height and seemed to lean toward each other. Every window above him was jammed with faces and protruding bodies. There must be hundreds of people in each building. The very weight of them must constitute a threat to walls and floors. The streets were so narrow the dwellers in opposite buildings could reach across and touch each other. If a building fell it would choke the street and crush everything in it. As he looked, someone above shouted and the faces disappeared at one of the windows. A pair of arms holding a large earthen bowl appeared and tipped the bowl's contents into the street. He ducked and cowered, robe over his head, cringing as the disgusting spatters struck. Then there was a sudden easing of pressure and the guards moved forward.

"Its a fire all right," said the centurion, nodding his head.

"There goes the fire squad." Several men ran across the street trundling a large wooden cart in which leather buckets were piled and leather hoses coiled. The men screamed, the crowd running before them screamed and the people being held up by their passage screamed, until all was absolute bedlam. Glancing down the street in the direction the men had run, Owain saw clouds of filthy black smoke and soot. He looked up, stung by a sudden burn, and saw soot and ashes floating in the air. The foul stink of burning filled his lungs. It was easy to believe the whole city would catch fire and burn all its inhabitants.

He shuddered and wished the guards would plod a little faster. Soon, however, they crossed in front of an enormous colonnaded building and entered a wide street leading up a steep hill. The street passed through a gate let into a massive brick faced wall. Soldiers guarding the gate waved them through and they continued along the street, which had now leveled off, the heavy wall through which they had passed paralleling the street to their left. The high buildings below gave way to lower ones, solidly built of stone and marble with only one or two stories. Each building was sealed from the street by walls with massive gates, and the centurion stopped before one of them and pounded its huge bronze knocker.

Bolts slid back inside and the ponderous gate opened into a large courtyard in which a line of armored guards held lances before them as if to repel an attack. When the centurion identified himself, the guards brought their lances into a vertical position and stood back against the marble walls and pillars. One of them led the way across the courtyard, which was closed in on all sides, and knocked on an ornately carved side door. There was no answer, so the guard opened the door and motioned Owain to enter.

"Sit down and wait," said the centurion.

"Can I wash myself?" asked Owain, holding out his grimy hands. "And clean my clothes?"

"Someone will come," said the centurion, giving him a heavy wink.

"Thank you," said Owain. The room was a small office. It felt hot and airless and numerous large flies buzzed around aggressively. A large desk littered with scrolls was against one wall and a small backless stool stood before the desk. There were two other chairs in the room, which had a single opaque window looking out on the courtyard and another door leading into the house. The window was richly hung with heavy curtains, elaborate tapestries covered the walls, and marble busts and plants stood neatly in corners. Owain sat down on one of the chairs and tried to control his trembling.

The sooner he could get this business out of the way and begin his journey home the happier he would be. He could barely stand the smell of his own body and looked down in disgust at his leather boots and trousers. They had been so neat and clean before he left the ship. His robe was frayed and spattered with filth, little burn holes and patches of soot all over it. His undergarments were stiff with dried sweat and added their smells to all the others that wafted from him. Who was going to meet him in this room, and what would they think of him? He hoped it wouldn't be Claudius. But fine as it was, this house was no palace. Perhaps they had brought him here first to talk to Narcissus. He hoped Narcissus owned a bath. It would be good to drink a cup of cool water and clean up before meeting the emperor once again.

He sat there for a long time. His agitation grew as he wondered what Bodin the Fox was doing in his absence, and whether Tetra and Rhys would be clever enough to attract more converts than Bodin. In his heart he knew Bodin would outfox them. Unless he got back to Britain quickly, Bodin would have convinced the Council that only he could devise a religion that would unify all the Britons. Maybe he could get Simon Peter to come to Britain again and speak to the Council. He got so engrossed in thinking about the church that he jumped in surprise when the inner door finally opened. A woman of great beauty dressed in a long white palla walked in followed by a heavy jawed youth and a melancholy looking man of middle years in a rumpled tunic and worn leather sandals. A black servant also came in carrying a palm frond. He proceeded to stir the air with it and the irritated flies buzzed angrily around Owain.

Owain got to his feet and bowed, blushing with embarrassment at his appearance in front of such a beautiful woman. He moved away, afraid that the palm frond might waft his stink to her. Her hair was black, her eyes brown and piercing, and her skin darker than a Briton's but wonderfully smooth and delicately molded. Her lips pouted voluptuously and her figure swayed sensuously as the man handed her into the other chair. Jeweled gold fibulae held her robe together, and she wore jeweled combs in her hair and a brilliant necklace around her neck. Bracelets and earrings of gold and ebony decorated her arms and ears, and her maroon leather sandals were studded with jewels. She sat down gracefully and looked at Owain with as much interest as if she were examining a gatepost. His heart beat a little faster. Even over his own stink he could smell the perfume radiating from her. The youth, who seemed too young to be dressed in the adult toga, sat down on the chair that Owain had used and looked at Owain scornfully, his delicate nose pinched as if the air were not pure enough for him to breathe. A gold bracelet was on the youth's right arm, and it looked to Owain as if the skin of some reptile had been embedded in it. His left arm was wrapped in the rumpled toga and his hand peeked out from its folds, showing he had not yet learned to carry it properly.

"You are the British Druid Owain," said the man, speaking in colloquial Greek. "I am Narcissus, humble freedman of the Emperor. Do not mind this lady's presence, or her son's. They are merely waiting while we conduct our business."

Owain remained standing, there being no chairs left. He wondered why Narcissus had not introduced the lady and her son. Perhaps, he thought grimly, he was not considered worthy enough to be introduced. He was on the same level as the man waving the palm frond. Narcissus sat down on the stool by the desk, put his hands together in an attitude of prayer and then cracked all his knuckles so loudly that Owain jumped.

"You have brought the scroll?" said Narcissus.

"I have brought a copy of the scroll."

"A copy will not suffice. We must have the original."

Owain looked at the woman, who looked back at him with no expression. A fly walked across her forehead and he felt an urge to shoo it away. "We have followed the instructions of King Caratacus," he said, watching the fly, "and the original will be delivered to you as soon as his freedom is publicly granted and the ransom paid."

Narcissus cracked his bones again and looked fierce. "You realize, of course," he said, "that we could have King Caratacus and his family, and you also, executed immediately? No one would be the wiser. Our people expect an enemy of Rome to be thrown into the Tarpean dungeons until he is driven insane and then executed for their amusement. They will be disappointed if it is not done."

Owain nodded gravely. This man, in spite of his high station, he knew to be a clerk, and he was not going to be intimidated by a clerk. He would have to be careful but not intimidated. "It is within Caesar's power to have King Caratacus executed," he agreed. "But the world would know that the Roman Emperor had been a prisoner of King Caratacus and had broken Roman law by not paying the agreed upon ransom. And it would know that the Emperor purchased a sword and shield from King Caratacus and did not win them in battle."

"He has never claimed that he won them in battle," said Narcissus.

"I am glad to hear that," said Owain.

There was a silence, while Narcissus continued to frown and look angry. "How do we know," he said at last, "that once the ransom has been paid and the man's freedom granted, the scroll will not fall into the wrong hands?"

"To guarantee that it won't," said Owain, "King Caratacus

will pledge himself to stay here after his freedom has been published and his ransom paid, until the original has been delivered into the hands of your governor in Britain, and from his hands into yours."

Narcissus looked at the woman and Owain saw through the corner of his eye that she nodded. She was not just waiting then. She had some role to play in this. Narcissus clapped his hands and a servant appeared at the door. "Bring in the baggage," said Narcissus, and the servant entered carrying Owain's leather bag in which were all his clothes and the copied scroll. The guards must have sent his bag by some other route instead of holding it at the guardhouse as they had said. Why? And where was Fergus? "You will show me the copy of the scroll," said Narcissus.

The servant dropped the bag on Owain's feet and Owain crouched down and opened it. He saw immediately that it had been emptied and refilled. Narcissus must have known the scroll was a copy and not the original. If it had been the original he would never have seen Britain again. He felt around anxiously. His extra crimson robe was still folded neatly but his precious soap had gone. "Someone has stolen my soap," he said, angrily. A fly landed on his nose and he shook his head.

Narcissus shrugged. "Only barbarians use soap," he said. "Rome is full of them."

Owain pulled out the scroll and handed it to Narcissus.

"A hundred thousand aureii," said Narcissus, looking sideways at the woman. "And three elephants. Elephants are out of the question. What does it mean—'in real gold?'"

"The Emperor brought a lot of coins to Britain," said Owain, "that were not gold. They were of lead painted to look like gold."

Narcissus sneered. "That was Gaius' doing. He used them to gamble with."

"It's too much," said the woman in Latin, and Owain looked at her, surprised. Her voice was agitated. Narcissus seemed surprised also and a little put out by the woman's comment. He rolled up the scroll and tapped his forearm with it. "It's little enough for an emperor," he said, also in Latin, looking sideways at Owain. "And this could hurt him."

"Let me see," said the boy, and Narcissus handed him the scroll. "This must not be published," said the boy, scanning it quickly. He held it out to show the woman and she gave it a brief glance. The fly was still on her forehead.

"It's too much," said the woman. "Give him fifty thousand sesterces. No, thirty thousand."

"And his freedom?" said Narcissus.

The woman shrugged. "His life costs nothing. What do I care about his life? He must not have money."

Narcissus took back the scroll from the boy and laid it on the desk. "Perhaps it would be better," he said, "if I talked to this Druid alone." The woman stood, and the fly abandoned her forehead as Narcissus opened the door for her. Owain wondered if Narcissus knew that educated Britons were fluent in Latin as well as Greek and wanted the woman out of the way before she revealed something she shouldn't.

"Not an ass more than thirty thousand," she said. She went out, the boy right behind her. Narcissus closed the door and approached Owain. Then he backed away with a sniff.

"Who was that lady?" asked Owain.

"It doesn't matter," said Narcissus. "What matters is that this king of yours does not make a fool of himself by asking for more than thirty thousand sesterces. In the circumstances that is an extremely generous offer. You will now sign a document accepting that sum in the name of Caratacus."

"I cannot do that," said Owain. "I have no authority to speak for King Caratacus. I am here simply as a messenger to arrange for delivery of the ransom note upon payment of the ransom and publication of King Caratacus' freedom."

Narcissus cracked his knuckles and looked fierce again. This is a play, thought Owain. I wonder if that woman is listening at the door?

"Let us be quite frank," said Narcissus. "You must know

that if we executed all of you and that scroll were to be published it would simply be a small embarrassment to the Empire. It would be denounced as a forgery and few would argue with such a ruling. We are willing to make an exception and grant Caratacus his freedom but you must cooperate. Caratacus will not condemn you for acting so wisely in his behalf."

Owain shook his head. "The publication of that scroll would not be a small matter to an emperor who is an erudite and prolific historian, conscious of Rome's traditions and his role in history and anxious to leave for posterity a reputation unblemished by such a stain on his character. And I must repeat that I cannot commit King Caratacus to any course without his prior knowledge and full consent. If you wish me to act in any way for him, you must first let me see him so we can discuss the matter fully."

"Then you will not sign the document?"

"No."

Narcissus clapped his hands. There was a scuffling on the other side of the door, probably the woman getting out of the way, thought Owain. The door opened and the servant who had brought in Owain's bag entered. Owain felt himself trembling as he wondered what was to happen next, and fought to appear calm and unafraid.

"Take him away," said Narcissus, and turned his back while the servant led Owain out of the room. They went down a long corridor that crossed a large inner courtyard and turned left into another corridor with alabaster windows facing on the inner courtyard. The servant opened a door and ushered Owain into a small room devoid of furniture and with no window. The servant started to close the door, but Owain stopped him. "I am thirsty and I need to urinate," he said. "Bring me water to drink and a bowl to wash in." The servant nodded and closed the door. The room was dark, except for a thin band of daylight coming under the door. Owain tried to open the door but it was barred on the outside. The room was so hot and stuffy he found it hard to breathe. One insect made a high-pitched whine as it flew into his ear and he slapped at it so hard his head rang. With a discontented sigh he groped his way to a corner and relieved himself then sat down on the floor with his back to a wall. Before long, he fell asleep.

The opening of the door awakened him. The same servant stood in the doorway holding a candle. It was dark outside and he wondered how long he had been asleep.

"Come," said the servant, and he got up. His body was stiff and he staggered then followed the servant into the corridor. They walked back the way they had come previously, and he thought he recognized the door to the room where he had talked with Narcissus. Stone oil lamps stood at regular intervals along the corridor, and through the translucent windows he could see the flickering coronas of other lamps outside in the courtyard and the dark shadows of moving figures. The servant opened a door and stood to one side while he entered. He gasped with surprise and pleasure. It was a beautifully decorated bathhouse tiled with marble and hung with soft drapes and towels. Gold sconces on the walls held lamps that cast a softly diffused light throughout the chamber. Water trickled continuously from a lead pipe into a marble basin and below the basin into another catch pipe that conveyed it under a marble latrine. He ran to the basin and drank eagerly, cupping the water in his hands. Satiated, he looked around to see that the servant had disappeared. In the center of the room, a light mist of steam rose from a huge square bath in which for the first time he noticed an enormous black man dressed only in a cloth wrapped about his loins. The man stood up to his knees in the water and his steam drenched muscles rippled in the flickering light of the lamps. In one hand, the man held a curved piece of bone. With the other, he beckoned to Owain to get into the bath.

"I must use the latrine," he said, pointing to it in case the man didn't understand, and the man put his hands on his hips and frowned while he waited. When he had finished he ripped the filthy clothes from his body and entered the warm bath, lying down so that the water closed over his head. He sighed and blew bubbles out of his mouth as the water calmed his troubled spirit, but a large pink-palmed hand reached down and pulled him by the hair into a sitting position. He cried out with shock as the black man scraped his skin with the bone but soon grew to like the regular motion of the implement driving out the impurities gathered on his long painful journey. When the man was through, he was so enervated he could barely rise from the bath and had to be led to a wall from which protruded a short golden bar. He seized the bar and let the side of his face rest against the wet marble wall, so relaxed he almost collapsed. Then a douche as cold as the coldest mountain spring he had ever drank from hit him in the side and he roared with shock. Again, the man threw cold water over him, and suddenly he felt himself coming back to life. His body tingled with renewed energy and he grinned as the servant rubbed him down vigorously with the towels. But when the man had finished rubbing him he stood back and cracked the damp towels over Owain's buttocks and sides. Owain jumped and shouted with pain, looking down at the red welts on his skin. The man stopped, a surprised look on his face. "You no like?" he said.

"I no like," said Owain, backing out of range.

The servant threw the towels down on top of Owain's dirty clothes. Then he went to a cedar chest, pulled out a pair of thin leather sandals and two white garments. One garment was a shift, which Owain pulled over his head. Then the servant helped him wrap a voluminous tunic around himself and tied a cord about his middle. Both garments smelled of the urine in which they had been washed. The sandals were large for his feet but he was able to keep them from slipping off by curling up his toes.

"What about my clothes?" he asked.

"You leave. We clean."

He wondered if he would ever see his battered crimson robe and his good British boots again, but he went to the door in response to the black man's gesture and opened it. The other servant had been waiting outside and he set off immediately down the corridor, Owain shuffling along behind as quickly as he could. Once again they passed the door where Narcissus had interviewed him, and this time the servant opened a door that was now guarded by two legionaries. The room into which he stepped was bright with light and Owain saw through momentarily blinded eyes that a huge bronze lamp stand stood in each corner, ablaze with many small lanterns. The room was hot and hazy from their heat and smoke, and smelled of olive oil. Between the two lamp stands facing him stood a guard in armor, his back to the wall. A large table around which several people sat took up the center of the room. Before he could focus his eyes upon them a well-known voice boomed out.

"By Duw, tis my favorite Druid!" said Caratacus, violating Owain's right to speak first. "Didn't I tell you they wouldn't chop off his flaming head."

Fergus banged his stick on the floor as Caratacus rose from the table and other voices shouted greetings. Owain realized he was among his own countrymen. Queen Genvissa and her daughter Eurgen sat on either side of Caratacus. And next to Genvissa sat King Linus, Caratacus' younger brother, and Prince Salog, Eurgen's husband. Across from Salog sat a young maiden with white blond hair who must be Caratacus' youngest daughter Claudia, still wearing the little cap that denoted her status as a maiden, and a youngish man wearing the broad purple of a Roman senator. With a lighter heart he hurried forward to greet Caratacus, but a golden-headed body he hadn't at first recognized intercepted him and threw her arms around his neck. "Gwendolyn!" he said, shocked, and involuntarily clasped her to him.

She looked up at him, eyes wet with tears of joy. He saw at once that the insanity had gone. She put her lips to his and as the warmth and the joy and the softness and the urgency of her seeped into him he forgot that Caratacus was waiting to greet him. "Gwendolyn," he said again, his own eyes filled with tears. He had not seen her since she had lost her mind. He had thought her dead, or imprisoned in the care of some old witch hired by

Rhys to protect her from her own madness. And here she was in Rome, well and lovelier than he had ever known her to be. She was sane. She was his wife. And the blood began to rush through his veins.

"Well, now that the Druid has spoken," said Caratacus, waking him from his reverie, "though not with the words of wisdom we might expect, I suppose we can greet him too. Unless he means to bed his flaming wife here before the lot of us."

Face hot, Owain put Gwendolyn aside and clasped his arms around Caratacus. "So you agreed to a reduced ransom, Sire?"

"It was that or your head. But I wouldn't take less than fifty thousand in gold without the elephants. Narcissus stormed out of here like a screeching hen, swearing by all his gods he would have you torn in pieces. But I knew he wouldn't."

Owain tried to look reassured. "What else did you agree to?"

"We can't go home for seven years."

Owain was horrified. "Does that include me?"

Caratacus, his mouth full, shook his head.

"Only him and Salog," said Genvissa. "I suppose we ought to be grateful. Pudens here thinks we can go to Blonwen's in Corinth after all the excitement dies down." The senator, red haired and vigorous, stood to greet Owain. "This is Pudens Pudentius Rufus[16]," said Genvissa, and Owain remembered the young man who had visited Britain with Claudius. "Pudens, this is Lord Owain Longhead, son of Eulltyd of Caer Went, the Druid Pencerdd and High Council member of whom you've heard so much."

"We have met before," said Pudens. "At Camulodunum."

Owain bowed, pleased to be remembered.

"That horrible Narcissus was going to have Caratacus put in a cage," said Genvissa.

"And he would have, had I not mentioned the little arrangement Claudius and me worked out when he was my prisoner."

"But he locked him up for weeks and fed him next to nothing

until you arrived," said Genvissa. "Just look at him." Caratacus indeed seemed thinner and frailer.

Owain felt a tug on his tunic and Gwendolyn led him around the table to her chair and stood behind it to wait on him, fetching him wine, cuts of meat, game birds and fish, and kissing him at each fetching. He didn't notice the wine's potency until the room grew hazy and indistinct and he felt comfortably tired yet excited by the many caresses Gwendolyn gave him. He gorged until he could eat no more. He made small efforts at conversation but soon gave up as he paid more and more attention to Gwendolyn. She had blossomed into a beautiful woman and he wished he could be alone with her. He hoped that Gwendolyn had a room where he and she could sleep together. "Did Rhys look after you well in Caer Leon?" he asked, conscious that his voice was slurred, remorseful that he had never been to see her and wondering how she had recovered her mind.

She crouched down by his side, forearms on his thigh, and looked at him with soft inviting eyes. The heat of her began to expand within him like wine. "A friend of aunt Blonwen's healed me," she said. "Blonwen brought her when she came to visit us shortly after we got here. Her name is Priscilla, but we call her aunt Prisca."

Another Elsa, he thought. Maybe there were others here who could heal. Gwendolyn must bring them back to Britain. With a few healers in Tetra's church, Bodin would find it hard to convince converts that he and not Owain had the right church. And with healers in Tetra's church there would be less competition from the Nazarene College. Looking down at Gwendolyn's wide blue eyes and moist red lips, however, he decided this was not the time to bring up such matters. He kissed her. "Is your aunt Blonwen still here?" he asked.

"No. She went back to Corinth and took Prisca with her. Claudius banned all Christians and Prisca would be arrested if they caught her."

"Christians?" said Owain, his interest piqued.

"That's what they're calling Nazarenes now." Her eyes were large and her mouth soft, so he put his hands around her neck and into her hair and kissed her again.

"Of course," he murmured. Christians. Little Christs. There was a ring to it. He must send a letter off to Tetra in the morning to tell her that he would bring some healers back with him and that Christian must be the name of her new church. As soon as he could get away he would take Gwendolyn and this Priscilla back to Britain. He kissed Gwendolyn again and wished the meal over so he could be alone with her. Now that she was sane he would make sure that Morfudd saw them together and witnessed how happy they were.

* * *

The procession ground to a halt. Owain had tried not to look overly impressed and gazed in a dignified manner at the grand buildings as they passed. They shimmered in the oppressive heat and seemed alive and menacing. He would have liked to see Rome without its Roman rabble, which hung from its walls and shrubbery and jabbered like a horde of agitated monkeys. For the first time a realization of the enormous wealth and power of Rome sank into his inner being and he began to doubt that the Britons could ever defeat such an enemy. Even to visualize anything on such a scale as this city, he realized, was beyond the most sophisticated Briton. And yet, Rome consisted not only of highly organized and efficient legions, immeasurable wealth and marvelously designed and beautiful architecture, it also included this disorderly rabble. He had thought the Roman populace would be disciplined and orderly, supercilious toward the enemies brought home for it to gaze at. But every time Caratacus waved at the crowd it cheered and hurrahed as if he were a Roman general coming home with news of his conquests.

Flushed by the crowd's adulation, Caratacus obviously enjoyed himself. Dressed in the full regalia of a High King of

Britain, he was a magnificent sight. From the golden crown on his head to the finely tooled jeweled leather boots on his feet he far outshone the plainly dressed nobility of Rome. Even he himself, thought Owain, dressed in his clean crimson robe fastened with the white jeweled clasp that showed his status as Pencerdd, his gold chain, red cap with the white feathers, black trousers and brown jeweled boots, must present a startling picture to this soapless mob, most of it dressed in dirty white tunics of coarse cloth. A sudden jerk on the rope that bound him to Caratacus broke his reverie, and the procession moved forward slowly down the narrow lane made for it by their guards. Ahead of him he could see the massed ranks of the Praetorian Guards, the standards of Rome and the heads of dignitaries sitting on some raised platform. This must be the tribunal that would decide their fate.

As they drew closer, Caratacus pulled on the rope. "There's Plautius," Caratacus hissed. "I wonder if he'll come over and say 'hail.' And there's the big man himself. He looks older and by Duw he looks worn out. Look at him drooling. If that's his wife by his side, I don't wonder."

"That's the woman who was with Narcissus," said Owain, shocked to see her sitting by Claudius' side. She must be the infamous Agrippina, Claudius' niece and latest wife. And the heavy jowled boy must have been her son Nero. With all the wealth that she and Claudius must command, why had she been so upset about the size of the ransom?

A hush fell over the crowd as the procession again halted, and Owain found himself, with Caratacus and his family, standing at the foot of the rostrum on which Claudius, Agrippina and many senators sat or stood. Claudius, a military cloak around his shoulders, made a half-hearted effort to rise but sank back into his chair with a sigh. Owain looked closely at the emperor's face and was relieved to see it was bland. Until the emperor pronounced their freedom they could still be executed if anything made him angry. He held his breath as Claudius opened and closed his mouth and ran his tongue around his teeth a few times.

"Rome is hon-honored," said Claudius, his face turning from side to side to address the august senators, "to have such a vavaliant enemy in its mimidst as the great B-British king, Cara, Cara, Caratacus. Nevertheless, he is ac-accused of crimes against the Roman imp-imperium in that he has raised his s-sword against its legions." He turned his face toward Caratacus. "How p-plead you to this charcharge?"

"As Pendragon and Arviragus of Britain," said Caratacus, "titles as proud in my domains as is Caesar Augustus here, I too possessed authority, separate from Rome's though not its equal. My ancestry is as ancient and honorable as that of any Roman prince. I was dictator of nations and had armies, arms, wealth, palaces and forts. I did not choose to make war on Rome, Rome chose to make war on me and on those who appointed me to protect them. Authority among nations rests upon arms, as the people of Rome well know, and without battle, authority is indeterminate. Would Caesar have me surrender my sword and my people to an authority unproven by battle?"

Claudius inserted the little finger of his right hand into his ear and wiggled it violently.

"Do you now agree," said a senator, "that the imperium of Rome has been established by battle, and that for a Briton to raise a sword against its legions is a crime of treason?"

Caratacus bowed to the senator. "A crime is a crime if those who view it as such are able to enforce their view by punishing whomever they declare to be criminals. No one can doubt the ability of Rome's legions to enforce the authority of Rome."

"Ah," said the senator. "But would you consider it a crime to raise your sword against a legion of Rome?"

"Aye, my lord senator," said Caratacus, without hesitation. "I would consider it a crime because it would break my taboos. I have cast away my sword and cannot raise it again."

There was a loud cheer from the crowd, and the senator

nodded as if satisfied. "It is appropriate, Caesar," he said, looking at Claudius as the noise quieted, "that this great king, whose spirit would do credit to a Roman, be set free as a token of Rome's mercy and forbearance toward those who have fought valiantly and who now acknowledge the authority of Caesar."

"Is that the w-w-will of this tribunal?" said Claudius, wiping the sweat from the side of his face.

"It is," said the senators.

"Th-then I order the release of these p-prisoners."

"Welcome to Rome!" shouted a voice, and the crowd repeated the cry.

"It is not a voluntary visit," said Caratacus to the crowd, and Owain could see that he gloried in the mob's adulation and feared it might lead him to say something unwise. "If I might offer a friendly word of advice," said Caratacus, "don't trust the ladies. It's because of one of them that I am here."

The crowd roared its approval and Caratacus winked at Owain as he waved at them. "It serves me right," roared Caratacus. "I tried to bed my own niece and she betrayed me."

A sudden hush filled the square. Owain looked at Agrippina, whose face was black with anger.

"What did I say?" hissed Caratacus.

"Agrippina is Claudius' niece," Owain hissed back. "They passed a law to let them marry, but most don't approve."

In answer, Caratacus pulled on the rope that tied him to Genvissa until she was at his side. He put his arm around her shoulders and faced the crowd again. "This is my lovely wife Genvissa, Queen of my domains," he said. "If anyone can keep me honest and true it is my lovely wife. When still a young maiden princess, she was fostered to the court of your great Caesar Augustus Tiberius." The crowd roared with approval again as Genvissa waved to them with great dignity. "When she was there," shouted Caratacus, "she befriended the great Claudius Drusus Germanicus, your present emperor." He waved frantically until the crowd's roar died down. "So you see," he said, "that we are not all of us strangers to Rome."

Owain saw out of the corner of his eye that Agrippina, a heavy frown on her face, was looking right at him while talking to Claudius, who looked bemused.

"And," went on Caratacus, waving at Eurgen, Gwendolyn and Salog, "these are some of my lovely children." The roar of the crowd was deafening, and Owain was relieved to see Aulus Plautius come to the edge of the rostrum. He tugged on the rope and Caratacus turned to face his old enemy.

"The British King Caratacus," said Plautius, addressing the crowd, "has been the greatest adversary faced by Rome since Hannibal. Fortunata's face has shone upon us, and we must offer prayers of gratitude to her and our great Jupiter, that we should lose so clever an enemy at so little cost. With the capture of King Caratacus, our war in Britannia can be considered over. King Caratacus was the will and spirit of the Britons, and now that he is taken from them we can look forward to the early return of at least two of our legions."

Caratacus took a deep breath and scowled as the crowd cheered, and Owain sensed he was about to tell Plautius that the war was far from over. He jerked on the rope and Caratacus looked startled. "Don't say anything, Sire," he hissed. "He said that to undercut Scapula. They're enemies."

"You're right," agreed Caratacus. "I will hold my tongue between my teeth lest we all lose our heads. Better yet I will close my eyes and ears lest I bite off my tongue."

Plautius walked along the edge of the rostrum until he reached a pile of arms and other trophies that had been thrown there to symbolize the defeat of Britain. He reached down and selected a long iron sword and turned toward Caratacus, holding the sword in both hands. "By order of Caesar," he said, "I am commanded to return to you your sword as a symbol of Rome's mercy toward a valiant enemy."

"By Beli Mawr," said Caratacus, his voice drowned in the

roar of the crowd. "It looks like Togo's old sword. They've straightened out the kink in the middle but it's still bent. I wonder if I'm to get his flaming shield too?"

"And by Caesar's command," said Plautius, bending to give the sword to Caratacus and pausing for effect as the crowd hushed in anticipation, "I order the fetters to be stricken from these prisoners. The only conditions are that King Caratacus and Prince Salog swear before their gods and ours that they will bear arms only in defense of Rome, and that they will not return to Britain for seven years. King Caratacus and Prince Salog will be allowed to receive the income from their estates while they are in exile."

The crowd roared its approval, but hushed as Caratacus put his foot against the sword that Plautius had given him and bent it until its blade formed a right angle. Then he cast it from him. "Thus I renounce my weapons," he said. "I need no sword among Romans."

The crowd cheered again as Claudius struggled to his feet, holding on to Plautius' arm.

"N-now that you are f-free," he said to Caratacus. "What th-think you of this great generous Rome, G-Goddess of the earth and of, of its people?"

Caratacus bowed. "I can think of no better place to make great soldiers," he said. Claudius bowed to acknowledge the compliment. "The scale and grandeur of your buildings put our poor palaces to shame, and must stimulate within your generals a desire to emulate in conquest what your architects have achieved in stone. The swarms of flies and rodents with sharp teeth that live here must have equipped your legions with the fortitude necessary to brush away our puny efforts to make their lives miserable. And the terrible heat and fetid smells must do much to persuade your young men to seek their fortunes elsewhere than in Rome. It is little wonder to a royal visitor such as myself, that all roads lead out from that golden milestone yonder to where the air is fresher and the grass is greener, and where the children are loved for their own sakes, and there is time to play and sport. Rome is a grand city, but I would not trade it for one of my rivers or for one of my mountain fastnesses, or for one good game of hurly on a bright May morning.

"Had we not been invaded by Rome's legions, I should have been proud to enter this city as your friend and ally instead of as your captive, and you would have welcomed me as a king should be welcomed who is descended from the great Cassivellaunus who twice repelled the Caesar Julius from Britain's shores. Is it any wonder that I who could have been a friend of Rome became an enemy to fight for the freedom of my peoples? Now that by a woman's treachery I have been your slave, and now that by your clemency I am freed, our friendship is forever abrogate, for how can friendship extend from one who views himself as master to one he views as manumitted slave? You will say that Rome has many friends, but I say that is not true. You have those who lick your boots and steal what they can while your power is on the rise. But the day will come when Rome will need true friends, and then it will well note the cost of its desire to rule the world.

"I am grateful for my freedom, but I grieve that it derives not from friendship freely given and freely accepted, but from the self interest of a master anxious to enhance his own renown. If you had had me killed, as your traditions allow, neither my fall nor your triumph would have become famous. But by saving my life, you have made me an everlasting memorial to your own clemency."

While Caratacus spoke, Owain saw Narcissus come behind Claudius and speak to him. Claudius shook his head several times as if refusing a request but when Agrippina said something he nodded. When Caratacus had finished, Claudius sat down heavily in his chair. Owain wondered what Narcissus and Agrippina had been saying to him. With a start, he noticed Claudius staring at him and bowed. But when he looked again, Claudius had turned his face away. He must have recognized me, thought Owain. Why did he not acknowledge me? He was so friendly in Britain. Perhaps Caratacus' speech had offended him.

There had been much in it to cause offense, and he wondered at Caratacus' temerity.

The guard detailed to free them reached him and cut away the rope tied around his waist. The crowd milled around them and continued to cheer. Glad as he was to see that they were free, he felt sad and disappointed. He would have liked Claudius to acknowledge him and talk to him once again. Caratacus' speech had made that impossible. While he agonized over it, Gwendolyn forced her way through the crowd. He clasped her to him and a tear trickled down his cheek.

"I'm so happy," said Gwendolyn.

"Yes," he said and wiped the tear away. "Do you think your friend Priscilla would come back to Britain with us?"

She looked startled but didn't say anything. Then the crowd hushed as one of the senators on the rostrum launched forth into a long speech comparing Claudius' treatment of Caratacus with Scipio's treatment of the Numidian Prince Syphax. Another senator made a longer speech in which Claudius' treatment of Caratacus was compared with Aemilius Paullus' treatment of the Macedonian King Perseus. Claudius had dozed off and Owain almost dozed off himself as the speakers went on and on. When the speeches were over and the senators began to break up, he saw Narcissus talking to Caratacus and pushed forward to hear, still clasping Gwendolyn. But Narcissus left before he could reach them. He stretched to touch Caratacus through the throng and Caratacus turned to him.

"Salog and me have to go to Jupiter's temple to swear our oaths," shouted Caratacus in Celtic. "Then we have to get you out of here in the morning. Claudius is going to issue an order for your arrest at noon tomorrow. You'd better be far away from the city by then. I think you upset Claudius."

"I upset Claudius!" said Owain. In shock and indignation, he looked wildly up at the rostrum. Claudius was being helped into his chair, his face bland and expressionless, his eyes glazed. He liked me, he thought. We got on well together. He invited me to visit him in Rome. Why has he done this? And then he saw Agrippina, dressed in finery exceeding that of her husband, standing in cold conversation with Plautius and other senators. They're fawning on her, he thought. She is the real power. She ordered my arrest, not Claudius. But why? What have I done to offend her? Does she blame me because Caratacus got a bigger ransom than she specified?

Gwendolyn tugged at his arm. "What is it?" he said, unable to take his eyes off Agrippina. Gwendolyn nodded toward Caratacus, pushing his way through to them. He suddenly felt resentful. How could Caratacus have the gall to say that he, Owain, must have upset Claudius? If anyone had upset Claudius it was Caratacus. Why should Caratacus and his family be set free after insulting Claudius and extracting a huge ransom from Narcissus while he Owain, who had come here only to help, was condemned to run from the city like a common criminal? It wasn't right. It wasn't the fitness of things.

"You'd better go to Blonwen's in Corinth," said Caratacus. "They'll look for you in Ostia so you're better off heading east. Pudens will get you on your way. You'd better stay with us, Gwendolyn."

"No," said Gwendolyn, "I am going with my husband." She pulled on Owain's arm and he followed after her without a word to Caratacus.

Chapter 6

Dedreth and Marius

Tristram whinnied. Dedreth, on her back in the river, bent her head backward to look up at him. The late afternoon sun sparkled through the treetops and bounced off the water rippling around her, forcing her to squint. He put his head down and blew on her.

"What is it?" she said, half asleep. The burbling noise of the river and its welcome coolness after the heat of the summer sun had made her drowsy. They were well inside Prasu's palace grounds and there was no danger here. She had ridden hard and wanted to rest. But Tristram whinnied again and tapped the ground with his right forefoot. She rolled over on her stomach, grunted as she pressed against a hard stone, and put her chin on her hands to keep it out of the water. She bent her knees so that her feet broke the surface, and curled her toes in the warm air. "What is the matter with you, Tristram?" she said, looking sleepily around the forest clearing. Her clothes and bow and quiver still lay in a pile by the bush where she had left them, and there was no sign of life. But the horse whinnied and tapped the ground again, something he only did when there was danger.

"There's no-one here," she said. There couldn't possibly be danger but she felt obliged to see what worried him. She got slowly out of the water and stretched, then put her arms around his neck, the warmth of his hide good against her wet breasts. Her hair spread all over her face and shoulders, and a thousand little rivulets ran down her body. There was nothing in the clearing, but something in Tristram's stance made her let go of him and look across the river. At first she saw nothing, her eyes dazzled by the sunlight dancing on the river and part blinded by her own hair. She pulled back her hair with both hands and then shaded her eyes to see more clearly. Several motionless men on horseback watched her from among the trees and suddenly fearful she ran behind Tristram so that only the top of her head showed above his back. Who were these men?

One wore royal colors, and as she watched he waved to dismiss his men and they rode away. As soon as they had disappeared among the trees, the strange king urged his horse into the water and picked his way through the rocks toward her. She looked behind her to see how far away were her clothes and weapons and made Tristram edge sideways in their direction. She still had some distance to go when the king emerged from the river and halted on the other side of Tristram. He looked down at her and she couldn't restrain a gasp. There had been something familiar about his build, but it had been so long since she last saw him. He looked older, wiser, sadder, and she knew a great change had taken place within him.

"It is the Lady Dedreth, is it not?" he asked. "I am your old adversary Eudal Cyllinus Marius, whom once you thought an arrogant idiot prince."

"And now you are High King of the Silures. You were never an idiot, Sire, but I must agree that you were arrogant."

Marius got down from his horse and stood on the other side of Tristram. "I am High King in name but not in fortune. I am merely looking after my father's domains."

"Fortunes are more often than not misfortunes. Gold is the root of all evil."

He shrugged. "Gold was never important to me. I will not inherit until my father Caratacus dies, and Duw willing I may see him once again before he does." Her hands were on top of Tristram's back and he put his on top of hers. "And if I could I would not wish to take his place," he said. "King Venutius leads our armies. I have nothing to do with warfare."

"Have you become a Nazarene?" she said, suddenly excited.

"No. I was not fit to be Arviragus. I was not fit for a prince when I killed your father, though it was an accident and not a murder as you thought, and had to fight a duel with your champion. What I am fit for, if there be anything, I have not yet learned. I hope it is to be a good king. Perhaps it is to become a Nazarene. But I don't know that I am fit even for that."

Her heart went out to him and then she remembered her nakedness and wondered how she would get to her clothes. It was strange being naked in front of this man she had once lusted to kill. He was taller than she and she wondered if he could see her breasts. She pressed herself against Tristram, caught her breath and shivered.

"You are cold," he said.

"No," she said. "I am overwhelmed by the change that has come over you. I can assure you that you are indeed fit to be a good king and a Nazarene, and that there is nothing higher to be."

He pressed down on her hands. "Then if there is nothing higher to be," he said, "you must be a Nazarene. I have thought often of you since we first met. I was thinking of you today as we rode to visit my sister and then I saw you rise from the foam like Venus Anadyomene."

She thought too of that day ten years ago they had first met, and the horror of her father dead at Marius' hands. Drunk, as he often was, he had drawn his sword at Marius' insult and Marius had defended himself with a stroke that cut her father down. Marius had claimed his sword had glanced off her father's and that he had not intended to kill him, but she had believed neither Marius' nor Boudicca's protestations. In those pre-Nazarene days, her temper had been white hot and she had tried to kill Marius herself. Now, she was willing to feel that it really had been an accident. She shuddered again. The air did feel cold against her drying body. "I am a Nazarene," she said. "And you have become fit at least to turn a pretty compliment. But now I must ask you to turn your head that I may put on my clothes."

Marius did not remove his hands from hers. "I have already seen your nakedness from across the river," he said. "Though it was from too great a distance and for too brief a time. Your beauty pierced my heart before I knew at whom I gazed. May I not see you naked again?"

She frowned. "You are either ingenuous," she said, "or think that I am. If need be, I will stand on this side of my horse until it grows dark, and then I will put on my clothes."

Marius wrapped his hands around hers and lifted them from Tristram's back. "But if your horse should move away," he said. "What then?"

Tristram, no longer restrained by her hands, took a step forward. "Stay," she hissed, pulling Marius' hands down until they rested again on the horse's back and he stopped. She tried to pull her hands out from Marius' grip but couldn't. He smiled at her, and in spite of her anger at being thwarted her breath came faster. All of itself her nakedness reached out to embrace him. She blushed, sure he could read her thoughts. Angry with herself, she bit her lip. She, a Nazarene, could not have such thoughts.

"If you would see me naked," she said, "you must let go of my hands and stand away."

"Gladly," he said, letting her go. He stood back a pace from Tristram and in a flash she was on the horse's side, arms around his neck and one leg over his back, galloping through the trees toward the trail. She glanced back and saw that he was not following. She mounted properly and rode as hard as she could until she came to the round wattle hut of Prasu's falconer. He would not be in it at this time of day but his wife would be. She slid from Tristram's back and ran into the hut. The woman screamed when she saw her naked visitor.

"Hush woman," said Dedreth. "Lend me a shift."

***

The great hall at Thetford was filled with smoke and the noise of reveling. Dim shapes moved through the smoke seeking companionship, food and drink, and from time to time a face loomed out of the haze and spoke to Boudicca. She sat on a stool at the head of Prasu's couch and her tiny foster sister Dedreth, who had once been betrothed to Owain Longhead before he married Gwendolyn, sat on the floor by her side. Her arm was around Dedreth's shoulders and her fingers caressed her hair. She had not seen Dedreth for five years and it made her happy that her little heretic elf had come to visit. It was unfortunate that her brother Marius had also come to sympathize over her recent illness. Marius and Dedreth had been bitter enemies after Marius had killed her father and tried to claim her and all her father's property as the spoils of combat. Dedreth's father was a fool and met his death by accident but to Dedreth it had been murder. She had tried to fight Marius but Dedreth's King Seisyll had insisted that Marius fight a duel with Selyf, one of his knights, to determine the truth of his claims. The duel had gone on for hours with no result. Marius had lost face, and as far as Boudicca knew he still hated Dedreth and she still hated him. Small as she was, Dedreth was a stubborn tiger and must be kept apart from Marius or they would fight again.

Prasu too had been ill. He sat on his couch by the firepit and gazed at the fire, eyes dull and half-closed, still mourning Subidasto. A Fidchell board with its pegs in place rested on a stool at his side. Gwenda, now seven years old, had learned to play the game but her lack of skill gave him little pleasure.

Venutius had recovered from the wounds he got when attacked by the Merrimar Gunes. They had killed Owain's messenger and tried to kill Venutius on the day Cartimandua betrayed her father to the Rummies. Everyone suspected

Cartimandua had paid the Gunes to kill Venutius so she could marry Scapula. Now that he was Arviragus, Venutius was in the south with his armies and Boudicca had not seen him since he recovered. Without him her life was empty. Owain had gone to Rome to try to gain her father's release, but each day she dreaded news might come that Caratacus had been executed. No wonder she had been ill.

There was a loud roar of laughter from the cubicle holding Marius' party and her head turned involuntarily in that direction. Her hand slid down Dedreth's cheek and Dedreth pressed her head against it then kissed it. "Why doesn't King Marius share his jokes with us?" asked Dedreth.

"It is better that he stays where he is," said Boudicca.

"I met him this afternoon. He is much changed."

"Yes," said Boudicca, remembering poor Marius' failure as Arviragus. "He has changed." And so has my little elf, she thought, to speak of Marius so mildly.

They lapsed into silence and she found herself thinking of Sabinus and the way he had wept when he saw her injured. For a Roman, he showed much love for this country he'd been sent here to rape. She owed him a service for ransoming her and keeping her identity secret. He had convinced her not to try to rescue her father, guarded as he was by an entire legion, and in many other ways she had yielded to his advice. But their growing friendship worried her. Might it take the edge off her resolve to get the Romans off her soil? She'd even had a kind word for one or two of the Romans who came to visit the palace now that the dark cloud of suspicion had been partially lifted from poor Prasu. Maybe the illness had changed her.

She bared her teeth at the thought. If the Rummies hurt or killed Caratacus the Rummies would soon find out how she felt. The Britons would revolt and she and Venutius would lead them. The hand that passed through Dedreth's hair with its message of love stiffened as if it unconsciously gripped a sword. Dedreth yelped, and Boudicca bent forward to kiss her, full of contrition. "What was I thinking about?" she said.

"Romans," said Dedreth. "Or Queen Cartimandua."

"Yes," said Boudicca with a sigh. "I don't know whom I hate the most, the Rummies or that traitorous witch."

Prasu stirred uneasily and peered into the gloom. "You must not speak of the Romans like that," he said, his voice plaintive. "They are our friends."

She patted his arm. "Then I will hate only Cartimandua," she said. Two figures loomed into view and she felt her heart beat faster. One was Ingenius and the other Sabinus. The tribune, handsome in his armor, bowed to Prasu and Boudicca then paused, looking at Dedreth. "This is the Lady Dedreth," said Ingenius. "I had forgotten that you had not met her." Ingenius was richly dressed but looked older and careworn. Dedreth gave her hand to Sabinus, who kissed it, his eye on Boudicca.

Prasu seemed overjoyed at the Roman's presence. He clapped his hands and waved to a servant to place chairs next to his couch. Sabinus sat down, his knees touching Boudicca's. "I was sorry to learn you were ill," he said to Boudicca. His eyes were bright but soft.

"You and I both know the nature of my illness," said Boudicca, "and what it will take to cure it."

"Alas," said Sabinus, "I cannot agree with your cure. If we Romans were to leave we would lose much that we have learned to love. I had rather we took the advice of our Nazarene friends to cease fighting and learn to love each other. But I have come to bring you news that should speed your convalescence."

"And that is?"

"Your father has been freed by the emperor's clemency."

She clasped her hands together and tears filled her eyes. Sabinus laid a gentle hand on top of hers, and she put it between hers.

"Now that you are well again," said Sabinus. "I must warn the Governor to put his legions on guard."

"I understand he has been awarded the *insignia triumphalia* for my father's capture. He must be pleased with my cousin Cartimandua for working so diligently in his behalf."

Sabinus shrugged. "Everyone on the staff of Aulus Plautius got one after the invasion," he said. "I believe our governor expected something more for sending your father to Rome."

"He has not left Colchester for some months. Has he had a falling out with my cousin?"

"I understand she is having trouble with her own kings and he could not go to visit her."

"That must be disappointing for him."

Prasu patted Sabinus' arm. "Please convey our congratulations to the governor on his award when next you see him," he said.

Sabinus smiled agreeably.

"Is my father banished from Britain?" she asked.

"For seven years," said Sabinus. He laughed softly. "They say he made quite a speech in front of the tribunal. The emperor's wife has not yet forgiven him for it. It was a speech that you might have given."

"I am my father's daughter," she said. "And like him I do not take lightly the slavery of my people."

"Slavery!" said Prasu. "How can you use such a word in front of Lord Sabinus? We are clients of Rome. There are no slaves in Iceni. Look at Ingenius here. Would you call him a slave?"

"Ask my Lord Sabinus," she said. "By his law all Britons are now slaves."

"But all Roman law is not enforced," said Sabinus.

"That is true," she said. "I most of all know that. I am afraid, my Lord Sabinus, that you do much to unsettle my hatred of Rome. I would all Romans were alike so that I could hate them uniformly, but it is difficult sometimes to distinguish you from a Briton."

He colored but said nothing. His hand still lay between hers and suddenly she knew he was in love with her. He was about her age, perhaps a little older, and he was a noble of patrician blood. His eyes were fixed on her to the exclusion of all else. Her scalp prickled. The thought of his love did not offend her. Could it be that she had encountered a Roman she could tolerate, perhaps even love? But what about Venutius? Her eyes widened and she wondered at her treasonable thoughts.

Ingenius coughed and looked embarrassed. Does he see? she thought, alarmed. He bent down so that only she could hear. "The Council's courier just brought news from Mona," he whispered. "Your grandfather the Archdruid is dead. He will be buried in the royal grave at Gosbecks."

Then that is where I shall lie, she thought. She sat for a long time in silence, absorbing the fact that the grand old man she had not seen for so long had passed out of her life. She had long since forgiven him for making her marry Prasu. His death would cause problems for the Council. Who would be the new Archdruid? How would Bodin make sure Owain was not elected? Bodin had just arrived at Thetford accompanied by the courier and the Druidess Morfudd. He had brought Boudicca a new sword and a banner that was to be used to identify the Council with his church. He and Morfudd were talking to Marius, an habitual sneer raising Bodin's upper lip. She decided she didn't like him.

Dedreth spoke to Ingenius, who squatted by the fire. "Have you found a new wife yet?" she asked.

"No," he said. "I can't forget Elsa."

Sabinus looked down at Dedreth. "You know Elsa?" he said, his hand still in Boudicca's. "She healed me of terrible wounds. To the Ninth legion she is a goddess. Because of her, many of our legionaries have become Nazarenes."

"Then you must not let her hear you call her a goddess," said Dedreth. "It is bad enough that our ignorant Britons are making her into one. They call her Brigit. Yes, I know her well. I wish I could be one ninth the Nazarene that she is."

Hearing a noise Boudicca turned to see three men wheel away and disappear into the haze. It was cousin Elidurus and two of Guderius' nobles. They must have wanted to talk to me, she thought, and turned away when they saw Sabinus. She put off Sabinus' hand with a smile, stood up abruptly and followed them. As she did, Bodin and his priestess Morfudd moved to intercept her. "I must beg an audience with you and King Marius right away," said Bodin. "We have news from the High Council." The man took it for granted she was at his disposal.

"Later," she said, looking at Morfudd. The woman was unusually good looking and refined for a priestess. But cold like a snake.

"It is important," said Bodin.

"I must join Lord Kincar and my cousin King Elidurus," she said. "When we are finished I will speak to you." She turned her back on him and walked away before he could protest further.

"It was Elidurus and two of Guderius' nobles," said Ingenius, peering after Boudicca. After watching them together there was no longer any doubt in his mind that the tribune was in love with Boudicca. "I wonder what they wanted?"

Prasu shook his head wonderingly and turned to Sabinus. "And what other news have you from Rome?" he asked, but Sabinus got up with a muttered excuse and left.

A slim figure came out of the haze and sat swiftly on Boudicca's stool, between Ingenius and Dedreth. It was the Druid priestess. He started to rise, but the woman put a restraining hand on his arm. "Please don't," said the Druidess. Her voice was soft but over modulated as if she were trying to keep some deep agitation under control. "And please, Sire," speaking to Prasu, "forgive me for interrupting. My name is Morfudd, and I must speak with the Lady Dedreth, if you will permit me."

Prasu smiled and nodded, and Morfudd turned to Dedreth, leaving her hand on Ingenius' arm. It felt strangely warm and comforting and her beauty and grace charmed him. Her hands were long and slender, her features delicately wrought, and her fine-spun golden hair fell down her back in three weighted braids. Her bright gray-green eyes moved swiftly and sharply like a hawk seeking its prey. This was an unusual priestess, he thought, not like others he had met. "Forgive me again," said Morfudd to Dedreth, "but you were pointed out to me as one on familiar terms with Lord Owain Longhead."

Dedreth frowned, and Ingenius remembered how infatuated Owain had once been with her. "I know Lord Owain," she said, "but I have not seen him for many years."

Morfudd looked baffled. "I must send a message to him," she said, glancing at Ingenius then back to Dedreth. "It is very urgent. I hoped that you might know where he is."

"He was in Rome with King Caratacus," said Dedreth. "He may still be there. I really don't know."

Morfudd clasped her hands together, her agitation showing.

"Can I help?" said Ingenius.

"Do you know where he is?"

"No," he said. "But I can ask my friend Sabinus to find out."

Morfudd seized Ingenius' hand and kissed it. "Please ask him," she said.

Ingenius stood up and bowed to Prasu and Dedreth. Then he took Morfudd's hand and raised her up. "Come with me," he said. "We'll both ask him."

Morfudd looked gratefully up at Ingenius, her body brushing his as they went past Prasu, now staring gloomily at the fire. Her body felt light and yielding and he suddenly wanted to hold her in his arms. It had been so long since he had been with a woman and she smelled so fresh and looked at him as if he could be someone special to her. As they threaded their way through the crowd to find Sabinus he felt light headed and hopeful. His financial troubles with Catus and Seneca seemed of less consequence. Surely such wealthy partners would not stoop to cheat him of what to them must be a pittance. He had simply been alone too long. He must marry again.

***

The great hall had grown quiet and Dedreth decided to go to bed. Prasu, Boudicca and most of the guests had disappeared, though some slept on couches or on the floor. Ingenius stood talking to Morfudd in a doorway holding her hands against his chest. It looked to Dedreth as if Ingenius had found someone new to love. She walked around to see if anyone else she knew was still in the hall but recognized no one. Marius' cubicle was deserted. Vaguely disappointed, she went out into the crisp night air. Marius had not thought her important enough to bid good night to. But she quickly lost her resentment. He was a High King and erratic to boot. Even though meeting him had stirred her blood, she was not going to slow her journey to the Kingdom by getting involved with someone as unattainable as he.

It was cold and she ran toward the round guesthouse. Why had the Druidess been so anxious to find Owain? She didn't seem the kind to waste her time being in love with Owain, married as he was to Caratacus' daughter, but if the agitation was not that of a lover, what could it be? Then she remembered the Archdruid's death. Of course! A new Archdruid would have to be elected. Morfudd must be trying to get Owain to come home so he could press his own candidacy. But why should Morfudd be interested in that?

Inside, she took a candle from the servant in the vestibule then passed by the smoking firepit to reach her room, a cubicle screened off from others like it by heavy drapes. She drew the curtains behind her and placed her candle on the small wooden chest by her bed. Then she saw the pile of clothes on the floor. On top of them lay her bow and quiver full of arrows. Marius must have had them brought back from the river, and at the thought she blushed furiously. If he had given them to a servant to place here what must the servant have thought? It would not take a genius to reason that she had been naked in his presence.

And if she had been naked it was reasonable to assume they had lain together.

She stamped her foot in anger. Was this her reward for months and years of celibacy—to be thought of as a woman who would lie with a man of an afternoon simply because he happened along and was a High King? She stamped her foot again and as she did so saw the curtains move where they abutted the wall. Quick as a flash she grabbed her bow and loaded it with an arrow. "Come out, whoever you are," she said. "Or I will fire into you."

Marius pulled the curtain aside and stepped into her room. Strangely enough she was not surprised. Who else could it be? Even though she had tried not to think about it she had halfway expected some further move after their sudden parting, and here he was, dressed in simple black trousers and a linen shirt, leather slippers on his feet. Without the finery he had worn in the great hall he looked younger and less remote. She was still angry because of the clothes but at the same time pleased that he had not ignored her.

"I was a fool," he said, "to leave a huntress' weapons where she could reach them. Won't you lower your bow?"

"Then you placed them here? And my clothes?" She lowered the bow but didn't take the tension off the arrow.

"You didn't think I would give them to a servant?"

Relieved, she let the arrow slide through her fingers and fall to the floor. "I should be honored to find a High King hiding behind my curtains," she said. "But why?"

"Why not? That is my room next to yours. It is my curtain as well as yours."

"Queen Boudicca does not place High Kings, especially her eldest brother, in guest houses such as this. Even I slept in the palace until you came along to dispossess me."

"But she places in them people I ask her to place in them, and then I ask the people she has placed in them to exchange places with me. It is all very proper." He came further into the room until he reached the foot of her bed and stirred the sheepskins on it with his toe. "May I sit down on your bed?" Without waiting for an answer he sat down.

"You must have gone to great pains to find my room and exchange yours. But you have not answered my question. Why?"

He lay back on the bed, hands folded behind his head, one foot still on the floor and the other resting on his knee. "You cheated me," he said.

"What do you mean?"

"You said I would see you naked."

"You did."

"I saw nothing but a white blur and the rear end of a horse."

"That was more than you deserved." She sat down on a stool and rested her bow against the wall. "You held me hostage and would have made me wait shivering behind my horse until dark."

"You could have come out to dress at any time," he said. "I will admit that the white blur was beautiful while it lasted. But you owe me the sight of more than that."

"I'm sure your sister the Queen will arrange for you to see any number of white blurs your heart desires."

"It is not a wench I would see," said Marius. "I would see you."

She bristled. "But I am not to be seen naked for your pleasure," she said. "You mistake me if you think otherwise."

He sat up and she tensed, ready to run from the room, but he bent forward and drew lines with his finger on the hard packed dirt floor. His long blond hair hung down and concealed his face. He really is good looking, she thought, but strange. She had heard that his sister Gwendolyn had gone mad after she married Owain. Was Marius a little mad too?

"You remember when first we met?" he said finally. "When I killed your father? I had the right not only to see you naked but to lie with you. There have been many times I wished I had. I wanted to, even though we hated each other."

"If you had lain with me I would have killed you. I was not a Nazarene then."

"I was a terrible general but I am not that easy to kill."

"I would have managed."

"Is it because you are a Nazarene," he said, "that you won't let me love you? Or do you still hate me?"

"You speak of loving me as if it were the same as seeing me naked. I am not a wench to be bought with flattering words. You are a High King and if you seek love you must seek it among those of your own station."

"It is because I am High King that I seek it where I seek it. I seek to see you, lie with you and love you."

"If you seek such here you will be disappointed."

"Then you have not forgiven me."

She went on her knees by him and clasped his hands in hers. "I did hate you," she said. "But Simon Peter healed me of it and I forgave you years ago. Nazarenes cannot hate. They can only love. But true love is not carnality. You speak of seeing and having and loving as if they were all the same thing."

"But they are."

"They are not."

His hands still clasped in hers she looked straight into his eyes and marveled to herself at their blueness and clarity. Then his hands were out of hers, one around her neck and the other at her side pulling her to him. His lips were against hers and her eyes closed as her body took fire. The Kingdom, the Kingdom, she said to herself, but it disappeared as his hand slid up her side and covered her breast. She gave a sharp sigh as he pulled her closer to him then froze as she heard a commotion in the vestibule.

Saddened and angered by the long story of his people's distress that Elidurus poured into her ears, Boudicca was irritated when she came into the hall with Elidurus and his people and saw Bodin still waiting for her. She had hoped he would have gone away by this time. But she had promised and must comply. Ingenius stood talking to Morfudd the green robed Druidess but as Boudicca approached, Morfudd disappeared into the darkness.

That Druidess looked dangerous. Ingenius would have to keep a sharp eye out. "Come," she said to Bodin. "We will go to King Marius."

Marius was not in his room. The room was barren and nothing disturbed its pristine neatness. Where had he gone—to some wench's room? A servant bowed. "He has taken the room next to the Lady Dedreth's, my lady," he said. "In the guest house."

Surprised, she set off through the hall, Bodin, Elidurus and the others trailing behind. As they walked to the guesthouse Morfudd joined them carrying a bulky package. A servant jumped up in surprise as they entered and pointed to the curtains covering Dedreth's cubicle. She pulled the curtain aside and there was Marius holding Dedreth in his arms.

"And I tried to keep you two separated," she said to Dedreth, "because I feared you might fight each other again. I had to ask the servants where you were." She looked at Marius none too kindly. "Lord Kincar is here with Elidurus. He has brought word from Venutius. The Twentieth has moved into the mountains and he has destroyed a foraging party and its cavalry. He says he can destroy the entire legion with your help. You must ride tonight."

"I saw Kincar and Elidurus," said Marius. "Why have you waited this long to tell me of this?"

"Elidurus has been telling us about his poor Trinoes. The Rummies are raping them. They're starving."

"We'll get food to them," said Marius. "But Venutius does not need me. He has full authority over my armies."

"You are head of all father's nations in his absence. They will follow Venutius as Arviragus but not without you at their head. Now get dressed for the journey."

Marius turned to Dedreth. "What do you say? Must I, Britain's worst general, obey my sister and go to war?"

Dedreth blushed. "I would not counsel you to make war on anyone," she said, "but to be High King is a higher duty than to be a general. King Venutius can move your peoples' bodies, but you must move their souls."

Bodin stepped past Boudicca into the candlelight. He bowed, first to Marius and then to Dedreth. "A queen could not have spoken better words," he said.

"Then I must make her my queen," said Marius.

"This is my Lord Bodin of the Council," said Boudicca, looking at Dedreth, whose face was on fire. "In my surprise at finding you both here I violated his right to speak first. But I have no doubt he will make up for it. Lord Bodin, this is the Lady Dedreth of Carys."

Bodin's face changed and Boudicca sensed an immediate hostility. Had he heard Dedreth's name before? Did he know she was of the heretic Nazarene College? Bodin approached Marius, beckoning to Morfudd to follow. Morfudd carried a folded banner on top of which lay a sword with a copper sheathed and ruby laden hilt. When she reached Bodin, he took the sword from her, held the point in one hand and rested the weapon on his forearm so that the hilt was proffered to Marius. Marius made no move to take it.

"I have been commanded by the High Council to present to you this sword and banner," said Bodin. "I am to ask that you kiss this sword and bear this banner and swear to defend Britain in the name of the Holy Nazarene church."

Marius folded his arms. "I lead no-one into battle," he said. "Take your sword and banner to King Venutius."

Bodin looked again at Dedreth. "This sword and banner are merely symbols of your allegiance to Britain and to our holy church. It is but a formality to accept them." He gestured with the sword hilt as if demanding that Marius seize it, but Marius remained immobile, his face wooden.

"Show my lord king the banner," said Bodin to Morfudd, and Morfudd unfolded it for all to see. On its white face a red cross had been sewn. "The Lord Jesus said that his followers should carry his cross," said Bodin. "Will you not swear to carry it for him and kiss his sword?"

"I have already sworn to defend Britain," said Marius.

"Because I know what Britain is. I do not know what your church is or why it should have a sword and banner."

"Do not quibble over trifles, good brother," said Boudicca. "The Council has decided the armies will fight better if they think Christ is on their side. Bear the banner and kiss the sword."

Marius turned to Dedreth. "You have told me my duty as High King," he said. "And you have told me you are a Nazarene who is against war. Should I kiss this sword and banner and swear to defend Britain in the name of your church?"

"Lord Bodin's church is not my church," said Dedreth.

"Be careful what you say, my lady," said Boudicca. "You made a pretty speech a moment ago and we thank you for it. But do not stand between Kings and Council. Remember your place and do not presume above it."

"She does not presume above her place," said Marius, "when she answers my questions. If Lord Bodin's is not your church," he said to Dedreth, "then what is your church?"

"I am a follower of the Cyndaf, Prince Joseph of Arimathea," said Dedreth. "He was great-uncle and friend to the Christ, Lord Jesus of Nazareth. Our church is of the spirit, not the flesh. It renounces both banner and sword."

"She is of the Nazarene College," said Bodin. "It is supported by treasonable Druids who seceded from the Council and put themselves in opposition to it. It has been declared heretic and traitorous because it spreads the poison of defeatism and abject surrender to Rome, and its members are subject to arrest and trial. The true Nazarene church is loyal to the Council."

"If it is a true Nazarene church," said Dedreth, her eyes blazing, "then how can it raise a war banner and kiss a sword as a symbol of he who said we must love our enemies and turn the other cheek if smitten? Why not be honest and call it the church of Camulos or the church of Mars?"

Boudicca stamped her foot. "That is enough!" she said. "The Nazarene church is an instrument of war. When this war is done we will follow Christ in your way. Keep your flame alive for all of us but do not burn with it our defense against Rome."

Bodin looked as if he were about to argue but stopped when Marius seized the sword and lifted it. "If this be but a symbol," he said, "then I will wear it to please my sister. But I will neither kiss it nor swear upon it." He threw it on Dedreth's bed and turned to Bodin. "Does that please my Lord Council member?"

Bodin's look was black. He bowed but said nothing.

"And now," said Marius. "If I am to do my sister's bidding I would ask that you allow me to take leave of Lady Dedreth."

"There is one more thing," said Boudicca. "Our cousin, King Elidurus, seeks a favor from you."

"Then he shall have it," said Marius, "in honor of the Lady Dedreth."

There was no doubt about it. Marius was infatuated with her elf. When had this taken place? "Be careful what you promise," she said, "Remember you must lead your nations."

King Elidurus' face was drawn with suffering and his hair quite white. He knelt at his cousin's feet.

"Nay, cousin," said Marius. "You shall not kneel to me." He tried to lift Elidurus to his feet but Elidurus would not budge.

"I will not rise unless you grant my request," said Elidurus.

"Whatever it is," said Marius, "it is granted already."

"You swear it?" said Elidurus.

"Ask him what it is first," said Boudicca.

"I swear it," said Marius, not looking at Boudicca.

"I invoke my favor in the name of our grandfather Cunobelinus, may he find much hunting in the Otherworld. And in the name of my uncle and your father, King Caratacus, and in the name of my uncles, Guderius and Belinus, and in the name of your mother, Queen Genvissa, and your sisters and brothers."

"Cousin, your favor is granted. Tell me what it is."

"I am a sick man. I cannot live much longer. My nation is ruined and my people are starving under the yoke of Rome. If something isn't done right away, Trinovante will disappear and be remembered no more."

"What would you have me do?"

"My Trinoes ache to fight but they have no-one to lead them."

"You would have me lead them, cousin?"

"No," said Elidurus with vigor, and Marius' eyebrows shot up. "I would have my son lead them."

"Brennius?" said Marius.

"Yes," said Elidurus. "We quarreled and he went away, but I forgive him. You must bring him back. I will make him High King and he can lead our armies against Rome."

"Where is Brennius?"

"In Hibernia."

"And you want me to find him and bring him home?"

"You have sworn it." Elidurus looked around the room. "He has sworn it," he said. "Therefore he must do it. And do it now."

"I will do it," said Marius. "Because I have sworn it. But why send me? I can send men to get him for you."

"You have sworn to do it."

Marius looked at Boudicca, his eyes blank.

"Do not look so at me," she said. "I warned you. Now your rash promise has cost us victory over the Twentieth."

Marius put out a hand and helped Elidurus to his feet. "Will you head the armies in my place?" he said to Boudicca. "You are twice the man I am and nine times the king. My nations love you as their own. They will accept you at their head if you tell them why I cannot be there."

"Aye," said Boudicca, making her voice bitter. "I will take your place because we cannot afford it unfilled. But who will take my place?" She wheeled and left the room, and the others followed one by one, leaving Dedreth alone with Marius.

Boudicca had felt angry, looked angry and acted angry. But she should be angry with herself at her own deceit. An insane sense of joy had come over her when Marius asked her to lead his nations. The Silures, Ordoes and Demetes, trained by Atak and her father to be the best armies in Britain, now under her command. The Twentieth Legion to fight and Venutius to fight it with. What more could she ask?

She heard nothing of what Bodin said, but hurried to the stables leaving them all standing in Prasu's hall. She must ride at first light.

* * *

It was the second day of the journey back to Joseph's village. Dedreth led the way on Tristram and right behind her plodded the men sent to escort her home. She pictured Marius traveling west to find Brennius and herself going to the Severn estuary to tell Joseph of her betrothal to Marius. What a strange erratic man was Marius. But how lovable! She closed her eyes and felt the hardness and the softness of him again, and shuddered at the intensity of her feeling. She wanted to be in his arms. What she felt was not of the Kingdom, but the Kingdom would come in its own good time. She could teach Marius to be a Nazarene and help him become a king worthy of Christ. They would find the way to the Kingdom together.

About midday, while they were still in the heart of the forest, two of the men behind her came up on either side. One put a finger to his lips cautioning her to be quiet. He reached out and seized Tristram's bridle, bringing him to a halt. All three horses became still, side by side, and those behind stopped also.

"What is it?" she whispered. The men shook their heads. Nothing seemed to move but she could sense the presence of men watching them. She felt fear rise within her so she closed her eyes and began to pray. When she looked again, a circle of dirty unkempt men surrounded them. There must be fifty of them and they held clubs in their hands. One or two were armed with swords.

"Tis the Gunes of Merimar," hissed one of her men. They unsheathed their swords and trembling she pulled an arrow from her quiver and loaded it in her bow. So these were the men who almost killed Venutius. Should she defend herself or rely on God to save her? She took the tension off and put the arrow back in its quiver. "Sheathe your swords," she said.

She looked down the forest trail beyond the Gunes. Would it be possible to charge through them? Even as she weighed the possibility, several horsemen appeared down the trail. They wore robes like Druids but they were not of Druid colors. One of them rode toward her and the Gunes stood back to let him through. Numbness stole over her and she knew what the man was about to say. He drew up his horse before her and looked at her, contempt in his eyes.

"You are the heretic traitress, Dedreth of Carys?" he asked.

Chapter 7

Paul

The bed covers tucked under his chin, Owain lay on his back and glowered at the low ceiling above him. The room lacked a door, and from somewhere above an unintelligible conversation and a strange white light came into it making it impossible for him to sleep. Gwendolyn lay at his side breathing softly and it made him angry to think that she always slept so well. People with slight intellects always seemed to sleep better than those with minds equipped to grapple with the abstract and complex. Gwendolyn might have been healed of insanity but her stupidity was still intact.

He placed a tentative hand on her stomach but she turned away with a grunt. He wondered if Priscilla had filled her mind with all these thoughts of celibacy. Or perhaps it was Paul, the ex-Pharisee healer and missionary who lived on the top floor. It hardly seemed fair, now that his days of loneliness and deprivation were over, to find that the wife whose only redeeming virtue was her body wanted to give up carnalism for the Kingdom. The few times she had indulged him she had reminded him—right in the middle—that carnalism was sinful.

The bright picture of Morfudd often came to disturb his sleep and he found himself wondering why she left him and went to Bodin. Had it been fear that drove her into the clutches of that upstart? Perhaps he should have been more assertive. If he had vigorously denounced Bodin in the tent that day she might have stayed with Owain. But then what would he have done with Gwendolyn? He sighed, thinking of his quiet tent in Mona, and decided a celibate existence was best for the pursuit of deep uninterrupted thought. He must tell that to Paul in the morning. In the meantime he moved restlessly in the bed, irritated when Gwendolyn sighed but did not awake.

He hadn't had a decent night's sleep since leaving Britain. In Rome, the nights always roared with the shouts of juvenile gangs on the prowl and the shrieks of their victims, and with the clatter of wheels against cobblestones as merchants rushed their carts down the streets. His resentment at having to be smuggled out of Rome to escape arrest had been eased but not erased by Gwendolyn and himself being escortedto Corinth.

Corinth was quieter than Rome but this particular house was a veritable bedlam. There must be two hundred people in it and not one of them ever seemed to sleep. Judging by the noise they spent their nights talking, arguing, singing, cooking, sawing wood, hammering nails, shifting furniture, pounding on doors and dragging heavy objects up and down the stairs. The house always reeked of the heavy oils and spices the Corinthians used in their cooking. It never grew dark or quiet at night. There were always lights or voices going past their door, and often people would walk into the room and hold a candle to his face or shake his shoulder to ask his name. Once, a heavy set man with a coarse beard tried to climb into bed with them and it had taxed Owain's patience to get the man to leave.

When they first arrived in Corinth, Blonwen, the sister of Caratacus, welcomed them into her small but crowded villa on the Acro-Corinthus. Sitting below the edge of its narrow peristyle garden he had been able to see the city and in the distance Parnassus, the mountain home of Apollo and the Muses. Blonwen had found some scrolls for him to read and for three days he knew relative peace and quiet, his nights disturbed only by the parties thrown by Blonwen to show Gwendolyn and Priscilla off to her friends. On the fourth day, Pudens came to say Gwendolyn and Owain had been invited to lodge in the large house of a wealthy Christian, Titius Justus. Justus was in Judea but his son Samuel had extended an invitation in his father's name. Tired of being crowded in Blonwen's overguested villa and expecting more spacious and private accommodations, Owain readily agreed. What a shock to find that Justus' house, four times larger than Blonwen's, was occupied by ten times as many people.

The strange white light that filtered into the room died down along with the conversation and he turned on his side hoping to sleep but once again a vision of Morfudd appeared in his mind. She stood in front of him and kissed his fingers with soft lips, her stomach against his. He groaned and gritted his teeth, wondering if she had married Bodin the Fox.

The sullen thump thump thump of a large mass of material being dragged down the staircase awakened him. The noise stopped outside the bedroom and he could tell that someone stood in the doorway. He sat up in bed and yawned groggily. Would he never get a night's sleep? The faint gray light of dawn filled the room so he realized he must have been asleep for some time. The dim light revealed a small familiar bushy haired figure standing in the doorway. It was Paul. In one hand, Paul grasped an end of the leather tent he had just dragged down the stairs.

"Will you ever finish that tent?" asked Owain, irritable at being awakened.

"Probably not," said Paul. "But every man is expected to work for his living. We're having trouble with some of the brothers in Thessalonica who won't work because they think the Lord is coming back to take them to heaven. Are you getting up soon? Priscilla is cooking the morning meal already and I would like to continue our discussion. Then you must come with me to hear brother Mark recite the sayings of Jesus. You Druids aren't the only ones versed in memorization, you know."

"Yes," sighed Owain. "If I can't get any sleep I might as well get up and argue with you some more."

"I haven't slept at all," said Paul.

Feeling movement beside him, Owain looked down and saw Gwendolyn squinting at Paul. She pulled the covers up to her chin and peered over the top of them. "What was that strange light?" asked Owain. "I couldn't shut it out. Not that I would have been able to sleep anyway with all the noise."

"You saw the light? That is very good. Most people could only see him when he was in the flesh."

Owain, pleased at the compliment, frowned. "See whom?" he asked.

"Jesus. He was up there talking to me. The first time I met him, all I could see of him was light so bright it blinded me. It was like coming out into the sunlight after spending years in a dark cave. All I've ever seen of him is light, but by now I've put off enough of the old man to be able to stand it."

"If all you saw was light," said Gwendolyn, "how did you know it was the Lord Jesus?"

"Oh, you know all right," said Paul. "You know."

"But I understood from Philip," said Owain, "that he was killed and went back to heaven."

Paul shrugged. "He's in heaven all right but so are we. We live and move and have our being in it. God's Kingdom is spiritual."

"Then it is what we call the Otherworld. Few can see it but some who are more spiritual are able to go in and out of it at will. We all go there when we die."

"It's not something you go in and out of. It's the only place there is. We see it through a glass darkly because the carnal mind sees only fleshly things. We must put it off and let in the mind and love of Christ. As we do we get a clearer view of the Kingdom and can express the dominion God gave us. It gives us the power to heal."

"I wish you would come to Britain and use your power to

destroy this man Bodin I told you about," said Owain. "He's frightening people into believing that Duw will strike them dead and keep them out of the Otherworld if they don't obey his priests. Surely, it must be the will of God that such a man be struck down?"

Paul dropped his tent and came to the foot of the bed. "God is a Spirit, the Mind of Christ, not a big human being sitting on a throne ready to throw thunderbolts at whomever we ask. That's what the carnal mind thinks God is and you must put off such thoughts. Now is it too hard to understand that we cannot love God or image God's power if we cannot love God's own image and likeness? Our warfare is not with people but with the carnal mind, to destroy its grip so that we can see what God really created. We must learn to love because love makes us aware of what is around us. Hatred makes us feel deficient and blinds us to it."

"You seem obsessed with this carnal mind."

"I am. It's Satan: enmity toward all things spiritual. It keeps us focused on our bodies, trying to make them feel good and last forever instead of forgetting them so we can learn to see the kingdom. And the more we focus on our bodies and fear what can happen to them the more blind and deaf to God we become, the more sick and diseased we get and the more we descend into conflict and warfare. That's why the Master called Simon Peter Satan when he tried to stop him from proving that death can be overcome. All Peter could think of was saving the Master's body. There are no bodies in the kingdom. That's why we can't see Jesus anymore, only light. Flesh and blood cannot enter the kingdom."

"But how can we get rid of it?"

"It's simple, so simple in fact I fear its simplicity will be corrupted and lost. The Christ hates iniquity and loves righteousness. If you feel angry, hateful or jealous you must put them off and replace such feelings with love. As you put off the carnal mind's hatreds and jealousies and judgments, which are all based on a sense of self-deficiency, and learn to love without discrimination just as God loves, you become at one with God's power and recognize that you have no deficiencies. Remember the parable of the prodigal son's brother and how deficient he felt when all that his father had belonged to him? How could the image of an omnipotent God have any deficiencies? This is the truth that makes us free. The evil works of the carnal mind are destroyed by God's love and as you grasp this and hold fast to it you will never be sick or die. When Jesus rose from the dead he proved once and for all that there is no power, not even death, able to defeat the love of God. You must learn to lose your faith in carnal works and put your faith only in the power of God's love. Is that too hard to understand?"

Owain shook his head. "I tell you honestly," he said. "Nothing is ever that simple. To tell this to people must confuse them."

"You may be right," said Paul, covering his face. "Many of those who listen to me go away confused because they believe that if they are the image of God, then God must a big bumbling human being as blind and deaf to His own perfect creation as they are. Only when we have put off the carnal mind's blindness and deafness to the truth will we fully image God's nature and power." Paul sweated profusely, obviously overwhelmed. He reached out and grabbed Owain's wrists. "Can't you help me make this clear? This is a thorn in my side, that I cannot make apparent to people what I see so clearly myself."

"Perhaps I can help you better communicate it," said Owain. "What you're really saying is that the carnal mind makes us see and do that which we should not see and not do, and to not see and not do that which we should see and do."

Paul leaned back, his eyes wide. "I like that," he said. "Do you mind if I use it in one of my talks?"

A woman's voice sounded from far below. "That's Prisca," said Paul. "I must go. Come and talk to me later on." He set off, dragging his tent behind him. On the other side of the doorway, he stopped and looked back. "The good that I would do I do not and the evil that I would not I do," he said. "I like that." He nodded to himself and disappeared. Owain could hear the thump thump thump of the tent on every step all the way to the bottom.

"He's a nice man," said Gwendolyn, looking up at Owain with big eyes and soft mouth.

"Yes," said Owain. "A little strange perhaps. He never stops preaching. I wonder if he ever brushes his hair?"

When they went down for the morning meal, Owain led Gwendolyn to a side table in the dining hall far away from the place of honor in the center. He chose this place every morning because Samuel loved to raise his hands in delighted shock and move them closer to Titius Justus' table. This morning, however, instead of moving them, Samuel served them barley bread, salt fish, goat milk, fruit and locusts dipped in honey right where they sat. He looked nervous and his hands shook. A dark haired girl in her teens, quite pretty and composed, followed him around. At first, Owain was offended at not being asked to move closer to the head table but it quickly became obvious that Samuel was not himself.

"I haven't yet met your father," said Owain, hoping to put the boy at ease. To his horror, Samuel jerked upright, upended the basket of food, knocked over a freshly poured cup of goat milk and twisted around to face the door. He clutched the girl as if in fear. All eyes in the vicinity turned on them.

"Where is he?" said Samuel. The girl struggled in his arms but he held on grimly.

"Where is whom?" said Owain. The milk ran toward the edge of the table and he stood up quickly so it wouldn't drip on his robe.

"He thought you meant his father had come in," said the dark haired girl. "You frightened him."

"I thought he was looking for me," said Samuel. "He's back from The Land[17]." He let go of the girl and mopped up the milk so vigorously he splashed Owain's robe. "Can Sarah sit with you while you eat?" said Samuel, appeal in his eyes. "I have to see where my father is." Without waiting for an answer he dashed off.

"Please join us," said Owain to Sarah as he brushed the drops of milk from his robe. Always careful not to offend his hosts, he washed his hands using water from a bowl on the table. "Can we offer you some bread?"

"You haven't prayed yet," said Sarah. "The man who eats without having blessed his food desecrates a holy thing."

"I was just about to pray," said Owain, sharply. Her words made him cross. He closed his eyes, folded his hands and rocked his upper body back and forth as he had seen the others do.

"She can't eat with us anyway," said Gwendolyn.

"Yes I can," said Sarah. "I'm not afraid of eating with foreigners. But I've already eaten." She sat down and folded her hands in her lap. Owain felt he should say something to put her at ease but realized she was already at ease.

The people nearby no longer stared at them but he could sense tension in the crowded smoke filled kitchen. If Samuel's father had returned from Judea, perhaps the guests feared being thrown out. No sane householder would let this many people lodge in his house. They must all be friends of Samuel. He blushed. Suppose Justus threw Gwendolyn and he out? How embarrassing that would be. "Hurry and eat your food," he whispered to Gwendolyn. "I think we should get out of here."

Before they could finish, a huge livid bearded man rushed into the kitchen followed by several servants. He carried a large barrel of fruit in his arms and with a howl of rage he threw the barrel on the floor. Fruit flew in all directions and the barrel crashed against the master's table, knocking it over. Samuel had come in right behind the man. He lifted the table into its proper position and stood wringing his hands as the bearded man pulled on his hair in rage. Owain stood up to watch as the guests scattered.

"It is Samuel's father," said Sarah. She didn't appear frightened by the commotion. "Samuel says he often gets angry."

So this is Titius Justus, thought Owain. I was right. He's upset about all these people. His attention was momentarily drawn to the doorway through which Justus had just entered. A scrawny man stood there holding a scroll. His weather beaten hangdog and tattooed face identified him as a low Briton, most likely a sailor. Had the sailor been sent to find him? Perhaps the scroll contained urgent tidings from Britain. He was about to wave to get the sailor's attention when Justus started throwing fruit. A large melon sailed through the air and smashed itself into pieces so close to their table that Owain jumped back in fright. "As this fruit is scattered," roared Justus. "So will the fruit of my son's loins be scattered."

"Father," said Samuel. He tried to touch his father but Justus knocked his arm away.

"Get me another barrel of fruit," said Justus to his servants. "Take it to the street and smash it. All will see what I think of my son. My own son has betrothed himself to a Samaritan behind my back. And such a lovely girl I had picked out for him."

"But father," said Samuel

"Shut up," said Justus. He climbed up on the table and waved his arms. The people nearest him, who had earlier backed away in fright, pressed forward again because it was obvious that Justus' anger was directed at his son and not at his guests. Justus kicked at some of the fruit on the table and sent it spinning into the crowd. "This is how it will be," he howled. "I will not recognize his wife. I will not recognize his children. How could I if she's a Samaritan?"

"She's a Christian," said Samuel, wiping the tears from his eyes.

"Helen is a Christian," said his father, jumping up and down on the table. "And she's from a good family. How can a Samaritan be a Christian? What is this girl's family? I spit on her family."

"You will love her if you'll let me bring her to you."

"How can I love her? Samaritans are bone kickers. I spit on bone kickers. They defiled the Temple. I spit on defilers of the Temple. I spit on Samaritans."

"But I don't love Helen."

"How can you not love her? I picked her out myself. Isn't that enough? You think you pick better than your own father picks? I spit on your pick. I pick you a good girl. Her father is my good friend. He is a Christian. You are a Christian. Helen is a Christian. What more can you want from me?"

"I want you to love Sarah," roared Samuel. Owain looked down at the girl sitting calmly across from him, hands still folded in her lap. The suspicion dawned on him that this little girl might be the cause of the argument. He nodded to himself, pleased at his own acuity. "I'm going to marry Sarah," said Samuel, "and I want your blessing. She is here. Let her kiss your hand."

"She is here?" roared Justus. "She is in my house? How dare she be in my house? Where are my servants? I want her thrown out."

"If you throw her out," said Samuel, "you will throw me out too. We will never come back. You will have no grandchildren to play with when you are old. You will have no one to put a pillow behind your head and bring you a cup of wine when you are tired. And you will be shamed among all your friends for not having your son and his wife and their children to care for you. Let her kiss your hand and give us your blessing."

"If she kisses my hand I will have it cut off and then I will spit on it."

Sarah stood up and smoothed her clothes. "They will go on like this all day," she said.

"Be careful," said Gwendolyn as Sarah walked firmly toward her betrothed. The room grew still as all eyes, including those of Justus, focused on her. Owain waved at the sailor and the man stared back glassily and nodded vaguely. So the man must have a message from Britain. Owain wondered what it could be and hoped this scene between Justus and his son would be over quickly. Suddenly, he couldn't wait to get out of this city. He wanted to be back in Britain. And with that sudden longing came the determination to leave Gwendolyn behind. She would be much happier with her father and mother. A quick picture of Morfudd came into his mind but he dutifully dismissed it.

Sarah stood next to Samuel and looked up at Justus. "You should be ashamed of yourself," she said. "Why are you spoiling all this good fruit? Instead of kicking and throwing it you should be on your knees to thank God for all the blessings that have been showered on you that you should have such fruit, and you should be gathering all of it you can to feed the hungry and the sick. It is your bad temper you should spit on. It is your anger you should spit on and your contumaciousness."

"I should be talked to like this in my own house by a Samaritan? And not only a Samaritan but a Samaritan woman? And not even a woman but a mere girl? Is that respect? I shall sell my house and go back to the Land where I am treated with respect."

"The days are past when a woman must give way to a man," said Sarah, "or a Samaritan to a Jew. In Christ all are equal. There is neither Samaritan nor Jew, male nor female, bond nor free. The only bond on us is that we speak truth and act in love. Now get down from that table and thank God for giving you such a son as Samuel and for giving your son such a wife as me. I will be a good wife for Samuel and I will be a good mother to his children and a good daughter to you." She reached up with her hand to help Justus jump down. "Show me that you are a Christian. Give me your hand and I will kiss it."

"You hear her?" said Justus, addressing the room at large. "Am I to be insulted in my own house by a female? Am I to be told I have bad temper? Am I to be told I am not a Christian?"

"Yes," said many voices from the back.

"She is a good girl," said a voice.

"You have a bad temper," said another voice.

"Let her kiss your hand," said another.

Justus jumped to the ground. "Marry her then," he said to Samuel. "If I'm to get no respect in my own house, if I'm to be told I have a bad temper, then I don't care who you marry. I spit on caring about who you marry. I'm going back to the Land." He began to march off, and Owain thought the scene was over, but Sarah ran around Justus, fell on her knees before him and put her arms around his legs so that he almost fell.

"You do care," she said. "You must let me kiss your hand and love you. You will never lack respect from your daughter or your grandchildren." She looked up at him, eyes wet with tears. Justus stood motionless while the room became absolutely silent, then without looking at her, put his hand by her face and she seized it and kissed it. Samuel ran to them, threw his arms around his father's neck and kissed him. Justus bore it all in silence, eyes closed, nose flared and head raised. But his cheeks were flushed. Sarah got to her feet and Justus marched sedately off without a word, kicking one last piece of fruit out of his way. Samuel would have followed him but Sarah stopped him. "Let him go," she said as Justus disappeared through the doorway. "He will come around."

As the crowd gathered to congratulate the young couple, Owain edged around it to the doorway where the sailor still waited. "Have you been sent to find me?" he said.

"Who wass ee?" said the sailor.

Owain straightened his robe with a flourish. Surely the ignorant man must realize that he addressed a High Council member. "I am Lord Owain Longhead of Caer Went," he said. "Member of the High Council of Kings and Druids. Is that scroll addressed to me?"

The sailor scratched his tattooed cheek with the edge of the scroll and looked dubious. "You wass Lord Owing Longred?"

"That's right."

"And you wass just in Rome?"

"Yes." Owain reached for the scroll but the sailor put it behind his back. His little beady eyes narrowed.

"How do I know you wass Lord Owing Longred?" he said.

"Don't you know what this robe signifies?" said Owain. He grabbed the front of it in his hand and shook it.

"Keep you warm?" said the sailor.

"It is the robe of a member of the High Council, you fool," said Owain. "Didn't they tell you I was a member of the High Council?"

"Didn't tell me nothing about you," said the sailor. "They said I wass to find Princess Gwendoling and give her this here scroll. They said she wass with you."

The shock of hearing the scroll was not for him was almost too much to bear. But he couldn't show his disappointment in front of this idiotic messenger or the word would get back to Rome. He made a great effort to control his emotions. "The Princess Gwendolyn is my wife. Give me the scroll and I will give it to her."

"Ar," said the sailor. "Pull the other one."

"Then come with me you idiot and give it to her yourself." Angry, he marched off in the direction of the table where he had left Gwendolyn but stopped before he had gone very far. "What is your name?" he asked, trying to sound more agreeable.

"I wass Buell."

"And who is your master?"

"Privatus wass my master. He be captain of our zip."

"Ah yes," said Owain.

"It wass King Caratacus what give me the scroll."

"Good," said Owain. Gwendolyn still sat at the table eating. "This man is called Buell," said Owain. "He has something for you from your father." Gwendolyn smiled at the man and held out her hand.

"You wass Princess Gwendoling?" asked Buell.

"Yes."

"King Caratacus said I wass to ask you the name of your sister."

"Why?"

"So I would know it wass you."

"Claudia."

Buell looked crafty again. "That wass not the name."

"Eurgen? Boudicca?"

Buell clutched the scroll to him and looked sideways at Owain. "Those wassn't the names," he said.

"Those are the only sisters she has," said Owain, rapidly losing his temper. "Give her the scroll, you clot, or you'll never see Privatus and your ship again. You have my word that she is the Princess Gwendolyn. That is enough."

Cowed, Buell handed the scroll to Gwendolyn. Hurriedly, she broke the seal and unrolled it. Inside was another scroll, heavily sealed. "It's addressed to you," she said, handing it to Owain. His heart leaped with excitement as he took it and he walked quickly to an empty table where he could read it undisturbed.

"It wass Gladyss!" shouted Buell. "Gladyss wass her name."

He looked back with a patronizing smile for the unfortunate Buell. Gladys was Gwendolyn's family name. Caratacus had probably told Buell to ask for it and the ignorant man had forgotten. Gwendolyn sat hunched over her own scroll, laboriously spelling out the words. He sat down and broke the seal of his scroll with trembling hands. The crabbed Greek handwriting adorned with splatters from a splintered pen he would know anywhere. It was Morfudd's.

> To Lord Owain Longhead, son of Eulltyd of Caer Went and Exalted Member of the Druidic High Council.
> My Dear Lord Owain:
> I know that your great kindness will let you forgive my presumption in writing to you. I am in desperate fear not simply for my own life, which is of small consequence, but for the lives of many who have grown to depend on your protection, and for the cause to which you have devoted so much of your intellectual and spiritual resources. That cause is in dire jeopardy. Deprived of your steadying influence the Council is rapidly being corrupted by him on whom I was foolish enough to think I

might exert a good influence (I will not sully this letter with his name). The church you established might have saved us but it is floundering like a lamb being led to slaughter. The Wolf (Fox is too mild an appellation!) will devour all in consummating a strategy that is as clever as it is devilish. Rather than coercing Britons into joining his church, the Wolf has simply declared all Britons to be Nazarenes and any who try to leave the church to be subject to cruel punishment including burning. He has published a creed to which all must swear obedience. Those who resist are tortured or killed. He has caused catastrophes to occur and has attributed them to Duw, so that the people cower in fear of His holy Name. He has instituted a reign of terror and has captured or slain some of the Nazarene healers. One of them was the Lady Dedreth, who I believe had the honor of your acquaintance. (One of which? thought Owain in his agitation: the captured or the slain? Why didn't she make it clear?)

The messenger who is to carry this to you is waiting, so I must bring it to a close. Dear Lord Owain, please return to those who love and need you in this hour of great trial. You cannot know how much I loved our warm relationship or how I wish I had stayed with you as your humble student. I am in hiding from him, but I will be waiting for you at the inn in Marazion[18] when you arrive from Morlaix. I will watch every ship in the hope you will be on it. May Duw and His Christus guide you safely.
Your devoted student,
Morfudd.
PS: The Archdruid is dead and if you don't return quickly the Council will most likely elect the Monster!

Owain grabbed his hair in both hands and sat hunched over the table. The scroll rolled itself up and lay between his elbows. He looked down at it unseeingly. The tabletop near where the scroll rested was made of open grained wood and he could trace on it the outlines of an ancient red stain. Something, perhaps the blood of an animal, had been spilled on it, and the scrubbing since had not been able to erase all trace of it. The stain had paled but was still visible at the bottom of each grain it covered. So the Archdruid was dead, and here he was several weeks journey away! Morfudd was right, Bodin would probably get himself elected. No one he knew of was strong enough to stand up to the Fox—the Wolf, as Morfudd now called him. So the memory of him was still dear to her and she wanted to be close to him again! She had been willing to forget him forever, until she found out what a monster Bodin was. Now that Bodin had revealed his true colors she was trying to resume the relationship she'd broken. Well, he didn't know if he would stand for it. She could watch the ships coming into harbor forever as far as he was concerned.

A strange feeling came over him as he thought of Dedreth dead. Try as he could, the picture of her astride her horse that used to haunt him in the depths of his love would not come back. Instead he could only see Morfudd reaching up to adjust his clasp. His throat burned and he opened his mouth to get more air. Dedreth dead! The stain on the tabletop disappeared under his right elbow, so he lifted it from the table to see how far the stain traveled. When he did, he became aware that Gwendolyn stood by him. He looked up and saw her face filled with concern.

"What has happened?" she said. "Is it bad news?"

"Yes," he said. "Very bad. I must return to Britain immediately." He looked around sharply. "Where is that stupid sailor?" Buell had been given food and was saying his prayer before eating it. It was a long prayer and Owain tapped his fingers impatiently. Gwendolyn wept but he would not let himself look at her. "Where is your ship?" he said, when Buell finished.

"Zip wass at Lickem," said Buell.

Good, thought Owain. Lechaeum was on the west side of the peninsula and days closer to Marseilles. "And where is your ship going to?"

"We wass taking olive oil to Marsee."

"Run to your captain as soon as you have eaten. Tell him he must wait for me. I will join your ship before morning."

"Am I not to come with you?" said Gwendolyn.

He stood up and embraced her. "It would be better not," he said. "There is much trouble in Britain. There is war not only with the Romans but among the Druids. It would be better if you stayed here with Pudens and Blonwen. When things settle down I will send for you." He pressed her to him as he talked, kissed her forehead and felt her soften against him. But he was thinking of the coming journey and Morfudd waiting at the inn. The ship should make Marseilles in two weeks, then two more weeks to cross Gaul to Morlaix and three more days by ship to reach Marazion. From there, he and Morfudd could be in Mona within five days. Six weeks from now he could be in his old familiar tent.

"We must thank Samuel and his father," said Gwendolyn.

"Yes yes," said Owain. "Of course." He noticed that she still held her scroll. "And what news did your father send? Better than mine, I hope?"

"Pudens has to go back to Rome and my father says we should go with him. But now that you are going back to Britain, I will go by myself."

"It will be best," said Owain. His heart felt lighter already.

***

Owain put down the leather bag. The pony and cart that Aquila had borrowed to take him to Privatus' ship stood outside the door to Justus' mansion. Justus beamed as he hugged Owain. "My house is always open," said Justus. "Sarah will learn to cook and give you food fit for a king."

"Sarah can cook already," said Sarah.

Owain turned to Gwendolyn and clasped her in a close embrace. Surprised at how sad he suddenly felt at the prospect of leaving her, he felt his eyes mist and held her longer than he had meant to while they dried up. "I'm glad you will be going to your parents," he said. "You will be much safer there."

Gwendolyn's eyes were dry when he stood back from her, but she looked sad. "I will never see you again," she said.

"I will send for you," he protested. "As soon as it is safe."

"I had hoped you would stay to become a Christian."

"I will become a Christian," said Owain. "But I am also a Briton and a Council member. As soon as it is safe I will send for you and we will live in Caer Leon near your brother Eudal Marius."

She smiled wanly and shook her head. "We will never meet again," she said. "I am too stupid to be your wife. Remember that I loved you as best I could."

He looked around, anxious for the scene to be over. His throat burned and constricted and he felt he would weep if he had to look at Gwendolyn much longer. He had meant to ask her to send Priscilla and Aquila to Britain but now he felt he could not. He would write to her about it later. "Where is Paul?" he said, his voice choked.

"Paul is in the kitchen," said Sarah. "I was giving him a hair cut." She waved him to follow and set off for the kitchen.

Paul sat at a table near the wall, head buried beneath his crossed arms. A trough from ear to ear had been cut in his bushy hair leaving only a few small tufts in front. Sarah had obviously been called away before she finished cutting the rest of it. Near one elbow a plate held food that had barely been nibbled on. Near the other were several sealed scrolls. As he got closer, Owain could see that Paul wept. He stood before the table, not knowing what to do. Sarah picked up the plate of food and went away with it. After a while Owain coughed and Paul raised his head.

"Forgive me," said Paul. He rubbed his eyes with his wrists and sniffed. "I didn't hear you."

"Is there anything I can do?"

Paul lifted his tear-streaked face and smiled sadly. His remaining hair, still damp with sweat from his exertions, had been pushed into strange patterns. He ran his fingers tentatively over the trough that Sarah had cut and looked puzzled. "I was weeping over my own failures," he said.

"With your ability to heal, how can you say that?"

Paul looked down at the table and turned his head from side to side. "My food has gone," he said. "I was just about to eat it."

"Sarah took it away. Shall I tell her to bring it back?"

Paul shook his head. "What is more important is that your words have touched my heart and now I too fear that I confuse people. The truth is so plain to me, I cannot grasp that others may not see it as clearly."

Owain nodded agreement. "I understood you," he said. "But in all modesty we Druids are used to thinking in abstract terms. What you see so clearly must be incomprehensible to those who have not disciplined their minds. To teach such primitives you must have explanations that can be understood at a very low level of comprehension and accompany each step in the explanation with rituals that will be easily remembered. Those rituals will ultimately, after much repetition, recall the explanation itself to mind. We also find explanations are more readily grasped if arranged in groups of three and accompanied by little ceremonies such as puffs of colored smoke or ringing bells. It helps too if the individual providing the explanation is dressed in an impressive costume that arouses fear in the beholder, as this tends to reinforce the importance of the ritual and explanation to the primitive mind."

"That is why I weep. Explanations that the carnal mind can readily grasp lead away from the Kingdom instead of toward it. What a task!—to make the simplicity that is Christ apparent to the confusion that is the carnal mind. If it cannot comprehend a God who is not a big human being must we give it a God with three heads and a knowledge of good and evil as you suggested so God seems more powerful?"

"Not three heads," said Owain, offended. "Three natures."

"The Lord our God is one and one alone. Must we make

God's mind and nature sound like a human mind and nature so that people will feel more comfortable? Must we do what is wrong so that what is right may come of it? What a dilemma this raises! If we make God and Christ acceptable to the carnal mind then how will we put off the carnal mind?" He beat his fists against his head, and Owain placed a hand on his shoulder to comfort him.

"It will take many wise men a great number of years to comprehend what you have told me," he said, "and convert it to teaching that will make the uneducated understand. And that will take an organization. If you're unable to convince the Jewish organization to do it then you must form a new one."

Paul howled so loudly that Owain jumped. "Christ would become unrecognizable in two generations," he said. "Organizations take on a life and purpose of their own. The reason for their existence becomes lost through competition for power and status within them. This has happened already to the church we set up in Thessalonica. The faith of men and women must rest not on hierarchies, rituals, man-made laws and fancy costumes but on the spirit and power of God."

Owain shrugged at Paul's impracticality. "I agree that an organization will pollute your teaching, but without an organization there will soon be no teaching at all."

Paul stood up and ran a hand through his hair as if to smooth it. He frowned as his fingers retraced the trough cut by Sarah as if still unsure how it got there. "Something within me, probably my training as a Pharisee, wants to agree with you," he said. "But it is part of the old man that I must put off. It is our ways and thoughts, not God's, that demand an organization of ambitious priests and manmade laws to bring the people to Christ. What we need are missionaries able to preach and illustrate the true gospel through healing so that every man can learn to work out his own salvation." He stamped his foot on the hard packed dirt floor. "I will have faith in God and not in human works," he said, clapping Owain on the shoulder. "I will go to Gentiles such as yourself and trust their minds will open to have faith in God's power and presence. If, God forbid, I fail, I will think about your advice. And now, hurry back to your healers. Tell them what I have told you about how to love in the name of Christ even such as Bodin. The Christ power is the impersonal love of God and God's image, and it is such love and only such love that destroys evil."

Paul turned and selected a scroll from those on the table. "On your way up through Gaul," he said, "would you please give this to our brother Zacchaeus[19] at Rocamadour. The directions are written on the outside. Write to me about your churches and I promise to write in return. God willing, I shall some day come to your island and rejoice with you in your success."

Owain took the scroll from Paul and shook his hand. "I will deliver your scroll," he promised. "And I will write. I am grateful for all that you have taught and shown me." He smiled at Paul but inwardly he felt relieved that he was leaving. Paul might be a great healer but he was a difficult, intense man to deal with, and his ideas were wild and uncoordinated. If anything made a case for needing clear doctrine and an organization it was Paul's behavior. If he had to listen to Paul much longer, he too would grow confused and full of doubts. If Christianity were to gain acceptance and grow it would take Druid discipline, clear doctrine and a well-managed organization to make it happen.

Chapter 8

The Twentieth Legion

The short wintry afternoon darkened and Atak shivered as he looked over the cliff's edge at the valley below. It would soon be night and the feeble warmth that had struggled all day to get through the clouds would give up in defeat. Across the valley the mountains were obscured by mist and the air felt wet. He drew his tartan cloak closer around him, pulled on his wet beard and thought of Tetra and their warm bed.

"Look at them," said Boudicca. "They think they have won their war." A tartan cloak covered her lanky figure also and she lay stretched out on a rock at the edge of the cliff so that only the top of her head showed to any watchers below. Her hair had been braided and fastened with three silver clasps to keep it all together and the end of it was tucked under her arm so it wouldn't fall over the edge and betray her. Behind them in the ravine up which they had climbed, Venutius and his advance guard waited with their horses. The great red, green and white Pendragon flew at its head along with the red and white Nazarene banner sent by the High Council. The rest of the armies waited below out of sight.

He leaned over and looked down at the valley. A long train of horse drawn carts laden with stones, grain, nuts, vegetables, salt and the carcasses of freshly killed animals jerked and rattled along the stony bottomland. The noise of its passage reached them clearly even at this height, as did the curses and laughs of the auxiliaries guarding it.

The small number and complacency of the Roman auxiliaries spoke plainer than words. Their only concern was to get to the camp and into their warm tents. Over twenty thousand British warriors had infested the mountains around them and no sixth sense seemed to warn them. Another twenty thousand horsemen, chariots and foot soldiers under King Guderius were less than forty miles to the northeast. The Rummies were getting sloppy. Now that Caratacus had been captured they thought British resistance was over. They were in for a surprise.

A pebble rattled past him and went over the edge. He looked back to see Venutius had come to join them. He put a hand on Atak's shoulder as he too peered over the edge. "Only a squadron," said Venutius "Tis an insult. By Beli Mawr we should destroy it."

"And let the garrison know we're here?" said Boudicca. "That would be foolish. How many are in that camp, Atak?"

Atak grimaced as he saw the black look cover Venutius' face. He looked over the edge so he wouldn't embarrass Venutius by witnessing his discomfiture. This was a base camp, headquarters to foraging parties and fort builders. The Rummies were heading up the Usk to Brecon as part of Scapula's threat to eliminate the Silures, who had been blamed for Venutius' attacks on the Twentieth's foraging parties. "There are tents for eight hundred," he said.

King Galga of the Decies looked over. "Are they full?"

"They'll have building parties out. Maybe they're half full. We should send out scouts to see what they're doing."

"Can we get down there without em hearing us?" said Galga.

"I don't care if they hear us," said Venutius. "We have men enough to make short work of a few hundred Rummies."

"What do you think, Atak?" said Boudicca.

The flat tone of her voice told Atak she didn't like Venutius' plan and wanted Atak to tell him so. He turned a wary eye on Venutius. "Surprise is worth a cohort."

"And will cost us less men," said Galga.

There was a silence. Venutius was a good general when it came to harassing Roman units in the open field, but he had neither Caratacus' subtlety nor his concern for husbanding resources. His victories cost more than they should, and Boudicca had formed the habit of picking holes in his simple plans. When Boudicca and Atak first began to make suggestions, he grumbled but in most cases went along. As proxy for her brother Eudal Cyllinus Marius, Boudicca commanded the larger part of the armies and Venutius could not take her suggestions lightly.

After a while, however, Atak could tell Venutius felt annoyed by Boudicca's constant criticism. It took much longer now to get him to change his mind, and Boudicca's irritability grew in proportion to Venutius' mounting resistance. She seemed to have lost some of her old love for the Arviragus. She no longer held hands with him.

Atak had advised her to find better ways to make suggestions and she had grimly acquiesced. But when she couldn't think of a better way she would retreat into silence. She would not be content until she was Arviragus.

"My guts tell me to go down there and smash em," said Venutius, "but I'm tired of arguing. We'll do it at midnight."

"Wouldn't it be better to get the Rummies to come out?" said Boudicca. "There's a ditch and a berm all round the camp."

Venutius snorted. "Are you telling me that with twenty thousand men we can't make short work of eight hundred Rummies? Even with a berm and a ditch around em?"

"We'll make short work of em," said Boudicca. "But we'll lose less men if we can get them out in the open."

Venutius walked away. "Fear of Rummies is eating your stomach."

"I am not so fearful," she shouted after him, "that I will waste men to cover it."

Venutius cursed and pulled his hair.

It was long past midnight and Atak felt nervous. If Venutius didn't move soon some Rummy scout must blunder into them. Maybe Venutius had been right. If they had attacked right away they would have lost more men but the battle would have been over. Now they were tied up in knots of their own making. Venutius sulked over Boudicca's angry words and his delay was a way to pay her back. Atak sighed. This war showed no sign of coming to a close. It had been seven years since the Rummies invaded and they still controlled less than a quarter of Britain. The Rummies could not overcome the Britons with the forces they had and the Britons did too much bickering among themselves to defeat the Rummies. And both sides were losing too many men to the Nazarenes.

He shivered as his stomach made loud noises. Like the rest of Venutius' army he had eaten only fruit and stale bread for the last two days and his hunger made him think more highly of Venutius' original plan to charge the camp. There must be food in it to feed their army for a week. He thought fondly of Tetra's comfortable house and regretted the summons from Boudicca that had brought him down here. He must be getting old and tired. Someone bumped into him. It was Boudicca.

"They know we're here," she said, her voice ominously flat.

"The Rummies?" he said. Women were able to foresee events hidden to men, and if Boudicca sensed that the Rummies knew of their presence she might very well be right.

"How could they know?" said Venutius, so close by that Atak jumped.

"They've baited a trap for us," said Boudicca. "The Rummies are waiting for us at the foot of the pass."

Venutius snorted. "You can see through rocks?"

"I tell you they're down there. That camp prefect is playing games. If you'd read Caesar you'd know. They act like we're not here while they send for reinforcements."

With a curse, Venutius got up to look over the edge. "I can't see anything," he said.

"We should have attacked right away," said Boudicca.

"By Beli Mawr!" shouted Venutius. "You talked me out of it."

"You're the Arviragus."

By this time, all the kings and generals were milling around in the small area near the ridge. Atak could feel their nervousness and wished Boudicca had not sounded so positive.

"What shall we do?" said Galga.

"By Gorry," said Venutius. "We shall attack like we should have done at first. When we get to the foot of the pass we'll break for the valley and smash through anything waiting for us. Don't stop to fight till we're all out. Then keep after em until we've got em all. I want no more advice and I want no survivors."

***

Atak tried to slow his horse but couldn't. The enormous mass behind him moved at its own pace and nothing the size of his horse could do anything about it. He was in the front ranks of the trotting horsemen and Boudicca very near to him. The black walls of the valley fell away on either side and the decline grew less steep.

If the Romans were waiting in ambush, the noise of the army's advance must have given them plenty of warning. Had they formed a wall or were they flanking either side of the pass? If they had formed a wall they could not be much further away or the widening pass could not be blocked. In either case, to break through a solid wall of legionaries or to survive attack from both flanks, speed was essential. They needed a good run so their momentum would carry them through.

A horseman pushed his way through to them. It was Venutius. "You ready?" he said.

"Aye," said Boudicca.

"Then go. Galga will take the right flank and I'll take the left." Venutius disappeared.

"Blow the horn," said Boudicca, and a dimly seen warrior raised the tall cylinder and blew a great blast. The metal tongue at the top of it clacked horrendously.

With a bloodcurdling scream, Boudicca kicked her horse into a gallop and Atak roared as he followed. Behind them, bedlam broke out as the horses plunged forward. The air was filled with hubbubs, the rattling of hooves against stone and the din of trumpets. It was an impressive noise and Atak could imagine the legionaries ahead sweating with fear as they grimly held their lances at the ready.

Atak also sweated with fear. A collision with a rock or a misstep and he would be under the hooves thundering along behind. He closed his mind to the thought and squinted ahead, trying to pick up any indication of the Rummy disposition. He drew his long British sword and held it close to the horse's side wishing he still had his short but tougher Roman sword.

The pass leveled out and they found themselves in the valley, traveling at high speed. The rough trail bent to the right to join the road that led past the camp to Brecon, and the mass of horsemen swept around the curve, close on Atak's heels. Another mile and they would be at the camp. He could see the faint glow from its lanterns and fires. "There were no Rummies," he shouted at Boudicca. "We should stop."

"I know," she screamed. "Where's the trumpeter?"

"I dropped me trumpet."

"Then scream, you fools. Tell em to stop."

Atak shouted as loud as he could, as did Boudicca and the others nearby, but the horsemen behind must have thought they were being urged on. The noise got louder and the pace increased.

"We'll have to attack the camp," screamed Boudicca.

"I hope they remember there's a ditch and a berm."

"Try to fan out when we get close so they can see it."

Ahead of them, the outline of the camp rapidly grew visible as fires stirred into life, lamps began to move and legionaries scurried around preparing its defense.

The tower guarding the closest corner of the camp came into view and Atak swung to his left while Boudicca headed down the road past the camp gate. He could sense the men fan out behind him and there was a sudden flurry of yells as the first horsemen plunged into the ditch and drove their animals up the berm, lances thudding into them thrown by the legionaries in the tower and behind the berm. He turned his horse into the ditch and scrambled toward the top as the viciously twisted head of a lance glanced off his thigh.

White faces of legionaries were suddenly in front of him and he hurled his horse at them, chopping with his sword as he burst into the camp. All around him, horsemen plunged through and among the tents, hacked at legionaries, screamed at the top of their voices. A dense knot of legionaries drove down on them, chopping, chopping, chopping; going down under the overwhelming number of Britons. Horses near him reared, shrieked and fell, hamstrung or disemboweled by vicious Roman swords. His mind screamed fear and bloodlust as he drove sword or hooves into anything that blocked his path.

There was pain in his legs and he wondered blindly why he hurt. His legs and the side of the horse were sticky. Then he was in the square, around which bonfires blazed and horsemen wildly pranced. His horse came to a halt by itself and he saw there were bodies under its hooves. Slowly, everything ground to a halt. His hand and arm trembled uncontrollably and he had to lay the sword across his thighs so he wouldn't shame himself by dropping it. His legs throbbed with pain and he was afraid to look at them. A great hush fell over the camp, broken only by the crackling of the bonfires, the shuffling of a few tired hooves and the ocean-like hiss of breath from winded and wounded men and beasts. It seemed an age before movement broke the stillness, an age in which his mind ceased to function and he sat staring at a bonfire without seeing it. Then a horseman pushed through to the center of the square and raised a sword. "And so shall all bloody Romans die!" she said, and only after the Britons cheered did he realize it was Boudicca.

For the first few days after the battle Atak could barely move. He lay on his back in a repaired Roman tent and listened to the cold wind and rain pound its leather sides. The cuts in both thighs and his right calf had been deep and he had lost a lot of blood. The Druid told him cheerfully he would limp forever. Two weeks after the battle his legs felt like tree trunks, encased as they were in Druid herbs and linen, but now he could hobble about and help repair some of the damaged chariots.

The Roman strength in the camp when they attacked had been several hundred legionaries and Thracian auxiliaries. Their dead had been buried along with the British dead. Most of the tents had been slashed to ribbons or ridden into the ground. Debris lay in piles and much of it had belonged to the Britons. Thirty or forty wounded Britons had been left to recover in the camp, and a hundred British warriors had been left behind to protect them.

Wagons had been loaded with food and drink and taken with the army, but plenty of it remained behind for the wounded and their protectors. When the cold rain fell too heavily for them to work on the chariots he would sit in his tent with the others and drink mead while they wondered out loud what great battles were being fought to the east. Then one day Cruker rode into the camp. He stood in the doorway of Atak's tent, water streaming from him and blowing in around him.

"Can you ride a four legger?" said Cruker to Atak.

"We can all ride," said one of the wounded.

Atak put a cup of mead into Cruker's hands. "What happened?"

Cruker squatted. "The Rummies sent two cohorts quick marching from Usk right into us," he said. "We laid low in the trees and split em in four pieces. Ate em one at a time. No survivors."

Atak whistled. "That means the Twentieth's lost a third of its men. Any sign of King Guderius?"

"He's up the Wye eating fortlets. He's to join us tomorrow."

"Is King Venutius going to attack Gleuum[20]?"

Cruker downed the rest of his mead. "That's why Queen Boudicca sent me. She wants every wounded that can swing a sword or push on a lance. She said if need be we was to bring you in a chariot."

"I can ride," said Atak.

"So can we," said the other wounded.

Cruker stood up. "We'd better go," he said. "She said waste no time because the Rummies sent to Wroxeter for help."

***

It was midday and the rain had stopped. A weak sun, low in the sky, peeked through hazy spaces between the clouds and made everything sparkle. A light mist rose from Severn, along the west bank of which Venutius' battered army rested. Atak pulled on his beard when told the British losses. The Twentieth had lost a third of their men but the Britons had lost five for every Rummy. Without armor or lances that could defeat Rummy armor the Britons had only their long iron swords and flimsy shields, their hot tempers and sheer weight of numbers with which to break up dense Rummy formations. A ratio of two or three Britons to each Roman was usual, five to one unacceptably high. They could not think of attacking before Guderius arrived.

"Where's King Guderius?" he asked.

"Should be here by nightfall," said Venutius.

The Roman camp was to the south of them and Atak set off across the river to survey it with Venutius and Boudicca. His stiff legs stuck out at an angle from each side of his horse and yawed uncomfortably when he rode. Boudicca and Venutius and the guards bearing Pendragon and the war horns kept their distance so they wouldn't collide with one of his legs. "It's been well sited," said Atak as it came into view.

"Granted," said Venutius. "What's the best way to get at em?"

Atak scratched his hips and stomach. They itched from the herbs and wrappings. The fort had been sited on the east bank of the Severn. The river marsh came up to its walls making it difficult to attack from that direction. A road ran through the middle of it from north to south and another road came out of the eastern wall so three gates gave access to the fort. Sturdy wooden towers at each corner protected the palisades.

Unlike the temporary camp they had just destroyed, this looked permanent with its heavy timbered buildings, deeper ditches and heavier ramparts. Artillery would be behind the ramparts ready to heave rocks on an army massing for assault. At regular intervals he could see ballista set to pour an enfilading fire of iron bolts on invaders struggling up the glacis from the ditch beneath. A line of legionaries around the rampart faced the river, and behind would be reserves: three or four cohorts and what was left of the Thracian auxiliary. This would not be an easy nut to crack, even though the Britons yelling insults across the river at the imperturbable Rummies might think so. "You have scouts out?" he asked.

"Of course."

"If the Rummies think we're all that's against em," said Boudicca, "maybe they'll come out. Then we can make a run for Guderius and trap em."

Atak shook his head. "They'd be fools to come out. We can attack the north gate after nightfall and Guderius can attack the south gate with half his men at the same time. With a few hundred men we can go over the western rampart from the marsh and get the eastern gate open for the other half of Guderius' men."

"You don't think they'll come out then?" said Boudicca.

"Why should they? A fort like that is worth three thousand men. We'll lose a lot but we can stand the losses better than they can."

"I suppose you're right," said Venutius. "But I'd hoped we could get em to come out. Boudicca seems to think we lose less men if they're out in the open."

Was he being sarcastic? Atak thought. By the icy look she gave Venutius Boudicca must have thought so. Sarcasm was the worst form of insult to a Briton. Were these two no longer in love? As if to match Boudicca's darkened face the sun went behind a cloud. It was suddenly gray and cold, and the wind felt wet. Atak shivered. Boudicca raised a hand. "What are they doing?"

A group of legionaries had climbed up on the bridge that had been built over the gate. Under attack, the bridge would be full of defenders firing down into the attackers with lances, arrows and bolts.

"Do they think we'd attack with twenty men?" said Venutius.

The gate opened and a single man walked out and came toward them. The gate closed behind him, but not quickly enough that Atak didn't see the glint of armor behind it. "It's a tribune," he said. "There are men formed up in the square. He might try to get us closer so they can spring a trap."

He looked back at the huge Nazarene banner and Pendragon, telling the Romans that their enemy's commander sat unprotected within easy reach. "We ought to fall back," he said. Nobody answered him and he glanced at Boudicca. Her eyes were fixed on the advancing tribune. Her face seemed unnaturally pale and her lips trembled.

"It's Sabinus," she said, her voice hoarse. "Why is he here?"

Venutius' head jerked around and he reined in his horse with a violent tug, so that the animal reared on its hind legs. "Who is Sabinus?" he said. "How come you know one Rummy from another?"

"He is a friend of Prasu's," said Boudicca.

"You speak as if he is a friend of yours."

"He is a friend. He saved my life and brought word of my father."

"By Beli Mawr," said Venutius, his face contorted with rage, "if you would make friends of a Rummy then I will make a corpse of him." He drew his sword, but Boudicca reached out and grabbed his sword arm with both hands. Atak fretted that he could do nothing to pull them apart and tugged at his beard in frustration. The guards moved to close in around the two struggling royals, but he waved them away. "Keep your eyes on that gate," he said.

"You will not harm him," said Boudicca. "You will listen to what he says." They stayed locked together by Boudicca's grip, eyes flaming, horses slowly circling, until the tribune got within ten paces. Then Venutius yanked his arm from Boudicca's grasp and sheathed his sword with a curse. The tribune halted. He seemed at ease, but his eyes traveled from Boudicca to Venutius as if he were not sure what was about to happen.

"Why are you not at Longthorpe?" said Boudicca.

"I had special duties that brought me here," said the tribune. He spoke familiarly as if from long acquaintanceship. Atak wondered why no one had ever mentioned this Roman. The man was well built and good looking, not much more than Boudicca's age. "More to the point," said the tribune, "why are you not at Thetford with your daughters?"

"A Queen too has special duties."

"That I can understand, but I am grieved to see you again in the field. No good can come of it and I fear for your safety."

"You had better fear for the safety of the legion you are visiting. We intend to destroy it."

"I fear neither for the legion nor myself. I fear for you. Whatever you accomplish here, Rome's vengeance will be terrible and thorough. I beg you to leave at once and go home. I came out because no Roman has yet identified you with this adventure, and if you leave now, none will. You have my word on it."

Venutius urged his horse forward until he was between the tribune and Boudicca. Atak moved his horse closer.

"What is it to you," said Venutius, his harsh voice barely audible, "if this queen be identified or no? You are a foul Rummy, scum of the earth. Now get back to your masters yonder and tell em that the Queen of Iceni is here at the head of her army. Go, or by the great Duw Himself I will strike you down."

The tribune took a step backwards. "If you wish to strike me down," he said, "get off your horse and meet me man to man."

Venutius had his leg halfway over the back of his horse when Atak stopped him with a shout. "The gate's opening," he said.

"By Duw, they're coming out," said Venutius, still halfway off his horse. The gate was now wide open and Thracian cavalry began to move through it. It looked to Atak as if several cohorts were formed up ready to quick march on the cavalry's heels. "You said they wouldn't do it."

"They're doing it," said Atak. "Let's get out of here."

At a signal from Venutius, the great horn blasted and Venutius and his guard galloped for the river crossing. Atak wheeled to gallop after them when he saw that Boudicca had moved next to the tribune and was speaking to him in a low voice. "Get out of here," he shouted.

The tribune waved her away, his face showing as much anxiety as his own, and Boudicca kicked her horse into movement. She galloped alongside Atak but without spirit. Her face seemed set in stone. What was between her and the tribune?

Across the river he looked back. The Romans were nearing the other bank at a rapid pace. Venutius waved at his captains and the disorderly Britons began to lope northward toward Guderius. Then he looked at Boudicca sitting listlessly on her horse and spat on the ground. "Get away with the chariots," he said to her, "and harass those Rummies while I see if they can keep up with Britons."

Boudicca shook her head as if to clear it then raised her sword and rode to the head of her chariots. The trumpets sounded and the mass of chariots surged away to the west as if in full retreat, the Thracian cavalry not far behind them. Atak was about to join them when Venutius stopped him. "Let her be," he said. "She'll lead em a merry chase. In the meantime we'll stay far enough ahead of the Rummies to keep their tongues hanging out until we meet Guderius. But as soon as they're well on their way, you and me will go back and look for that tribune. If I clap my eyes on him he shall not live through this day."

***

Boudicca had never seen Venutius so angry. His lips quivered uncontrollably and she thought he was about to strike her. She had pushed him too far this time and bitterly regretted all the criticisms she had not suppressed. It was her fault and she must bear the blame. Oh Venutius, she thought. Do as I say this once and I will never question your judgment again. But do not do this stupid thing.

Beneath them in the valley were the remains of the Twentieth Legion. Less than three hundred legionaries, many of them wounded, sat on the ground surrounded by thousands of the victorious Britons. In the center their commander and his guards stood erect, still holding the sacred aquila and the legion standards. If she knew aught of Romans, those guards would lay a waste of bodies around them before surrendering what they held.

Venutius had slowly headed the Britons toward the mountain passes and the remaining cohorts of the Twentieth had quick-marched around his left attempting to cut him off when they found themselves trapped as Guderius' army appeared on their flank. Cavalry might have saved them, but her chariots had kept the cavalry engaged on Venutius' rear. It had been sloppy generalship on the part of Manlius Valens, the legion commander, but even as she had exulted with Venutius and Guderius about the victory, she had found herself worrying about Sabinus and hoping he had stayed at the fort. And then Venutius had announced what he was going to do with the defeated legionaries. "They shall pass under the yoke," he said.

The men had cheered and set to work constructing the yoke,

a light tree trunk held horizontal by lances driven into the earth. Only four feet above ground, each legionary would have to stoop to pass beneath it. It was the most degrading form of humiliation feared by Romans, and legions would die to the last man before submitting to it. When he saw what was happening, Atak came lumbering up on his horse. "No," he said, as they helped him off the horse. "Don't do it."

"I will take no advice from you," said Venutius. "By Duw, I am Arviragus and I will decide what shall be done."

Ready as she had been to punish the Rummies, Boudicca had seen immediately what concerned Atak. "Atak is right," she said. "If we pass these men under the yoke, next year there will be six more legions to face. This will not help our cause."

Venutius had almost gone berserk. "You have done nothing but tear me down in front of my men," he shouted, spittle flying from his mouth. "You question every decision I make. Well by Duw you shall not question this one." He had turned from her to Atak, shaking with rage. "And you," he said, "had better decide whom you serve. By Duw, it is bad enough that a queen of Britain makes love with one of their foul tribunes. Will you now desert me also?"

She had almost screamed with rage at the insult, but restrained herself. She had brought this about and must undo it.

"I serve Britain as you well know," Atak had said, folding his arms. "If we defeat enough Rummies they might get discouraged and leave. They'll never leave if you humiliate them."

And now, here they stood immobile: anger, repentance and reason struggling for dominance, the British warriors standing around dismayed that their leaders fought among themselves after such a victory. Venutius could never let reason prevail over his anger after the petty humiliations she of all people had subjected him to. Atak could do nothing. If Britain were to be saved she would have to act.

She unfastened her sword belt and dropped it on the ground. Then she faced the British warriors. "I have been unjust toward our Arviragus," she shouted. "I have criticized decisions he has made and he has turned out to be right and I have been wrong. If I had not counseled him to wait when we were in the mountains, our battle on the Usk would have been over more quickly and at less cost. Now he has won this great victory over the Twentieth legion and has proved himself a great Arviragus. I honor him and in penance for my sins against him I pass myself beneath that yoke and ask his pardon."

She stripped the cloak and tunic from herself and strode forward, breasts bare to the cold wind, the warriors backing away to let her pass. She stooped and passed beneath the yoke, walked back to Venutius and crouched at his feet. "Forgive me for all I have said and done against your honor," she said. "Grant me this one request and I will be ever your true wife and loyal servant."

Venutius bent forward, tears streaming down his face, and raised her up. He clasped her to him and kissed her as the warriors cheered. "Get thee dressed," he said. As she pulled on her clothes he turned to the warriors. "These foul Rummies have been taught a lesson they will long remember," he shouted. "Now let them crawl home to their governor and tell him what it is like to face a British army."

There were groans of disappointment from those who had looked forward to seeing their enemy humiliated, but a wide avenue gradually opened up between the Romans and safety. For a while, the legionaries did not react, but as the significance of the Britons' movement made itself plain they formed up and marched out of the valley carrying their wounded.

Chapter 9

Owain Comes Home

The ship heeled under a great blast of icy sleet laced wind, and Owain held shivering to the cordage surrounding the creaking mast. He had refused to stay below and so that he wouldn't be washed overboard a sailor had wrapped a line around him and tied it to the mast. His hands were so cold he could no longer feel them, and the gray tunic that Zachaeus had given him was wet through from the sleet and spray. His crimson robe would have kept him warmer but it now doubtless protected the muscular brigand who had held him by the ankles and threatened to drop him off the high cliff at Rocamadour unless he surrendered it and his hat and gold chain. Every once in a while he would look uncomprehendingly at his drab gray tunic. The accouterments he had lost were not only protection from the weather but his true identity. He was no longer a high ranking Druid but a simple plebeian in a workman's tunic. He found it difficult to comprehend how he must look to others.

At Paul's request he had sought out Zachaeus at Rocamadour to give him Paul's scroll. He had stayed more than a week in Zachaeus' cave on the high rocky plateau, watching as Zachaeus healed the scores who sought him out. So inspired had he become that he had agreed to let Zachaeus baptize him a Christian, as circumcision was no longer required of Christian men.

Unlike Paul, whose mind darted in many directions at once, often confusing his listeners, Zachaeus was direct and to the point. "Clear your mind of trash," he said. "Get rid of the jealousies and resentments and ambitions that cloud the mind. God is perfect indiscriminate love and we must image that perfection and nothing else. As we let God's love govern us we begin to see and speak with authority as the Master did. Sickness and evil cannot stand in the presence of the love and power of God that we image. The Master said we would do greater works than he did as we follow his way and destroy the carnal mind and its works. This is God's truth, the Christ, and this is what makes us free."

There was no longer any doubt in Owain's mind about the power of the Christ. The many philosophies he had studied, including his own Druidic philosophy, provoked admiration for the intellectual arguments employed but provided no means for verifying the truth of what was contended. If the Christ was truth, and the power it gave to heal verified its truth, then the Druid goal, which was to seek truth, had been met. What was needed now was to properly organize the thousands of converts flocking to Christianity. Apart from missionaries wandering aimlessly around (which seemed to be Paul's preferred method) and a few bishops setting up competitive fiefdoms there seemed to be no hierarchy of leadership, no system of dress as in the Druid order. Without proper accouterments it was not possible to determine the status of whom one encountered, and without such knowledge how could leadership be enforced?

He pondered much during his stay in Rocamadour on how he could best help get these people organized. Should he do it as a simple Christian or as a high-ranking Druid? Druid discipline could bring the Christ truth to others in an organized way but he had to admit Druidism was a little overpowering to the simple, such as those who flocked to Paul and Zachaeus. He had almost made up his mind to become a simple Christian organizer during a solitary walk one morning when he met the brigands who robbed him. His first reaction had been rage, especially when Zachaeus tried to soothe him by saying that all things would work together for good if he loved God supremely.

After he had calmed down and Zachaeus had found this drab tunic for him, he decided that he could best serve Christ as a Druid. He would return to Britain as quickly as possible and obtain the clothes that would restore his dignity. His service to Christianity would be enhanced if he brought to it the prestige of a Pencerdd Druid and High Council member. He left Zachaeus with a promise to keep him posted on the progress of organized Christianity in Britain, hurried to Morlaix and bought passage on a trade ship.

The captain, whom he sensed suspected that Owain was not the simple plebeian he appeared to be, had warned him that the wintertime crossing would be rough and even perilous, but thinking often of Morfudd's promise to wait for him at the inn at Marazion he would let nothing delay his return. Now, as the ship heeled so much he had difficulty standing even while holding on to the mast, he wondered if it might not have been wiser to wait. When the ship's bow pitched down into the wave's trough and the little triangular patch of leather sail attached to the foremast momentarily ceased to block his vision, the shore loomed grimly through the driving scud. The constant flashes of white he knew were waves breaking on rocks.

It seemed as if they were being driven remorselessly onto them, and that nothing could prevent their being dashed to pieces. Fear welled up in him, and then a picture of Paul holding his bushy hair in both hands came into his mind. Use the sword of the Spirit, he heard Paul say. Put off the old man and put on the dominion that God gave you. The Kingdom is within. Trust God.

As he clung to the mast he got the eerie feeling that the ship was about to do a cartwheel. He closed his eyes grimly and prayed Thy Kingdom come. So lost did he become in his prayer that he barely noticed the ship's motion had eased. A rough hand untied the line around his waist. The wind had softened and the flying scud had turned into an erratic drizzle. The ship had lost its heel and pitched ponderously in the following sea as it passed an island to its right.

"That be Ictis[21]," said the sailor who had untied him. "Thought we'd never get in the lee, but we be tying up before long."

He went to the side of the ship to be out of the way of the sailors. The sailors acted as if everything was normal and he felt a pang of disappointment. He had half hoped they would see that his prayers had brought them home safely. He could see the ship was now in the bay of Marazion and through the gloomy drizzle he could spot the wooden pilings of the wharf in the distance. The wind had become fluky, causing the little storm sail to flap noisily, and the sailors took down the sail and put out two large sweeps. The ship steadied and he went below for his travel bag as the ship slowly approached the wharf. After four days on this wretched vessel, sleeping on rough slimy planks and unable to wash thoroughly or change his clothes, he longed to get to the inn where he could bathe before meeting Morfudd.

Several figures and some horsemen stood on the wharf and he wondered if Morfudd were one of them. They were wrapped up against the weather but as near as he could tell all were males. Other passengers came on deck as the ship hit the wharf with a heavy thump and the sailors leaped overside to fasten the vessel in place with lines. His heart pounded at the thought of Morfudd being so close. He knew he could not be his natural self for a while because of her misadventures with Bodin but if she were to completely surrender he would quickly relent. Tomorrow, he would ask to be taken to King Tenvantius, who would give him clothes befitting his rank and have he and Morfudd escorted to Mona.

A rough plank was hoisted against the ship's side and Owain walked toward it. Before he could get to it several of the men who had been standing on the wharf ran up it onto the ship. They were unusually short and dwarflike and he gasped indignantly when one of them, a lout with an evil face, seized his arms and peered up into his face.

"Get your hands off me," said Owain, bitterly regretting the gray tunic that concealed his true identity. They would not have dared touch him if he had been wearing the robe of a Council member. The man let go of him with a curse and with another dwarf grabbed other passengers and scrutinized them. A struggle began, but fortunately the captain had his sailors seize the men.

"What's going on?" said the captain.

"You got a Druid on board, capting?" said the dwarf who had grabbed Owain. The captain gave a quick glance at Owain, and Owain was about to announce his identity when something restrained him. These louts could have no business with Druids.

"Why do you people keep looking for Druids?" said the captain. "This is the fifth time you've come aboard my ship."

"You sure there aren't none, capting?"

"There are none. Now get off before I have my men throw you into the bay."

The small louts walked off the ship and crossed the wharf to join the waiting horsemen, louts like themselves. They jumped on their horses and disappeared into the trees. Where had he seen or heard of little louts like that before? The Gunes of Merrimar! He had heard that it was they who had waylaid Venutius. Why were they looking for a Druid? What possible connection could they have with the Druids?

Almost immediately he thought of Bodin, the only Druid capable of hiring such trash. But why would Bodin have the Gunes meet ships and look for Druids? As far as he knew, he was the only Druid out of the country. Had Bodin hired these men to kill him? With a shudder he walked up the narrow dirt road to the inn. He looked constantly over his shoulder and around each building, but the Gunes seemed to have gone. Thank God he wore a drab gray tunic and not his crimson robe. If he had worn his robe he might be dead now. He wondered what Morfudd would have to say about it. She had said she would have every ship watched but she must have missed this one. No matter, he thought, I will bathe and send for clean clothes before I let her know I've arrived.

Later that night, clean, refreshed and dressed in a newly laundered linen tunic, he asked the innkeeper about Morfudd and received a blank look. No Druidess had ever stayed at his inn. Was this her watch—to have the Gunes lie in wait for him? Was she still working for Bodin?

Chapter 10

Scapula Reports

To Tiberius Claudius Drusus Caesar Augustus Germanicus, Emperor, High Pontiff, Consul and Protector of the People.

Written from the oppidum of Queen Cartimandua at Barwick, in the heart of the Brigante nation.

Hail Caesar!

In response to your command, here is a summary of each legion's status and a report on the defeat of the Twentieth legion. Let me say at the outset that the root cause of all problems is the way in which my direction has been undermined by insubordination and incompetency and also by your own directions to keep Vespasian's Second Augusta up to full strength at whatever cost to the other legions.

I understand your desire to bring the western peninsula under control, but Vespasian couldn't do it and the weakening of the other legions (Vespasian always insists on having the best veterans and equipment) has made our task in the north more difficult. I have spent several weeks of hard labor here getting the Brigantes under control and I cannot rely on my commanders to take the right kind of initiative in my absence. I know you will pay no account to the slanderous rumors circulated against me by those jealous of my leadership.

The Second is at full strength in winter quarters at its new fort (which is not of regulation size) on the river Brit. Flavius Vespasian has only built fourteen forts and I'm told they are not even spaced correctly! He pulled back to the river Brit because (he says) it is more defensible (I hope his non-regulation fort holds up!). He would show more promise as a legion commander if he were placed under my direction so that I can make sure he at least builds and locates forts correctly. I have recommended this before, but now that our position has been weakened by his constant demands for reinforcement I hope you will agree I have been right all along and make him my subordinate.

The Ninth legion is at three quarter strength and is mostly in winter quarters at Longthorpe (I have two cohorts from the Ninth here at Barwick during my negotiations with Queen Cartimandua). The legion has not built as many forts and fortlets as would have been the case without Vespasian's constant demands for manpower. The Druids have stirred up unrest and I have ordered my legions to extirpate them. There have been problems among the legionaries of the Ninth themselves. Several, including four senior centurions, deserted to join this Nazarene sect that I have also given orders to extirpate. Caesius Nasica tells me this sect is no longer active in his area, but he has made such statements before and if he cannot build his proper quota of forts I do not trust him. It is time to think seriously about replacing all the commanders and I have attached names of senators who would be fully supportive of me so we could bring this war to a speedy conclusion. Without such steps, I cannot assure you that our objectives will be attained.

The Fourteenth legion is at half strength and is in winter quarters at Viroconium[22]. Of all the legions, this is the best even though it has been sadly reduced in effectiveness by the constant demands of Vespasian. It has built over a hundred forts and fortlets, which is twice more than all the other legions put together, and each is built to regulation and at the correct distance from each other. I spent two months pacing off these structures so I can assure you each is where it should be.

The Twentieth's fort at Gleuum[23] having been destroyed it has returned to winter quarters in Verulamium. Most of the survivors are still recovering from wounds suffered in a battle with more than two hundred and fifty thousand barbarians. Manlius Valens foolishly left the security of the Gleuum fort to attack a small army across the Severn. The barbarians fled so slowly that he was able to force-march ahead of them and was about to surround them when he found himself flanked by a large army concealed in the forest. It was a gross tactical error on the part of Manlius Valens, but it does not surprise me.

Valens has resisted every effort on my part to get him to properly train his men. Early last year his men built a fort near the Usk that was over a quarter of a mile further from the next fort than it should be. His feeble excuse was that the fort would be subject to flooding if located according to regulations. It took three months to get him to move it to its proper location and since then he has not ceased to complain that it is underwater most of the time. It is easy to see how the barbarians would hold his legion in contempt and seek to destroy it. Of all my commanders, he is the least competent and the most likely to spread vicious rumors. I urge his recall with the utmost expedition.

With my legions brought up to strength, plus the two additional ones I requested, and with new commanders, the campaign this year will be decisive.

Salutations from your right arm in Britain!
Long live Caesar!
Publius Ostorius Scapula
Legatus Augusti Pro Praetore

Chapter 11

Coilus

Still filled with remorse over the way she had pecked at Venutius, Boudicca's heart swelled with love at the way he had accepted her repentance and backed away from his foolish plan to humiliate the Rummies and thus bring down the full wrath of Rome on their heads. She would never criticize him again, even if she did see more clearly what needed to be done. "I cannot go back to Prasu," she said. "We'll live as husband and wife should. We have never had time to be alone together." Venutius beamed.

"I have never seen the land your father gave me when he made me a lord," said Atak.

"Then we'll go there and forget this ceaseless war."

For two days and nights the little party struggled up through the mountain passes. The cold rain and sleet turned to snow and at night they could barely stay warm in their tents. At last they emerged into the small valley that Caratacus had given Atak. It had stopped snowing and it was possible to see the lake and even parts of the other side. Atak looked at it and pulled his beard. The winter rains had swollen the lake so that it surrounded the small stone house.

"It's not deep," said Venutius, splashing around in the hall. "Let's get some fire then we can warm our innards and outtards."

The guards soon had a roaring fire going but she would let none of them stand around it. The piles of moldy skins on which they would have to sleep had to be shaken out and held before the fire to dry. Firewood had to be chopped and stacked, logs brought in to sit on, the red earthenware and iron pots washed and the rations sorted. When they had eaten she would send to Caer Leon for servants, and Atak and Venutius would go out to hunt for fresh meat. She felt like a housewife but it made her happy.

From now on Venutius would be her lord and master and she would exist only to please him. This little home, rough as it was, would be their heaven and they would stay here for a year, true wife and true husband. She had found a platform for them above the hall, and the straw was clean and the skins aired. Never before had she felt she wanted him so much as on this night. They had made love in the tent, but it had been so cold their movements had seemed arthritic. After they had all sat around the fire for a while, drinking wine mixed with honey and singing the songs that soldiers loved to sing, she took Venutius to bed on the platform, pulled his head to her breast and locked her long legs around him until he gasped for mercy. She would never let him go. She had made up her mind to become pregnant again, to give Venutius a son of their very own. He was her true husband, her true love, the only man she could ever give herself to without restraint. But someday, she promised herself, she and not Venutius would be Arviragus. Much as she loved him, his vision was neither broad nor focused enough to comprehend what was needed to get the Rummies off British soil. In time, with a little encouragement from her, he would yield his title.

Atak and Cruker soon left with their men, homesick for their own fires, but Boudicca and Venutius passed the winter there, fishing, hunting, taking long walks, fighting in the snow, making love. It was idyllic, but as spring approached and it became obvious she was pregnant, the old itch began to surface. They had grown too used to war and the Rummies had been left in peace for too long. She found herself growing irritable with Venutius, finding little faults in what he did or didn't do so that he became irritable also.

One day, after Venutius had stormed out in a pet to go hunting, there was a pounding at the door and in walked Elsa, Goronwy the ex-Druid bard and Sabinus. Sabinus was dressed in a plain tunic and looked almost like a Briton. "I have left the army," he said in response to her look. "I've been invited to join Joseph's colony."

"King Venutius is out hunting," she said, trying as best she could to convey a warning. If Venutius caught Sabinus here he would kill him. She had tried to explain their friendship to him, but Venutius was insanely jealous of the Roman. She must get rid of her visitors before he came back.

"I fear King Venutius does not feel kindly toward me," said Sabinus, smiling. He took her hand in his and pressed it.

"He has good cause not to love Romans," she said. "But some day he will recognize those who would be our friends."

"Lord Sabinus is not only our friend," said Goronwy, "he has become a Nazarene like us, a Christian as we are now being called."

She laughed. "You mean an Arimathean Christian," she said. "You will have to distinguish among those who call themselves such for political reasons and those who truly believe."

"Rather," said Elsa, "we must distinguish among those who love the Christ and those who are enemies of it."

She bristled. "You would class me an enemy of Christ?"

"You bear Lord Bodin's banner. He burns in the name of Christ."

She bit her lip. Bodin, aggressive and ruthless, had persuaded the Council to call all Britons Nazarenes, and to declare Joseph's people subject to punishment, but this was the first she had heard of burnings.

"The banner I carry," she said, "is not Lord Bodin's but the Council's. I carry it because that is the policy of Britain. If Bodin burns Britons he desecrates himself and Council both, for burning is not the policy of Britain."

"The banner you carry desecrates the Christ that gave you back your daughter. Christ is the way to peace and that banner is for war. I beg you will burn it and cease to call your soldiers Nazarenes. To call them such dishonors Christ."

Even as the anger at Elsa's words boiled up within her, she knew Elsa was right. The banner and the name did nothing for Britain, and what Elsa was and could do showed the presence of a power that was greater than she or any king could wield. The banner had simply been something to rally around. Now she saw its dishonesty. It polluted not only Elsa's Christ but her own armies and leadership. If they were to defeat Rome they would do it with unsullied weapons. She drew the ruby encrusted sword that Bodin had given her, put her foot against its blade and bent it into uselessness. Then she flung it into the firepit. "I will burn the banner," she said, "and no more call my warriors Nazarene."

Elsa came to her and went down on her knees to kiss her hands. "You are no enemy of Christ," she said. "Because your heart is true you will not let evil become the policy of this state."

"I will speak with Lord Owain when he returns from Rome," she said. "He and I will bring it before the Council."

"I beg you to do more than that. The Merrimar Gunes captured Dedreth and they tried to get her to renounce Joseph. She was almost burned. The Gunes are in Bodin's pay."

"She is all right?"

Elsa nodded reassuringly and she felt a flood of relief. "She is at your father's palace in Caer Leon."

"She disappeared on her way back from Thetford," said Goronwy. "The Gunes took her to Brigante. She was chained to a tree waiting her turn to be burned when the Gunes were surprised by a Roman patrol and fled into the forest."

She wondered what the Rummies were doing in Brigante while her anger at Bodin simmered. Cartimandua had a treaty that kept them out of her borders. Had she invited them in again? Why? "Is Marius with her?" she asked.

"King Marius is still in Hibernia looking for Prince Brennius," said Goronwy. "One of our bards told her how to break the chains and got them both away before the Gunes came back."

A picture flashed through Boudicca's mind: Ingenius showing her the chains he had made for Catus. "She broke the fifth link," she said, and Goronwy beamed in surprise.

"All British chains are made that way," he said.

If that had been a proper chain, she thought, Dedreth might be dead. But what were Rummies doing in Brigante? There was a noise and she turned. It was Venutius. His hand was on his sword and he glared at Sabinus. Before she could say anything Elsa stepped past her and seized Venutius' hand, lifting it from the sword. "Lord Sabinus has left the army," said Elsa. "He is now a Christian and has come with us to tell you that the Lady Dedreth is in Caer Leon. She was almost killed by the Merrimar Gunes."

There was a long pause while Venutius looked from Elsa to Boudicca, and from Boudicca to Sabinus. At last, his eyes came back to Elsa's. "They almost killed me once," he said. "It is time to be rid of them."

Thank you Duw, she thought. And thank you Elsa, for you must have prayed the hate out of him. She went up to him and kissed him. He was stiff but he did not push her away. "We must send for her," she said.

"This house is over full with Christians."

Sabinus bowed. "We will leave immediately."

She opened her mouth to protest but forced herself to shut it again. It was enough that Venutius had not attacked Sabinus. She would push him no further.

***

It was a bright summer's day when Coilus was born in Atak's house by the lake. Dedreth and the woman servant helped with the birth, and Dedreth wrapped Boudicca's new son in linen and placed him in her arms so that Venutius could come in and admire them both. It had been an easy birth, and the tears she shed when Venutius kissed them both were for joy. "I have given you a son," she said.

"He has your hair," said Venutius, running his finger through the light red wisps on Coilus' head. "And your eyes and nose. By Duw, his eyes are fiercer than yours and he has yet to see his first Rummy."

"He shall be a greater king than you or I."

Venutius shook his head gloomily. "He will never be a king," he said.

"I tell you he will," said Boudicca. "We shall foster him to Dedreth and Marius when they are married. When Prasu dies and I am High Queen, you shall divorce Cartimandua and marry me. By that time the Rummies will be off this land and all the southern nations shall become one kingdom. Our son shall rule it."

"By Duw Himself, you have grand ambitions."

"Sabinus told Dedreth the Rummies are discouraged since we defeated the Twentieth. The Germans defeated three legions at Paderborn and the Rummies have never invaded them since. If we can defeat two more they will go home. We have destroyed the Twentieth and by Duw we can do it again. We shall do it for Coilus."

Dedreth sat down by her side and placed a hand on Boudicca's arm. "Before you make your son King of all Britain," she said, "will you not first make him a Christian?"

Boudicca looked down at the little wizened face at her breast. Coilus' eyes were open but he stared off into the distance as if pondering his future. That little unformed nose with its high bridge, was not that her grandfather's nose? It would grow into a great hooked beak dividing those clear ice blue eyes that would see into the trembling soul of all who stood before him. Yes, he must be a Christian. Grandfather Cunobelinus, who had invited the first Nazarenes into Britain, would have wished it. "Send for Elsa," she said. "I will have none else baptize him."

When Elsa came to baptize Coilus, she brought with her Goronwy and he told them the news that had just been brought to Caer Leon. "The Council of Kings and Druids elected Doderin Archdruid," he said. "The Council feared Bodin's faction would secede if they elected Owain and Owain's supporters would leave if they elected Bodin."

"Poor Owain," said Boudicca. Owain wanted to be Archdruid as much as she wanted to be Arviragus.

"And Scapula is dead," said Goronwy, as they walked toward the shore of the lake where Coilus was to be immersed. "That Rummy patrol that Logan and Dedreth saw in Brigante were Praetorian Guards. They were sent to Cartimandua's fort to order him to commit suicide. They brought a ceremonial dagger for him to do it with."

"And he did it right there?" said Venutius.

"Well, no. He offered to cut himself off from Rome, declare himself Emperor of Britain and marry Cartimandua if she would have the praetorians killed and divorce you. Cartimandua agreed on condition she became Empress and got control of the legions, but a Briton called Velocatus was there and killed him with the dagger."

"By Duw, then Caratacus was right," said Venutius. "What did they do to Velocatus?

"Nothing," said Goronwy. "The Rummies thought Scapula killed himself. They gave him a state funeral in Colchester. The new Governor is to be Didius Gallus."

"And what did Cartie do to Velocatus?" said Venutius.

"Well," said Goronwy, embarrassed. "It appears he was Cartimandua's lover and killed Scapula out of jealousy. Then he threatened to have her kings throw her off her throne. To pacify him she called her council together and told it to declare her divorced. She said she will marry Velocatus after the divorce is complete."

Boudicca clutched Coilus to her. She could feel the heat rise within Venutius like molten lava. Divorced, he would no longer be a High King and thus could not be Arviragus of Britain. He stopped dead in his tracks. "Marry him? He was my man at arms."

"Her kings will never let her degrade her throne like that," said Boudicca. "They will depose her first."

"They will not have the chance," roared Venutius. "For I will kill her." He would have turned to leave but Boudicca stopped him.

"You will go nowhere," she said, "until we have reasoned out what to do." He stood rigid, eyes glazed with anger and venom. "We will not jeopardize Coilus' future kingdoms to avenge something that will most likely come to nothing. She has lost her chance to become Queen of all Britain and can take Velocatus to her bed without divorcing you or marrying him. Much as I hate her, she is not stupid."

He was silent a long time. Then he said "Aye. You are right."

Her heart warmed to him as she handed Coilus to Elsa. Her hothead was learning patience. But someday she and not he would be Arviragus and he must be brought to admit it. Much as she loved him he was not the one to prepare the way for Coilus.

Chapter 12

The Loan

"He must be wealthy indeed," said Boudicca. She stood at the gate to Ingenius' impressive house in Colchester, Venutius at her side. It was after midnight and only one window was dimly illuminated. A stone lantern burned near the door to the house, and in its faint light she could see a covered chair such as high Roman officials used. Their own guards waited down the street, and there was no sign of life around the house. "Let's get him up," she said at last and went to the door.

It took much knocking but finally the door creaked open to reveal Friggit, Cunobelinus' old steward. Ingenius must have taken him into his service. "Whisht my lady," said Friggit when he recognized her. "There's Rummies here."

"This late?" she said. "Is Ingenius with them?"

"No," said Friggit, waving them in. "They be asleep and he is in his own room. Come quick and quiet."

He tiptoed through a hall barely illuminated by dim candles, opened a door and ushered them into a room that was a little better lit. Friggit pounded on the tile floor with his pole.

A figure reclining on a couch sat up violently, hands pressed to his temples. "Stop it," he shouted. It was Ingenius. Friggit stopped pounding. "Who is it?" asked Ingenius.

Friggit lifted his pole up and down as if he were banging it on the floor. "Queen Boudicca and King Venutius," he said.

As if with enormous effort, Ingenius stood up. A servant girl who had been lying with him also stood and grabbed his arm. "Let go," he muttered irritably. She let go and went behind the couch.

Boudicca walked up to him. "Are you all right?" she asked.

"I would bend a knee," he said, "but I cannot."

"We've come at a bad time," said Venutius.

"No," said Ingenius. "I have a headache."

"Too much wine," said Boudicca. "Your face is blotchy and puffed up." She sat down on the couch and Ingenius sat by her while Venutius remained standing.

"I don't believe I drink that much," said Ingenius. "These headaches have been getting worse. It is so good to see you both again. When you disappeared, I wondered if you were together."

"I'm sure many people wondered that," said Boudicca. "Since we destroyed the Twentieth the Rummies have barely stirred. Our armies have mostly disbanded and gone home. Yes, we were and are together. I have left Prasu."

"And your daughters?"

"Goneril and Gwenda will join us when Prasu dies." Which, she thought, won't be long from what I hear.

The servant girl came from behind the couch and picked up the cup and amphora.

"Leave it," said Venutius. "I will have some wine."

"I will get fresh," said the girl. She began to walk away with the amphora and cup.

"Leave the wine, Regan," said Ingenius. "Bring more cups. Can I offer you food?" Boudicca shook her head. Regan put the amphora and cup back on the table and walked quickly out of the room.

"What about you?" said Boudicca. "We hear you're very close to the new Governor."

"He's asleep in the dining hall," said Ingenius. "He comes here to meet Britons who like to game."

"You should get married again," said Boudicca. "You'll lead a less dissolute life." She held up a hand for Venutius to grasp.

"I almost did," said Ingenius. "I was betrothed to Morfudd the Druidess but it didn't work out."

"Morfudd?" echoed Boudicca. She remembered the good-looking Ovate who had brought the flag and sword to Marius. "I thought she belonged to Lord Bodin."

Ingenius flushed. He had thought, when Bodin didn't get the Archdruid post he had schemed for, that Morfudd would never go back to him. It had been a crippling blow to lose her and he still cringed at the memory of it. He must have spent a small fortune showing her off to influential Romans. She had lulled him with flattery and promises until she had milked all his reserves. Then she had repaid him by going back to the former lover who, she told him earlier, had mistreated and frightened her almost to death. It had been a long time before he could face the pitying smiles of his friends. The thought of her duplicity still made him angry. But even in his anger he could still feel her in his arms, still smell and taste her body, still want her even though he knew she would make his life miserable. "She left Bodin but then went back to him," he said. "I'm glad to see you and King Venutius together, but I know there must be complications."

"There are complications," said Boudicca. "We now have a son to care for. We need your help."

"Is his name to be known?"

"His name is Coilus Galahad," said Boudicca. "Dedreth was with us at the birth. And Joseph of Arimathea and his son Galaad."

"You have joined the heretics?"

"No. We serve the Council's Nazarene church for Britain's sake. But we had Coilus baptized by Elsa for his sake. She has gone back to the mountains with Galaad and Goronwy. Joseph's eldest son Josephes and his wife have also gone with them."

Ingenius looked pained. Boudicca sensed the question in

his mind. "Galaad and Elsa are not as Venutius and me," she said. "They are beyond the demands of the flesh."

Ingenius flushed. "And Atak?" he said.

"Atak has settled down with Elsa's mother in Mona. But he spends a lot of time with us. Scapula brought in some of his old German Chatti warriors before he got killed and Atak convinced them to join our side and made a cavalry troop out of them."

"Where is that servant girl?" said Venutius, picking up the amphora. "I would drink Coilus' health." He filled Ingenius' cup with wine. "To Coilus. May he be a better king than his father."

Ingenius got up and shouted for Regan, while Venutius drank and then held the cup for Boudicca to drink from. "We will not ask you to join us," she said, "since it has made your head ache." She sipped and made a face. "Your wine tastes a little strange." Venutius refilled the cup and she took another sip. "We need a large sum of money. It will be a loan, not a gift. We have just found out my brother Marius is held hostage in Hibernia with my nephew Brennius, who is king now that Elidurus is dead, and we must have the money to free them."

There was a noise at the door and it was a servant. Regan was nowhere to be found. "Then fetch us more cups," said Ingenius.

"Marius is to marry Dedreth," said Boudicca. "They will foster Coilus."

"I thought Dedreth and King Marius were enemies."

"They were. Now they obviously are not."

Ingenius sat silent and her anger began to rise. She had not expected him to simply hand her the money but he seemed to be weighing whether or not he should lend it at all.

Venutius shared another drink of wine with her and refilled the cup. Then he stood before Ingenius. "I can't repay you," said Venutius. "But you will be repaid."

Ingenius started then blushed. He must have read their thoughts. "How much do you need?"

"Twenty million in gold," said Boudicca.

There was a dead silence. He smiled, but it was a hollow forced smile. "When must you have it?"

"Now," said Boudicca. "As you well know I have sufficient resources to repay you. I'm sure you can imagine, though, why I can't at present claim what is mine. Marius, once he is freed, will repay you."

"I have no fears about repayment," said Ingenius. "But what wealth I have left is tied up with Catus' and Seneca's in trade goods and buildings. I will have to borrow and it will take time to raise the money."

"There is no time," she said. "You must have the money in Hibernia in two weeks or Marius and Brennius will die."

"Two weeks!" he gasped. "It will take a week to get it there. I cannot raise that much in a week."

She stood up and stared down at him. "I will tell you how to do it," she said. "Prasu is desperate to see the Governor so he can be restored to favor before he dies but Didius Gallus won't see him. Arrange it. He'll be so happy he'll be glad to invest in your trade. That should provide cash for the ransom."

"Any money we got from King Prasu," said Ingenius, "would go straight into my partner's pockets. I wouldn't see any of it." Now he sounded angry.

She rubbed her suddenly aching forehead and frowned. Ingenius stood much in her debt. If she had not permitted it and made his way easy for him he would have neither a straight leg nor a fine house to live in. Where was his gratitude? "I would suggest you decide where your future lies," she said. "When Prasu dies I will succeed him. Before long, Venutius will step down in my favor and I shall be Arviragus of Britain. When the time is right I will raise the midriff of Britain and our allies will raise the west. If Cartimandua comes in with us she will raise the north, or we'll do it without her. Our destruction of the Twentieth proves that Rome's legions can be defeated. They will be driven from these shores once and for all, along with those who would rather lick their boots than help restore our sovereignty. Once they have gone I will have supreme power over half of Britain. Those who are with me now will be with me then."

"I am with you as you must know," said Ingenius. "But what if I can't raise the money from King Prasu?"

She looked at Venutius, who sat with his head between his hands. "My head," groaned Venutius. "It's splitting open."

"So is mine," she said. "There is too much smoke from this brazier. I tell you straight," she said to Ingenius. "Raise this money or you are no subject of mine."

Venutius got up from his stool and staggered over to the table. He picked up the amphora and held it to his nose. "By Duw," he said, his voice thick. "This stuff is poisoned. Your little servant wench is trying to do you in."

"Let me see," said Boudicca, and Venutius handed her the amphora. "It tasted queer," she said, "and it smells queer. No wonder she left in a hurry. How long have you had these headaches?"

"A month," said Ingenius.

"She's been feeding it to you in growing doses," said Venutius. "So you won't notice the one that kills you. That's why Boudicca and me got headaches so quickly. Where did you get her?"

"From Morfudd. She gave me Regan as a present."

"Why would a Druidess want you killed?"

Ingenius stood, horror on his face. "She had me publish a will leaving everything I have to her. I've been so apathetic since I got these headaches I've taken no steps to rescind it. I must do it right away." He rushed to the door but stopped short. Boudicca, right behind, almost collided with him and grabbed his arms. Then she saw figures plodding toward them and drew back.

"It's Didius Gallus," hissed Ingenius. She hid behind the door with Venutius. The Governor and two Romans stopped not three feet from them. Gallus wheezed as if out of breath from the short walk. From the brief glimpse she had of him he seemed as old as Prasu and as fat.

"I thought I saw someone," said Gallus to Ingenius. His jowls wobbled when he talked and a gray stubble of beard straggled around his chins. The front of his toga, where it jutted out over his capacious stomach, was stained with wine. He was accompanied by a guard and two of his legates: Arrius Maximus and Velius Valerianus.

"A couple of Britons, my Lord Governor," said Ingenius. "Looking for the latrine."

"I must return to my palace," said Gallus. "I enjoyed the game, though it cost me twenty thousand."

"You should be able to regain it next week, my lord," said Ingenius. "I will invite less skilled opponents."

"You would do that for me?" said Gallus. "I am not rich, you know. I lost most of my wealth with that damned Seneca. He pulled out before our venture collapsed, leaving my partners and me holding the bag. It doesn't seem right that such Romans and Britons like yourself are growing wealthy while I'm hard put to find twenty thousand when I lose an occasional game."

"It doesn't seem right," agreed Ingenius. "My lord, may I request a private word?"

"Shoo," said Gallus, waving the legates and the guard away. His eyes brightened perceptibly. He's expecting me to give him some money, thought Ingenius. "There is a British game called Fidchell," he said. "Only someone with a clear head can play it. Like yourself, for example."

"Yes, yes," said Gallus.

"It's the favorite game of King Prasu of the Iceni."

"Oh yes. He's been trying to see me. My legates said don't do it. Didn't his wife and one of his kings lead a rebellion?"

"King Prasu is quite harmless," said Ingenius, biting his tongue. He had almost said elderly and harmless until he remembered that Prasu and Gallus were about the same age. "He has been devastated by Rome's loss of confidence in him."

"Is that why he likes to play Fiddle?" said Gallus.

"He is extremely wealthy," said Ingenius, "and would do anything to get Rome's confidence in him restored. Anything.

For him to be invited to play his favorite game with the Roman Governor—well, I leave it to your imagination."

"Ah," said Gallus. "Now I get your drift. But I don't know how to play this Fiddle game."

"My steward is a Fidchell expert. He can give you lessons before each game. And if you made a point of letting King Prasu know that you had very little time to spare, he would not want to keep the Governor waiting too long while he made a move."

Gallus grabbed Ingenius by both arms, tears in his eyes. "My boy," said Gallus. "You're the first Briton—or Roman for that matter—who has done anything to make me feel welcome in this country of yours. I want you to know I appreciate it." He looked back at the waiting legates then again at Ingenius. "How much do you think I can make on each game?"

"I would think ten thousand a game to begin with. After that, well, King Prasu is a wealthy man who cares more for Rome's good opinion than he does for his wealth."

"Ah ah!" said Gallus. "Ah ah! Rome will have such a good opinion of him he shall not sleep nights thinking about it. When shall we have the first game?"

"If you wish to visit my home in the afternoon tomorrow, Friggit will give you your first lesson. King Prasu can eat with us in the evening, just a small gathering. After we have eaten I could suggest that he teach you his favorite game."

"Ah ah!" said Gallus. "Ah ah! Teach me his favorite game! You Britons have a sense of humor that would do justice to a Greek."

"Then I can expect you tomorrow afternoon?"

Gallus gestured for the waiting legates to join him. "I'd better see what these slave drivers have lined up for me. Well," he said to the legates, "I know you've been bursting with bad news all night. What is so important it can't wait a few more days?"

"There is trouble in Brigante," said Arrius Maximus. "Queen Cartimandua wants help with her underkings. She's taken some low gladiator type as her lover and says she's going to divorce her husband Venutius and marry him. Her kings are in an uproar about it and claim she would defile her throne. They want Venutius to come up there and dethrone her. That could be dangerous because he'd take her place and then we'll have the whole north against us."

Gallus turned to Ingenius. "What a woman that queen is," he said. "Somebody ought to have warned her about me. She tried to dilly dally with me like she did with Plautius and Scapula and what a waste of time that was for her." He turned back to the legate and prodded him in the chest. "I thought Scapula said Venutius was friendly to Rome. Why would he raise the north against us?"

The legate coughed politely. "I think Governor Scapula got the wrong impression. Venutius is the British Arviragus."

"So what do you propose?"

"We should send two cohorts from the Ninth up to the Humber. If Venutius sees we're ready to move he'll think twice about attacking."

"Who was it wiped out Valens' legion?"

"Venutius."

"Did he think twice about attacking the Twentieth?"

"That was different. He ran away and Valens chased him. He led Valens into a trap. Caesius Nasica does not run after barbarians and he will not fall into a trap."

Gallus shrugged. "It makes little difference if he does," he said. "We're going to be recalled anyway. The Empress thinks this is a waste of time and money and I agree with her. There is no money to be made here. But if it makes you happy send two cohorts.

"And we have to do something about the forts," said Velius Valerianus. "Scapula had so many built they've just about swallowed up all our legions. If we have to get an army together we'll have to close some."

Gallus prodded him in the chest. "So how many should we close?" he asked.

"A third at least."

"So close a third."

"We need to decide which ones to close."

"Close the ones we need the least," said Gallus. "Now, I have an important meeting tomorrow afternoon with King-" he turned to Ingenius.

"Prasu," said Ingenius.

"That's right," said Gallus. "Pratsu. So do what needs to be done. Don't bother me with the details."

The two legates bowed and stood back. Gallus grasped Ingenius' arms and rubbed them. "I thank you again for your hospitality, my young friend. I will have a room set aside for you in my palace and you must come and stay with me. Did I ever tell you about my campaigns in Africa against Tacfarinas?"

"No, my lord," said Ingenius

"Ah, those were the good days. And didn't you say you helped to build the water system here in Camulodunum?"

"I built many of the pipes for it." Ingenius stifled a yawn, but Gallus seemed not to notice.

"I must tell you how we did it in Rome. I was *curator aquarum* for ten years, you know. It was me who built the tunnel from Lake Fucine to the Ciris. The tunnel caved in but that was Narcissus' doing. He hired cheap contractors who gave him half of what they made. That freedman is a crook of the first order. He's about to be thrown into the dungeons."

"You really must have led a very interesting life, my lord."

"Yes. Well, the good days are behind and now I have to make some money to recoup my losses." He patted Ingenius' backside. "I can't wait to hear what King what's his name has to say. Ah ah! Come my gloomy advisers, let's go to our beds and get some proper sleep."

"By Duw," said Venutius, when Gallus and his attendants had left. "I knew I couldn't trust her or that bastard Velocatus. We shall raise an army and go there right away."

"We cannot waste our men and time fighting Britons when

there are Romans to be got rid of," said Boudicca. "What difference does it make if she beds him?"

"This, my girl. If she divorces me I am no longer Arviragus. You heard what Gallus said. The Rummies are going to be recalled. Guderius still has an army and we shall use it to destroy that low born clot who is after my wife."

"I thought I was your wife."

Venutius snarled. "You know what I mean."

Ingenius came back from seeing the Governor off. "You will have the loan?" said Boudicca, wishing her head would stop hurting.

He nodded, but still looked worried—or perhaps it was the headache. "I will get it some way," he said.

Chapter 13

Church Business

Tetra had just fastened the silver fibula in her new robe when the door burst open and Almedha came in. Almedha's eyes were bright with excitement and as always when she became excited, her left hand gripped her throat. "She's here," said Almedha.

"Who is here?" said Tetra, knowing full well who had arrived. Her own heart raced at the news but she wished to rebuke Almedha's excitement. Almedha was a second-degree Druid and a good assistant. She seemed to know the Hebrew Scriptures well but she became excited too easily and that was not good for the dignity of the church. She was also in a continual state of disarray, hair forever drifting over her eyes and her too loose tunic never neatly arranged.

Almedha must have sensed the disapproval in Tetra's voice for she took the hand away from her throat and composed her face. "Elsa," she said. "Your daughter Elsa is here with the Druid Goronwy. They crossed over from the mainland last night."

Tetra would not let her emotions show. She took the large white hat from the servant girl and placed it on her head, adjusting it as she looked into the polished bronze mirror held up by the girl. Owain had at first been reluctant to let white be used by anyone but a Pencerdd, but he had finally concluded that the

Bishop of his church could be an exception. To be on the safe side he had a large golden cross embroidered on the front of it. No Pencerdd had a cross on his hat and the crosses used by Bodin were red. "That is good," she said. "But I will have little time to talk with her before the meeting."

"The Archdruid is waiting," said Almedha. "And Lord Owain, of course, and Rhys."

"Then we had better begin right away. I will greet Elsa and Goronwy but we will have to talk later." She picked up one of Almedha's stray locks with her finger and thumb and tucked it behind the Druidess' ear.

The jeweled slippers that Owain had obtained for her were too tight, so her progress down the stairs was slow and stately. Her heart leaped when she saw Elsa and Goronwy waiting with Clotenus the long bearded steward. They were both dressed in plain tunics and leather sandals. Try as she might, she could not maintain her composure and wept when Elsa came into her arms after so many years. "My dear," was all she could say, and even the knowledge that her hat had tilted to one side could not make her relinquish the embrace.

"This be the Druit Goronwy and the woman Elsa," said Clotenus, banging his pole on the floor.

Tetra nodded irritably and waved the foolish man away.

"You look wonderful, mother," said Elsa.

"And you too," she said, unable to restrain a blush at the compliment, made as it was in front of Goronwy.

"You have always been beautiful," said Goronwy, taking her into his arms, "but never more so than now." After Atak's hard and gigantic frame, Goronwy's soft body seemed strangely comforting. She wondered if he still had tender feelings toward her and how he felt about her role as Bishop of the First Holy British Christian Church. Perhaps later she could get him aside and ask him if they had thought about joining her church. They must surely be tired of wandering all over the country. "Let me present Almedha, my assistant," she said, and was appalled when

Almedha followed her example and put her arms first around Elsa and then around Goronwy, kissing them both. Neither Elsa nor Goronwy seemed offended so she withheld the rebuke that had almost burst from her. She would talk to Almedha later about her behavior.

The room in which she was to meet with Owain and the Archdruid joined the hall not far from where they stood, and several of the new priests that Owain had recruited stood or squatted near the door. While she was still recovering from the greetings the door opened and Owain came into the hall. Seeing the little group he walked toward them, a dignified smile on his face.

"You remember my daughter Elsa, Lord Owain," she said, and was relieved when Owain took Elsa's hand in his and bowed politely. "And Goronwy," she added.

Owain's acknowledgment of Goronwy was more restrained but polite enough. "We have heard much of your great healing work," he said, addressing both of them. "We pray each day that we might find a way to persuade you to join our church." He paused as if waiting for them to agree but neither said anything. Then he turned to Elsa. "When I spoke to the Apostle Paul in Corinth, I told him of your healings and he said you must be a true disciple of Christ."

"You spoke to Paul?" said Elsa, her eyes wide. "Dedreth has spoken to Peter and you have spoken to Paul, and I have met neither one."

"Don't forget we were with Philip," said Tetra. "Philip is a great apostle."

"Indeed he is," said Owain.

"You have seen the Lady Dedreth recently?" asked Owain, and Tetra noticed the heightened color in his face.

"Why yes," said Elsa. "Only a week ago."

"And she's fully recovered from her ordeal?"

"Oh yes."

Elsa didn't know that Owain had been in love with Dedreth,

thought Tetra. She wouldn't have known of it herself if Atak hadn't told her. "And now," she said, putting her hand on Goronwy's arm, "I'm afraid we must part for a time. I have an important meeting with Lord Owain and the Archdruid and must leave you both in the care of Almedha. As soon as the meeting is over we can talk together in comfort."

Owain held up his hands. "I would much rather Elsa and Goronwy joined our meeting," he said. "Their views would be particularly helpful." Each of his hands grasped one of Elsa's and Goronwy's. "Will you not join us?" he asked.

Elsa looked sideways at her mother as if trying to read what passed through Tetra's mind. Then she turned and smiled at Owain. "I'm not sure we can help," she said. "But we're willing to try."

"Then let us join the Archdruid," said Owain, and opened his arms wide to usher them down the hall. Tetra straightened her hat and smiled as she passed him, but the smile felt a little wooden. She was not sure that she liked Elsa and Goronwy being present at the meeting. It would have been better, she thought, not to have them see how little a role she played in her own church.

Before she reached the door of the meeting room one of the priests, a fat man in a black tunic whose name was Badwin the Bald, passed around her and bowed to Owain. The man's oily smile repelled her. Owain stopped to talk to the man and Elsa turned to Tetra. "How is dear Atak?" she asked. "And what is he doing?"

"He's in the mountains somewhere," said Tetra, her voice grim. "We don't see him much anymore. He has some Germans of his own now and he's off with Boudicca and Venutius looking for a battle. He's disappointed because the Romans don't seem to want to fight anymore and the Britons have disbanded their armies."

"So he's no longer a Nazarene?"

"He's a Christian," said Tetra. "We don't say Nazarene."

Elsa looked puzzled.

"Lord Bodin calls his church the Nazarene Church of Britain," explained Almedha, and Elsa smiled to show that she understood.

Tetra sat at the other end of the table from the Archdruid. She didn't like the silly little man and wondered how the Council could have been foolish enough to elect him. Owain would have been the logical choice but the Council was afraid of another schism should it elect him instead of Bodin. Instead, she thought disgustedly, they had picked Doderin, the man who could never make up his mind.

Doderin was dressed in all the finery of his rank and half rose then sat down again as they trooped in. Owain was the last to enter and she grimaced as the fat Badwin came in with him. Badwin was ambitious and used Owain for his own ends. She would not even let her eyes rest on the man. After the introductions were over Doderin nodded so that the great white ostrich feathers above his head rattled, and then sat bolt upright as if afraid the feathers would fall off. He smiled at Tetra when she looked at him but Tetra made her eyes glassy and didn't smile back.

Owain poured himself a cup of water from the amphora on the table and took a small sip. "What we are here to decide," he said, and Tetra noticed he looked at everyone save the Archdruid, "is the direction our church should pursue. Lord Bodin the Fox has, I fear, coerced thousands of Britons into joining his church by threatening them with plague and fire and claiming he can keep them out of the Otherworld permanently if they don't obey his priests. He has burned Britons who would not obey him, claiming he is acting as God's emissary. If he goes on like this the entire country will soon be cowering in fear."

"Some of the Council didn't approve of that," said Doderin. "But then again, some did. It's hard to say what should be done."

"The Lady Dedreth would have been burned by him," said Goronwy, "if she hadn't escaped with Logan Bullhead."

"Quite so," said Owain. "If the Council cannot make up its

mind to stop Lord Bodin we must find some new way to show the people that ours is the true church. Then they will leave Bodin's church and flock to ours. Once they are in our church, we can lead them step by step to a proper understanding of God."

Rhys cleared his throat and stuck out his chest. "Instead of fire and plague," he said, "we could tell them Duw-Bran, I mean God, will strike them with hemorrhoids, boil-scars and itch from which they will never recover if they don't join our church." Owain glared at him and Rhys looked down at his feet. "At least it's better than fire and plague," he said.

"We need new doctrine," said Badwin. "Something different from Bodin's." Owain nodded agreement, and Tetra felt the fat man's eyes survey her but made no attempt to acknowledge him.

Elsa leaned forward and placed her forearms on the table, one hand on top of the other. "God does not send fire, brimstone or hemorrhoids," she said. "We bring those things on ourselves when we try to live outside God's law by not loving all that God created. When we empty our minds of carnality, and love and obey God as the Lord Jesus taught, God heals all our diseases. Why don't you tell them that? Isn't that new enough?"

Owain gave Elsa his patient smile, and Tetra knew right away what he would say. She had heard it so often. "What you say, my dear Elsa, is true," he said. "But for those of us trying to lead the nations in the right direction, it is not a practical thing to tell people. Paul himself became confused trying to explain it to me. Since we are not all able to show people what God is by healing as you do we must seek some middle ground between the evil of a Bodin and the pure idealism of an Elsa. We must tell them only what they can comprehend at the moment and lead them step by step to higher truths as they progress."

"But you can show people what God is," said Elsa, "and you can heal if you follow the Master's teachings. His teachings are very practical. Let me show you." She reached across the table, picked up Owain's cup of water and poured some onto the floor. "What happens when I pour the water out?" she asked.

Badwin sniffed contemptuously. "The cup empties," he said.

"No it doesn't," said Elsa. "It fills with air. The water keeps the air from getting in. When we empty our minds of carnal thoughts: anger, fear, jealousy, ambitions, hatred and unbelief, the holy pneuma—the mind of Christ and its power—floods in. Only carnal thoughts keep it out. When we purify our minds and love as Christ loves we become at one with God, the mind of Christ, and then we can heal. Surely, that isn't too hard to understand?"

Owain shook his head and gave her his patient smile again. You're wasting your time, Elsa, said Tetra to herself. I've been trying to convince this man for four years. You're going to convince him in one day? "Paul said much the same thing," said Owain, "but I believe at the end of our talks he could see that such a concept is much too simple to form a religion around. What seems so simple and practical to you and Paul is far beyond the people's comprehension. They must be taught only as much about God at one time as they can assimilate. To do this we must have a properly educated hierarchy of priests with appropriate dress to identify ranks within it, we must have a concept of God that people will respect and fear to offend, and we must have doctrine, rituals and liturgy to focus the people's minds on the majesty of His representatives here on earth. When we've done this they will be ready to hear you describe God as you and I know He really is."

"The people must be given something simple to begin with," said Badwin. "And there's nothing more simple than fighting for God and their nations."

"Why can't we do what Elsa says?" asked Doderin. "It sounds simple to me. But then, so does the fire and brimstone."

"One weak spot in what Bodin is preaching," said Almedha, "is his God with only two natures. The Hebrew Scriptures talk only of two."

"Elohim and Yahweh," said Badwin, nodding at everyone.

"As we all know," said Almedha, "a God with only two natures is not as powerful as one with three. If we had a three natured God He would be more awesome."

"Like the Three Morrigans," said Badwin.

"We've got to stick with Hebrew Scripture," said Almedha, pushing the hair back away from her eyes, "and not bring in our own gods if we want to get the Jerusalem Council to support us."

"Yes, we must keep their support," said Owain. "So we have to stick with Elohim and Yahweh. Have you found anything else in Scripture that would indicate a third nature?"

There was a heavy knock on the door, and Clotenus came into the room. He banged his pole ponderously on the ground.

"Yes," said Owain. "What is it?"

"Crowd of people outside."

"What do they want?"

"They be asking for Brigit."

Elsa's face turned bright red but she said nothing. Tetra almost spoke but stilled the urge. Owain looked angry. "There is no Brigit here. Send them away." He waved his hand in dismissal and Clotenus went out with a shrug.

"There is a Holy Spirit and a Lord of Hosts," said Almedha. "It's not clear whether either one is also Elohim or Yahweh. Sometimes they do good things and sometimes bad. It could be an entirely separate nature."

Owain reached across the table and gently smoothed one of Almedha's hanging tresses so it stayed behind her ear. "See if you can't make something out of it," said Owain. "You're a very creative person and I'm sure you'll be able to devise something. If we can show our God to be more powerful than Bodin's it will be easier to convince people that ours is the right church. To the people, three natures are certainly more powerful than two. And it will be closer to our ideal of Bran, Ceridwen and Mabon. Father God, Mother God and Young God."

"The Lord our God is one Lord," murmured Goronwy, and Owain looked at him superciliously.

"I'm aware of the logic," said Owain, "but again, we are trying to lift the people step by step from the three natures of Duw to a God they can recognize and fear."

"Sorry," said Goronwy.

"Three is more powerful than one," said Badwin. "But nine is even more powerful. Why not have a God with nine natures?"

"Are you familiar with Hebrew Scripture?" asked Almedha, and Tetra rejoiced to see the fat priest squirm.

"Not very," said Badwin. "My knowledge is not as broad on that subject as it is on others."

"Then your opinion is irrelevant," said Almedha, and Tetra nodded vigorously. That should put Badwin in his place. She smiled at Almedha. Her behavior was sometimes erratic and her hair was always in her eyes but her scholarship could not be faulted.

"Nine natures would be too complicated," said Rhys, joining in the attack on Badwin. "You just said yourself we should keep things simple."

Badwin glowered but retired from the conflict. Doderin's feathers rattled as he moved his head. "Why do we have to have three churches?" he said to Owain. "Why can't you and Bodin and Basil get together and make one church? One is simpler than three."

Owain sighed. "You would have us join Bodin in burning people?" he said. "We are trying to lead the people to the true God. Bodin is trying to become powerful by making them worship an evil god and is doing evil to bring it about."

"His church is bigger than yours," said Doderin. "He must be doing something right."

Tetra felt Elsa's eyes on her and blushed. Elsa must wonder what kind of a church her mother headed and why she said nothing to defend Philip's teaching. "If our priests would learn to heal," said Tetra, "people would flock to this church instead of Bodin's. They go to his out of fear. They would come to ours out of love."

This time it was Tetra's turn to receive Owain's patient smile. "I will not argue the point with you, Bishop Tetra," he said. "Of course they would flock to us if we had healers. I hope that someday Elsa will teach our priests how to heal." Tetra felt her face grow hot at Owain's words. What he had said was a criticism of the fact she herself could no longer heal. He had not said anything about it up to this point, but it must have been on his mind. "To get the people to come we must have a superior plan and priests to carry it out. The people will flock to us when we convince them our concept is best."

While Owain talked, Tetra became conscious of a disturbance in the hall outside. It grew louder, and she realized it was the sound of many voices. There was another heavy knock on the door and once again it opened to admit the heavy face of Clotenus. He didn't enter the room this time but merely extended into it the arm that held his pole and banged the pole on the ground.

"What is it?" said Owain, his voice sharp with impatience.

"All these people," said Clotenus. "They be asking for Brigit."

"What people?" Owain stood up and opened the door. The hall outside was filled with people. "What are all these people doing here?" he said, his voice now angry. "Who let them in? Go away," he shouted at the throng. "You have no right to be here. You must all leave at once."

"We wants Brigit," said a voice.

"Who is Brigit?" said Owain to Clotenus.

Elsa stood and put her hand on Owain's arm. When the crowd outside saw her the noise increased to a roar. "It's me they want," she said to Owain. "They call me Brigit even though I ask them not to. I will go outside and then they won't disturb you."

"No," said Owain. "They have no right to be here." Then he went out into the hall and the crowd fell back as Tetra and the others followed him. Elsa was at Tetra's side and it became apparent to Tetra that the crowd moved not in response to Owain's threats but because Elsa walked behind Owain. Slowly, the crowd passed out through the main entrance doors, and Tetra came out on to the steps behind Owain and Elsa. She gasped when she saw the size of the crowd. It filled the courtyard and spilled into the fields beyond, a sea of faces all staring at Elsa. For all its size it was strangely quiet. Some women nearby held up babies, and others in the forefront she could plainly see were diseased or lame. "Dear God," she said, her voice choked with emotion. "They want us to help them."

"The fields are white to harvest," said Elsa. "Come, Goronwy. We must let Lord Owain and mother get on with their meeting."

Owain's face was pale, and Tetra saw that even he was overawed by the size of the crowd. "You can't possibly help that many people," he said. "We must send them away."

"No," said Elsa. "We must do God's work. Please go back to your meeting." She stepped down into the crowd, Goronwy at her side, and Tetra's eyes filled with tears so that she could no longer see. She felt Owain's hand on her arm and followed blindly as he steered her back inside. Why was she going back inside? Atak rarely came to her any more. Why didn't she leave and join Elsa and Goronwy? She bumped against the door as Owain led her into the meeting room then sat down and covered her eyes with her hands.

"What did those people want?" said Doderin.

"They came to be healed," she said. She took her hands away and looked at Owain. He sat silent and morose, his hands clasped before him.

"They had no right to come in here like that," he said. "We must put more guards around the place."

Chapter 14

Fidchell and Other Games

"Look at them," said Catus, eyelids blinking at a rapid rate. "How long have they been playing that stupid game?"

"A long time," said Ingenius.

"We'll be here all night," said Spurius Vibius Rufus. Rufus was a friend of Seneca, the great speculator and playwright, and a partner in some of the ventures that Catus and Ingenius had joined. Prasu and Didius Gallus sat across from each other in Ingenius' great hall, a small table between them on which rested the Fidchell board. Prasu's hand weaved in circles and figure eights around the board, and Gallus' head weaved in harmony with it. A candle in a tall iron candlestick stood to Prasu's right, its flickering light illumining the board and the angular figure of Friggit, posted behind Prasu's chair in easy view of Gallus.

Whenever it became Gallus' turn to place a peg in one of the holes, Friggit would lean his head to the left or right or forwards or backwards to guide the Governor's hand, shake his head violently when Gallus held the peg over the wrong hole or nod it just as violently when the peg drifted over the right hole. What with Prasu's indecisiveness, thought Ingenius, and Gallus' inability to comprehend Friggit's head movements, the game was likely to last all night.

He, Catus and Rufus had sat close to the game when it began shortly after the evening meal and made encouraging noises to give confidence to the Governor. The Governor, however, made it apparent that the noises unsettled him so the encouragement ceased. Fidchell was not a fast moving game and seeing his other guests about to fall asleep over their wine, Ingenius suggested they retire to couches against the wall. After all, he thought grimly, the main purpose of the evening was not the game of Fidchell. He took a sip of well watered wine from his cup.

"Did you hear from Rome?" he asked Catus.

The little man puffed out his chest. "The Empress has confirmed my appointment as Procurator *Augusti Britanniae*," he said. "It should arrive shortly. I will no longer have to be bothered by that nitpicking ass Graecinius Laco."

"That should be good for trade," said Rufus.

"It will be good for our trade," said Catus.

"You'll be moving to London then," said Ingenius.

"My mansion overlooks the Thames and I shall be right in the thick of things. It's my intention to retire richer than Narcissus and you two will help me do it."

Rufus whistled. "If you want to skim off more cream than Narcissus you'll need a big spoon. But you must be careful not to end up where he's ended up."

Catus puffed out his chest again. "Narcissus was a fool," he said. "He crossed Agrippina and no-one who wants to stay alive does that. I will lick her boots and anything else she wants licked to get my rightful share of the empire's profits."

"But I hear she's going to pull us out of Britain," said Rufus. "What will happen to our trade if she does?"

"Nothing. Trade will go on just the same and I'll still be here to make sure Rome gets its fair share."

"And your fair share of Rome's fair share."

"That's right."

Ingenius took a deep breath. "How much silver did we manage to corner?" he asked.

Catus sneered. "All the British ore," he said. "For what it's worth, which isn't much. But we've tied up almost thirty percent of the Iberian. With what we pulled out last year the market's beginning to hurt and prices are rising. We'll start releasing it soon and make a killing."

"How soon?"

Catus looked at Ingenius and then at Rufus. "Why?" he said.

"I need twenty million."

"When?"

"Now."

"You won't get that from the silver. Maybe fourteen. And it will be three months at least. Why do you need the money?"

"It's a private venture."

Catus narrowed his eyes and rubbed his hands together. "It must be good if you're not going to let your partners in on it."

"It's not that kind of venture. It's a loan I've promised to make. It'll be repaid in a month."

Catus laughed so loudly that Didius Gallus looked up from the game and glared. Catus waved his hand at Rufus. "How many loans have we been told will be paid off in a month?" he said.

"Hundreds," said Rufus.

"And how many have we seen get paid off in a month?"

Rufus made a big circle with his finger and thumb.

Catus turned back to Ingenius and blinked his eyes. "You must be careful making loans for a month," he said. "You must have lots of security and charge lots of interest. Especially if you have to borrow the money yourself first." He leaned back and closed his eyes to mere slits. "I gather you want your partners to loan you the money against your investments?"

"Yes."

Catus shook his head. "Can't be done," he said.

"He only has forty five in the pot," said Rufus.

"But it will be worth twice that," said Ingenius. "You said it will be worth ninety in less than a year."

"The year isn't over," said Catus. "Anything might happen.

You know our rules. To borrow twenty you need sixty in security. If we sold you out completely you wouldn't have forty."

"Nearer thirty," said Rufus.

"We might let you have ten," said Catus. "Maybe twelve. Who is the loan to?"

Ingenius felt his face redden. He didn't want to reveal that it was Boudicca. Especially where Prasu might hear.

"If you don't trust us, don't expect any help."

"It's very secure," Ingenius whispered. "It's to Queen Boudicca."

"Ah!" said Catus. "The wife of our rich King of Iceni." He turned his blinking eyes on Prasu. "He's worth a lot more than sixty million. I know because I inventoried him." He turned back to Ingenius. "Why doesn't she get the money from him?"

"She is no longer his wife. She can't get her assets back until he dies."

"How is she going to repay your loan if she has no assets and can't get them from the man yonder?"

"He might live another five years," said Rufus, looking closely at Prasu. "Those fat old codgers fool you sometimes."

Ingenius cursed himself inwardly for having revealed the loan's destination. "Her brother, High King Marius is to pay it," he said.

"Isn't he Caratacus' son?"

"Yes."

Catus shrugged. "I haven't inventoried him so I don't know what he's worth. He's on the wrong side of our fence. Maybe he can pay it and maybe he can't. Maybe his father turned over his estates to him and maybe he didn't."

"He didn't," said Rufus.

"He's more wealthy than King Prasu," said Ingenius.

"Can he spend his money?" said Catus.

"It's not his to spend," said Rufus. He nodded at Prasu. "What's he worth?"

"Two or three hundred million or so," said Catus. He looked

at Ingenius and his eyes stopped blinking. "Why don't you sell him your share in the silver?"

"His advisers will tell him it's not worth twenty million at today's prices."

"Don't sell it for twenty. Sell it for twelve." Catus rubbed his hands on his stomach and beamed. "I'll draw up a note tomorrow. Get it signed and we'll lend you the rest."

"What about my investment?"

"You've sold it to our friend over there for a note you're going to give to us. We'll discount it and give you eight for it and because you're our partner we'll lend you twelve at the usual interest. When you get your twenty plus interest back from Marius you can invest in something else. We intend to make a killing on grapes."

"I'd rather be in silver," said Ingenius, playing for time while he calculated the interest on the twelve million and wondered if he would have the nerve to ask Boudicca to pay it.

"The silver might not pay as much as we thought," said Rufus. "More people drink wine than buy silver. Grapes are good."

"If there isn't a drought," said Ingenius. He didn't think he would have the nerve to ask Boudicca for the interest. But maybe he could drop a hint of the loan's cost to Venutius.

"We've shown you how to get your twenty mil," said Catus, "but if you'd rather stay in silver it's all right with us. Maybe Prasu will lend you the money if you tell him what it's for."

Ingenius turned to watch the game. Prasu had finally placed his peg in a hole and Gallus' hand moved in spastic jerks as he tried to interpret the wild dance being performed by Friggit's head. With his left hand, the Governor raised his cup to drink from it, but the cup was empty. "Friggit!" said Ingenius, angrily, and the steward banged his pole on the ground as he froze to attention. Gallus plugged his peg into a hole. "Send for more wine," said Ingenius. "Look after our guests."

Friggit called a servant and Prasu leaned back, a satisfied smile on his face. "I've won," he said.

"Jupiter be praised," said Rufus, standing up. "The stupid game is over."

"What do you mean, you've won?" said Gallus, glaring at Friggit.

"It's quite simple," said Prasu. "You put your peg in the sixteenth hole from the bottom and sixth from your right. That's ninety-six. My last peg was twenty-one from the top and fifteenth from my left. That's three hundred and fifteen. Now to go diagonally from either corner without using any hole I've already been in, the only holes you have left are six by three, fourteen by nine and twenty-one by eight. Subtracting ninety-six from three hundred and fifteen leaves two hundred and nineteen. The hole you have that comes closest to that is six by three, and you'd have to multiply that by twelve to come close. That means I have twelve more moves before you can make your next one, and the holes left to me will put me so far ahead you can't possibly catch up. If you don't see this, then we can continue to play, but I assure you it will be as I've said. Ask Friggit. He's our resident expert. It was Friggit who taught me the game."

Friggit avoided Gallus' glare and banged his pole on the ground. "Hurry along with the wine, there, aren't you?" he shouted.

"Perhaps you'd send Friggit over to teach me," said Gallus. "How much did you say we were wagering on this very first game?"

Prasu waved his hand politely. "We will call this an exercise in getting to know one another," he said. "I hope I can count on your Excellency to join me in many more games."

"What I should have done," said Gallus, "is put my peg here." He plugged in the peg. "That would have given me, let's see, nineteen by twelve is two hundred and twenty eight. What was your last number?"

"Three hundred and fifteen."

"That would leave eighty seven. Now if I had done that, what would you have had to do?"

"Oh dear," said Prasu. He pulled his peg out of the hole and began to circle the board again. Rufus snarled and sat down.

"How soon could I get the money?" asked Ingenius. He had thought it through. No doubt Catus had something evil planned for Prasu's note. If Catus did something bad with the note, Boudicca could end up losing many times the value of the loan. But if he did not get the loan she would ruin him. It was a choice between a large loss for her and a total loss for him.

"As soon as I get Prasu's note," said Catus. "You can have the money in two days."

"And you'll have it drawn up tomorrow?"

"I'll give you the note tomorrow."

***

Prasu pushed the Fidchell board away, unrolled the scroll and looked at it uncomprehendingly. "What would I do with twelve million in silver ore?" he bleated. "We already have large stocks of silver." He picked up his wine cup and took a long drink.

"You would not have to take possession of it, Sire," said Ingenius. "It is simply an investment. Lord Seneca's syndicate is buying large stocks of ore and holding it off the market. When the supply gets low enough prices will rise and then the ore will be sold at the higher prices. That way, the syndicate makes a profit. By making this investment you will be entitled to a percentage of the profits, and Lord Seneca's steward, Vibius Rufus, estimates that your twelve million would earn at least a million more, less the interest on the note. That's a million less interest simply for signing a note and waiting for two or three months."

Prasu sighed. He took another drink from his cup then set it down on the table. "I'm sure it's all very well," he said, "but I don't need another million. What would I do with it? I never spent the gold that Caesar Claudius so kindly gave me. It will all go to Goneril and Gwenda when I die. Besides, my treasurer is not here to advise me." He brightened up and smiled. "While you're here would you like to play a game of Fidchell?"

"I'm sorry, Sire, but I have to meet the Procurator at the Governor's palace. If you divide your kingdoms between the princesses, you know, they will each have only half of what you now have. Another million might make a difference to them."

Prasu reached out his free hand and laid it on the Fidchell board, moving it so that it lined up with his vision. "I have no doubt they will marry and marry well. Besides, they will likely inherit much of Queen Boudicca's wealth, and that is more than mine." He sighed again and let the scroll roll itself up. He looked so downcast that Ingenius felt sorry for the old king. "Have you seen Queen Boudicca?" asked Prasu.

"Not for some time, Sire." How could he tell Prasu that she was staying in his house and that he had spoken to her just before leaving it?

"I thought at first she had been killed in that terrible battle, but I've heard since that she is living in the western mountains. Why doesn't she come home to her daughters and me? We all miss her so."

"Perhaps she is afraid the Romans know she fought against them. She may fear that not only she but you and the princesses would be arrested if she came home to Iceni."

"Do the Romans know? Have you heard anything?"

"The fact that the Governor considers you his friend would indicate they don't, Sire."

"That's true. That's very true. Do you think Queen Boudicca might come home if she knew she were not under suspicion?"

"It's possible, Sire."

Prasu unrolled the scroll again and looked at it blankly. "I like the Governor," he said. "He's not very honest, but he has a good heart. He is coming here tonight. And he has agreed to play without Friggit making faces at him behind my back."

Ingenius blushed. So the old codger, as Rufus called him, had not been as blind to Friggit as he had seemed. "If you were a member of a Roman syndicate whose noble leader is tutor to Agrippina's son," he said, "and whose principal partner is the new Procurator of Britain, your standing with Rome would be unassailable. Queen Boudicca could draw no other conclusion."

"It hasn't been that way for a long time," said Prasu. He let the scroll roll itself up again. "For a long time I think they blamed me for Subidasto's rebellion, although he never dropped a hint to me about it. I don't know what got into him to do such a thing. And I do miss our games. I tried for months to see Ostorius Scapula, but I was always told he was up north somewhere." He always was, said Ingenius to himself, having heard about Scapula's infatuation with Cartimandua. "And I got the same treatment from Didius Gallus until this week when you so kindly invited me to meet him."

Ingenius steeled himself to press on with the matter. "I truly believe, Sire," he said, "that if you sign that note you will find your old relationship with Rome fully restored."

"Do you really believe so? I must confess that things haven't turned out the way we were led to expect. Governor Plautius assured me the whole of Britain would be Roman within two years and that we'd all be one nation at peace. It doesn't seem as if the Romans will ever get the west and the north under control. And now I hear they're talking about giving up and going home. That would leave us in a terrible fix."

"I don't think they will go home, Sire. They have too much invested here to think of abandoning it. Didius Gallus will get things moving again, and with your old relationship with Rome reestablished you'll be able to help restore peace."

"Do you really think so? Queen Boudicca has always spoken very highly of you and trusts your judgment implicitly. She was never too fond of Romans, which always grieved me, but if she saw that she was not under suspicion, you think she would come home?"

"I can't say, Sire. But if fear of being under suspicion is what is keeping her away, that fear would be removed."

"Ah yes," said the old king. "That is very true." He slowly unrolled the scroll. "All I have to do is sign it?"

"That's all you have to do, Sire."

"Then if you would be so good as to call Friggit, I will have him bring pen and ink."

Chapter 15

Catus Has a Visitor

The atrium of the Governor's mansion was crowded. Ingenius had to hold the scroll close to his chest to protect it as he wormed his way toward the legionaries guarding the inner doors. He heard his name shouted and waved vaguely in the direction of the sound but pressed on. Suddenly a strong hand grasped his tunic from behind, pulled him to a stop and then grasped his arm. It was Iorwerth, an elderly heavy set Trinoe noble who used to be part of Elidurus' court before the old king died. Two other Trinoe nobles pushed their way through and stood glaring at him.

"You're going to see Gallus?" said Iorwerth.

Ingenius tried to pry himself loose from Iorwerth's grip but the man was too strong for him. "I have to see Decianus Catus," he said. "He's waiting and I'm late."

"You can spare a minute for your fellow Britons," said Iorwerth. "You still are a fellow Briton?"

"What is it you want?"

Iorwerth snarled, and the hate in him was so vivid that Ingenius recoiled. "We want these Rummies off our back," said Iorwerth. "We gave up fair and square and didn't cry when they took most of our property. But now they're bleeding us of what bit we have left and we can't live."

"It's a bloody insult to make us serve as Flamines," said one of the other nobles, whom Ingenius had never met. "They're making us pay through the nose to call Claudius a genius and pay for his flaming temple services when we can't buy enough food to feed our servants. Why don't they pay for their own services?"

"I tell you," said Iorwerth, shaking Ingenius' arm. "We'll burn their bloody temple down for em if they don't back off."

"Why are you shouting at me?" said Ingenius. "What can I do? I'm a flamine too. I have to serve in the temple myself and pay for the games. I hate it as much as you do."

Iorwerth squeezed his arm so hard he almost cried out. "You're on their side, you little twit," he said, his eyes dilated with rage. "Now I'll tell you what you can do if you want to keep all your fingers. You can go to your friend Catus and tell him to back off or he'll lose his testicles and his temple both. You tell him that. You hear?" Ingenius looked toward the guards across the room, and that seemed to infuriate Iorwerth even more. "You get that little money grubber to back off or you'll find out how Britons handle traitors."

"I'm not a traitor," said Ingenius. He glared at Iorwerth.

"Prove it," said Iorwerth.

"I'll talk to him," said Ingenius. "But I can't make him do anything."

"You'd better," said Iorwerth, letting go of his arm, "or we'll take care of him and you both. Now get in there and try to remember where your loyalty lies."

"I'm as good a Briton as you," said Ingenius.

"Then prove it."

Trembling with anger, he pushed away from the three nobles and headed for the doors leading into the palace proper. When he reached the legionaries the centurion saluted him and waved to the guards to open the doors. He felt a glow of vindictive pleasure as he bowed his head in acknowledgment. Those Trinoe nobles who would have held him in contempt as a crippled misfit ten years ago now envied his power to get through these portals. Well, they could stew in their own sour juices. He would do nothing for them. Just before the heavy doors closed behind him, he paused and looked back but couldn't see Iorwerth in the crowd. With a shrug he went inside, and the doors closed behind him.

He walked down the marble floored inner hall past rooms occupied by the beneficiarii of Gallus' staff. Outside each room were small groups of men waiting to see the tax collectors or other administrators assigned to help the Governor. Some sat on stools or squatted, but most stood silent, perhaps cowed by their impressive surroundings. Catus had recently moved into a large corner suite, having convinced Gallus that his promotion to Procurator had been confirmed. As Procurator he would no longer be under the Governor's jurisdiction. Across from Catus' suite were the stairs leading up to the Governor's quarters on the second floor, and between the stairs and Catus' suite was a small room occupied by Gaius Marius Secundus. Secundus was a mysterious soldier turned policeman who ranged far and wide on special assignments, supposedly for Gallus. As Ingenius turned into Catus' anteroom, he noticed that Secundus' door was closed and that a legionary stood guard outside it.

Catus had his own beneficiarii, who occupied small rooms opening on to two sides of the anteroom. The third wall facing the door that Ingenius had just entered contained two large doors barring the way to the great man himself. Several British clerks sat at tables in the anteroom, and the chief of these was Sadoke, the sandy haired and balding Briton who had served Quintus Marcellinus at Longthorpe. Sadoke acted as a steward to Catus. He came forward rubbing his hands when he saw Ingenius.

"He's expecting me," said Ingenius. He was still angry from his encounter with Iorwerth and Sadoke irritated him further. He nodded abruptly toward the doors.

"Oh, I'm sure he is," said Sadoke.

"Then tell him I'm here."

"The trouble is," said Sadoke, "Someone's in there with him."

"Rufus?" said Ingenius.

"Oh, no," said Sadoke. "Someone quite different."

There was a pause while Ingenius tried to stare Sadoke down. Sadoke kept his eyes fixed on Ingenius and didn't blink. "Who is it?" asked Ingenius.

"Well, I don't know that he would want me to tell you. It would be fitter if he told you himself. Don't you think so?"

Ingenius shrugged and sat down on a chair near the door. "I'll wait then," he said.

"Yes," said Sadoke. "That would be fitter." Rubbing his hands he sidled off back to his table next to Catus' double doors and shuffled scrolls. From time to time he looked over at Ingenius, his face lit up in a smirk.

The twit, thought Ingenius, rubbing his arm where Iorwerth had gripped it. He could have told me who is in there. I wonder who it is?

His reverie was broken by a commotion in the hall and he went outside to see what caused it. It was the Governor, face flushed with anticipation. He rushed by with his guards as if hastening to meet a lover. Gallus did not see him and Ingenius watched the little party hurry down the corridor until it stopped short of the entry doors. A detachment of legionaries marched in escorting two men whose faces were obscured as Gallus rushed forward to greet them. The escort turned and marched out again as Gallus and his visitors headed back down the hall in Ingenius' direction. His eyes opened wide with surprise when he recognized them. Prasu walked along arm in arm with Gallus and right behind the portly king walked Friggit. Friggit carried the Fidchell board in his outstretched arms, and one of the guards at his side carried Friggit's pole. Gallus stopped short when he noticed Ingenius.

"My dear boy," he said. He dropped Prasu's arm and came forward to clasp Ingenius' arms. His pudgy fingers were remarkably strong. "I laid awake all last night thinking of that

Fidchell game and what I should have done not to lose it. I couldn't wait any longer, so I sent for King, King..."

"Prasu," said Prasu, a benign smile on his face. Prasu looked a little drunk, thought Ingenius.

"King Pratsu," said Gallus, "to come over right away and play another game. I think I have it finally worked out how to win." He turned to Prasu. "I intend to win, you know."

Prasu smiled happily. "Every player intends to win, Governor," he said. "If he didn't it would be a dull game."

"Ah Ah!" said Gallus, taking a hand off Ingenius' arm to poke him in the ribs and then putting it back on again. "What a sense of humor you Britons have. You heard me give him fair warning. Would you object to a little wager, now, King, King..."

Prasu leaned forward confidentially. "Prasu," he said. "No, of course I would not object to a little wager."

"Then a wager we will have. And you will not object to me asking Friggit for help from time to time? You had mentioned before that I could do that."

"He shouldn't tell you where to stick the peg," said Prasu, patting the Governor's arm with his soft hand. "He could perhaps give you a hint."

"He could say, for example, the left hand corner is a better place than the middle?"

"Yes, he could say that."

"And he could say, for example, between these two pegs over here rather than those two over there?"

"I think for one or two of the earlier games he might say that. Once you have become skilled you will want to stick them just where you think they ought to be stuck. You see, you will have a strategy that Friggit won't know about, and he might give you wrong advice."

Gallus let go of Ingenius' arms and glowered at Friggit. Friggit, unabashed, glowered back.

"Not intentionally, of course," said Prasu.

"I would hope not," said Gallus. Then his face lit up in a

smile and he patted Ingenius on the backside. "You must not forget our arrangement," he said to Ingenius. "You are to come here and spend a few days."

"Of course, Governor," said Ingenius. "I shall look forward to it."

"Then King Pratsu and me will go upstairs and play our game." The Governor put his arm around Prasu's shoulders and the little entourage moved off toward the staircase.

Ingenius turned and was about to enter the anteroom when Secundus' door opened and the legionary outside it came to attention with a crash of metal against metal. Curious, he stopped. The burly, ill-dressed and black browed Secundus came out first, then stood aside to let a tall red haired and red bearded man with bright blue eyes, obviously a Hibernian, sweep past him. Ingenius watched the lanky figure until it disappeared through the entry doors. He jumped when a hand grasped his arm, and turned. It was Catus, and he was about to hand him the scroll when the person who must have been in the room with Catus brushed by and headed down the hall. It was a slim and graceful female figure dressed in a plain tunic, a copper belt around its waist and three braids of golden hair swinging three copper balls from side to side as it hurried along. The familiar sight froze his blood. For a moment he was too shocked to move. Then he tried to break Catus' hold on his arm and run after the figure, but Catus' grip was too strong.

"Morfudd!" he shouted, but she paid no attention.

"Let her go," said Catus, and suddenly short of breath he didn't resist as Catus pulled him through the doorway out of sight of the fleeing Druidess.

"What is she doing here?" he asked, as Catus guided him past Sadoke and into his room. He sat down on a chair and stared dully at the Procurator-elect.

Catus closed the doors and Ingenius noticed for the first time that Catus was disheveled, not his usual tidy self. Catus blinked his eyes and grinned sheepishly when he saw that Ingenius had noticed, and smoothed his toga. "That is quite a woman," he said.

"Why was she here?"

Catus crossed the room, pausing on the way to straighten the couch that had been pulled out of line with the other furnishings, and sat down behind his table. On the table sat a bulging sack made of rough cloth. Catus pushed the sack toward him, and Ingenius got up to see what was in it. It was full of gold coins. "She came to give me that," said Catus. His eyes had stopped blinking and were fixed on Ingenius' face. "It's something you should have known about."

"How could I know about this?" said Ingenius. "Where did it come from and why did she bring it to you?"

"It came from Mona," said Catus. "She brought it to me as a token of good faith."

Mona? thought Ingenius. That's where the Druids keep their gold stocks. "Good faith for what? What does she want?"

There was a knock at the door and it opened slightly to admit the head of Sadoke. Sadoke opened his mouth to say something when he was pushed aside by Secundus, who walked into the room.

"It's true," said Secundus, closing the door behind him. He looked at Ingenius as if not sure whether to proceed.

"Go on," said Catus.

"Mona's full of it. O'O says it's the Druids' hoard."

"Who is O'O?" asked Ingenius, but neither of the two men answered him.

Catus rubbed his hands and blinked his eyes. "Then we must get Gallus to send a cohort after it."

"Are you sure?"

"I didn't say," said Catus, with a sly look at Ingenius, "that Gallus has to know what the cohort is going after. Sometimes, we get to know what we would rather not know, and sometimes we get to know not that which we would rather know."

Ingenius frowned. That sounded like something Morfudd had

said many times.

Secundus' head went back and he laughed, a deep gurgling chuckle. "He doesn't have to know anything about it at all," he said. "Maximus can send one from the fourteenth and have the gold shipped out to Morlaix. Seneca can handle it from there."

"Then tell Maximus," said Catus. "But don't tell anyone else."

Secundus put a finger to the side of his nose and walked out, slamming the door behind him.

"Disgusting man," said Catus, blinking rapidly. "But useful."

"What does Morfudd want for telling you about the gold?" asked Ingenius. "And who is O'O?"

Catus blinked suggestively. "She's starting a new religion and wants to put our gods in with hers so we'll protect it for her."

"Are you going to?"

"Why of course. The kind of protection I just gave her she can have anytime she wants. But it's nothing you need know about. In fact it's best if you don't know. O'O is one of Secundus' Hibernian spies. He thought we knew about the gold so we didn't disillusion him." He looked pointedly at the scroll in Ingenius' hand, and Ingenius handed it to him. Catus unrolled it and looked at Prasu's signature. He nodded, a satisfied sneer on his face. "That will do nicely," he said. "Come back in two days."

Chapter 16

Tetra Has a Visitor

The dawn was far advanced and Tetra could see quite clearly in the rose tinted early light. Save for the receding footsteps of Archdruid Doderin and his two assistants, and the busy chattering of the waking birds, all was quiet and peaceful. She leaned against the doorway and watched Doderin cross the courtyard, his white ostrich feathers bending sideways from the wind of his passage, and go through the now heavily guarded gate on his way to the Council meeting. Her smile was almost a sneer as she watched the funny little man hurry his assistants along so the meeting could begin at sunrise, its proper time. She glanced back at the staircase. If Owain didn't appear soon, he would be late for the meeting and that would spoil his day. She wondered what kept him.

With a discontented sigh, she pushed herself away from the doorpost and went back into the hall. She would rather have listened to the birds and prayed for the peace of mind she longed for, but she had a daily meeting of her own to attend. Owain's priestly recruits were milling around in a corner of the hall like a gaggle of hungry blackbirds. Soon, they would assemble to recite the morning prayers led by Tetra herself, and then be taught doctrine by Almedha. There must be fifty she thought, and Owain still sought more. He had divided them into three grades and devised examinations for them to pass from one grade to the next. She sighed again. After they had been taught Almedha's new prayers and Almedha's new doctrine and passed their examinations, what then? Would the Britons flock to her church because of these dull looking priests dressed in the black tunics that Owain had picked because black didn't conflict with any of the other colors in use? Would they come to hear Almedha's explanation of the three natures of God and to hear prayers that went on and on and never healed? Would they not rather stay in Bodin's church out of fear of being burned?

As she approached the priests, several of them bowed obsequiously and smiled at her. To her horror, Badwin the Bald blocked her way. Badwin's fatness was repulsively flabby and oily. His skin was too pale and folded over, and had a bluish tinge to it. The top of his head shone and she often wondered if he polished it. He had passed the examination for the third grade and acted as if he were superior to her. She had heard him wonder out loud whether she too should have to pass the examination. Whenever he addressed her she got the feeling he ridiculed her. She shuddered and decided to walk around him. He raised his hands as if in supplication, and the fat around his forearms quivered. "Is our dear Bishop to lead us in prayer this morning?" said Badwin.

She had intended to lead with one of Philip's prayers, but the sudden conviction that Badwin would ridicule it made her decide not to. "Almedha will lead the prayers," she said, then swept past him without pausing until she reached the high chair in the corner reserved for her own use. Seated on it, she would listen to Almedha's teaching for a while and then, when she couldn't stand it any longer, add a few thoughts of her own. Even though they often contradicted what Almedha had just said her words were always received with a show of respect. She wondered what Almedha and the priests thought about her, deep in the recesses of their own ambitions. There was no doubt in her mind that Badwin wanted to be Bishop himself and watched for an opportunity to discredit her. She wasn't sure what Almedha wanted.

Not seeing Almedha, she looked toward the stairs, but they were empty. It was strange that all the priests seemed to be here and yet there was no sign of Almedha. Where could she be? Her heart skipped a beat when it occurred to her that both Owain and Almedha were late in appearing. Were they together? Was there something between them? She knew that Owain thought highly of Almedha, and the man must be lonely, living as he did without a wife. He was forever lifting Almedha's hair out of her eyes and patting her on the head. What would happen if Owain and Almedha were to marry? What would that do to her status?

She had felt herself grow more resentful as the church developed, and she knew Owain sensed her growing antagonism. Perhaps Owain wished that Almedha and not she were head of the church. If he married Almedha it would not be long, she decided, before she was asked to give her white hat and cripplingly tight slippers to Owain's new wife. She looked down at the offending footwear and remembered that Almedha's feet were much smaller than hers. Had Owain had them made for Almedha's instead of her own feet? Had he always planned for Almedha to be Bishop? Well, she thought grimly, Almedha would be welcome to the slippers and the hat. If nothing else it would set Badwin the Bald on his backside and force her to follow after Elsa and Goronwy. Ever since they had left she had wondered why she hadn't obeyed the impulse to leave with them. She had been able to heal once, and away from this strange church that Owain and Almedha were building between them, she could learn to heal again. She could serve Christ and be useful. It would serve Atak right if he showed up for one of his infrequent visits and found she had gone. It would serve him right, but the thought of it brought a lump to her throat. Was her life to be completely empty of love?

There was a noise on the stairs. Owain clumped down them, awkwardly pulling at the fastenings on his Council robe, his face as red as the robe itself. He looked harassed and she wondered what had gone wrong. Two female legs appeared on the stairs behind him, and as the rest of Almedha's green clad body came into view, two more legs appeared behind her. These legs were also female and Tetra watched intently as the green hem of an ovate's robe gradually grew into a handsome woman whose graceful progress down the stairs drew all eyes to her. Tetra had not seen this woman before, and she got up to walk toward Owain, who had stopped in great irritation at the foot of the stairs to complete the fastening of his robe. "Let me help you," she said as she reached him, and he let his hands drop to his sides and glared at the ceiling while she seized the silver clasp that had defied him and clipped it neatly to the hooks on his belt.

"Thank you," he said, no gratitude in his voice. "I'm late for my meeting and must run, but let me present the Ovate Morfudd." He turned to the attractive woman who had now come to his side and waved his hand rudely. "This is Tetradia, Bishop of our church," he said to Morfudd, his voice curt and unfriendly. "I will let Almedha acquaint you with each other for I must hurry." He put his hand on top of his hat and ran out into the courtyard, which was now heavily tinted by the redness of sunrise. He had over a mile to run and wouldn't make it in time. She smiled. That would make him even more upset.

Morfudd, she thought, as she turned to greet the attractive young woman. Hadn't she heard that name connected with Bodin's?

"Morfudd came to us last night," said Almedha, clutching her throat as she spoke. "It was quite late so we thought it best not to awaken you. She has come to us from Lord Bodin's church."

Tetra felt her eyebrows go up.

Morfudd reached out and took Tetra's hands into her own and stroked them. "I have left Lord Bodin's church," said Morfudd, "because it is evil. I have come here to throw myself on your mercy and ask for asylum."

Tetra found herself gazing into Morfudd's eyes, unsure

whether they were gray or violet. Morfudd still stroked her hands and the sensation calmed her. Fragments of half grasped memories floated through her mind as she steeped herself in the aura of this woman's beauty and felt herself melting like a hard candle dropped into a vat of bubbling tallow. Hadn't Atak said something about this woman being betrothed to Ingenius? And hadn't there been something connecting her with Owain himself? She had often laughed at Atak's insistence that women drew the essence out of him, but now she felt the essence draining out of herself, flowing toward this sensuous female whose cleverness, she knew instinctively, far exceeded not only her own but Owain's. She felt her body lean toward Morfudd's and expand, aching to be caressed and stroked like a cat. If Almedha had not spoken, breaking the spell, she might have sunk into Morfudd's arms.

"Perhaps Morfudd may join us while we pray?" said Almedha. "The priests are waiting."

Tetra nodded dumbly. "Of course," she said, and found herself walking arm in arm with Morfudd as Almedha led the way to the priests. Morfudd's arm rested so lightly on hers that the woman seemed to float rather than walk. She sat on her high chair as the priests turned to face Almedha, and Morfudd stood by her side, her thigh lightly touching Tetra's.

"Let us pray," said Almedha in the flat tone she used for praying, and Tetra immediately stopped hearing. From indignation at the thought of praying to a three-faced God, her mind quickly drifted onto the subject of Morfudd and some of the stories she had heard. She couldn't recollect the stories, but she did remember they had a common thread. Morfudd enticed men to love her and then abandoned them. Perhaps she hated men. She became very conscious of Morfudd's leg touching hers and even though the touch was light she could feel its heat. Suddenly afraid, she moved her leg slightly and the contact lessened. Morfudd moved closer and this time she didn't move her leg.

Almedha's prayer went on and on, and she was tempted to interrupt in order to bring it to a close but didn't want to appear domineering in front of Morfudd. She looked up at her once during the prayer, and Morfudd quickly caught her glance and smiled as if she understood Tetra's impatience and approved of her forbearance. She found the hand that had been lying limply in her lap suddenly held within Morfudd's, and a warm glow passed over her body as the comfort of the caress sank into her being. She felt that Morfudd approved of her, even liked her, and closed her eyes with a contentment she had not felt for a long time. Atak never caressed her. Atak's lovemaking was quick to begin and quick to end. In the beginning she had never felt the need for caresses because she had always been ready enough to keep pace with him. But as his visits grew further apart and her life more lonely the fires within her died to smoldering ash. This sudden warmth from Morfudd made her realize her need, and without consciously willing it she wrapped her fingers around Morfudd's hand and squeezed it in response. Almedha's head was still bowed in interminable prayer as were the priests.' Suddenly, her hand was lifted and its palm pressed against the Druidess' warm lips. Her mouth opened in an involuntarily gasp and she turned slightly as Morfudd bent down, her head next to Tetra's.

"Protect me, dear Tetra," murmured Morfudd, her breath warm in Tetra's ear. "Promise that you will protect me. My life is in danger if you will not take me in and protect me."

"Of course I will protect you," whispered Tetra. She wasn't sure what Morfudd feared, but it most likely was Bodin. "You are safe here with me." She squeezed Morfudd's hand to reassure her.

"Lord Owain may not let me stay," Morfudd whispered. "He hates Lord Bodin and I fear hates me. I have no-one to turn to."

"You will stay with me," said Tetra. "You will help me." She squeezed Morfudd's hand again and Morfudd kissed it and put it back on Tetra's lap, then straightened up as Almedha's prayer came to an end. Her heart full of this new dependency, Tetra heard little of Almedha's dissertation on the three natures of God.

She wanted to be alone with Morfudd, to have this strange warm beauty tell her the truth about the stories she had heard. She wanted to hear what it was that Morfudd feared, and she wanted to assure Morfudd that she would have a secure place in her church. She visualized the long discussion they could have in her private quarters and the closeness that would develop from it. She had not realized how much she needed a friend, someone to whom she could bare her soul, and now God in His love had provided one for her. She and Morfudd would serve God together. If Owain rejected Morfudd they would both leave and join Elsa. She became so engrossed in her daydreaming that she jumped when Morfudd spoke in a hard clear voice.

"I am delighted," said Morfudd, addressing Almedha, "to hear your description of God. A God with three natures is certainly more powerful than a God with only one or two." Is she being sarcastic? thought Tetra. "But isn't something lacking? Even with three natures the picture you draw is incomplete."

"In what way?"

"The picture you draw is entirely masculine."

"God is entirely masculine," said Badwin. "He created Adam in his own likeness."

"Elohim created man male and female," said Morfudd, "and therefore must be both male and female. Elohim made a finished creation out of nothing. It was entirely good and Elohim gave men and women equal dominion over it. Yahweh made an unfinished creation. He made a male out of dust who then got lonely because he had no companion. A wife had to be improvised and then a snake got dominion over both of them. Yahweh's creation is well adapted to the male viewpoint but as for me I prefer Elohim's creation." Morfudd stared coolly at Badwin until he lowered his eyes, then smiled at Almedha. She reached forward and smoothed Almedha's hair back behind her ear. "You have just said, Almedha, that the Lord Jesus taught that God is Love. How can Love not be feminine? Your Holy Spirit must be Mother of all. How can we be the children of God if God is simply a Father and not a Mother? Doesn't the Hebrew prophet Isaiah say that as a Mother, God will comfort us?"

Almedha put her hand to her throat and pursed her lips. She nodded dubiously, her eyes on Tetra as if seeking approval. "If the Holy Spirit is Mother," said Almedha, "then one of the other natures must be the good Father Elohim and Yahweh the Father that is both good and bad. This could account for the fact that we have both good people and good and bad in the world. Elohim fathers the good and Yahweh the good and bad." Almedha paused, her eyes still on Tetra. Others looked at Tetra also. Clearly she had to take a position.

"Morfudd is right," said Tetra. "How could God create woman if God is not feminine as well as masculine? But there is no bad nature in God. God is only good."

"Then we're back to a God with only two natures," said Badwin, his voice resonating with triumph. "A female nature and a good nature. How can we convince our Britons that a God who is just a good Father and a good Mother is more powerful than Lord Bodin's God, who is Yahweh the Bad as well as Yahweh the Good and the Holy Spirit who sends fire? People are more afraid of a God with a bad side to Him. If they don't stay in Bodin's church they know they will get burned or thrown out of the Otherworld by Yahweh. They won't come to us unless we tell them God will do something bad to them if they don't. I don't think Lord Owain is going to agree to this. I think we're letting female nonsense divert us from what we're here to do."

"That's right," said some of the priests.

Tetra stood up in a rage and put her hands to her hat. She was about to rip it off her head and throw it on the floor when Morfudd's hand grasped her arm and steadied her.

"Dear Tetra," Morfudd whispered. "Don't let them upset you. It's what they're trying to do and if you leave they will have won." Tetra let her arms fall to her side and looked unseeingly ahead while she tried to control her anger. Morfudd was right. She must not let Badwin succeed in making a fool of her. Morfudd still stood as if ready to continue speaking, so Tetra sat down and tried to calm her trembling. As soon as Morfudd finished she would close the meeting.

"As to the three natures of God," said Morfudd, "the Druid concept is easily reconciled with that of the Jews'. Duw-Bran is Elohim, Good Father of all, Duw-Ceridwen is Holy Spirit, Mother of all, and Duw-Mabon is Jesus, the Young God."

Tetra felt her mind go blank. This was worse than Almedha's groping. Morfudd was brilliant and self possessed but she must get her alone and acquaint her with Philip's teaching. Before any of the priests could challenge Morfudd's theology she stood up and raised her arms. "We will close the meeting," she said.

Badwin heaved himself to his feet, and Tetra felt a wave of fear as he turned toward her. The man had not lost his self-possession and she knew he could take away every shred of hers. Instinctively, she reached out and put a hand on Morfudd's arm. Morfudd would know what to say even if it was wrong doctrine. "I would suggest," said Badwin, his voice ponderous but controlled, "that Lord Owain be apprised of these strange thoughts before any attempt is made to include them in doctrine." He turned on his heel and walked toward the door, a little knot of the priests hurrying to join him. Tetra heaved a sigh of relief.

Morfudd laughed contemptuously. "That fat man would like to be Bishop," she said. "He will run to Owain as soon as the Council meeting is over." She turned to Tetra as Almedha and the remainder of the priests drifted away, and her smile was suddenly as sweet as before. She took Tetra's hands in hers and Tetra felt the fear and resentment drain from her. She stood gazing into Morfudd's eyes and the essence flowed out of her in a great stream. "Can we go somewhere to talk?" asked Morfudd. "I do feel the need to talk to you before Lord Owain returns. If you do not befriend me, he will send me away, I know it. I feel a great warmth toward you, as if we'd always been friends. I want to tell you everything about me so that you will love me and be my friend. You will love me and be my friend, won't you?"

Tears welled up in Tetra's eyes and she pulled Morfudd's hands against her breasts. "You shall always be my friend," she said. "I will always love you."

Chapter 17

Atak's Last Visit

Morfudd moved quickly away from the open window in Tetra's room. "They're coming," she said, her eyes bright. "There are people and horsemen with them. Something must have happened at the Council. Come and see."

Tetra got up slowly and went to the window. She felt disappointed and fearful. She had no desire to confront Owain and Badwin. Even with Morfudd there, she knew she would not be able to hold her own. She would be made to look a fool in front of everyone. Even though Morfudd was now so close to her, she resented the younger woman's insistence on putting Badwin in his place. More and more she regretted being Bishop of Owain's church. All she wanted was a little peace and quiet and someone to love. Morfudd was far better equipped to be Bishop. Owain should let Morfudd be Bishop and she Tetra would be her assistant. She would propose this to Owain as soon as she could get him alone. If he agreed then she would tell Morfudd the exciting news. Morfudd would love her even more dearly if she let her be Bishop and became Morfudd's assistant. When she reached the window, Morfudd came behind and hugged her. She closed her eyes in ecstasy. This was all she wanted. To be loved by Morfudd.

"Look," said Morfudd, and she opened her eyes reluctantly.

The first thing that caught her attention was Doderin's headdress. Its white feathers shook and caught the evening sun as he approached the gate. Owain walked along at Doderin's side and she could see the flash of his teeth as he talked and waved his arms. Other council members crowded around the two men and behind them rode several horsemen. She gasped and pulled her hand out from Morfudd's embrace to hold it to her mouth. The size of that one was unmistakable. "It's Atak," she said, and she didn't know whether she was pleased or horrified. "It's my husband," she said, realizing that Morfudd didn't know Atak. "The big one at the end."

Morfudd released her and she turned in panic. "He won't stay long," she said. "He never does." Morfudd placed her hand against Tetra's cheek and she seized and kissed it.

"The fat man has seen them too," said Morfudd, looking down over Tetra's shoulder. "Look at him waddle. He must tell Lord Owain what bad girls we've been."

"I don't care what he tells him." She kissed Morfudd's hand again. "For all I care he can be Bishop."

"Oh no," said Morfudd, her voice harsh. "He is not going to take your Bishop's hat." She kissed Tetra. "Have no fear of Badwin. If there is one thing I have learned during my years of slavery with that monster Bodin it is how to defend myself and those I love."

"You have had such a terrible experience with that horrible man. But now you're out of his power. I shall always love and protect you. And you must never leave me."

Morfudd kissed her again. "My dear green-eyed Tetra, I will stay with you for the rest of your life."

They walked down the stairs together and went out into the courtyard, where Owain and the small crowd of followers and horsemen had gathered. Atak saw her right away and dismounted, giving his reins to someone to hold for him. His face was serious, but he gave her a smile as he came up the steps, put his arms around her and kissed her. He nodded good-naturedly at Morfudd while he still held Tetra. His beard felt rough as it moved against her face and he smelled of sweat. She pulled her head back sharply. For the first time she felt embarrassed at being held so closely by him. "Morfudd," she said, disengaging herself and turning to the Druidess, "this is Atak, my husband. Morfudd is going to help me with the church," she told Atak. She had not taken her eyes off Morfudd as she said this, and saw the Druidess' eyes look beyond her and her face take on a wooden look. Owain had come up the steps and at Owain's side was Badwin the Bald. Badwin's face sweated profusely. He looked discomfited and she guessed he had not been able to talk to Owain about Morfudd's strange doctrine.

"If you wish to spend some time alone with Lord Atak," said Owain to Tetra, his voice bleak, "I would suggest you do so quickly. He must leave right after the evening meal."

"What has happened?" she said.

"There is terrible trouble in Brigante. Cartimandua has divorced King Venutius and betrothed herself to Velocatus, King Venutius' man at arms. The kings have risen. They have called on King Venutius to overthrow Cartimandua and become High King in her place. Cartimandua has taken Prince Caswal and his wife and children hostage, and King Venutius has gone to Brigante to free them. Cartimandua has called on the Romans to help and the Ninth Legion is on its way north. Unless we raise an army quickly to help Venutius, we may lose our Arviragus."

"So I can't stay long," said Atak. "I have to go to Queen Boudicca."

"I thought you were with Queen Boudicca," she said.

"I was," he said. "I left to tell you to come to the wedding but they sent a scout after me. He brought me to the Council. And now I have to go back."

"What wedding?"

Atak pulled on his beard and looked at Owain. "Lady Dedreth is marrying King Eudal Marius."

She looked quickly at Owain to see if the news would upset

him but he seemed unaffected by it. He turned to her with a determined air.

"You must marry them," he said. "They must join our church. I'm sure that if you tell Lady Dedreth what is at stake here she will consent. She knows how evil is Lord Bodin's church. Think what it will do for our church if the first king in Britain and his wife are married in it and belong to it."

Was he going mad from the strain? she wondered. Dedreth would never join his church. "She belongs to Joseph of Arimathea's church," she said. "The one you and your Council declared heretic. She will ask Joseph or Elsa to marry them."

Owain's face turned red. "Arimathea is a foreigner," he said, his lip curled back in a snarl. "He has no interest in Britain. King Marius must be made to recognize his responsibilities now that his father is exiled. He is the first High King in Britain and must do all he can to unite the people. The unity of Britain must come before all else and he must support this church. It is the only one that can unify the people against the enemy."

"It is the only one that can teach his people properly," said Badwin. "King Marius must be made to understand that."

Tetra glared at Badwin and was about to tell him to shut up when she felt Morfudd's hand on her arm. "King Marius is not interested in teaching his people," said Morfudd, her tone contemptuous. Owain recoiled from her voice and his face turned redder. "He is only interested at the moment in raising twenty million for his ransom," she said. "He borrowed it from Queen Boudicca, who borrowed it from the usurers."

"What has that to do with the marriage?" said Owain. His voice was muffled as if he could barely open his mouth to speak to Morfudd. Why was he so angry with her?

"If Bishop Tetra's church were to give him the twenty million," said Morfudd, "it would have a lot to do with the marriage. He could not object to being married in the church that saved his sister from the usurer's clutches."

"The church give him twenty million! What of his own fortune?"

"He has no fortune until his father dies."

"Queen Boudicca has many times that amount. Why should she go to the usurers?"

"She has left her husband. She will not have her fortune back until Prasu dies."

Owain sighed impatiently. "And where, pray, would our church get twenty million?"

Morfudd raised her head to look above Owain's, her eyes fixed across the courtyard. Doderin stood between two arguing council members, his feathers shaking with each movement of his head as he agreed first with one and then the other. He was well out of earshot. "My dear Lord Owain," said Morfudd, her voice soft. She reached out and lightly touched his red council robe. "You and I know where there is gold far in excess of that amount."

"The Council's gold!" said Owain. He cleared his throat and looked at Morfudd suspiciously. What has he got against her? thought Tetra. "The Council's gold is no longer where you last saw it," he said. "Nor is it as large an amount. We have had great expenditures."

Morfudd's eyes narrowed. "Nonetheless," she said, "to the High Council, such a sum must be trifling. Could it be spent in a better cause?"

Owain pursed his lips and frowned. "How can you know what is and is not trifling to the High Council?" he said. "Twenty million is a huge sum."

Morfudd put her hands together in front of her chin and bowed submissively. "I am a pupil of the learned Lord Owain," she said. "He above all men understands what I know and don't know." So that was it, thought Tetra, relieved. She had heard there was some connection between Owain and Morfudd and it had been apparent that they had known each other well at some time in the past. So Morfudd had not been his lover but his pupil.

They must have had a falling out over Druid business. For some reason that made her feel better. "And above all men," said Morfudd, nodding significantly toward the Archdruid, "Lord Owain must know that the expenditure of such a sum to consolidate such a cause is a most worthy use of the Council's resources."

Owain grunted deprecatingly. "I won't argue that," he said. "But the Archdruid and the Council would have to be convinced."

"Perhaps they don't need to be convinced," said Morfudd.

Owain turned his head sharply. "What do you mean by that?"

"Isn't my lord Owain still charged with assisting the High Kings in fulfilling their responsibilities to the alliance? And can't he expend the Council's resources in an emergency?"

"There is no emergency."

"Surely my lord Owain would agree that if the marriage is to take place soon, the need to take action is urgent?"

"Urgent yes, but I could not call it an emergency. And even if I did I still cannot expend funds while the Archdruid is here. He would have to approve."

"Then the Archdruid must be persuaded to leave."

With one accord, everyone on the steps turned to look at the Archdruid, who still stood between the two arguing Council members, a confused look on his face. "And how do we arrange that?" said Owain, his voice sarcastic.

"If King Venutius cannot raise enough men to defeat Vellocatus," said Morfudd, "he will not be able to bring Brigante into the alliance. Surely the Archdruid should to go to King Guderius with Lord Atak and use all the power of his personal prestige to convince King Guderius to field his army before this priceless opportunity is lost."

Owain frowned, but Tetra could see he was impressed by Morfudd's words. She looked furtively at the beautiful Druidess and felt a glow of wonder that someone as clever as Morfudd could love someone as dull as she. She must convince Owain that Morfudd should be Bishop. Morfudd was far more able than she to handle the likes of Badwin the Bald. Even though Morfudd's theology sent shivers up her spine it was obvious that Morfudd was a true Nazarene at heart. She had never been exposed to Philip so could not be blamed if her understanding was imperfect. She had been ill used by Bodin but now at last she was free. From now on she would help Owain's church to grow as she had mistakenly helped Bodin's. Tetra reached out and touched Morfudd's arm, comforted by its smoothness and warmth. She must do all she could to make Owain like Morfudd so that Morfudd could stay with them forever. "I will be glad go to King Marius and Dedreth," she said. "And offer to marry them if that will help our church." Owain's face brightened. "And I will take Morfudd with me."

Owain's head jerked back and he frowned. "I'm not sure that would be a good idea," he said, not looking at Morfudd.

"Why not?" said Tetra. If Morfudd was not to go then neither was she. She was not going to be parted from Morfudd.

"It is because Lord Owain does not trust me," said Morfudd. "In his eyes I am the servant of Lord Bodin."

"But that isn't true," said Tetra to Owain. "Morfudd has severed all her ties with Lord Bodin. It is unchristian not to trust her when she has suffered so much."

"It is not a matter of trust," said Owain.

"Then why isn't it a good idea?"

"Lord Owain is concerned," said Badwin, "about giving such an important task to women. Perhaps I should accompany the Bishop. A masculine presence would lend stature to our church before King Marius."

"You will not accompany me anywhere," said Tetra. She would have said more, but Morfudd quieted her with a look.

"Lord Owain is still convinced that I conspired with Lord Bodin to have him killed," said Morfudd.

"What!" said Tetra.

"I wrote to him in Corinth promising to meet him at Marazion when he returned. The messenger showed my letter to Lord Bodin and he kept me locked up and in chains for months. He sent the Gunes of Merrimar to meet each ship that docked. I don't know what they would have done to Lord Owain had they caught him, but he escaped them. He immediately assumed I had enticed him to Marazion in order to have him killed. Little did he know that I was near death myself. When I finally escaped I ran away to Sir Ingenius, the only man so far who had treated me kindly, and we were betrothed. But even that turned to ashes when Lord Bodin threatened to have Sir Ingenius killed if I didn't leave him and return to his church."

Tetra's chest swelled as she saw tears in the Druidess' eyes. Impulsively, she seized Morfudd's hand and glared at Owain.

"I begged him last night to hear my explanation but he would not grant me that privilege," said Morfudd, her voice as suddenly soft as her demeanor. "Now, I ask him again to hear me explain what happened and let me tell him the urgent news I have brought. Lord Owain, will you not at least grant me an audience?"

Owain looked down at his feet and Tetra felt an urge to shake him. How could he treat a woman like Morfudd with such disdain? Was she of so little consequence that he would not deign to give her a hearing? If this was his attitude toward women as lovely and talented as Morfudd then she was ready to leave his church. Let him give it to Badwin and see what kind of a church that fat oaf would make of it. She took a deep breath. "Morfudd told me about herself today," she said, glad that her voice did not break. "I believe her when she says you have been taught to believe things of her that are not true. If you wish me to remain in your church, Lord Owain, then I must insist that you grant Morfudd what she asks. I believe it would be a Christian thing to do."

Owain raised his head and looked at Morfudd. He had a dogged look on his face but seemed unsure of himself. "Very well," he said. "I will yield to your advice, Bishop Tetra. As soon as the evening meal is over."

She nodded, satisfied. What could Morfudd's urgent news be? And why hadn't Morfudd told her about it? She gave Morfudd an encouraging smile, but Morfudd obviously did not see it as she bowed submissively to Owain. "Thank you, Lord Owain," said Morfudd. "And now, here comes the Archdruid."

"Ah yes," said Owain. He ran down the steps to intercept Doderin and guided him away from the others. They walked together around a corner of the building. As soon as they had disappeared, Badwin turned and went inside.

"Our fat friend didn't get to make his point," said Morfudd.

"Owain will get the Archdruid to go with Atak," said Tetra to Morfudd. "He's going to take your advice. I'm so glad he decided to listen to you. I can't imagine why he refused. But now that you've told him you have urgent news I'm sure he will. He will be kind to you when you tell him what you've told me."

She had hoped that Morfudd would give her a hint about the urgent news, but Morfudd smiled serenely through her tears and instead of looking at her looked at Atak. Tetra felt a twinge of alarm. Morfudd behaved almost as if she had some plan of her own that did not include Tetra. What could the news be that it must be kept a secret from her? And why should there be secrets between them? Perhaps it had been a mistake to press Owain into that private audience with Morfudd. Owain and Morfudd were both so much cleverer than she. What if they became fast friends? What would that do to her relationship with them? And what would she do if they quarreled again and Morfudd went away?

"If the Archdruid's coming with me," said Atak, putting his hand on Tetra's bottom, "he must hurry. I'm away after supper."

"If I were willing to wager with Tetra's husband," said Morfudd, giving Tetra a quick glance before turning her gaze back on Atak, "I would wager that you do not leave after supper. I would wager that you will spend at least one night here with your lovely wife."

Tetra darted a sharp glance at Morfudd, who still gazed serenely at Atak. What Morfudd said might be true, but did she have to say it just like that?

Atak grunted, then sighed. "You're probably right," he said.

"I won't get out tonight." He patted Tetra's backside. Not too long ago she would have welcomed the caress, crude as it was. Now she didn't know how she felt about it. "Let's go in," said Atak.

She put a hand out to Morfudd, and Morfudd gave it a gentle squeeze. Then Tetra went into the building, Atak close on her heels. Morfudd's eyes had been blank, devoid of interest, and she wondered with a sick feeling what had caused her to change like that. Atak put his arm around her waist and she wriggled out of his grip as they walked up the stairs. "Please don't," she said. "I don't feel like being touched right now." Atak pulled him to her even tighter and she pushed against his chest. "Sometimes," she said, trying to remember Owain's favorite words, "we have to do not that which we had rather not do, and do that which we had rather do."

Atak seemed puzzled then broke out into a smile. "So let's go do it," he said.

They made love in Tetra's room but to Atak it was unsatisfying. Tetra seemed preoccupied and wept throughout. "What's wrong?" he asked, but she only shook her head and wouldn't answer. It must be something to do with that Druidess, he thought. She was a beautiful woman but why did she suck the energy out of him with Tetra standing by? There was something strange and creepy about her. Seeing that Tetra had gone to sleep with a frown still on her face, he crept out of bed and got dressed. He needed a walk and some fresh air.

The courtyard was empty except for one or two emaciated looking men dressed in black. He wondered what they did as he went around the palace to the stables. His horse had been fed and rubbed down but the courier's horse was being led out. Like the courier, the poor beast had been given a quick meal and was now being sent off with its master to the next destination. Atak patted its rump as it went past him.

Going back into the palace he was about to climb the wooden stairs to Tetra's room when he passed a door and noticed that it was slightly open. He grasped the handle to pull it closed but heard a noise inside and on impulse opened the door and peeked in. His mouth and eyes opened wide in surprise. The Druidess and Owain, their clothes up around their shoulders, were making love on the floor next to a large table. Morfudd was on her back, head turned toward the door, and her eyes locked on to Atak's. She made no sign of alarm or recognition but simply stared at him with no expression, her body almost motionless as Owain heaved and groaned himself into ecstasy. Atak pulled the door closed and leaned against the wall while he recovered from the shock. Then he went back upstairs to Tetra. She was still asleep.

When they came down together to the main hall, the tables had been set up for the evening meal but most of them were empty. One or two of the priests smiled respectfully when they saw Tetra, but many seemed ill at ease. She wondered what was wrong. Had something happened to frighten them? As she and Atak got close to the table where she usually sat with the Archdruid, Owain and Almedha she moved more slowly and felt fearful, not knowing what to expect. The table was empty save for Almedha. Almedha stood up and clutched her throat as they approached: a sure sign that something was amiss. "Where is Lord Owain and the Archdruid?" asked Tetra as they sat down on the rough wooden bench. There was no sign of Morfudd.

Almedha sat down, still clutching her throat. She looked distressed. "The Archdruid called a Council meeting."

Atak raised his eyebrows. "It will be dark soon," he said. Councils never sat after dark.

Tetra leaned forward and tucked Almedha's hair behind her ear. She was about to ask what had happened, but right then a servant girl brought a basket of bread and an amphora of wine and set them on the table. Tetra watched dully as Atak grabbed a piece of the bread and began to wolf it down. For a moment she envied him. He had no aching voids that needed filling, no religious conflicts to settle, no Badwins competing for his place in life. Unlike her, he always knew exactly what to do and what would happen when he did it. Whatever needs he had were easily satisfied, and if he couldn't get them satisfied in one place he got them satisfied somewhere else. She felt tears coming to her eyes and fought to restrain them. Where had Morfudd gone? Had she abandoned Tetra? She almost feared to ask. "Where is Morfudd?" she said at last when the servant had gone. She poured wine into their cups. Her hand shook and she spilled a little.

"She went to the Council meeting. It was because of what she said that Lord Owain went to the Archdruid and the Archdruid called the meeting."

Relieved to hear that Morfudd was still nearby, Tetra lifted her cup to drink from it, but a thought struck her and instead she laid it down on the table. "Then she has already talked to Lord Owain? She didn't wait until after supper?"

"They were in the meeting room for a long time."

While Atak and me were making love, she thought. She looked at Atak and Atak gave her a strange sideways look as if he knew something she didn't. Morfudd must have known that's what I would have to do when I went upstairs with Atak. Was that why she had suddenly grown so cool and distant? And why she had left without saying a word? Atak pushed his empty cup toward her and she absently refilled it with wine. The servant girl reappeared carrying two bowls of hot stew on a tray. She placed one in front of each of them and Atak picked his up in both hands. He blew on it to cool the stew and cursed when it burned his lips and dribbled down his beard. "Use your spoon," she said, disgusted. "What did Morfudd tell Lord Owain that made him call a Council meeting?" she asked Almedha.

"She said the Romans had found out about the gold on Mona and a legion is coming to get it."

"What!" said Atak, holding the bowl away from his mouth and spilling the stew. "Which legion?"

So that was the urgent news! No wonder Owain and the

Archdruid had gone to the Council. But why had they taken Morfudd with them?

Almedha clutched her throat. "I don't remember, but she said it's on its way here."

"Was it the Fourteenth?" said Atak. "It's the closest."

"Yes. I think she said the Fourteenth."

"What kind of woman is this Morfudd?" said Atak to Tetra. "Is she to be trusted?"

"Oh yes," said Tetra. "She's a Nazarene. I would trust her completely."

"Well, I don't believe her. If the Fourteenth had moved we'd know." He stood. "I must get to the Council before they do something stupid." He picked up his bowl, took a great gulp of the hot stew and cursed again. "Did she say how the Rummies heard about the gold?"

"She had just come from Colchester," said Almedha. "She knows someone in the Governor's palace. They said a man named Secundus is the one who found out about it. There are spies among the Roman Nazarenes here on Mona who belong to him."

Atak shook his head disbelievingly. "I'd better go," he said. He squeezed Tetra's shoulder in farewell. "Save that stew for me. I'll eat when I get back." He pushed his way through the tables and went out of the door into the twilight. A few moments later she heard the horse's hooves clatter in the courtyard as he galloped off. So that was that, she thought. I won't see him for another six months.

After Atak left, Almedha watched intently through her hair while Tetra ate her stew. It was lamb boiled with vegetables and herbs, Atak's favorite. He would have enjoyed it. She would take his bowl up to her room, but it was unlikely that he would come back to eat it.

"Is Lord Atak right?" asked Almedha. She pulled her hair back revealing fearful eyes. "There is no legion on its way here?"

"He usually knows about those things."

"Why would Morfudd lie about something like that?"

Tetra paused, a piece of gravy soaked bread half way to her mouth. Had Morfudd lied to Owain? She shook her head to clear it. The truth would quickly be known. What would she gain by lying? "Maybe the scouts didn't see the legion leave," she mused. "Or they couldn't find Boudicca or Atak to tell them."

Almedha looked even more agitated. "Then it might be on its way here? What will we do if it comes on to Mona?"

"Lord Atak will find some way to stop it," she said.

"What will the Council do if the Romans take all the gold?"

"The Romans won't find it. The Council keeps it hidden and now they'll move it to a new hiding place. Did the Archdruid decide to go with Lord Atak?"

Almedha shook her head. "Their great concern was to get the gold moved and hidden right away," she said.

"Then why did Morfudd go with them to the Council?"

"Lord Owain seemed to expect her to go so she just went."

And now Morfudd will know where they've hidden it, Tetra thought absently. Owain must have lost the distrust he so plainly had when he last talked to Morfudd. What had happened to restore confidence in his old pupil? "Was Lord Owain civil with Morfudd?"

"Oh yes."

"Good," said Tetra, but for some reason felt uneasy. What had caused the change? If Morfudd had lied about the legion, what other lies had she told? While she ruminated, the girl who had served them came behind and touched her shoulder. Startled, she looked around, and standing next to the girl was a dark haired young woman, pretty and well dressed. She had large black intense eyes. "What is it?" she asked.

The strange girl smiled. She bowed her head but the bow was like that given by an equal rather than by a servant. "My name is Regan," said the young woman, her voice firm and clear. "I am servant to Morfudd. She told me to serve you. I am a gift from her."

Tetra felt her heart beat faster. So Morfudd must care for her. Her fears had been unfounded. But what would she do with another servant woman? "It is kind of Morfudd," she said. "But I already have a servant girl who looks after me."

"Send her back to the steward," said Regan. "Morfudd has given me to you because I will make you happier than anyone else can. Give me one day to show what I can do for you and then you will never give me up."

Tetra looked at Almedha, who laid her hands flat on the table and examined her fingernails with great interest. What was she to do? The girl was too self-assured by far and neither spoke nor acted like a servant. And yet she shuddered inwardly at the thought of Morfudd's displeasure should she not accept her gift. The bond between Morfudd and herself was not as firm as she had thought earlier. To refuse her gift might break it altogether. "Very well," she said. "I will accept."

"Then I will go to your rooms and prepare for you," said Regan. "Please direct this servant to take me there."

Tetra hesitated, dumbfounded. Regan spoke with authority, as if she had decided to take over Tetra's life, and Tetra wasn't sure that she liked the idea. Why did even the people she loved seem to make her life more complicated? She felt an urge to tell Regan she had changed her mind, but the words died on her lips when she looked into Regan's black liquid eyes. There was something about the girl that made her reluctant to offer a challenge. "Take Regan to my rooms," she said to the other servant. "I will be up shortly."

Uneasy, she stayed with Almedha much longer than she ordinarily would have. They talked about Morfudd's idea of a feminine side to God, and in spite of herself, she began to like the idea. Philip's concept of God had been a Spirit, a Mind of Christ that was both male and female, and that seemed somehow cold and cheerless. Almedha too had grown to like the idea and prattled on interminably about weaving it into her doctrine. While she prattled the servant girl made off with Atak's bowl of stew. She made a half-hearted attempt to halt the girl, but changed her mind. Atak would not come back. He never did. It grew dark and as the lamps in the hall were lit she found her mind drifting toward the Council meeting. What would they decide to do? Where would they hide their gold? Would Morfudd help them find a new hiding place? Something told her that Morfudd would be very good at that. And would Morfudd be able to get rid of the Archdruid and convince Owain to send the twenty million to King Marius?

With Morfudd, everything seemed possible, and she felt an inward glow at the prospect of being loved by such a bright and commanding woman. Morfudd was so far above her in every way that it made her feel like a child. She became so preoccupied that it took a little while for Almedha's silence to sink in. She realized Almedha had stopped talking some time ago and looked at Tetra in the faint yellow light as if she expected an answer to some question. "I'm sorry," she said. "Did you ask me something?"

"No," said Almedha. "If you will excuse me I will go to bed. Lord Owain is likely to be gone all night."

"Yes," said Tetra. "And Morfudd too. It will take them all night to hide the gold, if that's what they're doing."

***

When he arrived at the hill where the Council held its meetings, Atak saw moving lights ahead and came amongst a bevy of horse drawn carts and what seemed like scores of Druids scurrying around in the twilight carrying heavy packages like ants. They must be moving the gold. He dismounted when he found Owain with Morfudd and the fat Badwin watching servants load heavy bags on a cart. "I will send six guards with you," said Owain to Morfudd. "You must make it clear to King Marius that the marriage must take place in our church."

"I will, my dear Lord Owain," said Morfudd. She turned and saw Atak. "Why," she said, "Here is Lord Atak come to tell us he is leaving. And that I would have lost my wager if I had made it with him."

"What wager was that?" said Owain.

"She said I would spend the night with Tetra," said Atak. "What's all this about the Fourteenth coming?"

Morfudd put her hands against his chest and looked into his eyes. He could smell a faint perfume coming off her. "We're not sure," she said, "but it's better to be safe than sorry. Isn't that so, Lord Owain?"

"Yes," said Owain.

"I'm sorry that I lost my wager with you," she said. Her hands lightly massaged his chest and he felt her stomach lightly brush against his. Was she after his essence? "I must make it up to you."

He grunted and pulled on his beard. This woman was too deep. "I must get off," he said to Owain.

He rode away feeling that Morfudd held him in contempt. The Druidess was a cold passionless calculating female. She had looked right at him as she lay inert on the floor with Owain on top of her and had seemed equally unemotional and unembarrassed. How any woman could make love and not move a muscle was beyond him. She must feel nothing. She had lied about the Fourteenth coming and she was up to something. Oh well, he thought, Owain must look out for himself. I have work to do.

***

The hall was almost deserted. Most of the priests must have gone to the Council meeting. Tetra climbed the stairs wearily. Near the top she had a sudden conviction that she would never see Morfudd again and paused. The conviction was so strong that she wondered again why she had not left all this and gone with Elsa and Goronwy. What would she have really given up? A ridiculous hat, a pair of tight slippers and the title of Bishop? She had once promised to leave all for Christ but instead had hung on to heartache and dashed hopes. Even Atak whom she had once loved so frantically had ceased to please her. How much happier she would have been with Elsa and Goronwy. But the opportunity had long gone and she must do the best she could with the life that had been given her. She was tired, and things always seemed blackest when she was tired. The day had placed great demands on her and she looked forward to covering herself with sheepskins and losing herself in oblivion. Tomorrow would be a new day and there would be happiness in it for her. Morfudd would be back by morning and Tetra would tell her about her plan to let Morfudd be Bishop. For such a sacrifice, Morfudd must see how much she was loved and be kind in return. She would tell Morfudd how she had been hurt by her coolness, and beg her to always be the same toward her, to always love her as she had promised. To please Morfudd she would even give up Atak.

She had forgotten all about Regan and it was a shock to enter her room and find the girl waiting for her. A single oil lamp in the corner cast a warm yellow glow over the furnishings and its flickering light seemed to make Regan larger than life. She closed the door behind her and paused, unsure of herself, almost afraid as Regan came toward her. She lifted her hands protectively, but Regan laughed and held them within her own.

"You mustn't be afraid of me," said Regan, drawing her gently away from the door and toward the pile of skins on which she and Morfudd had lain that afternoon. "You must take off those warm sticky clothes so I can bathe you with these soft cloths. Here, smell the perfume in them." She held a damp soft cloth to Tetra's nose as she gently urged her down into the skins and then tenderly wiped her face and neck with it.

The perfume was heavy but pleasant, and Tetra felt her senses yielding as the hat was lifted from her and the robe drawn over her head so that only the thin shift remained. Losing her fear, she lay back against the skins and felt the tension of the day dissipate as Regan pulled off those horrid slippers. She stretched her toes and watched the graceful girl fold her robe and place it and the hat on a chest. "You don't talk like a Briton or a servant," she said. "Have you always lived in Britain?"

Regan sneered, but even her sneer was graceful. "I'm no more a Briton than you," she said. "Britons are stupid." She picked up a large silver cup in both hands and brought it to Tetra, kneeling before her and holding the cup. "You must drink this," said Regan, her large dark eyes softly gleaming above the cup's edge. "It's a wonderful nectar made in a secret way known only to Druid priestesses, and after you have drunk it I will bathe your body and brush your hair. You will think you are in heaven. Morfudd wants you to be in heaven always."

She drank slowly from the cup, her eyes fixed on Regan's. Regan's eyes seemed to expand and fill the whole room as the smooth creamy fiery liquid entered her body and took away all her strength so that she drifted away from the cup and sank deeper into the softness beneath her. "Drink more," said Regan, and she felt her head gently raised until her lips found the cup. Her body seemed to expand and rise, to lose any sense of weight or burden. Her mouth fell open of its own volition and she could feel without caring a trickle of the nectar make its way down her chin. Her arms fell to either side of her body and she couldn't make the effort to raise them again. She wanted to say something but couldn't. Her mouth moved but then stopped. A great corona of light edged her vision and through the central darkness she watched as Regan laid the silver cup on the floor and wiped the nectar from her chin.

She tried to smile but couldn't. Her body seemed to have stopped working, but she didn't care. She felt as if she were suspended in a heavy liquid and that no movement of any kind was required of her. She vaguely felt the shift drawn from her body and the smooth soft perfumed cloths gently caress her, wiping away all the cares she ever had. She was an infant being mothered by Regan, and as the reddening corona blotted out all darkness and all vision she thought: Tomorrow, tomorrow, Morfudd will come for me and all will be well.

Chapter 18

Brennius Fights

Several months later

The black wind drove the sleet so hard that a great cake of ice formed on Boudicca's stomach. She rode head down against the storm and wondered dully if she would be colder without the cake of ice than with it. It kept the wind from blowing straight through her, but its dank frigidness chilled her being so that all her movements slowed to a crawl. It was only noon but it might just as well have been midnight.

Around her plodded the remnants of Guderius' army. Ahead of them plodded the remnants of Velocatus' Brigante army. Venutius should stop campaigning and go south for the winter but he would have none of it. Not even the prospect of visiting their son Coilus, fostered to Marius and Dedreth since their marriage, would move him. His mind was closed to anything but Velocatus dead. Cartimandua had declared herself divorced from Venutius and betrothed to Velocatus, and already it was being said that her action stripped him of his right to be Arviragus. Much as she loved him she wished that he would be stripped of it so that it could be given to her.

Governor Didius Gallus was more interested in playing Fidchell with his new friend Prasu than conducting campaigns, so the two cohorts from the Ninth Legion that had been shadowing them for the past six months was the only Rummy activity to be concerned about. Without the essential haranguing of an Arviragus attuned to the main task of getting the Romans out of Britain there was no inducement to Kings and Council to maintain hungry armies in the field. Except for this ragtag that fruitlessly chased Velocatus most had been disbanded and thus a priceless opportunity to combine the British armies in an attack on the lethargic legions had been lost. She had tried to get Venutius to see this but his consuming hatred of Velocatus blinded him to reason.

She rode on grimly yearning to be Arviragus and at the same time yearning to see Goneril and Coilus again. Goneril was eleven now, growing into a beautiful warrior maiden out of her mother's sight. She ached to hold Coilus again, imagining him in Dedreth's arms instead of her own. Thinking of Dedreth reminded her that she had not yet been able to thank Ingenius for raising the ransom for Marius and Brennius even though she had been a little put out by his attitude. Could raising such a sum, large as it was, really threaten his security? She sniffed. He had become wealthy, and like most wealthy people, hated to part with what he had accumulated. By this time, Marius must have repaid him, but nonetheless she owed him her thanks and must give it.

Almost asleep, she plodded on until her horse collided with the one in front and stopped. She raised her head, eyes squinting against the wind and sleet. All the riders had stopped. A few horses whinnied in displeasure.

"What is it?" she asked a Catuve.

The Catuve shrugged apathetically and went back to sleep.

They sat like that for a long time, most of the men around her, like the Catuve, asleep. The sleet still whipped around them, but jammed together as they were it didn't seem as cold. She wondered why they had stopped. Then she too fell asleep.

Movement woke her up. Horses backed up and some shied. A dark shadow loomed ahead as a rider forced his way through to the rear. It was uncle Guderius, his gloomy features barely recognizable through the ice that clung to his face and beard. "We're camping here," he shouted as he pushed through. He pointed to her right and disappeared in the sleet, still shouting at the riders.

The mass of horses broke up as the army headed for cover. There was a river ahead, fast moving but shallow, and the horses picked their way through it, pausing to drink when they reached the other side. She felt the shelter of the cliff before she saw it. The sleet whirled aimlessly, no longer driven by the furious wind and soon even the wind ceased. Against the cliff it was windless and comfortable. She picked her way forward to find Venutius. His men already had a tent up and she crawled into it gratefully and stretched out on the ground.

Venutius awakened her. "Brennius has come," he said. "We're going to have a council."

Brennius, freckle faced, burly and with unkempt red hair and beard was in the tent brushing the snow from his clothes. He looked at her with his crossed eyes and she gave him a grim smile. Why had he followed them here? "I came to thank you for raising my ransom money, Aunt Boudicca," he said, as if in answer to her thought. "And wasn't it a fine thing for you to do."

"Thank your uncle Marius," she said. Brennius looked puzzled by her answer so she looked around the tent. Guderius was there, her younger brother Linus, Marius' underking Afan and two of Venutius' captains. "Where's Atak?" she said.

"Back with his Germans," said Linus.

"I'll get him."

Atak had talked some of his old Chattis into leaving the Rummies and joining the Britons. It made him happy to have his own guard. She staggered out of the tent and walked down the long line of men nestled against the cliff. The sleet had stopped and the sky said it was late afternoon. Hungry horses rooted in the snow for food. She found Atak among his Germans. Seeing him lying there it dawned on her that he was getting old. "Get up," she said and kicked his foot. He only grunted so she kicked him again.

"I'm stiff," he said.

"We're all stiff." She set off walking and he lumbered along behind her. They came to the tent and Brennius whirled to face Atak as they approached the circle of men.

"And who by the great Gum is this?" said Brennius. Atak yawned but said nothing. "Will you not answer me then?" said Brennius. He went over to Atak as Atak was about to squat and brought his fist around in a great swing against Atak's chin. Atak landed on his back and Brennius knelt by his side.

"And are you all right then?" said Brennius. "I would not have hit you but it came over me like a flash to wonder if such a man as you could be knocked off his feet by such a man as I, and before I knew I was going to do it I did it and sorry I am for the inconvenience of it, falling flat on your back as you did. Would you like to get up and take the swipe at me now?"

Atak shook his head.

"If you would," said Brennius, "twould be no bother at all."

"That's all right," said Atak, sitting up.

"This is Lord Atak," said Boudicca to Brennius. "He's been with us since the beginning. Atak, this is Brennius of the Trinoes, my nephew. He is High King now that his father has died. He was hostage with Marius in Hibernia and it cost us a fortune to get them both ransomed." Actually, she thought, it cost Marius a fortune.

"We'll have to raid the Ninth for food," said Venutius.

"Where are they?" said Atak.

"Ten miles up river," said Venutius. "All in winter tents and lots of provender. But we can wait till we get Velocatus."

"No we can't," said Boudicca. "Our men and horses haven't eaten a decent meal in two weeks."

"That swine is worse off than we are," said Venutius. "His men are exhausted and he's losing horses. If we raid the Rummies first they'll follow us and then find Velocatus. They'll join up with him."

"How far away is he?" asked Atak.

"Two or three miles. Our scout says they're all asleep."

There was a sudden shredding rip and a cold blast of wind. She leaped to her feet along with the others and they all drew their swords. An entire side of the tent had been cut so that a great section of it hung down and several dark heavily cloaked figures stood outside, one holding the sword that had cut the tent open. As they faced the figures, swords at the ready, there was another tearing rip behind them and they spun around to see more figures on the other side.

"Velocatus," said Venutius. He rushed out of the tent with Boudicca and the others close behind. So they're all asleep, she thought bitterly. A circle of men stood outside, swords pointed inward. Where were the men who had been guarding the tent? With Venutius and the others she crouched in the middle of the circle holding her sword for what seemed an eternity. Atak had disappeared and she wondered where he had gone.

Suddenly, Atak's Germans were on the outside of the circle and Velocatus' men wavered, holding their swords in one direction and looking the other. Then the leader threw down his sword and the men with him did likewise. "We didn't come to fight," said the man to Venutius. "I am King Grud. We bring a offer from King Velocatus."

"King?" said Venutius. "The only Velocatus I know is a servant."

"Oh he's a king all right. He's betrothed to Queen Cartimandua and she's made him as much a king as you ever was."

Venutius raised his sword as if to strike the man. "Watch your filthy mouth, you clot, or we'll kill the lot of you."

Grud flinched but stood his ground. "Well, he's a king anyway. When she marries him he will be High King of Southern Brigante."

"That is what I am you fool."

"I know naught about that."

"So you help Velocatus," sneered Venutius, sheathing his sword. "A king to help a servant. Well, what's his offer?"

"You and him should settle all with a fight."

"I should fight a servant? I am Arviragus of Britain."

"If he kills you your brother Caswal and the others will be freed and your army must go home so he can marry Queen Cartimandua in peace. If you kill him you will be High King of southern Brigante."

"I am already High King of southern Brigante," said Venutius. "Even if I were to disgrace myself by fighting him how can he offer me what is already mine?"

"Because it won't be yours if he marries her."

"I think you should do it," said Boudicca. "You should kill him and get this silly campaign over with."

Venutius whirled on her. "You think I should dishonor myself by fighting a servant?"

"Tis a good offer," said Guderius. "King or no, it will get this lot over with and we can go home."

"We have better things to do than traipse all over this Duw forsaken land," said Linus.

"You're all against me?" said Venutius. "You would have me sully my hands with servant's blood?"

"I'll fight in your place," said Brennius. "I care not whether his blood be royal or common. It will run the same off my invincible sword." Brennius drew his bright sword and waved it in the air. "This I won fair off King Feradach Finn Feactnach, son of the King of Connaught himself when I was hostage for the hundred cows spotted with white with their calves coupled together with yokes of brass, the hundred red javelins and the sixty barrels made of yew tree, the hundred brightly colored lances and the five hundred war cloaks, the fifty copper boilers and the hundred different colored horses the Aithech Tuatha said I owed for causing them to break their taboo when I rode their great bull for twenty miles into the lands of the Ulstermen and encouraged him tired as he was to service the six white cows of Fiacha. Tis a fine sword indeed, invincible it is, and there is no British sword the like of it. Fight in your place I will and cut the naughty man in pieces."

"To have a king fight in my place against a servant," said Venutius, "is as great a dishonor as to fight him myself. You will bring Velocatus here," he said to Grud, "and I will thrash him and let him go if he promises to stay away from my wife."

"She is not your wife," said Grud. "She divorced you."

"But I did not divorce her," said Venutius. "She is married to me. I am High King and she will not challenge my rights."

"That has naught to do with me," said Grud. "What must I tell King Velocatus? Is cross-eyes here going to fight for you?"

"Cross eyes!" roared Brennius. He grabbed Grud by the throat. "Tis yours that will be crossed after I rip the skin off your bones and strangle you with it." Still holding Grud he handed his sword to Atak, but as he turned Grud joined his fists together and brought them down on Brennius' neck, felling him to the ground. Brennius started to get up but Grud came at him with joined fists and knocked him down again.

"Let him get up," said Venutius.

"By Gorry and by Gum," said Brennius, getting to his feet, "if tis Velocatus you won't let me fight, let this kingly clot take his place. I will be you and fight him, and he will be Velocatus and fight me. Give me my invincible sword, and his guts will be sliced in nine hundred pieces." Atak handed him the sword. To Atak it looked flimsy.

"I will fight cross-eyes," said Grud. "But Velocatus must agree."

"Then send to him," said Boudicca. "Tell him King Brennius will fight for King Venutius and that you will fight for him. You will stay here as hostage while one of your men fetches him."

Venutius glowered but nodded agreement and one of Grud's men went to his horse and rode off.

"We must find a ford," said Brennius. "Such a battle as this must be done right and proper."

"The river only comes up to the horses' ankles," said Boudicca. "If you want a ford you'll have to go where it's deeper."

"The whole river's a ford," said Venutius. He scowled as if doubt had just filled his mind. "You can win this battle?" he said.

"This sword," said Brennius, raising the weapon above his head, "was blessed by the King of Connaught himself, and before that it was blessed by the blessed Bran himself. It will have his head off and his entrails scattered before his eyeballs have told his brains to get his bowels to empty themselves in the sheer terror of seeing its coming. Before his pitiful sword makes its first swing his arm will be dislocated from his body, his legs cut out from under him and his genitals flying through the air like a covey of pigeons with the Three Morrigans after em. Twill be the carving up of a pig for the feast."

"Then you will win?" said Venutius, doubt still on his face.

"He will win," said Boudicca, slapping Venutius on the back. "Marius has told me that Brennius is a great warrior."

"Would Marius know a warrior if he saw one?" said Guderius.

"By Gorry, he had better be," said Venutius. "If he is not I stand to lose what I can ill afford. If I am no longer High King of south Brigante, I am no longer Arviragus of Britain."

"He will win," said Boudicca, but doubt crossed her mind as she looked at Brennius. Could he stand against an old campaigner like Grud?

"There must be a bard," said Brennius. "There must be such a song of this that men will sing of it for nine thousand years."

"Get the Druid Mahel," she said, and a soldier went off to find him. Please Duw, she prayed. Please God, let Brennius win.

When Velocatus showed up heavily cloaked against the rain that had begun to fall, he had six horsemen with him. It was almost dark and Velocatus came close before he stopped. One of his men walked his horse before Venutius. "King Velocatus says he will accept King Brennius as King Venutius," said the horseman, "and King Grud will be him."

"If neither be killed," said Mahel the Druid Ovate, "the one defeated must surrender his claim to be husband or betrothed of Queen Cartimandua and High King of Southern Brigante."

"Aye," said Venutius.

"Aye," said the horseman.

"And it must be fought in the ford," said Brennius.

"Aye," said the man. "It matters little where tis fought." He turned to Venutius. "King Velocatus says that for old time's sake he is willing to give your army two days to get out of Brigante after King Grud has killed your champion."

"Tell that low born ex-servant of mine," said Venutius, raising his fist to the man on the horse, "that I will thrash him for his insolence as soon as his so-called champion has been sliced up and scattered to the wind."

"Can't do that," said the horseman. "The fight's the fight and that's all there is to it. You can't go after King Velocatus and he can't go after you."

"It would not be the fitness of things," said the Druid.

King Grud climbed on his horse ready to ride away. "The fight will begin at sunrise," Boudicca told him. "You will be here at dawn to fight in the river."

"In the river?" said Grud. "That water's like ice."

"King Brennius will fight no place but in the river," said Boudicca, and Grud glumly shrugged.

"It won't bother cross-eyes," he said, "because he'll be dead. I'm the one will have cold feet when it's all over. But if cross-eyes must die in the river, so be it."

As Velocatus and his men rode off, Boudicca returned to the ruined tent and squatted in the dark with the others against the front of it, the only part still not torn. Brennius seemed to have formed an attachment for Atak for he found Atak in the dark and squeezed in between the two of them.

"Let me feel that sword, again," said Atak, and Brennius drew it from its sheath and handed it to him. "What makes you think it's invincible?" said Atak, running his thumb along its edge.

"And wasn't I told so by Feradach Finn Feactnach himself," said Brennius. "And him the son of the King of Connaught. Why would such a man tell me what is not the truth of things?"

"If it is the truth of things," said Atak, "why would such a man part with such a weapon?"

"I won it from him fair and square. And he won from me the sword given to me by my great-uncle King Caratacus. That was a fine sword with gold and jewels on the hilt, but thicker and uglier. And twas not invincible."

"No sword is invincible," said Atak. "If it is, it's the man wielding it that makes it so. This feels a bit thin and over sharp. Use mine to fight Grud. It's thicker and stronger."

"No," said Brennius, taking back his sword. "I will trust the word of King Feradach Finn Feactnach himself, and I will trust my sword to be invincible. Better I trust it than me, for I know I am not invincible."

"That's a good thing to know," said Atak. He stretched out his legs in the mud. "With that in mind we duck faster."

The rain came down in torrents all night long, and during the short lulls when its force slackened and the lessening of its noise awakened her Boudicca could hear the roar of the river increasing as it rose in its banks. It wouldn't be one big ford by morning, she thought sleepily. Brennius and Grud would have to fight on the bank. Once during the night, when Atak's snoring awakened her, she thought of him getting knocked down by Brennius. He was getting too old to fight. The next fist he was unable to duck might be holding a sword.

The dawn broke as Boudicca and Atak followed Brennius to the river. A light rain fell but there was no wind. To their right a solid block of men and horses stretched all the way from the cliff to the riverbank. Velocatus' army. Upriver, their own men and horses milled around in the dim light as they formed up. Soon, the two armies faced each other. A wide space was left between them forming a broad avenue down to the river. Two horsemen approached and dismounted. One was King Grud and the other his man at arms. Mahel the Druid splashed through the mud toward them.

"May right prevail," said Mahel.

"It had better," said Linus, "or we shall have no Arviragus."

"Why is your army here?" said Boudicca to Grud.

"They want to see me kill cross-eyes," said Grud.

Brennius stood looking at the boiling river, hand on his hips. He moved a few feet to his left and made a mark in the mud with his foot, then turned as they came up to him. "And isn't this the ford of fords," he said. "Where is the bard to witness every stroke of my invincible sword as I fill the river with Brigante blood?"

"The Druid Mahel is here to see right is done," said Boudicca. This morning she felt horror struck by what they had agreed to. Her confidence in Brennius had sunk to its lowest ebb.

"'Tis not right to fight in that," said Grud, looking at the river. "'Tis roaring like the bull that jumped over a wall that was too high for all of himself to clear. We'll fight on the bank."

"Nay," said Brennius. "We fight in the ford."

"There is no ford," said Grud.

"Let the Druid decide," said Boudicca. "The fight was accepted on condition it be fought in the river. Shall that condition be set aside?" If they fought in that river and Brennius' sword was as useless as it looked, the river might let Brennius get Grud off balance so he could kill him before his sword broke.

"The condition imposes the same hardship on both," said Mahel. "Let the condition prevail."

"The water is but three feet deep," said Brennius. "Are you too old and feeble and craven to get your feet wet?"

"By Gorry," said Grud, drawing his sword. "No man shall call me craven, let alone a stripling runt with crossed eyes."

"Then stop your caterwauling and come at me," said Brennius. He drew his sword and raised it above his head. Grud made to lunge at him and Brennius jumped into the river. There was enough of a hesitation before he jumped to show he had picked a place to jump to. Brennius landed with his legs apart, the water up to his groin. He staggered under the force of the current and then regained his balance. "Come, you craven old crock," he roared. "Even with your rheumy eyes you can see the water comes barely above my knees. Jump in and fight."

Grud peered at the swiftly rushing water and hesitated.

"Come, you chicken hearted coward," roared Brennius. "Will you sacrifice your army and your king for naught? Jump." A roar of anger welled up in support from Velocatus' army.

Grud jumped. He landed as far out as Brennius, but Brennius must have jumped on a large submerged rock. Grud went in up to his chest and was bowled over by the current. Both his feet came out of the water as he somersaulted. When his head reappeared he was far downstream. Another roar of anger welled up from his army, but the roar died away as Grud got himself a firm footing and raised his sword, head barely above water. "Come down here and fight," he shouted.

"I was first," shouted Brennius. "You must fight here."

"'Tis easier for you to get to me than for I to get to you," roared Grud.

"Nonetheless," said Brennius. "You must fight me where I stand. Ask the Druid. Is that not so?"

"That is so," said Mahel. "First in sets the place of combat."

Grud roared in disgust but began to battle his way upstream toward Brennius. Several times he lost his balance and was almost swept away but recovered and kept grimly on. Boudicca felt better. Grud would be tired by the time he reached Brennius and that would be in their favor. She looked up at the sky. It was gray but patches of white showed through and the rain had stopped. Maybe the sun would break through. A sudden roar broke her reverie and she saw that Grud had got himself within striking distance of Brennius. The fight was about to begin.

Grud swung first. His sword made a great arc that would

have disemboweled Brennius had Brennius not leaned back to avoid it, losing his balance as he did so. Brennius' feet came out from under him and he fell backward to disappear under the water. Grud moved forward to press home his attack, but he too fell forward before he reached Brennius and disappeared under the surface. While under it, he must have found Brennius' rock, for he climbed upon it and slashed at the water around him with his sword trying to find Brennius, who had disappeared from view.

With a great shout, Brennius suddenly emerged from the water downstream of Grud and came at Grud from behind. Grud turned crabwise on the rock and the battle waxed fast and furious, Grud kneeling and holding on to the rock with one hand while slashing with the other. Several times, the swords met with a clang, and each time she winced, expecting Brennius' sword to break. Brennius kept working his way around Grud as they fought and once Grud almost lost his grip on the rock when Brennius' sword came too close and he had to duck.

To this point, neither one had wounded the other, but it seemed that Grud's blows were getting wilder. Suddenly, Grud struggled to his feet and lowered his sword as he swayed back and forth on the rock. "Tis not right," he roared to the Druid. "I cannot fight a man with crossed eyes. I do not know at which eye to look. Make him cover one eye."

"Nay," said Brennius, lowering his sword. "How can I fight with but one eye? Tell him to stop caterwauling like a goat in heat and fight."

"The fight must go on," said Mahel to Grud. "You knew he was cross-eyed when you agreed to fight."

With a snort of rage, Grud took a wild two-handed swing at Brennius. Brennius put up his sword to counter the blow and with a sharp crack his weapon broke off leaving just a third of it above the hilt. Boudicca grimaced. The fight was over unless Grud did something stupid or Brennius something clever. Sword raised to strike the finishing blow, Grud leaped off the rock as

Brennius looked at his ruined weapon. He came down in the water by Brennius with a great crash but the sword missed by more than a foot.

As Grud staggered forward from the impetus of his own blow, Brennius seized his own ruined sword by the remnant of its blade and brought the hilt down on Grud's neck. Grud disappeared under the surface and when he reappeared he was a long way down river. He rolled over and disappeared. A watery sunrise broke through as if to celebrate Brennius' victory, and a roar of joy rose up from Venutius' army as Brennius struggled ashore still holding his broken weapon.

"What is your verdict, my lord Druid?" asked Boudicca.

"King Brennius has won the battle," said Mahel, "and King Velocatus must give up his claims."

There was a roar of anger from Velocatus' army and Velocatus himself rode forward to halt beside Boudicca and her companions. "It was not right," he said, "that King Grud had to fight a man with crossed eyes and in a river."

"Nonetheless," said Boudicca, "those were the conditions you agreed to and you must abide by the consequences."

"We'll see about that," said Velocatus. "Tweren't a fair fight."

"You will disperse your army at once," said Venutius, riding up. "You are lucky that I do not thrash you here in front of your men. Now get them out of here and yourself out with em."

"Why don't you get yourself out of here," said Velocatus. "It weren't a fair fight."

"By Gorry," said Venutius, his face red with fury. He turned on Boudicca. "You see what happens when you treat with servants? They have no honor. Their word is worth nothing." He turned back to Velocatus. "Get back to your army," he said. "We will destroy it and you with it."

"I wouldn't be too sure about that," said Velocatus. "You'd better look behind you."

Venutius turned to look upriver. To see better, he stood precariously on the horse's back. What he saw set his face in stone. She and the others also turned to look, but being on foot could not see beyond their own army. "What is it?" she said, going to Venutius.

As if to answer her question, trumpets blared out in the distance, and her heart sank. Those were Roman trumpets. They were trapped between the cliffs and the river, Velocatus on one side and the Roman cohorts on the other. Velocatus must have appealed to the Rummies and sent men out to kill Venutius' scouts so Venutius would not be warned of the Roman's advance. There was no way out of this trap. Faced with Velocatus alone they might have prevailed, but with this much stronger force combined against them there was no hope. She looked up at Venutius. His face was bleak.

Chapter 19

Ingenius Brings News

Atak's hands were so cold he could no longer feel the sword. It dropped to the ground and he stooped to pick it up.

"Why don't they attack?" said Boudicca. "They have more men and they're fed and rested." All the kings stood around her in a knot looking at the Romans. Atak sheathed his sword and hoped no one had noticed its fall.

It was growing dark but there were few clouds and the moon was already visible. The cold and hungry Catuve army had stood at arms all day, ready to defend itself against the mass of Roman armor on one side and the rag tag army of Velocatus on the other. At midday the river had begun to fall and Atak thought they might be able to escape across it during the night. But the Romans forded it higher up and now an entire cohort faced them on the other bank. By itself the cohort was stronger than their army and there was yet another facing them on this side.

On the cliffs above their heads, Brigante warriors carried supplies down to Velocatus' army. Watching their foes being fed while they starved enraged the Catuves, so that it took all Guderius' and Venutius' will power to keep them from attacking.

"As soon as it gets dark," said Boudicca, "I will take Atak's Germans and get us some food."

"Where from?" said Guderius.

"We'll take it from Velocatus," she said, pointing to a fissure in the cliff face. It promised enough footing to get to the top. "If the Rummies haven't attacked during the day, they won't at night. We can at least get our men fed."

"I'll get them together," said Atak.

"You're not going," said Boudicca.

"They won't go without me," said Atak, offended.

"They will if you tell them to. You're too old for this, Atak. You proved that last night."

"You mean when Brennius hit me? I was squatting."

She shrugged. "Your fighting days are over."

Atak pulled on his beard. Boudicca must have seen him drop his sword. He would never have dropped it if his hands hadn't been so cold. "You didn't say that when Grud's men had you surrounded and I put my Chattis around them."

Her eyes got colder. "Are you going to tell your Germans to follow me or not?"

A great temptation welled up in him to walk away from her, but he couldn't bring himself to do it. So this was her thanks for all his years of service—to be told he was too old to fight? He just hoped she didn't need his sword at her side again as she had so often in the past. A quick vision passed through his mind of a naked and frightened young Boudicca in the burning shipyard at Boulogne, about to be raped by a Roman legionary. She had not quibbled about his age then. Too old to fight? He would never have been too old to swing a sword for her. "All right," he said. "I'll tell them." He brushed by Venutius and marched off to find his Germans, body more erect and step more vigorous than usual.

"You hurt his feelings," he heard Linus say.

Later, he stood glumly watching as Boudicca climbed up the fissure and disappeared into the darkness, his Chattis right on her heels. He hoped she would be able to handle them if they got excited. He felt a wet hand on his shoulder and turned. It was

Brennius and Brennius was soaking wet. He held a long piece of iron in his hand and the metal glinted in the moonlight.

"I found me invincible sword," he said. "You would not believe how many rocks and caves and holes there are in that river, or how strong the water is and how it hurries to get to the sea, but by the great Gum himself I found it. Took me a whole day and I thought once I was a gonner but there it was shining away with the holy light that Bran the Blessed bestowed upon it and it drew me to it because it knew I was its master and its little soul belonged to me. Was there ever such a fine sword, now?"

"It's too thin and sharp," said Atak, avoiding Brennius' cross-eyed look. "What are you going to do now you've found it?"

Brennius stuck his face in front of Atak's so that he was forced to look at him. He felt his own eyes cross in sympathy with Brennius' and could see why Grud had such a hard time of it during the fight. "And aren't I going to have the hilt put onto it?" said Brennius. "Twill be shorter but just as shiny bright."

"It will be stronger if it's shorter," Atak agreed.

Brennius grabbed him by the arm and steered him over to the cliff away from the others. "It's your advice I'm wanting," he said. "But not about swords."

They squatted at the foot of the cliff and Brennius jabbed his invincible sword into the earth so that it stood upright. He leaned so close that Atak could feel the water in Brennius' clothes soaking into his own. "When my father King Elidurus sent my uncle King Marius to find me in Hibernia," he said, "and me in hock for innumerable cattle, hides, war cloaks, copper boilers and barrels because I rode the great bull into the lands of the Ulstermen to service the six white cows of Fiacha, he sent me a message in case by the time I got back to become High King of the Trinoes, which I am, he was dead, which he was, and may his saintly soul rest in peace in the Otherworld."

"What was the message?" said Atak.

"He said that because our nation had been raped and pillaged by the foul Rummies, and our lands taken away from us and our treasuries emptied and our holy sites desecrated and our nobles humiliated and our slaves impressed, he had pledged to bow the knee to Aunt Boudicca whenever she called the nations to rise and throw the Rummies back into the water that bore them to our shores. Now the advice I would ask of you, my wise old German friend . . . "

"I am not that old," said Atak. "I am as hale and hearty now as I was thirty years ago."

"Then be my wise and ageless German friend and may your sword arm never falter in the service of our cause. The advice I would ask of you is should I indeed do it? No sooner had I arrived back in my own palace, beholden to Boudicca as I am for my ransom, and talked to my own kings and nobles, sad and sorry lot they are what with not eating regularly and hatred of the Rummies gnawing at their vitals like a horde of hungry rats, than she sent word she looked upon me and my own kings as bound by my father's pledge. I didn't say that I would not, nor yet did I say that I would, nor have I yet said either way though she prods me day and night about it. Now I ask you, do you see any sign that if the nations rose she would indeed be able to throw the Rummies back into the foul ocean that bore them here? Would she be any better than Venutius at leading us against the Rummies?"

"Did someone send you to find this out?"

"Aye, the Druids of the Council at Mona. There are those who say Boudicca would be a better Arviragus than Venutius, but how would either one of them, they say, who can't get a grip on Velocatus, hope to get a grip on the Rummies? And if neither one can get a grip on the Rummies, where in this blessed island are we to look for an Arviragus? Many have come to the thought that such a person cannot be found in this army, bottled up as it is like a bee in a barrel with its head missing and its wings broken and its sting pulled out of it."

Atak pulled on his beard. So Brennius had been sent up here to find out what was going on. What were they all doing up here in the far north, cut off from any news of what was happening in the south where all the action was? How had they got themselves into this morass?

His anger rose again when he remembered Boudicca's cutting words dismissing him as too old to play a part in this silly venture. He knew how desperately she wanted to lead the armies of Britain. Here was a good way to balance the books. A few words from him could ruin her chance of ever becoming Arviragus. Brennius and the Druids were right. Venutius had lost both his wits and his leadership ability, obsessed as he was by his desire to avenge himself on his old man at arms. Yesterday, he would have said that Boudicca would make a much better Arviragus. Now, he wasn't sure what he would say.

"Well?" said Brennius.

Before he could answer, a great black object fell to the ground just a few feet from them. With a loud crash it flew apart and something struck Atak a heavy blow on the side of his head.

"Watch out below," shouted a voice from above as two more black objects hit the ground even closer than the first one. With a curse, Brennius jumped to his feet and ran, Atak close on his heels. Other crashes told of more objects landing, but they stopped running when they cannoned into men running the other way.

"It's food," someone shouted. "Boudicca's got food." Atak and Brennius ran back with the men toward the cliff. A horde of men and horses were already scavenging among the supplies that Boudicca had dropped from above even though crashes and an occasional scream told of more supplies being dropped. Atak picked up something from the ground and saw it was a large piece of salted meat.

"Back!" shouted Brennius at the men. "Get back will you and let the cooks at the flaming food. Light fires and we'll put grease on our knives and hot food in our bellies."

Guderius and Venutius ran to the scene and shouted also, but the hungry soldiers continued to wolf down the uncooked food. After a while, the kings sat down with their backs to the cliff, each with a piece of salted meat in his hands. Brennius called to Atak and as he went to join him he saw that the large object, a piece of which had struck him, was a cart. Two of the wheels were missing. He sat down and began to chew on his salted meat.

"Well?" said Brennius. "Do we have an Arviragus or is it another one we must look for? And if tis another then who is it to be? Must we get Cartimandua herself?"

Atak belched. The meat was rancid. The Romans must have passed along their spoiled food to Velocatus' men. Boudicca should have taken his Chattis the other way. He laid the meat down on the ground and began to chew on an ear of corn. As he did, Boudicca walked past on her way to join Guderius and Venutius, a piece of the spoiled meat in her hand. She looked tired and fretful. His Chattis had probably given her a hard time. "Give me till morning to think about it," he said.

Atak grunted and moved his foot, but the insistent kicking went on. He found it harder of late to wake up in the mornings but he finally opened his eyes and sat up. The sun had risen behind the cliff and the snow on the hills in front of him glowed in the early morning light. Brennius continued kicking until Atak threw off his sheepskin and got stiffly to his feet. He stood glowering at the cross-eyed young king.

"Do ye see anything across the river?" said Brennius. Atak shook his head. His horse stood in front of them rooting among the remains of the food and blocked most of his view. His stomach rumbled from the tainted meat and he was too tired to move to a better vantage point.

"Do ye see anything to our right?" said Brennius, and Atak peered to his right. But for their own men sleeping nearby, the ground between the cliff and the river was empty as far as he could see, save for dead horses, wrecked wagons and much litter.

"Velocatus," said Atak, pulling on his beard. "He's gone."

"Aye, he has that. And don't you remember the Rummies waiting across the river for us?"

Atak shook himself awake. He pushed Brennius and the horse aside. Across the river there wasn't a Roman in sight.

"Now," said Brennius, putting his hands on his hips. "Look to our left, will ye, and tell me what you see."

Atak could see nothing but the backs of their own men staring off in the direction of the Romans and chattering excitedly. He heaved himself up on the horse's back. The Romans had not gone, but they were forming up. He almost kicked the horse into motion to join Venutius and Boudicca, but restrained himself when he saw the Romans were formed up not to attack but to march. As he watched, trumpets sounded and the leading cohort began to march away from them. "They're leaving," he said. "Why?"

"Should I call them back then?" said Brennius. "Should I challenge the leader of such a fine body of men to fight me in the ford, his little meat carver against my invincible sword with the new hilt I have yet to have put on it? Or should we let them go and see how much food they've left behind?"

"I'm going to see what happened," said Atak.

"And I will come with you," said Brennius.

Venutius was also on horseback watching the departing Romans, as were Boudicca and Guderius. Atak threaded his way through the excited soldiers, Brennius behind and to his left, and stayed his horse at Venutius' left. He could not bring himself to talk to Boudicca. "What's happening?" he asked.

"As soon as we know for sure where those Rummies are headed," said Venutius, "we're going after Velocatus."

"Then you will go by yourself," said Boudicca. "I have had enough of this foolish campaign."

"Me too," said Guderius.

"We have lost enough time and men already," said Boudicca. "Only a fool would lose more."

"Then I am now to you a fool?" shouted Venutius, his face brick red. Boudicca said nothing, but moved her horse away.

"Look," said Guderius, pointing. "Rummies are coming."

A small group of horsemen had separated themselves from the main body and came toward them at a walk.

"They're not all soldiers," said Atak. The two men leading the group were unarmed and unarmored. The armored men were probably an escort.

Boudicca gasped and threw a quick alarmed glance at Venutius. "It's Sabinus," she said. "And Ingenius is with him." She backed her horse around so that her sword arm faced Venutius and put her hand on the hilt of her weapon. "You will not move toward him," she said.

Venutius' face blackened, but he said nothing.

Sabinus and Ingenius stopped their horses a few feet away and Ingenius dismounted. Sabinus looked at Boudicca and Venutius and nodded gravely. Boudicca nodded back, equally grave. Ingenius' face was serious and he looked ill. He glanced at Atak with a wan smile and walked over to Boudicca. "I have come with news for my queen and King Venutius," he said. "And with sad news for Atak." Tetra, he thought. Tetra's sick.

"And what has your companion brought?" said Boudicca.

"I have brought news that Claudius is dead," said Sabinus. "The legions can do nothing until the new emperor declares his policy toward Britain. The Governor believes the legions will be withdrawn to Gaul. If so, there will be no further need for you to take the field."

Boudicca said nothing for a few moments, then looked down at Ingenius. Atak wondered what Ingenius' sad news was. "And what is your news?" asked Boudicca.

"The High Council requests that the Arviragus return as quickly as possible to Mona," said Ingenius, turning to Venutius.

"Why?" said Venutius.

"There is to be a meeting of Kings and Council."

"What is the meeting for?" asked Boudicca.

Ingenius reddened and looked uncomfortable.

Boudicca turned to Venutius, her face angry. "It's to appoint a new Arviragus," she said. "Why else would they have Kings and Council? Do you still insist on this foolhardy chase?"

"The Council asks that King Venutius leave Brigante with the utmost speed," said Ingenius. "Queen Cartimandua has said she will not join the Alliance unless this is done."

Venutius jerked on his reins so that his horse reared. Atak quickly edged his to one side, forcing Brennius against the cliff. What he had feared was coming true. Venutius looked as if he were about to go berserk. "By Duw!" roared Venutius. "That woman has tried my patience for the last time. She has never intended to be in the Alliance, and now she works the Council to get me dismissed. She has sullied her throne by betrothing herself to a servant, but by the Three Morrigans she shall sully it no more."

He drew his sword and raised it over his head. "She shall die," he said, urging his horse forward. "And by Duw," he said, "so shall your Rummy lover." He brought his horse up against Sabinus' and drove his sword through the tribune's midriff.

Boudicca shrieked and dismounted to run to Sabinus. Venutius withdrew his sword with a snarl, and was holding it straight before him, Sabinus' blood dripping from it, when one of the armed escorts, who had ridden forward when Venutius charged, brought his sword down on Venutius' sword arm, almost severing it at the wrist. The sword flew from Venutius' hand and he sat his horse watching the blood pour from him, a puzzled expression on his face, while the escorts rode off after the retreating Romans. Boudicca caught Sabinus as he slid from his horse and lowered the ex-tribune gently to the ground, tears streaming from her eyes. Ingenius ran to them, while Atak dismounted and went to Venutius. His first thought was that a crippled Venutius could no longer be Arviragus. But would the Council appoint Boudicca if the Romans were about to leave? "Raise your arm," he said, as he, Brennius and Guderius brought the dazed Venutius down from his horse and laid him on the ground. "It will slow the blood."

The Druid Mahel bent over the prostrate Venutius and poured

liquid between his teeth from a small amphora. "Hold his arm up," he said. He looked around at Atak. "I need something to wrap it." Atak pulled off his shirt, tore it into strips and handed them to Mahel. Mahel wrapped the strips as tightly as he could around Venutius' wrist and hand. The strips quickly became blood soaked. He held some twigs and herbs against the wrapping and twisted more strips around those. "Keep the arm up," he said.

Venutius nodded slightly, his face white and eyes glazed. His arm started to fold against his chest but Guderius caught it.

Atak went over to Boudicca, who still sat holding Sabinus' head. Her weeping had stopped but she too seemed dazed. One glance told him Sabinus was dead. Ingenius was on his knees by Sabinus' side, eyes wet with tears. Boudicca looked at Atak but said nothing. "The Druid said Venutius might lose the use of his arm," he said. He turned to Ingenius. "What's the sad news for me?"

"Tetra," said Ingenius, and Atak nodded. He had known it must be about Tetra. "She's dead," said Ingenius.

"Dead?" He pulled on his beard. "Dead? When?" He was not able to take it in. "How did it happen?"

"Owain said it was the night the Council moved their gold to a safer place."

"That's the night I left. We ate together." And I never went back, he thought. He had meant to but had come on this stupid campaign with Boudicca instead.

"Owain said she just died in her sleep."

How could she have just died in her sleep?

Boudicca looked down on Sabinus. "It is strange," she said, "that I could ever feel kindly toward a Roman but I did. He was a good man and would have become a Briton." She got to her feet. "We will bury him here," she said. "Then we must go to the Council."

Atak followed her as she walked over to Venutius and knelt by him. Venutius had lost consciousness. "He has been well and truly punished," she said. "Dear God I wonder what my punishment will be for having driven him to this." She bent over and kissed Venutius then slowly got to her feet. Atak felt her light touch on his arm and looked unseeingly at her. "You must be my right arm," she said. "You must forever be my sword."

Part III

58—61 A.D.

(Three years later)

Chapter 1

Owain Corresponds

From Lord Owain Longhead to King Caratacus in Rome. Sire:

Hearing that your son King Linus is to visit you in Rome I have sent with him this hasty epistle.

Didius Gallus' term of office has expired and we do not know who is to take his place nor the policy to be implemented by the new Governor. The High Council would welcome any information you can acquire. Under Gallus' governorship we have enjoyed a reign of comparative peace as the new Emperor Nero seems to have forgotten about Britain. Gallus and King Prasu became great friends and much of Gallus' time was usefully spent (as far as we are concerned) in arranging Fidchell contests among high Britons and Romans. Gallus also, at King Prasu's request, gave a full pardon to Queen Boudicca, who had been under a cloud because of her suspected role in destroying the Twentieth Legion.

When King Venutius was forced to relinquish Pendragon because of the wounds he received in his unwise invasion of Brigante territory, Kings and Council decided not to appoint a new Arviragus in the fear that the status quo with Rome might be disturbed. It was a decision neither Queen Boudicca nor I concurred in, but we were overruled. Many felt that besides the Romans, Queen Cartimandua also would be offended by her appointment and thus might not join the Alliance. Since the decision, Queen Cartimandua has still not consented to join, and because of the general lack of pressure from the Romans and in the absence of a commander charged with maintaining our armies our warriors disbanded and all operations against Rome ceased. With this change in governors, however, the Council has decided it must take some precautionary action. Queen Cartimandua is still opposed to Queen Boudicca being appointed Arviragus, and as your seven-year exile will end next year, the Council has asked me to request that you will accept responsibility for the defense of Britain when you return. Please let me know if this is possible.

A small body of Romans invaded Mona under cover of darkness about three years ago and absconded with a significant amount of your gold as well as a little of the Council's. It is not clear how these men heard of or found the gold as it had only recently been moved to a more secure hiding place. The Council has since placed the remaining gold in the care of your son, King Eudal Marius, who has hidden it in the western mountains. It was a great disappointment to the Council that, having provided the ransom that freed King Marius and King Brennius, your son ignored the Council's request that he be married in the First Holy Christian Church of Britain and elected instead to be married by those the Council has declared heretic. The Council hopes you might be able to persuade your son to better support his nation's proper institutions.

Please give my love and respect to your wife the Queen, the Princess Eurgen, my wife the Princess Gwendolyn and her friend Priscilla and especially Paul, whom I hope has finished the tent he was making in Corinth. Please ask Gwendolyn to tell Paul that our church is growing apace now that we have explained to the people the three natures of God as defined in Hebrew scriptures. I had hoped to pay another visit to Rome and Corinth now that Claudius is dead, but what with pressing Council and church business I have not had the time.

Hoping that we will soon see you once again on these shores,

Your son in law, friend and loyal subject,
Lord Owain Longhead of Caerwent

***

Reply from King Caratacus in Rome, dictated to his daughter the Princess Gwendolyn and delivered by the sailor Buel.

Dear Lord Owain Longhead of Caerwent:
My father directs me to write as follows—
Gallus has arrived here. I can see why he got along well with Fat Prasu, they're two of a kind. Nero made him dance for everyone and now he has to learn to play the harp. The new Governor is to be Quintus Veranius, a skinny man with teeth. Nero hasn't forgotten Britain. Veranius has been told to capture the western mountains and wipe out Brigante by next year. He says he can do it, but not if you have an Arviragus worth a bucket and a half of watercress. He's been taking care of some buildings here but now they're saying he's a diplomat. All I've seen him do is show his teeth. It's a good set of them he has but I don't know that he can bite with them.

How can you tell it was my gold that was stolen and not the Council's? When is the Council to make up my losses? And what makes you think Marius will guard it better than you did? Everyone here knows it's in the Western mountains and Seneca is laying odds of four to one his man Catus finds it first. To be on the safe side I've written to ask my cousin King Silent to bring his stealthy men over to help when Veranius arrives. You may have to lend him the widow Angarad again for his trouble but whatever you have to give him will be worth it. As for asking me to be Arviragus again, the Council must be out of its gourd. Six years of Roman living has done me in. I am coming back to spend my last years at Caer Leon with Genvissa so tell Eudal Marius to have it ready for me. Tell the Council Boudicca's the only man left among the kings I know of who can tell a salmon from a snake and she should get Pendragon. Put her in charge of the gold or we'll all lose our tunics.

Caratacus, Hammer of the Cymry.

P.S. Thank you for your kind thoughts and we are all glad you're doing well. In case you were concerned I will not be coming back with mother and father as Priscilla has invited me to share her home. All who met you in Rome and Corinth send their good wishes for your church, although none of us here understand what you mean by the three natures of God. Paul has not yet finished making the tent. His travels with Timothy keep him very busy and he says carrying it around with them is a thorn in his side. He also gets upset because Timothy keeps adding paragraphs to his letters and mixing up the pages.

Love, Gwendolyn.

Chapter 2

Veranius Makes a Proposition

It was the first time Owain Longhead had been in Ingenius' house. The servant who admitted him led him into the crowded great hall and then disappeared. Nobody paid any attention to him and he momentarily regretted the decision to exchange his red robe of office for the plain dress of a British lord. Ingenius had advised that all attendees wear plain clothes as the retired legionaries in Colchester would rough up any Briton whose dress indicated a high station. The new Governor was to be introduced to what he thought were loyal subjects and Owain reluctantly agreed it was wiser not to draw attention to his rank. He hoped the other kings and Druids also had enough sense to disguise themselves.

He peered over the heads of the Romans and Britons jostling each other as they drank wine and chattered, but couldn't see any of the kings or queens whom the Council had asked Ingenius to assemble. He wondered if the messengers had been waylaid, as so often happened, and whether, after all the trouble of coming here, there would even be a meeting of Kings and Council later on to decide what to do about the new Governor.

He sat down on a polished wooden bench near the door and looked with lowered brows around the highly decorated and wonderfully furnished hall, unable to restrain a sniff. Ingenius was barely thirty years of age. How could such a comparative youth afford a house fit enough to entertain kings and queens and Roman Governors? Owain was approaching his forty-ninth birthday and what did he have to show for all his hard work and sacrifice? He and Almedha merely occupied living quarters in Doderin's ramshackle old palace on Anglesey. And the doddering Doderin showed no signs of relinquishing his post as Archdruid. He gritted his teeth and clutched his throat with his right hand, then immediately blushed and took his hand away.

A servant saw the motion and brought him a cup of wine. He had picked up the habit of clutching his throat from Almedha and would have to gain better control over himself. When he became Archdruid, he thought grimly, he would have built for himself a palace that would put Ingenius' house to shame. And then he would have to decide what to do about Morfudd.

On the afternoon of the day the Council moved its gold, overcome it seemed with grief because of his mistrust of her, she had placed her hands in his then gone limp in his arms, body pressed to his, breath coming quick, eyes closed and mouth partly open as if suddenly consumed by passion. Slowly and gracefully she had sunk beneath him to the floor. Driven almost out of his mind by the softness of her body and the heady aroma of her perfume he had opened her robe and found her naked beneath it. With not the least sign of resistance she had accepted his frantic caresses and let him enter her. Only when he was approaching the last extremity of his pleasure did she move as if awaking from sleep and cried out with horror, pushing him away unsatisfied. She had accused him of raping an innocent woman who had fainted in his arms, and though he suspected that he had been seduced he had no defense against her. From that moment she had been mistress of his church.

She had repelled any advance yet she constantly teased him sexually to worm one concession after another from him. He suspected she must have told the Romans where the Council's gold had been hidden but he had grown so dependent on her teasing that he had been afraid to question her when so much of the gold suddenly disappeared. When the news came that Bodin had married Sibyl, the wealthy daughter of King Divicorix of the Parisi, she vowed to destroy Bodin's church and teased Owain until he made her bishop in lieu of Badwin, who like Tetra, had suddenly died in his sleep. Since then she had remade the church in her own image and it had tripled in size. Some of the growth had come about because she now offered guarantees of admittance into the Otherworld. Ten more Holy Christian Church buildings had been erected in the last year, while some of Bodin's had mysteriously burnt to the ground.

Many of the warriors who avoided the other churches had joined Morfudd's, which at first had pleased him greatly, but now he was no longer sure what she or the many priestesses she had engaged did. Even Almedha seemed unsure about what went on at the frequent love meals that were celebrated. At least, he sniffed, she would not tell him what went on. Perhaps it was just as well he didn't know. He had been shocked to find out that statues of Roman gods were in several of the churches. When he became Archdruid, he would pluck up his courage, get rid of Morfudd and her creepy black haired servant Regan, and put Almedha in her place. Almedha lacked Morfudd's beauty and grace but at least he knew where he stood with her. Someday, after he had got rid of Morfudd and the Roman gods, and Caratacus had died and he could divorce Gwendolyn, he would marry her.

There was a sudden press in front of him as more newcomers crowded into the room. A tall, gangly man with unkempt red hair and beard, dressed in a simple brown tunic, stepped back from the press and brought his booted foot down on Owain's, at the same time bumping his cup so that the wine spilled. Unable to repress a roar of pain, Owain dropped the cup and jumped to his feet. The red haired man turned to face him as the people nearby scattered, and grabbed Owain's tunic with both hands, pulling him forward so that Owain's face almost buried itself in the man's beard. "And is your foot broken then?" said the man, and Owain forgot the pain in his foot when he looked into the green eyes of the man who held him and his own eyes began to cross. It was the young freckle-faced cross-eyed Brennius, High King of the Trinoes. Brennius' eyes lit up. He must have recognized Owain. He let go of Owain and held a finger to his lips. "Whisht," he said, "I am but a visiting British lord. And aren't ye the . . ."

"Whisht!" said Owain, looking away and putting a finger over his own lips while he rubbed his throbbing foot against the back of his calf. "I am but a visiting British lord also."

"The thing I would ask of you," said Brennius, "as one lord to another, is: did I break your foot when I stood on it?"

"It was nothing," said Owain, grimacing with pain.

"If twas nothing, then that was a mighty roar you let out to signify the nothingness of it."

"I meant you didn't need to apologize. Of course it hurt."

Brennius nodded his head with a satisfied smile. "Good," he said. "Then I am getting on me again the weight that I lost when I went back to Hibernia and got myself captured again by Feradach Finn Feactnach. And him the son of the King of Connaught."

So that's where Brennius went, thought Owain as he rubbed his foot. Brennius had disappeared shortly after Venutius was wounded. He had never reported to the Council his findings on the conduct of Venutius and Boudicca. Without his report, Doderin's predictable ambivalence had convinced the Council not to act on Boudicca's petition to become Arviragus in Venutius' stead. Because of Brennius and Doderin there had been neither an Arviragus nor armies to lead for almost three years now.

Owain sniffed mentally. Of all the Druids, Doderin was the least fit to be Archdruid, and most of these hare brained kings forgot what they were about before they were half way through doing it. Boudicca should have been made Arviragus three years ago. By this time, the Britons would have been equipped to resist any attempt by the new governor to enlarge the boundaries of the Roman conquest.

"And aren't you going to ask me why I went looking for the son of the King of Connaught himself?" said Brennius.

Before Owain could answer a hand appeared on Brennius' shoulder. It was Eudal Marius and with Eudal Marius was his wife Queen Dedreth. They also were dressed in plain clothes. No wonder he hadn't recognized them. Dedreth, even without the accouterments of a Queen, looked lovelier than he had ever seen her and her beauty brought a lump to his throat. She smiled at him and he tried to smile back but couldn't. He still had not forgiven them. They had accepted twenty million in gold from the Council to pay Marius' ransom and then let Joseph of Arimathea marry them instead of his own church.

"I heard the mention of King Feradach Finn Feactnach," said Marius, nodding at Owain, "and I knew of only one man who would still mention the name as if he were not the greatest blackguard within the seven waves that ring our islands."

"Indeed he is," said Brennius. "But you must admit the man carries out his blackguardery with a fine air of fun about him."

"And you went back to see him?"

"I went back to wrap around his scrawny throat the sword he said was made invincible by the blessed Bran himself. It broke when I fought the great battle with Grud you must have heard of."

"Indeed we have," said Marius, "for you have never ceased to tell of it."

"And it broke again even after it was shortened to such a shortness and dulled to such a dullness and rehilted with such a hilt that Atak himself, who thinks that even Rummy swords are too long and too sharp and too hilted, agreed it should be short enough and unhilted enough and dull enough to rip out the intestines and chop up the liver of any adversary foolish enough to get in the way of it."

"And is that how you broke it the second time?"

"It broke the second time when I pulled it out of its sheath and waved it in the air to frighten my adversaries with its invincibility. It split up the middle and came away from the hilt and fell to the ground in three pieces."

"And did Feradach Finn Feactnach give you a new sword?"

"That he did. At least, I have his holy word of honor as son of the King of Connaught that he will. After his men caught me and my men climbing over the wall that surrounds the wall that surrounds the wall that surrounds his palace, my new sword that is to come cost me two years of feeding his pigs and the promise of another visit from the widow Angarad, which is something you'll have to do to protect the honor of your cousin. When the widow has crossed the sea and got through the three walls, and the six white cows of Fiacha have been serviced by the great bull Banger after Angarad herself has put her hands on him and got him interested again in his work, by his honor he will send me by one of his very own knights the sword held by Eremon himself when he whipped the Tuatha de Danann at Taillte and took the fair land of Hibernia to his bosom."

Unimpressed by the conversation, Owain continued to rub his sore foot on the back of his calf and let his eyes drift around the hall. Boudicca had just entered, leaving the huge Atak by the door. He waved at her.

Dressed in a plain tunic, Boudicca made her way through the throng. She saw Owain with Brennius, her brother Marius and his wife Dedreth and edged over to be near them. Dedreth came to her side and raised her face for a kiss.

"How is my Coilus?" said Boudicca.

"Coilus is already a king," said Dedreth. "Even our Silures defer to him. And how are Goneril and Gwenda?"

"Goneril is too much like me and Gwenda too much like her father. She has become a slave to Fidchell now that her father has lost Gallus as a playmate."

"So you are still with Prasu at Thetford?"

"Aye. I am a dutiful queen with nothing to do."

"Except train Goneril for war."

There was disapproval in this but Boudicca shrugged it off. "She is my daughter and like me will be a knight."

"And Venutius?"

She shook her head bitterly. "He's changed since his injury. He is hiding in the mountains and will barely come out to face anyone." She would have said more, but there was a stir at the end of the hall and the blast of trumpets.

"Tis Quintus Veranius Dentatus himself," said Marius. "And we are now to find out what kind of a Governor he is to be."

The room fell quiet as the doors at the end furthest from them opened and the new governor strode briskly in with his legates and guards, Procurator Decianus Catus and his host Ingenius. He came to a halt precisely in the center of a pool of diffused sunlight entering through one of the high alabaster windows. Veranius was dressed in a broad banded paludamentum hung carelessly over his body. The garland on his head was pushed back and tilted to one side to reveal his fine brow and the ringlets of shiny dark curls that framed it. He was tall for a Roman and extremely good-looking if a little on the swarthy side, and had a fine set of teeth. Their whiteness was apparent even from this distance and they were in full view at all times for the Governor's smile never left his face. The smile, the jaunty carriage and the casual style of dress told Boudicca the Governor wished to be everyone's friend. Quintus Veranius did not emit the aura of a man bent on vigorous warfare. She felt disappointed. The Council might not feel the need to appoint her Arviragus after all.

Ingenius, richly dressed in his red flamine robe but looking pale, introduced the Governor. When he had finished his short but fulsome speech, Veranius lifted his right arm and grinned at his audience. "Friends of Rome," he said. "I salute you."

There was a general murmur as the greeting sank in and Veranius apparently took it as a reciprocal greeting for his smile grew wider. He obviously thought everyone in the hall was friendly to Rome. Veranius Bigtooth would be surprised if he knew what manner of men and women had come to take the measure of him. "I wish to greet each of you," said Veranius, "and will as soon as I have told you my policies."

Boudicca turned to speak to Marius when the sudden vision of a man passing by stopped her. It was a tall and broad Hibernian king with golden hair and beard and piercing blue eyes. There seemed to be other Hibernians moving through the crowd nearby. She shook her head in disbelief when she could no longer see the strange king or the other men. Were her eyes playing tricks on her? She must be tired from her journey. She glanced quickly around but could see only Romans and Britons.

"I have been told," said Veranius, "that Britons are reasonable people. Together, we can do what the emperor wants with no trouble at all. Together, we can make him happy. If the emperor is made happy there will be gifts and loans at favorable interest rates."

Veranius spread his arms wide as if to embrace everyone in the room and made his smile even wider. "What does the emperor want?" he asked. "He wants us all to play music and sing. He wants everyone here to learn to play a musical instrument so that when he comes to Britain we can entertain him just as he will entertain us. Now, can anyone guess what else the emperor wants?"

Veranius' question was greeted by stony silence, and Owain found himself looking into Dedreth's face. She smiled at him again, and this time he managed a weak smile in return. Somehow, it seemed almost sacrilegious that he had once aspired to marry her, first lady in the land as she now was. Aspired? he thought grimly. He had lusted after her so that nothing else could enter his mind. Who could tell what effect his love for her must have had on Britain's defense, pre-occupied as it had made him? He sighed and turned his gaze back on Veranius' teeth. The Governor's next words chilled him and made him regret again not having made Boudicca Arviragus.

"The emperor knows your friends on the other side of our

border have concealed gold in the western mountains," said Veranius. "That gold is the lawful property of Rome by virtue of the conquest of Britain. Now I ask you, is it unreasonable that the emperor should want his gold? Of course it isn't, and it is my job as your Governor to see his wishes are promptly carried out. Even as I talk, my legions are preparing to march. We know where the gold is, and it won't take us long to find it.

"What I propose is this. I would like some of you to get together and fetch the gold. If your friends up there hesitate, just tell them what will happen if they hesitate too long. In no time at all they'll give you the gold. If you agree to do this I will hold off the legions. Now what could be fairer? Just think about it for a while and it will sink in. Some of you come on back here with Ingenius and Catus and me and we'll work it out. In the meantime I'd like everyone to come up and meet me. We're going to be great friends."

Owain turned to Boudicca, a worried look on his face. "What are we to do?" he asked. "How serious is this man?"

"He's a fool," said Boudicca. "But a dangerous one."

Marius seemed unmoved by it all and simply shrugged. "We must meet him, I suppose," he said. "It will prove difficult to give him the gold, however, for there is none."

"What?" said Owain. "What do you mean, there is none?"

"We gave it all away," said Marius. "Queen Dedreth says it is the root of all evil so we gave it to the poor."

Boudicca pursed her lips. What kind of madman had Marius become? Joseph of Arimathea must have put Dedreth up to this.

"You gave away the Council's gold?" said Owain, his voice so shrill that many turned to stare at him.

"We are better off without it," said Dedreth.

"And will you be able to convince the Council that it can buy arms and food without gold?" said Owain, his teeth showing in a snarl. He was so furious that he almost struck Marius. High King or no, the man had betrayed Britain with his foolish Christian notions. And Dedreth must have egged him on. He felt his old love for Dedreth fade and something like hatred take its place. Why had she suggested such a stupid course to a man that she knew to be erratic? Was it she who had convinced Marius not to get married in Owain's church after it had paid Marius' ransom?

"The gold is gone," said Dedreth. "Now that it is gone, there will be no fighting over it. When Catus and the other Romans realize it is gone, they will stop looking for it. Our people have laid down their arms and will fight no more. When the Romans understand that, they will leave us in peace."

Boudicca took a deep breath to steady her voice. "Do you believe the Romans will take your word for it that the gold is gone?" she said. "They will tear the mountains apart looking for it. They will slaughter and burn and pillage looking for it and they will never cease looking for it. Far better the Romans had found it and taken it. Far better for your own conscience, when you see the price that will be paid for your folly." She turned on her heel and went back to the doorway where she had left Atak. She found him talking to Ingenius. Before she could say anything, Owain was at her side.

With barely a nod at Ingenius and Atak, he put himself squarely in front of her, his face working with rage. "Did you know that your brother had given away the gold?" he said.

"I did not," she said. "His friends of the Christian College must have convinced his wife and she must have convinced him. You have little cause for complaint, my Lord Owain. While the Council has dillied and dallied over the defense of this land and paid more attention to hiding its gold and arguing over which church is the true church than to appointing me Arviragus or raising armies, the Rummies have reinforced their legions with new auxiliaries and packed their colonies with veterans. Because of your vacillations we have not now the means to resist their expansion and you complain to me that you have lost your gold?"

Owain's face turned brick red and she thought he was going to have a fit. "You would have us let Bodin kill and burn to get people into his church?" he said. "We had to form another church so the Council in Jerusalem would not consider us a bunch of savages. The fact that Bodin's church is declining while ours is expanding shows we are the true church, a church founded on reason. The Council vacillated over making you Arviragus because it elected that fool Doderin as Archdruid."

"I care naught for your church nor Bodin's," she said. "Nor for Basil's church nor Arimathea's. The only true Christian I know of is Elsa. Neither Bodin's nor any other so-called Christian banner will ever fly at the head of armies I command. You may tell that to the Council. And you, my friend, must get rid of this idiot Doderin and get yourself made Archdruid. Atak will help you,"—Atak bared his teeth and made a gesture as if wringing the neck of a chicken—"and you will have my support and my gold behind you, but you must drop this foolish fighting over which church is to rule. By Duw, if Bodin will terrify his church into joining battle, then I will place a sword in every frightened fist. If Basil's church will fight with a candle in one hand I will place a sword in the other. And if yours will join for the sake of reason, then I will harangue them until they know no reason other but to die or win for Britain. But by fear or candles or reason, I want soldiers in the field and good ones at that. It will be your task and the Council's to make sure that Arimathea takes not one sword arm further from our cause."

Excited, Owain seized her hand and kissed it. "By Holy Duw-Bran and Mother Ceridwen," he said, forgetting in his enthusiasm that he was now a Christian, "with such a leader as you we cannot fail."

"Aye, we can," said Boudicca, her face grim. "But if we do we will fail with honor. We will fail like free men. And the Rummies will long regret the price of their victory. If we are not to fail I must have armies. I have pledges from the southern kings but first I must be made Arviragus of Britain."

"With this fool of a governor at our throats, Kings and Council will quickly make you Arviragus," said Owain. "I will do all in my power to bring it about. We are already assembling the Trinoes and Catuves."

"But will they fight?" said Boudicca. "Or are they made up of useless Nazarenes who are neither Nazarene nor soldier?"

"By Duw they will fight," said Owain. "They have nothing else to live for."

"I hope you are right," said Ingenius, "because Veranius intends to attack with all his legions if he doesn't get the gold."

Owain turned on Ingenius as if the red flamine robe infuriated him. He grabbed it in one hand and shook it. "I was not aware," he said, "that you had been elected to the High Council. Do you now speak for it or for your Roman masters?"

"Leave him be," said Boudicca, pulling his hand away from Ingenius' robe. "That red robe, as you well know, is his Rummy dress for attending Veranius. Ingenius serves us well, and as I believe, at great cost to himself."

Owain sneered and looked deliberately around as if surveying all of Ingenius' possessions.

"There is nothing here that is mine," said Ingenius, his voice bitter. "Decianus Catus and Seneca own it just as they own most of Colchester. My debts have made me their slave."

"Then why do they let you live like a king while Brennius and his nobles live in tents?"

"I am a show piece. I am an example to the Britons of what they can get if they invest with Seneca. Little do they know how accurate an example I am. They too will become slaves."

"Leave them," said Atak, "and join us."

"Then I would lose even my hope," said Ingenius. "I will stay while there is a chance I can recover some of what I owned. I cannot give up everything without a fight."

"Ingenius will serve us better here," said Boudicca. "He will tell us what Veranius is planning."

There was a stirring in the doorway as a legate and two guards forced their way through. She could see other guards pushing through the crowd in the hall and passageway as if searching for someone. The legate seemed fearful as he looked around, and she wondered what could have frightened him. Relief lightened the man's face when he saw Ingenius. He came over rapidly and grabbed Ingenius' arm, looking at Boudicca as he did so. He pulled Ingenius to one side and whispered. Ingenius looked startled and was about to rush away with the legate when Boudicca stopped him. "What is it?" she said.

Ingenius glanced at the legate before answering. "It's the Governor," he said. "He's disappeared. He went out to the latrine and vanished. No-one can find him."

Chapter 3

Arviragus

9 Months later

Queen Cartimandua, now that she had given up on owning her own Roman Governor of Britain, had finally joined the Alliance against Rome. To show her good faith she offered her palace in Colchester for a meeting of Kings and Council at which a new Archdruid and an Arviragus of Britain would be installed. Owain, just elected as Archdruid, could barely restrain himself as she stood before him and slowly lowered the golden tiara with its three towering white ostrich feathers on to his head. He knelt before her on a low stool with teeth gritted, hands clasped and eyes tightly closed. If he did not keep a tight grip he felt he would succumb to the insane urge that had come upon him to seize the diaphanously dressed and superbly shaped body that wafted its heated and deliriously seductive perfumes upon him and bury himself in it.

Until Cartimandua raised the tiara he had been fully in control of himself, thinking only of the gold Cymric cross on his back and the golden breastplate on his front, and the sword with its crystal dove that he would have to raise and lower by its point, and the Hirlas horn that he would have to blow, and the gold trimmed blue flag of John Bull that he would have to kiss, and the ring with its egg shaped stone that Morfudd would have to place on his finger, and the kings and queens and Druids behind him all watching him at this highest point of his ambition being crowned Archdruid.

But when she raised the tiara and held it for such a long time above him and he looked up from his kneeling position to watch for its descent and found himself unable to look higher than the lovely breasts that had suddenly become naked like the rest of her and between which passed the copper brown coil of her hair on its way to caress her waist, he was back in the warm water of the pool in which he had first met her long before the Romans came, her nakedness against his as she slipped between his arms and legs like an eel and wrapped the blackness of the Otherworld around his consciousness.

Although she had never indicated by hint or gesture that she had been the woman in the pool, the conviction that it had been Cartimandua had grown within him over the years until there was no doubt at all in his mind. She had seduced him and drawn from him the details of Britain's plans to prevent the invasion and he had almost resigned his post in consequence. But the bitterest pill of all to swallow, for one with such a trained memory, was that he had no recollection of making love with her. They must have coupled, but try as he might he could bring back no memory of what must have been sheer delight.

The cold ring of gold settled around his head and the warmth and softness of her hands as she adjusted it and smoothed and caressed the hair that it had misplaced sent shocks throughout his body. She placed a hand beneath his chin and gently raised his head so that he looked into her deep brown eyes, the breath coming between his clenched teeth in an involuntary gasp. His hands opened up as if by themselves they would seize her, but with a great effort of will he clasped them to his chest.

"There you are, my Lord Archdruid," she said, so that all could hear. "You are now crowned and ready to perform your duties." She leaned a little closer and spoke softly, barely above a whisper, her lips almost touching his ear and her warm breath moving the hairs within it as a soft summer breeze might ripple the grass. "But I wouldn't turn around just yet."

She stepped back from him and he remained kneeling on the stool, senses in turmoil, eyes closed and hands clasped before him as if in prayer while he struggled mightily to get her out of his mind. But even with his eyes tight shut he could see her naked form in front of him as clearly as if his eyes were wide open. Why did Duw-Bran, God that is, let him be beset by urges such as this, right in the middle of the holiest of all ceremonies, the one he had so eagerly anticipated all his adult life? Had Morfudd teased all control out of him? He could not shame himself by standing up in his magnificent new robe and revealing to everyone in the room that his thoughts had not been filled with humble contemplation of the great responsibilities being entrusted to him. He must remain kneeling and force himself to worry about Doderin, his predecessor.

A month after Veranius disappeared, Doderin had been found dead early one morning in the courtyard of the palace in Mona. Everyone assumed he had fallen out of his bedroom window and broken his neck, and at first Owain had eagerly agreed. But the more he thought about it the more convinced he became that Doderin had been thrown out of his window. His body lay too far from the wall merely to have fallen. Was this how Atak had fulfilled Boudicca's pledge to help him become Archdruid?

She had certainly come to his aid when the Council broke up into two warring factions: one supporting himself for Archdruid, and the other supporting Bodin the Fox, but now that he had been elected and given a new title: Unifier of Britain, he wasn't sure this was the kind of aid he really wanted. Her vigorous harangue had brought the majority to his side, but the smaller and more energetic group had seceded with Bodin. He shuddered, as loud impatient coughs from the audience awoke him from his reverie. Unclasping his hands, he got to his feet then turned and remained bowed in a great show of humility as the Council members, kings, queens and Druids, applauded.

Boudicca watched Cartimandua lower the golden tiara on to Owain's head and wondered irritably why he remained kneeling so long. Had he gone to sleep? Owain finally got up and went through the ceremonies of his inauguration, after which the audience went over to congratulate him. She put a hand on his shoulder. "I am glad you are Archdruid," she said, "but now we have an Arviragus to appoint." And it had better be me.

"May the three natures of God guide us," said Owain. He looked around briefly then cleared his throat to open the meeting. Before he could speak, however, the doors were slammed back in the vestibule and a crowd of angry men pushed its way into the room. It was Lord Iorwerth and his Trinoes.

"What is the meaning of this?" said Owain. He rose to his full height and rattled his ostrich feathers. "This is a meeting of Kings and Council. Where are the guards?"

Boudicca had not seen Iorwerth since he had helped her attack the Rummy fort at Verulam so many years ago. He nodded to her. "We're not leaving until this Council hears what we have to say."

"This Council is not met to hear you," said Owain. "You must leave immediately or I will call the guard."

"There is your guard," said Iorwerth, waving toward the vestibule where a group of soldiers stood leering. "They're my men and will do as I say. Now hear this. There isn't a noble left among the Trinoes and the Catuves who owns anything but debts on land and houses that have been theirs for generations. This bat eyed Catus has taken all we own and by Duw we are sick of it. It's got to stop, and if this Council can't get its brains to work there are those here who will find a way to make it stop."

"Is that all you have to say?" said Owain.

"No it isn't. I'm here to tell this Council that a Rummy house will get burned down every week until it does something."

Owain threw up his arms in horror. "You can't do that," he said. "The Romans will be about our ears."

Iorwerth shrugged. "It might frighten you to have Rummies about your ears," he said. "It doesn't frighten us. We're going to fire a house every week and soon we'll burn Claudius' bloody temple. If this upsets you, you'd better finish this war." He turned to walk out.

"Wait," said Owain. "You must not burn any houses. Only the Council can decide what to do." Iorwerth and his followers marched out through the vestibule without looking back.

"Iorwerth's right," said a Council member.

Owain raised his hands again to restore order. "Surely it is the will of this Council," he said, "that Lord Iorwerth be stopped? Since Quintus Veranius disappeared, things have been quiet. But we must take care not to arouse unnecessary reprisals. If bloodshed once begins it may never cease."

Amid the groans and cheers that responded to Owain's speech King Guderius rose to his feet. "It may be quiet here in Colchester," he said, "but tis the quiet of death. The Rummies have taken many hostages against their governor being brought back. Britons are dying all around us, starving because the Rummies confiscate their crops and cattle and sell em abroad. Iorwerth is right in his judgment but wrong in his timing. My Catuves are as ready to rise as Brennius' Trinoes, but twould be foolhardy to do it now. We need an Arviragus and we need armies. We must make a plan and we must make Iorwerth a party to our plan. When the time is right we will need all of Iorwerth's energy, bad temper and all in our cause. We must do nothing to rebuke Iorwerth but much to convince him we are going to bring this war to a conclusion."

"Aye, aye," said many voices.

"Then will this Council direct Lord Iorwerth to wait for the appointment of our Arviragus and desist from burning houses?"

The fierce black-eyed heavy browed Corio, High King of the North Dobunes, rose to his feet. "Instead of trying to convince

Iorwerth to do nothing," he said, "this Council must convince itself to do something. Iorwerth is already convinced and with good reason that this Council can neither see what needs to be done nor do it if it did. Let this Council appoint Queen Boudicca as Arviragus and commit to the raising of armies. Then Brennius can ask Iorwerth to wait."

Boudicca smiled. Thank you Corio. She had not wished to speak but she had been anxious for someone else to speak for her.

"Is it true Queen Boudicca has recovered the gold that Marius gave away?" asked Corio.

"Aye, it's true," she said. "My soldiers scoured the mountains and recovered more than three quarters of it. It will not be stolen nor given away again for I will guard it."

"But it is the Council's gold," said Cartimandua.

"It is Britain's gold."

There was a dead silence and all eyes turned on Owain. "I would propose," he said, "that High Queen Boudicca of Iceni, daughter of High King Caratacus and Queen Genvissa, be appointed Arviragus over the Alliance against Rome."

Boudicca's heart sank as Cartimandua rose smoothly to her feet, her natural height enhanced by the great mass of jewel studded copper hair coiled on top of her head. "Do I understand correctly?" she said. "For the Council to regain its gold it must first appoint Queen Boudicca Arviragus?"

"There is no connection," said Owain, "between the gold and this appointment."

"Then Queen Boudicca will not object to placing the gold back in the care of the Council."

"When it is in care of the Council," said Boudicca, "too many know where it is and have access to it. So long as it is in my care, none but I and my trusted servants know where it is."

"It was in your brother's care before and he gave it away. How does this Council know that you too won't give it away? And why should the Council trust your servants?"

Heads began to nod and Owain turned to Boudicca. "Will you agree to restore the gold if the Council guarantees its safety?"

Her eyes narrowed as she looked at Cartimandua. This bitch would do anything to jeopardize her appointment. She nodded.

"And now that we have the gold disposed of," said Owain, "shall the Council appoint Queen Boudicca Arviragus?"

"I would speak against it," said Cartimandua. "I believe the Council will agree that an Arviragus of the Alliance against Rome must be unequivocally an enemy of Romans, firm and fixed in hatred and unrelenting in determination to annihilate them?"

"Aye!" shouted almost everyone in the room, and some of the kings banged their knives on the floor and cheered.

"Far from hating our enemy, Queen Boudicca has enjoyed friendly relationships with them at her husband's court for years. There is strong evidence to indicate an even more than friendly relationship with Julius Titus Sabinus, a Roman Tribune who is now dead. If our Arviragus be not sure whether to hate or love Romans, how will she behave against them in the field?"

Fuming with anger Boudicca got to her feet but Guderius also rose and seized her arm to stop her from speaking. "What about you and Plautius and Scapula?" said Guderius. "Did you hate them when you bedded them? You have no right to complain of my niece's conduct."

"I," said Cartimandua, her composure unruffled, "do not seek the post of Arviragus."

King Corio rose to his feet. "This Council is no stranger to the consequences of stupid decisions," he said. "Before it makes another it had better think well on what it must choose among. First, if our Arviragus is not to be Queen Boudicca, then who else is it to be—Fat Prasu? Second, an Arviragus without armies is no Arviragus. Boudicca has pledges from all the southern kings to provide armies if she is appointed Arviragus. Is anyone else in possession of such pledges? I think not and the Council wastes our time with drivel if it does not move to do that other than which there is no choice."

The uproar this time was even more deafening and it was clearly apparent that most favored Corio's argument. When this is over, my black-eyed Corio, thought Boudicca, I will kiss you. But Cartimandua again stood to address the Council. "King Corio speaks," she said, "as if the sole kingdoms from which we had to choose were the southern nations. I remind the Council that, since I have joined the Alliance, there exists an area as large as the southern nations and as able to field armies. Within my nations are kings well qualified to assume this post. I propose that my husband, High King Velocatus, be given that responsibility. And I would remind the Council that King Venutius and Queen Boudicca acting together were unable to defeat King Velocatus during a campaign of over a year."

Boudicca gritted her teeth and would not rise to the bait. If she challenged Cartimandua the Council would divide and there would be no Arviragus. Cartimandua was trying to exact a price for joining the Alliance and the Council must decide whether to pay it. No one here could stomach the thought of giving the Alliance's highest post to one not a High King or Queen born of a lineage of royal blood. To make one of the servant caste Arviragus would forever debase Pendragon. Yet if Cartimandua's request were turned down she might withdraw from the Alliance and the loss of her armies could cripple it. The gloom was so pervasive that no one rose to break it and she could not afford to. Who would rise to keep Velocatus out?

King Rusticus, aged High King of the Belgies, struggled to his feet. "I would ask Queen Cartimandua," he said, "if she is still Client to Rome and if her treaties are still in effect— particularly the provision that her domains will not be invaded if she makes no overt attack against Rome?"

"They are still in effect," said Cartimandua, "and will be until I decide to break them." Despite the bravado, Boudicca detected a tremor in Cartimandua's voice. The perceptible hostility in the room must have convinced her that Velocatus would never become Arviragus.

"But they would be seen as broken," said Rusticus, "if a High King of Brigante were appointed Arviragus. Such an appointment can no longer be concealed from Rome as it was in the past, and your treaties would be abrogated. So long as your lands are inviolate, our task of defense is easier managed. The warriors you can spare by not having to defend your own nations can add weight to the armies that must defend ours, and their identity will not be readily detected by Rome. If, however, your husband is declared Arviragus, the restraints upon Rome would be removed and our defense problem magnified perhaps beyond our ability to cope. For these reasons I beg that you withdraw your husband's name and give the Council instead your authority to appoint Queen Boudicca as Arviragus."

King Corio got to his feet and moved to the center of the room next to Owain. "I propose," said Corio, "that if our much loved northern neighbor will accede to Rusticus' plan, this Council create a new title for her."

"What should the title be?" asked Owain.

"How should I know?" said Corio. "Think of something."

Owain knitted his brow while he methodically went through all the titles he knew. A sudden vision of a feeble Claudius being helped to his chair while Agrippina chatted with Plautius flashed into his mind. Of course! "The Council could confer upon High Queen Cartimandua the title of Empress of the Northern Nations," he said, keeping his eyes on Boudicca to see how she would react. "A special golden crown could be wrought for the occasion."

The cheering that followed convinced him that he had made a good choice. But he still kept a wary eye on Boudicca. She sat in her place with a wooden look on her face and made no move to object. From what he knew of her she was not likely to be jealous of Cartimandua's new title if she got her way about being Arviragus. Titles other than that meant little to her. When the cheering subsided, he turned to Cartimandua and bowed low. "If

Queen Cartimandua will accept the suggestion of Kings Rusticus and Corio," he said, "this Council will be ever grateful to her."

Cartimandua rose to her feet and surveyed the room with cool dignity. "I will accede to the Council's request," she said, "on one condition. I demand that Queen Boudicca provide a hostage until her hostility to Rome has been proved beyond cavil."

"And who is this hostage to be?" asked Owain.

"Her son by my former husband King Venutius." You bitch, thought Boudicca, just because you can't have a child of your own. "He is to be fostered in my household. Should this Council find Queen Boudicca remiss in her duties, his life is forfeit."

Boudicca remained squatted. Cartimandua would forever control her if she once got her hands on Coilus. But there was no way out for the moment. Her lips trembled but she nodded, and a sigh of relief filled the room.

"And now," said Owain. "Is it the will of this Council that Queen Boudicca be appointed Arviragus?"

The response was unanimous. "Aye, it is."

"Then let Pendragon be brought forth."

All rose as the regalia bearers entered carrying the staff on which Pendragon was furled. Boudicca knelt before Owain while he rested the ceremonial sword on her right shoulder. The tears coursed down her cheeks and she bowed her head. That bitch would not see her cry.

"It is the will of this Council," said Owain, "that you lead the Alliance against Rome. Will you accept this ancient and honorable title of Arviragus, and the allegiance of all the kings and queens and council members here gathered, and do you swear to do all in your power to drive the adversary from our shores?"

"Yes," she said. "I will and I do."

"Then in the name of the Council I declare you Arviragus of Britain, Commander of the Alliance against Rome. May your sword arm and courage ever serve the three natures of God and the peoples of this land."

Boudicca, the momentary tears gone, rose, strode firmly over to Pendragon and kissed the hem of the great pennant. As she did so, Owain blew a mighty blast on the Hirlas horn. The crowd cheered and Owain relinquished the horn as the Druidess Almedha came between he and Boudicca clutching her throat. "What's the matter?" said Owain, glassy eyed from blowing the horn.

"Sir Ingenius has found the Governor," said Almedha.

"What?" He looked at Boudicca as if unsure what to do as the kings and Council members crowded around to congratulate her.

Boudicca signaled him to go with Almedha. For the moment she had to smile and look pleased with the honor she had fought so bitterly for. But as soon as she could get away, she went outside to join Owain, Almedha and Ingenius.

"My servant found him in the latrine," said Ingenius. "Whoever kidnapped him put him back right where he disappeared."

"How is he?"

"He's dead."

At least this would postpone action by the Romans until next year. She would have time to raise her armies. "How did he die?"

"I don't know," said Ingenius. "Two of his teeth are gone."

"It must have been the knights of the Red Branch," said Owain, looking at Boudicca. "Your father said he would send for them."

"Then thank God for Hibernia," she said, thinking of that sudden glimpse she had had of the golden haired Hibernian king just before Veranius' speech. How did they manage to get around without being seen?

"Have you told the Romans?" asked Owain of Ingenius.

"I thought I had better tell you first."

Owain nodded. "You did the right thing. We'll take a look at him then decide what to do."

"There is one other thing," said Ingenius, looking at Boudicca.

"What is that?" she said.

"I think King Prasu's life is in danger. Decianus Catus has lost an enormous sum on a venture. If he can't make it up quickly he may lose his rank as Procurator."

"Good. But what has that to do with King Prasu?"

"Catus has a note from King Prasu. I overheard him tell one of his partners it's the only hope he has of quickly raising money. The army asked Catus to act toward Rome as if Veranius is campaigning in the west to give the army time to find him and the gold, so the army's beholden to him. He even issued edicts in the name of Veranius. Now that Veranius is dead, Rome will have to be told, but in the confusion the army can have King Prasu killed so that Catus can place a demand on his treasury."

"Raid our treasury?" she said. That little bat eyed clerk? "What kind of note does Catus have?"

"It was a note for twelve million to invest in silver, but Catus made it into a note for half King Prasu's estates. Being Procurator he'll be able to collect in Nero's name, not that Nero will ever see it."

She looked closely at Ingenius' drawn and worried face. "How do you know all this?" she said, and Ingenius burst into tears.

"I was the one who got King Prasu to sign the note," he said. "Catus wouldn't lend me the twenty million you had to have unless I got King Prasu to sign a note Catus could hold for security. King Prasu thought he was investing it in our syndicate. The loan was never repaid and I lost all I own."

"You were never repaid?" said Boudicca, horrified. She had assumed that Marius had paid it back to Ingenius.

Ingenius shook his head sullenly.

"But the ransom was paid," said Owain. "The Council sent the gold to King Marius."

"How could it have been?" said Ingenius, his eyes suddenly dry. "Queen Boudicca got it from me and I had to borrow it from Catus. I lost all I own to pay Catus back."

Owain froze, an icy chill spreading throughout his body. So

that's why Marius and Dedreth didn't marry in his church as Morfudd had said they would. The day that Morfudd had seduced him and helped the Council find a new hiding place for its gold she had talked him into releasing the twenty million into her custody. She and Badwin had set off for Caer Leon with an armed guard, and she had told him on her return that the gold had been delivered to Marius. She and Badwin must have hidden it somewhere. Was that why Badwin died so suddenly?

"Well?" said Ingenius, suspicion clouding his face. "Was King Marius paid by the Council?"

"I don't know," said Owain. "But I will find out."

"Prasu must be taken away and hidden while I find out about this note," Boudicca said. She would send him to the fort at Tas[24]. She turned to Ingenius, guilt nagging at her for having caused the poor boy's downfall. "Are you willing to get out from Catus' clutches and serve me as you once did?"

"Yes," sighed Ingenius. "I will never beat Catus."

"Ride to Caer Leon," she said, "then I will show you what I want done." She patted his arm kindly. "You have been valuable to us," she said. "But from now on you must be wholly a Briton."

"I always have been a Briton," said Ingenius, his face red.

"Good," said Boudicca. "Then you will have no difficulty in leaving all this to serve me. Serve me well and you will not find me ungenerous. When I can, I will repay your loan." She turned to Owain. "And you my good friend," she said, "must also help your Arviragus if you would have her win this war."

"Anything," said Owain, wondering in his agitation what she had in mind now.

"My first task," she said, "is to raise levies and mold them into one army. You have always preached unity and your lessons have been well heard. Unity requires oneness of purpose, oneness of direction and oneness of execution. There will be one army and one commander and one battle plan."

"Excellent," said Owain. "Excellent. Under your leadership we will be one."

"Good. Then you will see the need to have but one church. I can raise levies and train them to war, but I cannot allow the time of my generals to be wasted or the energies of my warriors dissipated in endless arguments over whose is the true church. The Christ has become too great an issue in the peoples' mind to ignore and our warriors will fight better if they think they're fighting for Christ."

"We have been trying to unite," said Owain, "but . . . "

"I know what you have been trying to do, my Lord Archdruid and I am not interested in hearing why you have not succeeded. What I want is your assurance that you will bring this silly warfare with Bodin to a quick end and join your churches into one. And I want you also to include Basil. Now that Cartimandua is joined to us I want nothing to disturb that relationship. What I demand is your assurance that you will bring about this unity."

Owain could not suppress a groan. She had no idea of the complexities involved: of Morfudd's hatred for Bodin and his new wife, of Bodin's contempt for all religious values, of Basil's utter incompetence, of Arimathea's growing ability to siphon off converts in need of healing. "What about Arimathea?" he said. "He does all he can to attract people away from our cause."

"Arimathea you will leave alone," said Boudicca. "Those who flock to him are not and cannot be warriors, and there will come a day when there will be enough of them to bring all wars to an end. The church I speak of is that which will unite our warriors behind our cause."

"I will do my best," said Owain, horrified at his own words. How could he possibly unify his church with Bodin's?

"I do not ask for your best," said Boudicca. "I demand that it will come to pass. Before this year is over Rome will send a new governor bent on avenging Veranius, and I want a unified army and a unified church before that happens."

Trapped, Owain could only nod. "I will unify the churches," he said.

Boudicca patted him on the cheek. "Good."

Almedha had been moving about nervously, looking over their shoulders, and finally she tugged on Owain's sleeve. Her hair had come loose and hung over her face. "What is it?" said Owain, pushing her hair back and hooking it behind her ear, and they looked where she pointed. A thick greasy black pall of smoke rose from within the city, not far from Cartimandua's palace. The noise of people shouting in alarm could be heard as they ran through the streets toward the blaze. "By Holy Duw," said Owain. "Iorwerth has set fire to a house. I told them he should be arrested."

"Iorwerth is doing something," said Boudicca. "The time for talking and dancing is over, my Lord Archdruid. You and I have been promoted today. Let us now make Britain free of this Rummy plague."

Owain set off with her toward the palace shaking with anger at Iorwerth's disobedience, but some of the Council members had already come outside to see the fire. Soon, all the Kings and Council, guards and servants jostled each other before Cartimandua's doors. Seeing Guderius with Brennius, Owain pushed toward them. "You must arrest Iorwerth," he said to Brennius. "He must be kept from doing more of this or the Romans will be about our ears."

"Tis a heart of gold he has," said Brennius, "as well as many followers. We cannot arrest the likes of him unless you want the Trinoes buzzing around here like flies around a honey pot."

"You must talk to him," said Guderius, placing a hand on Owain's shoulder. "Make him listen to reason."

"I thought you were going to talk to him."

"I said the Council should. You're the Archdruid. You do it."

Owain shuddered as he visualized again the heavyset beetle browed Iorwerth striding into the Council meeting, knocking Council members sprawling. How was he to convince such a hard head that the Council had things under control? Archdruid Belinus and that idiot Doderin had never been called upon to do the things he was being called upon to do. He scowled and pushed his way through the entry doors, Almedha fluttering along right behind him.

In the vestibule he almost collided with Cartimandua. She seized his hands and smiled, her body close to his. "I have not properly congratulated you on your triumph," she said. "I am so glad that you are now Archdruid as you always wished." So that confirmed she was the woman in the pool, he thought. She was the only one to whom he had ever revealed his ambition. To his great surprise she let go of his hands, pressed her body to his and kissed him full on the lips, making his ostrich feathers rattle, then went out through the doors to mingle with the throng and watch the fire. He stood there shaking until Almedha put her hand on his arm.

"She thinks much of you," said Almedha, smiling nervously. The comb holding her hair had come loose and he could barely see her eyes. Afraid to touch her in case he lost control he snarled and went up the stairs to the guest rooms.

I have nine months, Boudicca thought later, before a new Governor can land. That is the right amount of time to bring forth the baby I would bring forth: an army equal to defeating Rome. Ingenius shall make weapons and Atak shall train my generals. And my poor dear crippled Venutius shall be at my side to give me warmth when all else is bleak. He will hide Prasu for me and devise some means to keep Coilus out of that woman's clutches. By Duw, we have learned enough by now to stop Rome. There are enough in Rome itself questioning this conquest that we need not defeat more than two legions. If we can defeat but two we will have defeated Rome, for they will not pay a larger price for that which has cost them so much and brought them so little. Two legions. We have already defeated one in the field. Surely the defeat of two is within our grasp.

Chapter 4

Caradawg

When she and Venutius dismounted in front of her father's palace at Caer Leon, Boudicca felt her anger rise at Marius and Dedreth. A great fire-blackened hole in the side of the palace made during a Roman raid had not been repaired. From inside came the screams and shouts of children at play. The much-loved compound was decrepit and full of tents and children. Even the great square on which so many chariot races had been held was covered with them. Only an area near the middle had been left clear, and on that a huge firepit had been built. Smoke curled up from it to be chased and whipped by gusts of wind. In the firepit, women tended several cauldrons and looked up curiously at the horsemen. The few men who stood around looked too old to fight.

Grim faced, Boudicca threw her reins around a rusty iron bar and walked inside with Venutius. She stopped in the vestibule, hands on hips, as Atak and Almedha hurried to join them.

"Caratacus would tear his hair if he saw this," said Venutius, putting his good arm around her waist. The cubicles were littered with clothes, skins and straw mattresses. Leaves and other debris rattled along the floor in the breeze. The rich tapestries that had divided the cubicles from one another had been pulled down for bed coverings. The big table used so often for their war councils was shoved against a wall and more clothes and food piled on top of it. Children, dogs and women abounded, and a few old men sat near the fire pits playing Fidchell. Around the fire pits poles had been driven into the ground and lines stretched between them from which hung newly washed clothes.

As she stared at the disorder a small urchin with black hair and eyes ran into the vestibule carrying a short heavy stick. He was barefoot and dressed in a dirty smock and looked about seven years old. For a horrible moment she thought it was Coilus, but the boy had black hair and was swarthy. Without warning the urchin began pounding on Atak's sore legs with the stick. With a roar of anguish Atak hopped away while Almedha put a hand around her throat and shrieked. Venutius tried to seize the boy with his good hand and got a blow on the head for his trouble. Then the urchin disappeared up the stairs.

"So my army's already routed by an infant," she said. "Come, Marius and Dedreth must be in one of the guest houses." She went outside and waved at Cruker, who wheeled and led his troop of horsemen back toward the gate to camp outside the grounds.

In one of the round guesthouses she found Dedreth and Marius. Neither wore the gold torque of their rank, and both wore the plain clothes of nobles. She hugged them, but her hug was mechanical and they must have sensed her displeasure for their faces lost their initial joy at seeing her. Marius drew Venutius and Atak to one side to drink some wine, but Dedreth ran to Atak and threw her arms around him. "Atak!" she said. "I was so sorry to hear about Tetra."

"Yes," said Atak. He pulled on his beard and edged closer to Marius, who held out a cup of wine.

"Atak is too busy to be lonely," said Boudicca, looking at Almedha. "This is Almedha," she said. "She has come to take my Coilus and give him to Cartimandua as hostage."

They all looked at Almedha and Almedha clutched her throat. "I wish it were not me," she said.

Dedreth went up to Almedha and embraced her. "Nobody

blames you," she said, putting a finger under a lock of Almedha's unruly hair and smoothing it back over her ear.

"I'll send to King Pelinore of the Selgovies," said Marius. "He's nearby and will keep an eye on Coilus."

"Where is he?" said Boudicca.

"He's out with Elsa and Goronwy," said Dedreth. "They will be back before dark."

"And how is he?"

"Before he left us last year, Joseph prophesied that Coilus would be sire of a line of great Christian kings."

"So Joseph is dead?" She felt sorry, but at least with him gone fewer warriors would be lost. "By the way," she said to Marius. "No-one ever repaid Ingenius for the loan of your ransom."

Marius looked dumbfounded. "I thought you had raised the ransom."

"I borrowed it from Ingenius. Now you must repay him."

"We have no money," said Dedreth.

"We gave it all away," said Marius.

Boudicca was about to vent her anger on them when a clod of earth hit Atak in the neck. He spun around to see who had thrown it and must have twisted his legs, which Boudicca knew to be still tender from the time they defeated the Twentieth. He roared and fell forward on his hands and knees. It was the same urchin who had hit Atak with the stick and she caught him and held him struggling in her arms. "Why did you do that to Lord Atak?" she demanded, shaking the boy, but the boy simply cursed until Marius pulled him away and pinned his arms to his side.

"He's an orphan," said Dedreth. "We tried to put him with a family but he won't stay."

"If he were older I would give him a sword," said Boudicca. "He has more fight in him than most of my generals." The boy was darker than a Briton, probably the son of some legionary by one of the British women. "What is your name?" said Boudicca.

"He has no name," said Marius, "We call him Caradawg."

"Then I will give him a name." She put her hand to the boy's chin and glanced at Almedha. "He shall be Coilus Caradawg of Iceni."

The boy howled with rage as if she had insulted him.

"Coilus?" said Marius.

"My Coilus is Coilus Galahad, after Joseph's son. Coilus Caradawg shall be my foster son. Atak and Almedha will take him to Cartimandua for me." Almedha looked worried. "Do not fear," said Boudicca. "Cartie has never seen Coilus. It will be a great joy to think of what he will do to her household." Almedha shook her head doubtfully and looked at Atak, still on his hands and knees. Almedha helped him struggle to his feet.

"Do you know who I am?" said Boudicca to the boy. "I am Queen Boudicca and you will be my son. You will live in the household of my cousin Queen Cartimandua and be educated as befits your new station. But I warn you. If Queen Cartimandua finds out you are not the son of my blood she will kill you. Do you understand?"

Caradawg glared at her.

"If King Marius lets go of you, will you behave?"

The boy scowled but said nothing.

"Let him go," said Boudicca. Marius put Caradawg down then stepped back. The boy rubbed his arms and glared at Boudicca and Atak. Then he rushed at Atak as if to kick him but Atak, firm on his feet by this time, scooped him up and put him under one arm.

"Call your servants," said Boudicca to Dedreth, "and have Coilus Caradawg bathed and dressed."

"We have no servants," said Dedreth. "All in our nation are equal." She smiled, and some of the old elfhood shone through. "But we have reserved a nice guest house for our royal visitors. And somehow, we will raise the money to pay Ingenius."

"If all in your nation are equal," said Boudicca, looking at Marius, "then you will not object if I try to raise an army among them. There must be some not yet so Christianized they will refuse to wield a sword in their country's defense."

"You are welcome to recruit all you can," said Marius. "Many will be in the square tonight for the love meal. There must be some who are spoiling for a fight."

When Elsa and Goronwy arrived with Coilus, Boudicca snatched him up. He was slender but his body was hard as a boy's should be. She kissed him but he pulled back and looked at Dedreth. "I am your mother," she said, hurt by his withdrawal. "And this is your father, King Venutius."

"Have you come to take me away?" said Coilus.

"Would you like to come with us?"

Coilus shook his head. "I want to stay here."

"Very well," she said, putting him down. She was hurt but she could not blame the lad. She would have to make friends with him again. It had been two years since she last saw him. Without a sound, Caradawg materialized and tapped Coilus on the shoulder. The two of them disappeared into the haze.

"I wish you would come with us and Caradawg to Brigante," said Atak to Elsa, who had just kissed him.

Elsa patted Atak's cheek but looked at Boudicca. "You are taking Caradawg to Brigante?"

"He is to be fostered to Cartimandua," said Boudicca.

"Did he agree?"

"He will agree," said Boudicca, "when Dedreth and you have convinced him. I cannot risk my son in the hands of that witch. Caradawg will be the gainer. He will be brought up in a royal household if he does not wreck it first."

"He will not gain if he loses the love he has here. Nor will he be the gainer if Cartimandua finds out and has him killed."

"Pah!" said Boudicca. "She would not dare have him killed. She demanded Coilus to save face before the Council. With Caradawg as her hostage her face will be saved and my son will be with my own family where he should be."

"And when Queen Cartimandua lets him go, will you accept him as a true foster son?"

"I will make him a knight and soldier. He has already defeated your stepfather and Venutius."

"With your leave," said Elsa, "I would like to talk further about it with Dedreth and Marius."

"You would talk against me?"

"I would talk for Caradawg. I want him to understand what you have proposed. If he agrees, I will have nothing further to say. If he does not agree and you take him anyway, something bad will come of it."

"What?" said Boudicca.

"I don't know. You will lose something you'll regret."

Boudicca shrugged. "What is one more loss, one more regret? Do your talking with Dedreth and leave me with Lord Atak."

As Goronwy and Elsa went off with Marius and Dedreth, Boudicca turned to Atak and Almedha. "Whatever happens," she said, "You will leave with Caradawg when I tell you to. You will take him straight to Cartimandua."

Their hangdog looks didn't make her feel any better about stealing Caradawg but she couldn't afford to risk Coilus in the hands of Cartimandua. Caradawg would adapt once he was placed there and his life would certainly improve. She would see that he was properly rewarded when he came of age. In the meantime she must spend some time with Coilus and teach him about his mother and why she had to be away from him so much. His look at Dedreth while she held him had been like a dagger in the side. He must learn to love his true mother.

Chapter 5

Tutor

The sun had gone behind the mountains when Atak went out with Almedha for the evening love meal. His legs felt better than they had for years. Elsa must have noticed his limp and healed them. Moved by a sudden impulse he put his arm around Almedha. She looked up at him and smiled as he pressed her body to his. She must like him, he thought, for she began to draw the essence out of him. It had been a long time since a woman had done that—not since Tetra died. Now that he was getting old maybe he should marry again before he ran out of essence. Almedha had a lot of hair but she would be a good choice.

The square was full of men, many of them warrior age. They must have been working in the fields or up in the hills and had come home for the night. They sat in ever widening rings around the circle that had been left in the middle of the square by the fire pits, and Atak felt his stomach rumble when he saw what looked like red clay bowls full of stew being passed around by women and young girls. He sat down in a newly forming circle, Almedha next to him, and saw Marius and Dedreth sit down a few feet away. There was no sign of Boudicca and Elsa, or Caradawg and Coilus, and he scowled thinking of the trouble he would have finding and capturing Caradawg before they left. His scowl faded when a bowl of the stew and a half loaf of bread were thrust into his hands. He opened his mouth to take a great bite of the bread, but the man to his left put a hand on his forearm. He paused, mouth still open, and looked sideways at the man. He was a wizened old man, too old to hit.

"We pray first," said the man.

Atak scowled but lowered the bread. The smell of the stew made him ravenous and he longed to put the bowl to his lips and suck in great mouthfuls of it. He looked at Almedha and she smiled at him through her hair. "We do the same thing in our church," she said. "We pray to Young God and then we eat bread and drink wine."

"I hope they don't pray too long," said Atak. "The stew will get cold."

"I wish we could get this many to come to our church."

"Do you give away stew and bread like this?"

"No," she said, pushing back her hair. "Perhaps we should."

More women passed through the circles placing an amphora of wine between each two people, and then in the growing darkness Goronwy stood in the circle, his figure illuminated by the flickering light of the fire pits. He raised his arms so that everything grew still. "Brothers and sisters," said Goronwy, "this is our meal of Thanksgiving for the salvation brought to us by Jesus, our Lord and Christ. In this growing darkness symbolic of the ignorance and worldly lust that crucified him we will kiss each other in the bond of love that unites all who follow his teaching and example. When we have eaten we will sing and pray as our Jewish brothers have taught us. And may the unity of our prayers and singing bring down the world's ignorance as the walls of Jericho were brought down by the Israelites of old. Now: kiss, eat and drink, and then we will sing and pray."

"It's strange to hear them speak of Jesus in the old way," said Almedha, "instead of as Young God. They mustn't have been taught about the three natures of God."

Atak put the bread he had been holding down on top of his

stew and turned to kiss Almedha. Her mouth was soft and opened slightly from the pressure of his lips. Some of her hair was trapped between their mouths but it didn't bother him. He put a hand beneath her rib cage and pulled her to him so that her mouth opened wider. It was a long kiss and he would have made it even longer but for the stew's aroma. He pushed her from him and picked up the bread to wolf it down, but the man on his left put a restraining hand on his arm. "What now?" he growled.

"You're supposed to kiss me too," said the man, and Atak leaned to the left so they could peck each other on the cheek.

"Now can I eat?" he said, and without waiting for an answer dipped his bread into the stew and crammed it in his mouth. When he had finished he wondered how he could get more, but before he could ask a man stood up by the fire pits and began to sing. His voice was loud and clear and other voices joined in until the hills echoed with the sound. The singing was so infectious Atak joined in. Almedha sang also, and he was surprised when he saw tears flowing down her cheeks when he pulled back her hair. "Are you all right?" he asked.

She smiled at him and wiped away the tears with the back of her hand. "It's the music," she said. "I wonder why Basil never taught us to sing? If we had singing like this people would flock to our church. I wish we could get that man in the front to come with us and teach us."

Atak followed her finger and saw she pointed to the man who had led the first song. He remembered how soft her mouth had been and decided he would get the man for her. He put his arm around her waist. "I don't have a woman," he said.

She looked away from him without smiling, eyes glinting in the light from the fire pits. "I know," she said. She said nothing further and after a while began singing again as if he had said nothing. Atak pulled on his beard. Was that all she was going to say? Had she understood what he meant? What else should he say?

Before he could think of anything the music suddenly hushed

and people to his left rose to their feet and shouted in alarm. Several horsemen moved through the crowd and into the circle by the fire pits. One carried Pendragon, and stopped by the fire pits so that all could see the great banner in the light of the flames. The other horsemen cantered around the ring. He saw Boudicca pass by the fire, her face and gold torque glinting red in the firelight. She held a small body before her on the saddle that must be Coilus. The horsemen slowed to a walk and Boudicca halted by the fire pits, her arms raised.

"Men of Siluria," she said, her voice clear and harsh.

"We want to sing," said a few loud voices.

"I am Boudicca, Arviragus of Britain, daughter of your own great King Caratacus and sister to Eudal Cyllinus Marius your High King. And this is my son, Prince Coilus Galahad." Atak could see the small black arm of Coilus raised in greeting.

"We have neither kings nor princes," said a voice, "nor queens either. We are all equal before God."

The hills that had echoed the singing now echoed cheering. Boudicca waited patiently until it subsided. "I too am baptized in Christ," she said. "I am not here to talk of kings and queens but of generals and armies. As you must know, the Roman Governor is dead. They will send another and worse, and we must defend our island or they will take it and make slaves of us all."

"Our general is the Lord Christ," said the same voice that spoke before. Atak peered over the heads in front of him to see who it was but couldn't make out the man's features. "We fight not with swords and arrows but with prayer. We will not join your army but you may join ours. Lay down your weapons, become one with us and we will love you as a sister. Our prayers will keep us safe from the Romans if we all have the mind of Christ."

Again Boudicca waited for the cheering to die down. She urged her horse over to stand pawing the ground in front of the man who had been answering her. "I thank you for your invitation," she said, looking down at the man but talking so all could hear. "And when this war with Rome is finished I will accept it. I would not have you believe me ignorant nor contemptuous of the Christ or its power. My daughter was raised from death and Elsa saved my own life. I honor your desire for peace and I quarrel not with those who choose peace and prayer while others fight. But quarrel you not with those who take up the sword and risk death and injury to expel the Roman defiler from these shores so that you may continue to live in peace."

She raised her head and turned her horse slowly in a circle so that all could see her. "I ask none to give up Christ," she said. "I ask only that those willing to fight pledge themselves to fight with me should the Romans seek further conquest. If I have moved you to this end, let me hear your voices, for I cannot see your faces."

Atak grinned at the roar that went up. Many of those who roared would change their mind before morning, but the Silures loved a fight and many would pledge themselves and bring their brothers down from the mountains. He watched Boudicca and her horsemen pick their way through the crowd and disappear into the shadows as the man who led the singing began a new song. The singing didn't seem as loud and he wondered if Boudicca's words had silenced some of the singers. The pauses between songs grew longer, and soon people began to get up and wander off.

As the crowd dispersed, he went back with Almedha and the others to the guesthouse. He put his arm around her waist and pulled her to him. She smiled gently but though she said nothing he could feel her take a great surge of essence out of him. She must want him but why didn't she say anything? Maybe she hadn't understood him. He would tell her again in the morning that he had no woman.

Only a candle and the glowing firepit illuminated the guesthouse, and as everybody seemed ready to sleep he went to his cubicle and covered himself with the sheepskins. He was quickly asleep and dreamed of climbing a wall in a large wet cave with a soft sandy bottom. He heard the sound of singing and saw Tetra sitting on a rock shelf combing her hair. She saw him and gestured to him. He couldn't see any way to get to her, and below was an abyss. Something banged on his back. Maybe it was a bird trying to get to its nest in the cliff. If it kept banging on him like this he would lose his grip and fall. He could feel the rock crumble under his fingers and began to slide down the cliff face. Then he was falling, but whatever it was that banged on him had not left off. He awoke with a start and realized that feet and knees and elbows were pushing against his back. At first he thought it must be Almedha climbing into bed with him and eagerly turned. But the body pushing against him was too small. He put his hand on the head that had been butting him between the shoulder blades.

"Caradawg," he said. Caradawg pulled his head away and butted him in the side. "Hey," said Atak. "If you want to sleep with me you'd better be still." He settled back down on the mattress and pulled the skins over himself and the boy. Before long Caradawg was asleep against Atak's back and he was afraid to turn over and get more comfortable because he might wake Caradawg. He sighed, wishing he hadn't dreamed about Tetra.

A hand shook Atak's shoulder and woke him. It was Boudicca, her arm around the sleepy Coilus, and the dawn was not yet strong enough to overcome the dim glow of the firepit. "Venutius and Coilus and Cruker and me are going into the mountains," she said. "I have hundreds who will fight. Coilus and me will gather them and you will make them into an army for me. I want you and Almedha to get out of here today with Caradawg. I will leave two men to go with you. When you've taken him to Barwick, go to Tas as fast as you can. There will be much for you to do." She took Coilus into her arms and rose swiftly to her feet. Before Atak could ask her if Elsa had agreed to Caradawg's going she was gone, Venutius lurching sleepily behind.

***

"Watch me," said Atak. "See how I do it." He lay flat on the riverbank, a sharpened thin wooden stake in his right hand. Caradawg lay just to his left, hands gripping the edge of the little cliff eaten out by the river, his eyes fixed on the water. They had left Caer Leon three days ago and another would bring them to Barwick. Almedha sat further down the bank talking to Gareth, her back to a tree, and the two soldiers were even further down watering the horses.

It had been Gareth who led the singing during the love meal. He was much younger than Atak had thought and was tall and well built with blond hair and beard and a nose like a hawk. Atak was sorry now that he had had the man abducted. He had told the soldiers to remove the ropes that bound him, hoping he would run away and go back to Caer Leon, but Gareth seemed to like Almedha and Almedha certainly liked Gareth. They would sing together for hours, and Almedha clutched her throat whenever Atak interrupted them. He had told her again that he didn't have a woman but all she ever said was 'I know.' Perhaps she didn't want to marry him now that she had met Gareth. But if she didn't want to marry him why did she keep drawing the essence out of him?

"There," said Caradawg. He moved his head slightly to the right, upstream of them, and Atak peered anxiously in that direction.

"Where?" Then he saw the fish. It barely moved as it drifted toward them. It was a good-sized fish and two more like it would make dinner for the six of them. With a quick lunge he drove his spear into the water and cursed as he saw the fish leap away.

"You missed it," said Caradawg, scorn in his voice.

"Only just," said Atak.

"Let me do it."

"You're not big enough."

"Give me your knife then and I'll make a spear."

"Here," said Atak, giving him the spear. "I wouldn't trust you with a knife."

"I'm going to go in the water."

"It's deeper than it looks. Here, hold on to my hand."

Ignoring Atak's hand, Caradawg jumped into the river, the water swirling up above his waist. He went out a few feet from the bank and stood with his spear at the ready, feet apart to steady him against the current. "Mind you don't fall over," said Atak, and Caradawg struck.

"Got it!" he said, his spear driven firmly into the river's bed. He reached down into the water but couldn't get the fish.

Atak jumped in and got his hands around it. "Pull the spear out," he said then flung the fish onto the bank. Caradawg gave an excited cry and leaped out of the river to grab the fish. It was too big and slippery for him to pick up, but his cries brought the others running to see what he had done. Almedha clutched him to her and kissed him but he broke free and dashed back into the river. When he had caught six fish Atak told him to stop. "We never kill more than we can eat," he said and broke the spear across his knee.

"Tomorrow, we'll be in Barwick," said Almedha, looking at Gareth. "I suppose Lord Owain will be there." Gareth grimaced and Almedha turned to Atak. She frowned and put her hand to her throat then took it away again. "Do you think we could stay here another day? It's so lovely here, and at Barwick, what with Lord Owain being there and everything . . . " Her voice trailed off and she looked down at Caradawg, who was trying to break half of the broken spear across his knee as Atak had done.

"We'll stay another day," said Atak.

That night, Atak showed Caradawg how to cook his fish over a firepit dug into the side of the riverbank, and then they all sat around the fire to eat and sing. Even though Almedha sat next to Gareth and leaned her head on his shoulder, Atak enjoyed the singing. Caradawg fell asleep in Atak's lap and after the singing was over Almedha and Gareth disappeared, so Atak made up a bed near the soldiers and put Caradawg into it before he crawled in himself. He would have liked Almedha to be in it too, but it was comforting to sleep with Caradawg's warm body against his back. Tomorrow, he would make a small bow and some arrows and teach the urchin how to shoot. Maybe he could show him how to get a deer.

Cartimandua recognized Atak immediately even though it had been so many years since she last saw him. Before he could bend a knee she waved the salutation aside and took one of his hands in hers. "He is my cousin's redbeard," she said to Archdruid Owain, "only now his beard is gray. My cousin has been hard on him. He should have taken the post I offered him." She looked right into Atak's eyes and leaned toward him enough so that the warm perfumed air from her body enveloped him as he felt the essence rush from him to her. Why did all these women want his essence? "Do you remember when you stopped me from thrashing my uncle Caratacus?"

Caratacus had kissed Cartimandua and put his hand on her bottom. She had swung the great coil of copper hair that wrapped itself around her waist and struck him across the face with it. She had been about to do it again when Atak stopped her. "I grabbed your arm," said Atak. She had fallen against him and had looked up at him with partly opened mouth so that his mind went blank.

"And you almost kissed me. You would have if my cousin hadn't stopped you. Did you ever wish she hadn't stopped you?"

Atak pulled his beard. "It would have been nice."

Cartimandua let go of him abruptly and turned to Owain. Owain was dressed in his golden Archdruid clothes and wore a golden crown with three great white feathers attached to it. He seemed out of sorts, upset by something. Caradawg stood next to Owain, clean and dressed like a prince in the new clothes that Almedha had made for him, and right behind Caradawg stood Almedha. Almedha seemed nervous and upset, and frequently put her hand to her throat. Maybe she was afraid of Cartimandua. Caradawg's eyes were fixed on Atak, but his face was expressionless. "So this is my cousin's son," said Cartimandua, bending down to look into Caradawg's eyes. Caradawg returned her stare and then turned his eyes back on Atak. Atak felt uncomfortable. Why did Caradawg keep staring at him?

"Yes," said Owain. "This is Prince Coilus."

Atak felt the back of his neck prickle as Cartimandua continued to stare at Caradawg. Owain had not been told about the switch. The only ones here who knew, besides himself, were Almedha and Caradawg. He had told Caradawg that Cartimandua would have him killed if she found out who he really was. He hoped what he said had sunk in. If it hadn't, Cartimandua might have himself killed as well as Caradawg. He breathed easier when Cartimandua straightened up. She clapped her hands and the steward Atak remembered from Colchester came toward them dragging his pole. He too looked gray around the edges and a little worse for wear. Atak nodded at him grimly as he slowed to a halt and turned his sleepy eyes on his mistress.

"Take Prince Coilus and find him a room," said Cartimandua. "Get some proper clothes made for him and give him a servant." The steward jerked his head at Caradawg in a signal to follow him and then shuffled off. Caradawg did not move and the steward seemed not to notice. Neither did Cartimandua. She turned to Owain. "He is the only child in my court," she said. "You will provide a Druid to teach him."

"I will send Rhys," said Owain.

Cartimandua grimaced. "Why can't Almedha teach him?"

"Almedha wishes to be married," said Owain, his voice stiff. Atak got the feeling that Owain had wanted to marry her himself.

"Oh?" said Cartimandua. Almedha put a hand to her throat and the movement must have drawn Cartimandua's attention to Caradawg. "Where did that Massa go?" she said, but the steward had disappeared. "Run along and find him," she said to Caradawg, but the boy merely stared at her. She frowned. "Does he understand?" she said to Atak.

"Do as Queen Cartimandua says," said Atak.

"No," said Caradawg. He walked over to Atak's side. Cartimandua stared at him but Caradawg wouldn't be stared down.

"Am I to have as much trouble with him as I've had with his mother?" said Cartimandua.

"He'll settle down," said Atak.

"No I won't," said Caradawg. "I'm going with you."

"You can't," said Atak. "You have to stay here."

For answer, Caradawg set off running across the hall. When he reached one of the braziers used to heat the building he tipped it over so the hot coals scattered across the floor. Then he ran to a high narrow cupboard standing by the wall and pushed it over. He set off running again toward the next brazier but before he could reach it a guard caught him and scooped him up.

"Take him to Massa," said Cartimandua. She trembled with rage. "He's to be locked up until he learns to behave." The boy was carried off struggling by the guard and Atak felt his throat tighten and burn. A strange sadness came over him. He flinched when Cartimandua wheeled on him. "It's you he wants to be with," she said. "You must stay and be his tutor."

"I can't," said Atak. "I have to train soldiers."

She stood before him and put her hands on his shoulders. The perfume rising from her body made him feel dizzy and once again he found himself staring fascinated at the inverted bow shape of her partly opened lips and the unsullied whiteness of her perfect teeth and the soft mound of a delicate tongue partly exposed by her breathing. The essence in him struggled to rush out in a great flood. "Look after Coilus for me," she said, her voice low and melodious. "By serving me in such a way you will best serve my cousin. She will know that in your hands her son is safe."

He was tempted. His life with Boudicca would be one campaign after another and he was tired of war. He would like to go fishing with Caradawg. But he could visualize Boudicca's face when told of his defection and shuddered. "I can't," he said.

She didn't release him right away but let her hands slide

onto his chest. "Don't decide right away," she said. "If ever you decide to come, do. My offer is forever open."

The rain fell in a steady blinding downpour. It was almost dark so Atak left the trail and dismounted on the bank of a river. He waved at the two warriors with him and they too dismounted, leading their horses off in search of a place to sleep. He unfastened his bedroll and leaned back against a tree, the sheepskins rolled under his arm. Untended, the horse moved off to nibble on the grass. If he waited the rain would ease and he could look for a drier spot to sleep. But the rain kept on and soon it grew quite dark. He sat under the tree, knees against his chest, and pulled the skins around him like a tent.

He hadn't thought much about Tetra for a long time but now all kinds of pictures from the past flooded into mind. He had met Tetra and her little daughter Elsa in the Belgic village where he had run after Caligula condemned him. Venutius and Boudicca had shown up there with their army and he had been forced into single combat with their champion Gruffydd. He'd won but his hand was badly cut and Tetra had bound it for him. Then they had made love on the floor of the meeting hut. It had been so good the memory of it was still as fresh as if it had been yesterday. But then he went off with the Britons and she was first forgotten in the excitement of burning Plautius' ships in Boulogne and then abandoned when Boudicca told him Tetra's gods forbade remarriage by widows. Even when she had come to Britain with Elsa as Philip's disciple and found him again and they had married, he had been away from her more than he had been with her. He had never really been a Nazarene as she had wanted him to be. He wished she hadn't died. If she hadn't died he would have left Boudicca by this time and settled down with her. She would have liked that. If she hadn't died they could have looked after Caradawg for Cartimandua. Tetra would have liked Caradawg.

He slept fitfully, slowly heeling over until he was on his side on the wet ground, his head resting on one of the tree's exposed roots. He dreamed of Caradawg, and woke up once sure that the boy was pressed against his back. He flung back the sheepskins and sat up to see but there was no one there. The rain had stopped and all that could be heard in the dense darkness of the forest was the soft drip of water falling from the trees.

It was dark dark dark, and not a single person in the world, not even Boudicca, would notice if he died right here. He would be forgotten before a day passed. Caratacus had long since forgotten him. Ingenius too had forgotten him. They had been close once, but now that Caratacus was exiled and Ingenius rich his two best friendships had wilted away. He had thought that Almedha liked him, but all she had wanted from him was his essence and her hair tucked behind her ear. Even Elsa, whom he had loved as a daughter, would soon forget him. He had done nothing to make her want to remember him.

Shaken by his gloom he tried to stand up to shake out the sheepskins but slipped on the wet tree root and sat down with a crash, hitting his head against the tree and biting his tongue as he did so. He flung his arms wide and let out a great roar of anguish. His life had meant nothing. He roared again, then raised his knees and let his head sink forward on them, lifting it quickly when he felt hot tears running down his nose. There was a crashing noise and a curse near him, and he groped around blindly for his sword as a heavy body fell over him. It was one of the warriors.

"We heard you shout," said the man. "Are you all right?"

"I'm all right," said Atak. "You two go on to Tas as soon as it's light."

"What about you?"

"I'm going back to Barwick."

Chapter 6

Caratacus Returns

Some months later

Boudicca dismounted as the line of wagons and horsemen entered the clearing next to Ingenius' workshop. She almost put out a hand to help Venutius dismount but drew back. He would fly into a rage if anyone treated him like a cripple. He looked old, drawn and wan as he dismounted, and his damaged arm hung crookedly at his side. Her heart went out to him but she could do nothing. He didn't want to be left up here in the Silurian mountains but she could find no better task for him than to train soldiers. Ingenius must have heard the noise of the wagons for he came walking toward them wiping sweat from his forehead with the back of his hand and then rubbing his hands on his bare chest.

"I've brought you enough iron for fifty thousand swords," said Boudicca as he bent a knee. "How many have you made?"

"Almost five thousand," he said.

Boudicca shook her head and Ingenius looked aggrieved. "You've got to do better than that," she said. She ached to pick up a sword from a pile ready for shipment and balance it in her hand but it was taboo for her to touch bare iron. "Can you wrap the hilt? Iron will get slippery with Rummy blood."

"Those are just the way they come from the forge," said Ingenius. "Fancy swords will take more time."

"We don't have more time."

"Maybe you'd better get someone else to make them."

"They'll do," said Venutius. He touched Boudicca's arm with his good hand as if to say 'don't needle him as you did me or you may get no swords at all,' but looked at Ingenius. "The new governor is likely to move soon. He brought reinforcements."

Ingenius curled his lip. "Wasn't Veranius ready to move?"

"Suetonius Paulinus is no Veranius," said Boudicca. "He's as old as Atak but he's tough. We have to hurry. I want to hurt him this year before he gets acclimated. I need fifty thousand swords and I need them by Lughnasa[25]. Wouldn't it be quicker to make em shorter? Atak always said ours were too long."

"He wanted us to make Rummy swords," said Venutius. "Britons can't use Rummy swords. Without a wall of Rummy shields to go with em they're no good."

"Is Atak with you?" said Ingenius, looking toward the men milling around the wagons. Some unloaded the iron and charcoal while others loaded the finished swords.

"No," said Boudicca, thinking of Elsa's prophecy that she would lose something if she stole Caradawg. "Cartimandua stole him from us."

Ingenius looked as if he were about to ask what she meant but must have changed his mind. "They're longer than Rummy swords," he said, "but shorter and harder than before. If we make em too soft they bend. If we make em too hard they break."

"I'll leave Cruker with you and send fifty more men," said Boudicca. "I must have swords. We can't fight Paulinus with sticks and stones."

"We'll do it if it's possible."

"It has to be possible," she said. "I have talked to Marius and Dedreth about your loan for the ransom. They will repay it."

Ingenius brightened. "What about chariots?" he said.

"King Afan has the Parisies making those for us."

"Come and see one that I've made."

They followed him around the back of his workshop, really an old village meeting hut that Ingenius had converted. Behind it stood a Parisi two-horse chariot. Its body was larger than the Silurian chariots and made of much denser wickerwork. On each wheel two short blades had been fastened. She bent down to look at the edges and saw they were extremely sharp.

Ingenius pounded on the flat of the blades to show how firmly they were attached. "You'd use these for breaking up the legions," he said. "Run these at em and they'll break and run."

"They will that," said Venutius, touching the blades.

"They scream like banshees when the chariot's running," said Ingenius, his voice hoarse with pride.

Boudicca felt sick with lust. This is what they had to have to break up Paulinus. In rows six deep with their shields locked together the legions were unbeatable so long as they cohered. It took hundreds of British lives to force a hole in their line and then it closed up as soon as they penetrated. Chop them into segments with these monsters and they would quickly fall to the British long swords. If only she had more time. "How fast can you build them?" she asked.

"Fifty a month if you get the Parisies to make chariots with bigger stronger wheels like this one."

"How about our Silurian chariots?"

"They're too flimsy."

"It will take gold. And you'd have to go to the Parisies."

Ingenius nodded.

She stood up decisively. "How soon can Cruker take over?"

"Now. He knows how to make swords and lance heads."

"Then you must go to King Afan and show him what to do. Take these blades off so no one sees them. You can build a forge there." Ingenius rubbed his hands together and she could see he was excited. "It's a wonderful idea," she said. "It can win us the war."

"We'll need two hundred at least," said Venutius. "That's four months."

"I want four hundred. Afan must build them faster. We must get as much gold as it takes."

"Atak would be a big help."

"Atak's too old to help any more. I have been spared the task of telling him that." Why did her voice sound so bitter? she wondered. "Now I must go to meet my father. He will arrive in Colchester next week. Venutius will be close by if you need anything."

Ingenius walked back with her and Venutius to where her guard waited and Cangus her equerry held her horse. "Where is Pendragon?" he said.

She could read his thoughts. He was wondering if her father would become Arviragus instead of her. "Pendragon will not be flown until we take the field," she said. "My father is coming to die in peace at Caer Leon. Like Atak, he too is getting old."

"Take care," said Venutius as she mounted, and she reached down to squeeze his left hand. "Be careful in Colchester. A lot of Britons are being killed."

"I will," she said. She looked again at Ingenius. "Thank you for making those blades. Nothing is more important. Get to King Afan's as quickly as you can—and don't let anyone see that chariot. I will get gold to Afan to pay the Parisies." She wheeled her horse and rode off, Cangus and her knight-guards clattering along behind. She had never felt so excited. With Ingenius' new chariots the defeat of two legions was within reach. The only question was: where was she to get enough gold to pay the Parisies? Did she dare take it from Prasu's treasury?

Venutius had been holding a scroll and handed it to Ingenius as Boudicca rode off. Surprised, Ingenius took it from him. "When I was in Colchester your friend Spurius Vibius Rufus asked me to give you this," said Venutius.

After Venutius had left, Ingenius went into the hut to read the scroll.

> *Why did you leave? You shouldn't give up so quickly. Catus needs money. If you can raise five million bring it to Camulodunum as fast as you can. He will give you back your notes and you'll be free and clear. But make it fast.*
> *SVR.*

He crushed the scroll and threw it into the forge. It exploded into flame before withering into a crinkled black cinder. He had two million in bronze coins he'd made for the Rummies hidden away in Colchester. Where could he get three more million? It was such a small sum compared to what he'd had before, but how unattainable it seemed now! Boudicca had said Marius would repay the ransom, but when? Could he borrow against it? Before he did anything he should go to Colchester and see Vibius Rufus.

Cruker showed up the next morning with fifty men. "Like old times," said Cruker, kicking the hot coals of the forge with his foot. "I brought a few of the lads we had in Colchester. They'll learn this lot fast."

"If you divide them into two shifts," said Ingenius, "you can keep em at it night and day, but it'll be a miracle if you can get fifty thousand swords by Lughnasa. Why is she so set on Lughnasa? The Rummies won't do anything this year."

"Don't believe it," said Cruker. "This new governor's a flaming terror. He's going through the legions like a dose of Sullis' spring water. Anyone who can't run ten miles in full kit and then swim across the Severn he's sending back to Gaul and bringing over tigers to replace em. Word is he's heard the gold's in Mona and he's going for it before winter."

"The gold's not still there, is it?"

"They've hid it somewhere else is what I heard."

Ingenius leaned forward confidentially. "Listen," he said. "I'll work with you tonight until you get the hang of it, and then I'll leave early in the morning."

By the time dawn broke, the new men had begun to catch on and Cruker was soon stretched out on the floor snoring as only an exhausted man could. Ingenius quickly wrapped some clothes and a small sack of gold coins in a traveling roll that he tied to his back. Then he walked to the stable, mounted his horse and rode through the trees until he reached the trail leading east. The sun had just risen and was touching a dark gray band of clouds, turning them pink and mauve and green with its light.

***

The mob surged into Colchester like floodwater pouring down a sluice. It came up both sides of the river and drove everything before it, making a strange sound like the subterranean groan of a tiger about to spring. Seeing it approach, Boudicca told her guards to disperse among the light crowd waiting on the dock. Dressed in plain tunics, armed only with long daggers strapped to their thighs, her guards were indistinguishable from other common Britons. She herself had no mark of rank and no weapon.

Her father's ship was to tie up in front of them. As the mob came onto the wooden dock, Cangus pushed her into the doorway of a building and stood before her as the tide of people filled the quays and overflowed into boats and ships. Armored ex-legionaries were in the press, helmets glittering like sequins fastened to a seething multi-colored cloth of British hair.

She could see the mast of her father's ship as it slowly moved up river. It carried no sail so the crew must be rowing to the dock. As the ship approached, the crowd began a rhythmic chant: "Caratacus, Caratacus, Caratacus." It reminded her of the crowd in that long ago Gostedd, when the chant had been 'No, No, No' to her father's plea for Britons to support him against Cartimandua's contention that the Rummies would stop their conquest if he were dismissed. Now, she reflected bitterly, Britons had learned how right her father had been. Her heart pounded with excitement as the ship stopped. It had been eight years since she had seen that loved face. She longed to tell him of Ingenius' new chariot and how it would break up the legions.

Lines must have been thrown to shore to keep the ship in place but it did not come alongside the dock. Perhaps the crew was afraid the crowd would surge onto the ship and capsize it. She could not see the ship's deck for the throng, but when a full-throated roar sounded she knew her father must have appeared. How was her father to get ashore? How was she to get him away?

Above the noise of the crowd she heard the shrill chatter of lines running through blocks and saw the great boom that held the sail appear over the crowd's heads. The cheering grew louder and her father's head and chest appeared. He held on to a line with one hand and waved with the other. He must be standing on some kind of platform suspended from the boom so he could see above the crowd. How much older he looked! The once blond hair and beard were gray, the face etched with lines of age. She longed to put her head on his chest as of old and tell him that she loved him. She waved, knowing as she did that he would not be able to see her in that press.

The crowd quietened as Caratacus raised both arms. "My friends," he said, and she could barely hear his voice. It had once been so clear and strong. The crowd stood mute. "Tis a welcome indeed for one so long gone from these loved shores. I had not thought you would still remember your old Arviragus. Caratacus does not weep easily, but as you can see, the eyes of me will not stay dry. Tis wonderful to be so loved, and Genvissa and me will long treasure this day."

He paused to wipe his eyes, and the crowd began to chant again, a low chant, barely audible but powerful in its depth. "Arviragus, Arviragus, Arviragus." It stopped when Caratacus raised his arms.

"Nay," he said. "I cannot be your Arviragus. I have sworn never to raise a sword against the Rummies. I am an old man now and have come home to die in peace among my loved ones."

The crowd roared, but now the roar was angry. The chant began again: "Arviragus, Arviragus, Arviragus." Out of the corner of her eye Boudicca saw the glint of armor. Legionaries forced their way through the crowd toward the dock where her father must come ashore. She nudged Cangus and Cangus nodded as Caratacus raised his arms again and the crowd's roar subsided into a sullen murmur. "We must get to the dock," she said, and hung on to Cangus' belt as he forced his way through. She could see her guards worming their way toward her.

"I cannot be your Arviragus," said Caratacus. "There is one better than me and you know who she is. Serve her well and do her bidding. Now if these good sailors will lower me, I would come ashore and kiss the soil that bore me on its breast."

She reached the dock with Cangus as the ship was pulled alongside. As it touched, the crowd parted to let Caratacus come ashore, all the while chanting "Arviragus, Arviragus." She wanted to scream at them to shut up and leave her father in peace, but managed instead to worm her way behind Cangus to the edge of the crowd. Her father stepped ashore, Genvissa right behind him, older too and plumper, weary looking, her skin like the crust of underdone bread.

Caratacus got down on his knees not twenty feet from Boudicca and kissed the ground. As he got up she called to him and he turned toward her, a smile of pleasure on his face. She burst through the crowd and ran toward him, arms outstretched. Before she could reach him, the crowd disintegrated, shoved aside by legionaries. Genvissa seized Caratacus as if to pull him back into the ship, but there was the flash of swords and she and Caratacus sank to their knees as Boudicca reached them. Caratacus opened his mouth to greet her, his eyes already glazing, and collapsed against her legs as she knelt to catch him, a great death scream from her mother ringing in her ears. "Daddy," she said, but Caratacus was dead. Genvissa sagged forward and her weight against Caratacus brought them all to the ground.

She crouched beside them shaking with grief, Cangus over her with legs astride to protect her from the milling throng. She wept as if her heart would break, barely conscious of the animal sounds and screams and vicious movements around her. Then

Cangus was shoved aside and a body fell on her. It was armored and the armor dug into her side, knocking the breath out of her. The pain shocked her into awareness. She must put aside her grief. It would do her father and mother no good and Caratacus would be the first to tell her to get on with the job at hand. She shoved the Rummy's body away and saw it was headless. Not far from her hand, as she pushed against the ground to get to her feet among the press of bodies, was a bloody arm. The crowd was tearing the legionaries limb from limb. She seized the dead legionary's sword and struggled to her feet as Cangus and some of her guards fought their way to her side.

All around them Britons were going berserk. No Roman would survive in this melee. A rough hand grabbed her arm and pulled her around. It was Iorwerth, the firer of Rummy houses, his eyes glassy with hate and teeth bared in a snarl. The men with him were his knights. He held a Rummy sword and waved it. "Here's our Arviragus," he roared. "Gather round, lads. We'll burn the bloody palace."

Like a river suddenly turning to rapids, the crowd lurched forward, heading for the Governor's palace. She was swept along, Cangus hanging grimly to her, but she managed to grab Iorwerth and pull him close. "Forget the palace," she shouted. "Get your men to one side."

"The palace must be burnt," shouted Iorwerth. "And then we'll burn this Rummy city to avenge your father."

"If you would avenge my father," she shouted back. "Get out of this mob and follow me."

Cangus managed to get them to the edge of the streaming mob and into a muddy little street that led away from the river. Iorwerth howled with rage at being thwarted but one by one his knights and her guards forced their way through and joined them as the mob rushed by.

"That mob will fire the palace," she said. "And Paulinus' legionaries will do all to prevent it. We have more important work to do. Did anyone see what happened to my parents' bodies?"

"Our men carried them back on board the ship," said one of Iorwerth's knights. "They will get them to your grandfather's palace."

Her father and mother would rest at Gosbecks with Cunobelinus. She looked around her little band of thirty or so knights and at Iorwerth's still glowering face. "My heart is made glad by your love for my father and mother," she said to Iorwerth, "and your desire to avenge them. But burning the palace will not get the Rummies off this land. Now hide those swords beneath your tunics and we will burn something more important than the palace."

She hid the short Rummy sword under her tunic and marched swiftly up the little street to the street of shops, Iorwerth and the knights following. Ingenius had shown her the small building that held the Rummy archives. It was always guarded but with this mob on the rampage the guards had likely been called away to defend the palace. Before they reached the street, a cavalry troop clattered by at high speed, swords drawn, heading for the palace.

The street of shops was almost deserted and they ran down it keeping close to the buildings. To their right, down by the river, they could hear screams and shouts and angry roars as Paulinus' legionaries attacked the mob. Already there was a smell of smoke in the air. An elderly ex-legionary guarded the archive building. He drew his sword as she ran up the steps. His mouth opened in surprise as she lifted her tunic to pull out her sword, but the next moment he was headless on the floor as Cangus chopped him down.

Inside the building she paused to look around. It consisted of one large room with two smaller rooms at the far end. At this end by the door there was a desk at which sat a frightened British clerk. One of the guards grabbed him by the scruff and hustled him outside. The desk was littered with scrolls. Around the walls of the large room ran many shelves on which lay bundles of scrolls bound together. Urns were scattered around the floor out of which bundles of scrolls protruded.

"It's just bloody paper," said Iorwerth.

"These," she said, "are the deeds to all the Rummies have confiscated. All the loans made to Britons are here" including Prasu's too, I hope, "and Duw knows what else. With these gone the Rummies won't know what they have or where it is. They can't live or breathe without paper. Your deeds too, my friend, are in here. Get those torches off the wall and set the place afire. But first let's see what's in those rooms."

She ran down to the other end of the room, Iorwerth on her heels and opened one of the doors. The room was full of scrolls, probably to be sorted. The other door was locked, but Iorwerth and two of his knights quickly smashed it down. On the floor inside were many heavy sacks. She quickly pulled one open and her heart lifted when she saw it was full of gold coins. Her chariots! "Get these to the door," she said, "and send a man to steal a wagon."

As the knights piled sacks by the door, she and Iorwerth threw armfuls of scrolls in a heap next to the desk. A rumble outside told her a wagon had been stolen and the men loaded the sacks in it as she and Iorwerth took torches from the wall and threw them on the piles of scrolls. She saw they were well alight and that the desk had caught fire before she went outside.

"Do you have a hiding place for that gold?" she asked Iorwerth, and the burly noble nodded.

"Aye," he said. "We can hide it in my land."

"Then get on your way," she said. "Bury it well."

"Aye," said Iorwerth. He jumped on the wagon with the man who had stolen it and whipped the horse into action.

"And we will get back to our horses," she said to Cangus. Smoke poured out of the archive building's door as they hurried away. One of the streets they were to pass on their way out of the city was the one near Claudius' temple on which Ingenius had built his house in happier days. She was glad he had finally separated himself from Catus and Seneca. He might ultimately have turned against the Britons instead of making weapons for them.

When they reached Ingenius' street she saw some of the mob pouring up it from the river, a few panic-stricken legionaries running in front of it. Black smoke billowed up from Claudius' temple and the crowd rocked the statue of Claudius, trying to overturn it. The temple had been built on a holy Druid site and the Romans were fools if they thought their building would survive.

Before the legionaries reached Ingenius' house, three civilian horsemen galloped out of the gates coming toward the street of shops. She pushed her men back around the corner as the horsemen slowed to enter the street, then gasped. The first horseman was the plump Catus Decianus, a look of panic on his face. The Second was Vibius Rufus, a man she had seen often with Catus and Seneca. The third was Ingenius. They turned onto the street of shops without seeing Boudicca and her guards and galloped off to the north.

Why was Ingenius with those people again? Why was he here instead of on his way to build those chariots? And where were the three of them going?

Chapter 7

Prasu Takes a Journey

Unlike Thetford, Tas offered major obstacles to any hostile force attempting to take it. A deep ditch surrounded it and the ramparts on the inward side of the ditch rose steeply to the fort's perimeter and were stiffened vertically by dressed and slippery logs. Around the perimeter were stacked more heavy dressed logs and boulders ready to roll down on attackers climbing the fort's glacis.

As Boudicca and her guards rode around it to the removable log bridge that provided access, the narrow path they were forced to follow kept them all the time within range of the archers and lancers defending the perimeter. The undergrowth between the surrounding trees had been cleared to the water's edge where the fort followed the river and for several hundred feet into the woods on the other side. Any hostile force would be plainly visible as it massed for an attack.

Atak had done a good job of providing a serious defense. All the same, she remembered his warning that such a fort would not keep the Rummies out for long. Ballista would clear the perimeter and then the Rummies would charge up the glacis under a testudo[26]. Without artillery of their own they were powerless to stop Romans determined to get in. She rode over the bridge and up to the heavy log gate reddened by the setting sun. Several warriors grinned down at her from the wooden fighting platform above as the gatekeeper opened the gate. There were many knights and warriors inside and a general cheer went up when they saw their queen ride in and dismount.

"Is King Caratacus not with ye then my lady?" said the gatekeeper. "And all of us agog to see him?"

"King Caratacus and Queen Genvissa are dead," she said, grimly handing her horse to a servant. "The Rummies killed them. They are being buried at Gosbecks with my grandfather, King Cunobelinus."

There was a shocked silence. "They've killed King Caratacus?" said the gatekeeper, wiping the tears from his eyes with the back of his hands. "And him just home from Rummyland? Bad cess to the dirthy flaming Rummies that killed him. And him with his back to them and no sword in his hand either without a doubt. You'd be betther looking to your weapons, lads. There will be death doom and destructhion to do now our own queen has come home with her father and mother killed by the flaming Rummies."

A great shout of anger went up. The shout sent a shiver through Boudicca and moved her strangely. Her father had served Britain by the manner of his death in a way he never could if he had been allowed to die in peace. Was she then glad he had died such a death? Yes she was, and doubtless so was he. The murder of Caratacus and Genvissa would work on warrior souls as nothing else could, and the gatekeeper had spoken truly. She would have little trouble gathering the nations in one last attempt to throw the Rummies off the land for good. With this kind of rage at her back she could defeat the Rummies. But first she needed armies and those new chariots. She stamped her foot and the men around her drew back, seeing her anger.

"The people flocked to my father," she said, "and the Rummies remembered how great a leader he was and feared he would lead the people against them again. That is why they treacherously killed him as he opened his arms to me in greeting."

Another shout of anger, louder than before went up.

"Was my father a great leader?"

"Aye. That he was."

"Am I his true daughter?"

"Aye. That you are. You are our Arviragus."

"And will we avenge my father?"

"Aye. That we will."

She turned to go into the palace and an avenue opened for her among the knights and warriors. At the other end of it Goneril came toward her weeping from the news she had just heard. She was now a tall willowy girl with flaming red hair and bright blue eyes. A golden torque was around her neck and she wore a simple white shirt tucked loosely into tartan trousers, the ends of which in turn were tucked into finely tooled leather boots. A leather belt was about her slender waist, and from it hung a silver hilted dagger in a leather sheath. Seventeen, she was the same age Boudicca had been when she set off for Boulogne with Venutius all those years ago and she was just as wild a chariot driver. She clasped the girl to her, conscious of the supple firmness of that young body. Goneril too was a warrior like herself, but must soon be ready for marriage. Whom could she marry?

"It is good to see you, mother," said Goneril. "It is horrible that Grandda and Grandma have been killed." They kissed and wiped the tears from their eyes. "Rummies will die for this."

"They have and they will. Our Britons will not take this lightly. Your grandfather was well loved."

"Father too is very ill," said Goneril.

She put her newly awakened grief aside and looked closely at Goneril, wondering how much her daughter loved Prasu and what she would say when told Venutius was her real father. Goneril had never seemed as close to Prasu as Gwenda, who was his favorite. "Then let us see him," she said.

They entered Prasu's room, which had been darkened by hanging drapes over the window. Only a single candle gave light and the room danced with great dark shadows as they moved.

Prasu lay asleep on a deep straw mattress. His stomach made a large mound under the linen bedcovers and his head lay to one side among the pillows. Even in the uncertain light his face seemed gray and weary, stubbled hair covering his chins and cheeks, his head almost bald. His breath came irregularly through loose lips and his eyes were partly open, only the whites showing. He looked near death, and Boudicca stared at the old king's face as incidents from the past flitted before her. Was it so long ago he had gasped at seeing her naked for the first time and had played love games on their wedding night? He had been a wily stoat at times and a Rummy lover, but her anger toward him had softened over the years and indifference had taken its place. He had tried to be good to her and toward their daughters. He had earned the right to die in peace.

A sudden movement startled her and broke her reverie. A figure came into the room. It was Gwenda, and Boudicca smiled with pleasure as she took her into her arms. Gwenda was sixteen. Unlike her sister she had more typical white-blonde hair and her eyes were a lighter and less intense blue. She reminded Boudicca of her own sister Gwendolyn, who had been driven crazy by Owain and was still in Rome. She had the same creamy white skin and voluptuous figure, and her manners were unrestrained. She wore sandals and a simple white linen tunic, her only ornament the gold torque around her neck. Goneril told Gwenda of their grandfather's death, and Boudicca's heart warmed to the younger girl when she burst into tears and came into her mother's arms for comfort. This daughter was not a warrior, and the thought made her happy as she kissed Gwenda's hair. Unlike herself and Goneril Gwenda would have a full time husband and family, and live in peace once the land was rid of Rummies.

***

Boudicca sat in the wooden tub washing away the grime of travel with Habren's help when she heard Einon, grown white and frail now, pounding his stick on the flagstones and announcing a visitor. Goneril would take care of whoever it was. She was in no hurry to leave her tub.

When she did emerge from the bedchamber dressed in a soft tunic she was surprised to see Ingenius sitting on a couch, Goneril standing before him near the firepit. Her anger rose at the sight of him but she also felt relieved. He wouldn't be here if he didn't intend to make those chariots. Ingenius rose to greet her, bent his knee and bowed over her hand. She kept her voice cold. "I saw you in Colchester," she said, and his face flamed red, "though you did not see me."

"I had business there," he said.

"I thought your business was with King Afan?"

"I got Cruker started on the swords," he said, "then I stopped in Colchester on my way here. I am now on my way to King Afan." His voice stiffened as if he resented her suspicion. "If you will permit me I shall leave early in the morning."

She sat down on the couch and looked up at Goneril as Ingenius sat down. By Duw, she thought, she is as I was at her age. Was this fresh vision herself twenty years ago? She felt old and tired and wondered why she had wanted all these years to be Arviragus. How much better it would be to go back to Atak's little house by the lake and have Venutius and all her family with her. She sighed. It would never be.

Ingenius fidgeted. He must be uncomfortable feeling her displeasure. It would be good for him. He had made her feel uncomfortable for the past two days.

"The last time I saw you," said Ingenius to Goneril, his voice straining to make light conversation, "you were a little girl asleep in bed with your sister. I had come to tell your mother that Scapula, the Roman governor at that time . . . "

"I well know who Scapula was," said Goneril. "And how he died. May all Rummies die the same way."

"Scapula had gone to the north to attack your grandfather."

"And my grandfather was betrayed by Aunt Cartimandua. I am familiar with the story."

Boudicca felt a malicious pleasure at Ingenius' discomfiture. He would find Goneril a hard nut to crack. "I am sorry your grandparents were killed," he said, frowning.

Goneril looked at him solemnly. Only a little twitch at the corner of her mouth betrayed any emotion. She remained standing by the firepit and Boudicca marveled at the grace of her lithe young figure. "How did you know they were killed?"

"I was told by a Roman who saw it happen."

"How came you to receive word of it from a Roman?"

"He didn't tell me. I was with another Roman, and Vibius Rufus came to tell him."

"And who was this other Roman?"

"His name is Decianus Catus." Ingenius looked at Boudicca. He wanted her help with this ice-cold princess but Boudicca would not meet his eyes. Let him squirm.

"The Procurator?" Goneril's voice became as icy as her eyes. "You must be on easy terms with the Rummies if you visit the Procurator. Did you avenge my grandparents when Catus was told of their murder?"

A servant appeared with a tray on which was a cup of wine and a plate of meal cakes. He gave it to Ingenius and Goneril waved her hand as a sign that he should eat before he answered. He wolfed down one of the meal cakes and glanced again at Boudicca, but Boudicca was going to give him no help. Goneril had the black and white viewpoint of the young. People were either enemies to be hated and killed or friends to be loved and succored. She lacked experience and couldn't understand, as Boudicca had been forced to understand, that it could serve a British purpose to work with Romans even while other Britons tried to kill them. But even though Goneril's viewpoint was impractical its purity made Boudicca yearn. She had felt that way once, as had Venutius, and it had been the happiest period of her life. Ingenius took a gulp of wine and wiped his mouth. "I did nothing to avenge King Caratacus," he said. "Or his wife the Queen. The Romans fled before the mob could reach the house."

"Catus would not have fled from me," said Goneril. She drew her dagger from its sheath and held it with the point toward him. "This would have partially settled the score." She put the dagger back. "But you must have done something?"

Ingenius put the tray aside and stood up. He looked at Boudicca again and she smiled primly. "It would have done little good," he said. "I am not loved by the Britons and the mob would have killed me. When the Romans fled I fled also. Catus fled to Longthorpe and I fled here. You will learn someday that there is more to defeating Romans than plunging a dagger into them. I was once a captain of chariots under your grandfather, not much older than you and as eager to kill Rummies. I learned from experience that our armies were as waves dashing themselves to pieces against the rocks. The Rummies were far above us in every way. I learned how to join in their commerce and observe the way they govern those they conquer. It has been a dirty job but it has taught me their strengths so we too can learn to become strong."

"Bravo," said Boudicca. "Pray tell us what you learned from Catus that will help you build the chariots we need." Suddenly made guilty by Ingenius' stricken look, she turned to Goneril. "Sir Ingenius," she said, "raised the ransom that freed your Uncle Marius and cousin Brennius from the Hibernians, and for that our family will always owe him gratitude. He has also made a magnificent chariot that may win the war for us."

"One chariot will not win a war," said Goneril. "No matter how magnificent. But I am glad you raised a ransom for uncle Marius."

"Why did you go to see Catus?" asked Boudicca.

"I went to see Catus," said Ingenius, "because Vibius Rufus sent me a note saying that Catus would absolve my debts if I could raise five million right away. I went to see if I could get

King Prasu's note for it. I hoped if he would I could get the money from you so that Catus couldn't come against you."

"And would he?"

"No. He had already raised the money by the time I got there. What he wants now is the location of the Council's gold so he can get it before Paulinus gets it. If I tell him he will give me the note."

"And what did you tell him?"

"I told him I would try to find out where it is. He gave me a safe conduct. It might be useful to us."

She had been conscious of Goneril staring at Ingenius until he finished. Does she still despise him for not killing Catus? But Ingenius had not betrayed them and she would defend him against Goneril if need be. Tomorrow she would send knights with him to make sure he reached Afan and got to work on the chariots.

Goneril lightly touched Ingenius' arm with her hand. "Come," she said. "I will take you in to see my father. He is quite poorly so you can't stay long. Then you may bathe and change clothes and eat the evening meal with us." She turned to lead the way but stopped when Gwenda came up to them.

"This is my sister the Princess Gwenda," said Goneril, and Ingenius bowed. "This is Sir Ingenius," said Goneril to Gwenda. "He has come to help us." Gwenda gave him a weak smile, her dark eyes still showing her grief at Caratacus' death. "You argue well in your own cause, Sir Ingenius," Goneril said. "But the time for learning from Romans is over. You must now become wholly a Briton."

Ingenius bowed but remained silent. In showing him her dying father, Boudicca knew that Goneril was forgiving him and he seemed to recognize it. Goneril knew that Prasu had liked Ingenius, for through him he had met Didius Gallus, for many years his Fidchell partner as well as Governor of Britain.

When Ingenius returned, bathed and wrapped in a robe that Goneril had put out for him, his feet ensconced in comfortable leather sandals, he felt physically relaxed but mentally disturbed.

The verbal battle with Goneril had shaken the self-image he had built up over the years, and while sitting in the hot water so laboriously brought in by the servants he had taken inventory. As a crippled youth despised by his healthy peers he had mastered mathematics and engineering as a pupil of Caratacus' Greek engineer, and after Elsa had healed his twisted leg he had become a captain of chariots and fought bravely. His metal working skills had made him into a fine artist and artisan. He was able to visualize the energies released in combat and devise weapons such as the chariot he had designed for Boudicca that would channel such energies to change the shape of battle. He was able to teach men and inspire them to work together to produce whatever could be sold in the marketplace, and he had learned much about the operation of the marketplace itself even though he had not yet made it his servant.

It was a list of accomplishments any man could be proud of, but Goneril, with a self righteous purity unchallenged as yet by the need to solve problems in a cruel unforgiving world had weighed him in her balance and found him wanting. Had he become too much a tool of the Rummies? At first he had angrily assured himself that he had been using them to learn their weaknesses and strengths for Britain's sake. But the vigorous yet innocent face pictured in his mind, the eyes that looked into his soul and found so little substance there, caused an ache he had not felt since Elsa left him. His life had been wholly self-centered and selfish. Losing Elsa had brought this home but he had ignored the lesson and worked only to please himself. The tawdry experience with Morfudd and the trouble he had caused for poor Prasu had also warned him, but those lessons too had been ignored. He had become simply a tool for Seneca and Catus, and his face burned in humiliation at the things he had done in trying to win their approval when all they had to offer was contempt. Was it too late to start over again?

When he came into the hall, Boudicca was sitting on a couch near the firepit. The hall sparkled with candles and lamps for night had fallen. Goneril had exchanged her shirt and trousers for a white tunic the very plainness of which drew immediate attention to her creamlike complexion and the fiery red hair that fell so softly about her shoulders. Looking at the fresh beauty of her his ache intensified.

Gwenda held out her hands to greet him, her manner as soft and gentle as her body. "I am sorry I was not able to greet you properly when you arrived," she said. "The shock of the news overwhelmed me."

"I understand," said Ingenius. "To lose such grandparents is a heavy burden to bear."

"It is more than ten years since we last saw them," said Goneril, as briskly as Boudicca herself might have spoken. "We were still children."

"But a child's love never dies," said Ingenius. "There is nothing higher than such love."

"You speak like a poet," said Goneril. "Is this another skill you have learned from the Rummies?"

"The Rummies I have known," said Ingenius, "are a mercenary and humorless lot not given to poetic feelings."

"Do not mind my sister," said Gwenda. "Her heart is softer than her tongue. When you lived with us you were captain of mother's guard. Weren't you married to Elsa? She who healed Goneril?"

His face reddened. "Yes."

"But she is no longer your wife."

"No."

"Did you lose your love for her?"

"No. But I loved my ambitions more. I deserved to lose her and I did."

"And what are your ambitions now?" said Goneril.

Ingenius released Gwenda's hands and stood before Goneril. "I have three," he said. "One is to make clear once and for all that I am truly a Briton."

"There has been room for doubt," said Goneril.

"There will no longer be if I can do ought to assure it."
"And the second?" said Goneril.
"Is to serve your mother and do all I can to assure her victory."
"Then you must build my chariots," said Boudicca.
"That I will. And help you determine how best to use them."
"And the third?"

He took Goneril's hand in his and kissed it. "It is to earn the love of a pure woman." Goneril's face flamed red as he turned to sit by Boudicca.

Before they retired for the night, Ingenius drew Boudicca aside. "I learned something else from Catus," he said.

"Oh?" Their conversation during the evening meal had restored her confidence in him and she didn't want to have it shaken again. Goneril had ceased to needle him and like all of them she had been enchanted by his stories about the machinations of Catus and Seneca and the troubles of greedy Romans like Paulinus and Didius Gallus who got fleeced by the evil pair.

"Paulinus intends to eliminate Iceni after King Prasu dies."

She frowned. "Didius Gallus assured Prasu it would be maintained and that I would be High Queen."

Ingenius shook his head. "The only kingdom that will be left on this side of the border is King Cogi's new Regni."

She had feared something like this would happen. Prasu had been confident, now that his relations with Rome were fully restored, that his kingdom would survive after he died. He had even made a will leaving half his estates to Nero in the expectation that Boudicca and the princesses would be able to share the rest. But that wasn't the Rummy way. The Icenis would lose everything and be simply another batch of Roman slaves. The important thing was: what would this do to her plans?

"I'm sorry to bring you such news," said Ingenius.

She tossed her head contemptuously. "It will stiffen the backbone of those who thought they could lick the Rummies' boots and keep what they had. If we are to keep our lands and kingdoms we must throw the Rummies out. There is no other option."

"Where will you go?"

"To the mountains if I have to. I fear Prasu will die soon, but before he does we'll clean out his treasury. Galga will be here tomorrow with the other kings to plan our campaign. His men can take the gold and jewels to Afan to build your chariots." Thank God they had found that gold in the archive building.

Ingenius laid a hand on her arm. "If you do that," he said, "you will be in great danger. When King Prasu dies, Catus will seize the treasury. His men have inventoried it and if anything is missing you'll be arrested."

"He will have to catch me first. Mahel tells me Prasu is not likely to die for a week. We'll have time to clean out Thetford."

The next morning, the fort filled to overflowing with kings, knights and nobles ready to avenge Caratacus' murder. Their retainers made a small army outside. Goneril came to Boudicca as she stood talking to the heavy set, heavy moving Galga and her uncle Guderius, and stood waiting until Boudicca pulled her to one side. "Ingenius has told me our kingdom is to be eliminated," she said.

Boudicca was angry. Why had Ingenius told her that? "When your father dies, not before," she said.

"That will not be long," said Goneril. "But why must we leave?"

"You and Gwenda must go to your Uncle Marius in Siluria."

"While you fight."

"I am Arviragus. When this war is over you can come back to Thetford."

Goneril's eyes were like blue ice. "I am going with Ingenius to the Parisies."

Her eyebrows went up. "You are not."

"He has told me about building the chariots and what they will do. I want to help build them and I want my own fifty. It is my right to fight in this war."

"You are too young."

"You were my age when you fired the ships in Boulogne."

Boudicca pursed her lips. She didn't like Goneril going with Ingenius and she didn't like the idea of Goneril fighting. She didn't want this first beautiful product of her love for Venutius put at risk of injury or death. But she knew how she had felt at Goneril's age and wasn't sure what Goneril would do if she wasn't allowed to go. Most likely she would go anyway, and then there would be no one to protect her. "What about your father?" she said, playing for time.

"Gwenda will stay. She is his favorite, and I have said my farewell already. Mahel says he will not become conscious again. Gwenda can go to uncle Marius. She is not a knight."

"All right," said Boudicca, giving in. With tears in her eyes she clasped the young body to her. "Have King Afan send a messenger when you get there."

Ingenius and Goneril had barely left when Habren came to Boudicca, tears streaming down her face. The kings and nobles thronging the hall grew quiet, sensing the reason for the tears.

"He is gone," said Habren.

"Gone?"

"King Prasu is dead."

There was a mind crushing silence and then Guderius spoke: "By Duw, we will not have time to clean out your treasury. We must get to the mountains."

Boudicca turned on him. "Prasu is not dead," she said.

"He is dead," screamed Habren, putting her hands to her face. "He is dead."

Boudicca walked up to her and slapped her face, so hard that she would have fallen had not one of the nobles caught her. "He is not dead," she said. "You will put him in the four wheeled chariot. You will sit on one side of him and Gwenda on the other. I will ride before you and we will take him to Thetford with a full guard where he will recuperate from his illness."

"What if you get stopped by the Rummies?" said Galga.

Oh you slow man, she thought. "They will not come too close when I tell them of the plague that has stricken Tas. Now I would have you, Galga, go through the forest with your men and meet us at Thetford after dark. The rest of you had better disperse until we have the gold away. Then we'll meet again and decide how this war is to be won."

Chapter 8

Boudicca Takes a Journey

Heavy white clouds tinged with gray and yellow moved quickly through the sky dappling the ground with patches of sunlight and shadow. It was breezy and the air was damp. Boudicca had little eye for scenery or weather as she rode grimly on through the forest with Prasu's standard-bearer riding directly behind her. Gwenda drove the chariot. She sat on one side of poor dead Prasu while Habren sat on the other, holding him up. Einon the steward sat behind holding his pole. The chariot was a hundred feet behind Boudicca, and Cangus with her guard of knights a hundred feet behind it. They were barely half way to Thetford when she rounded a bend and saw the Roman cavalry patrol. The men had dismounted where a small stream crossed the trail and were sitting or standing around eating their rations while their horses drank from the stream or grazed on the undergrowth.

Her first impulse was to retreat but she was in full view and they would have chased her. There was nothing for it but to brazen it out. She raised a hand to stop the chariot then cantered down to the patrol. A centurion stood in the way as she approached and seized her bridle.

"I am Boudicca, Queen of Iceni," she said to the man, speaking in his own language. "If you are wise you will have your men stand well back from the road. My husband, King Prasu, and the two women with him are deadly sick of the plague and we are taking them to Thetford so that our Druids may heal them."

"What kind of plague is it?" said the centurion.

"There is more than one kind? Would you take a closer look?"

"I'm not that curious," said the centurion. He looked at her doubtfully but waved to his men and told them to take their horses into the trees upwind of the trail. When they were well away he left the trail himself but did not go very deep into the forest. He's suspicious, she thought. He motioned her to ride on.

She waved to Gwenda and waited for the standard bearer, blocking the centurion's view of the road as much as possible. She could almost feel the man staring as the chariot passed, seeing death written all over Prasu's face and wondering what to make of it, Habren weeping hysterically and Gwenda frightened but brave.

The chariot and the knight-guards got past and she rode on behind them. Would that suspicious centurion send to Tas to see if there really was a plague? As they approached Thetford, they passed several of the great fields where Prasu kept his horses, the famous Iceni blacks, Britain's best horses. The thought of leaving such a treasure in the hands of the Rummies made her nauseous. There must be some way to drive them into the Parisi lands. Such horses she must have for Ingenius' chariots.

The chariot stopped in front of the palace doors and Habren leaped off it and ran inside. Deprived of her support, Prasu's body fell sideways on the seat and Gwenda tried frantically to pull it upright again. Some of the knights ran forward to help.

"Leave it," said Boudicca, dismounting. "Take King Prasu inside and prop him up in bed," she said to the servants looking doubtfully at Prasu. "He's dead," she said. "But I don't want anyone to know. King Prasu is ill. Is that understood?"

"He'll smell up the place," said Einon.

"We'll have to put up with it. The death stiffness has left him. Take him into the bedchamber and cover the windows." She put her arm around Gwenda's shoulders and led the poor girl inside. "I'm sorry to put you through this," she said, as softly as she could, "but it's important that the Rummies don't know your father is dead or they'll confiscate everything we own. We must have time to empty our treasury and drive our horses over the border. Before we leave, we'll give your father a proper burial."

"Is there really an Otherworld? Will he get to play Fidchell?"

"Elsa assures me there is an Otherworld. It may not be as we've envisioned it, but I'm sure your father is there."

It was late at night and dark before Galga and his knights arrived. They had waited in the forest to be sure there were not seen entering the compound. Boudicca had Einon quarter Galga's knights while she took the slow moving Galga to Prasu's treasury, a small round stone building. The guards opened the door and lit several of the clay oil lamps dotted around the floor. Inside, the building felt dank and its musty odor mingled strangely with the fumes rising from the lamps.

Galga gave a long slow whistle as he looked around. "We'll have a job getting this lot out," he said. Boudicca bit her lips as she nodded agreement. It had been years since she was last in Prasu's treasury and she had forgotten what it was like. Piles of iron, lead and silver ingots were stacked indiscriminately around the walls and in the middle of the dirt floor. Here and there, large wooden partitions had been put against the walls like the spokes of a wheel, and between them hoards of gold, silver and bronze coins had been piled on the floor. A battered wooden chest lay between two piles of ingots. She opened it to see it was full of jewels and precious stones.

"We must sack this right away," she said. "We'll take the gold and jewels to Afan and leave everything else."

By midmorning all the knights and servants, even including Habren, were at work in the treasury tying the gold coins into sacks. Boudicca, Gwenda and Habren had worked all night cutting heavy cloth into doubled squares for bagging the gold. Haggard and groggy from lack of sleep, Boudicca would have loved to sink down on a couch but dare not. If she did, the work would stop. Besides, there was that nagging picture of the Iceni blacks. How was she to get them to the Parisies?

She made Galga mount his horse and urged him along to the fields where the horses grazed. As they rode they passed many Britons who gave them curious looks and waves. Where were they all going? She stopped on the road at the edge of one of the fields and a boy ran over to hold their horses. He was a bright looking boy, not more than twelve, and she smiled at him wishing she had her own Coilus with her.

Galga shook his head gloomily. "It's over a hundred miles," he said. "You'd never get all these horses that far without the Rummies stopping you." Why were all her kings so negative?

She glanced down at the boy. He looked far more intelligent than Galga. "Does your father look after our horses?" she asked.

"Yes, my lady," said the boy, ducking his head. "Him and me and my three brothers and my two sisters."

"Do you know where the Parisies live?"

"We have took horses there before this."

"Have you ever been stopped by the Rummies?"

"Not the way we go. We go through the swamps at night. Takes longer but they never see us."

"If you had to get all our horses to the Parisies," she said, "how would you go about it?"

"Take a hundred at a time. Have em all there in two months."

She reached down and patted his head. "You're a good boy," she said. "What is your name?"

"Coel, majesty."

"Coel, have your father come to me at the palace." If this boy could get her horses out she would see that he was made a knight. She glowered at Galga and set off back to the palace. The boys had more initiative than her kings. She ought to give Coel and Caradawg each an army.

Their pace was slowed on the way back by Britons walking along the road. There must be scores of them. One looked back as he heard their horses approaching so she stopped alongside him. "Where are you all coming from?" she asked.

The man gave her the knee when he saw her torque and Prasu's standard. "You are Queen Boudicca?" he said.

"Yes."

"We're from Colchester. The Rummies are killing hundreds because of the burnings when King Caratacus was killed. We cannot defend ourselves so we're getting out of there."

She nodded sympathetically. "And where are you fleeing to?"

"Why, to you, my lady. They say you have weapons for us and we're here to fight."

"We have no weapons," she said, aghast. "Who sent you?"

"I did hear that King Velocatus was saying it."

"King Velocatus?" This was Cartimandua's doing.

The man nodded.

She dug her heels into the horse's sides and plunged ahead, Galga right behind. The clatter of their hooves scattered the fleeing Britons as she bore down on them. Why was Velocatus putting out such a story? Why was he trying to stir up a premature rising? Was Cartimandua still working for the Rummies? As she neared the palace she slowed to a walk to thread her way through the thickening mob. Men recognized her and shouted to her, while others cheered. They must expect her to wave a sword and somehow defeat Rome's legions. Their hopes had been falsely raised and they would be angry when they learned the truth. But she must tell them the truth.

The crowd massed against the palace gates but a narrow avenue opened up to allow her and Galga to pass. She stopped between the two wooden pillars that held up the gates and turned to face the mob. The crowd quietened when it became apparent she was going to speak. She could see many more refugees hurrying from the road. A familiar figure on horseback pushed his way through to join her and she was surprised at how pleased she was to see him. It was her nephew, the cross-eyed King

Brennius. Seeing him she suddenly missed Venutius. He should be here at her side. It dawned upon her that they could now be married. She would send for him right away.

"Britons," she shouted. "The time to rise is not yet." There was a growl but it stopped immediately when she peremptorily waved her arm. "Do not be dismayed," she said, "nor lose your anger. I would have it kept at white heat until it burns the foul Rummies where they stand." Brennius waved his sword in the air and many cheered. "We are not going to attack until we are ready," she went on. "We are making swords and lances and chariots for an army of a hundred thousand and you will be part of that army. We have a new weapon being built that will break up the legions. There will be no more walls of shields to frustrate our best efforts. When our weapons are ready we shall strike and strike hard. But we will not jeopardize our cause by striking before we are ready."

Brennius waved his sword again and the mob sent up a mighty shout. "When? When will it be?"

"Give me six months and there will not be a Rummy in this land that will not taste British iron. We will slaughter the lot and clean our island of this plague." She raised her arm again to quieten the excited crowd. "In the meantime I would have all of you head for the western nations where King Brennius will form you into an army."

Brennius pushed through to her side and turned his horse to face the cheering crowd. "When?" he said, out of the corner of his mouth.

"Now," she said. "You must get them away from here. They will bring the Rummies upon us."

"If I am to be their Moses you will have to feed em first. Tis not for the likes of me to pound on rocks and have water come out, nor is it likely Duw will drop a little manna in our path. They will need grease in their stomachs and bread in their pockets for such a march, me leading them and all."

"Feed this many?" Of course Brennius was right. These people had been walking all the way from Colchester and would have to live off the land on their way to the free nations. But how would they feed this multitude? "Einon will have to open the granary and gather fruit and cattle," she said. "You must organize this for me. I must get our treasure north to the Parisies."

"Indeed I will," said Brennius. "It will look like Beltane when our bonfires light the sky and smell like Lughnasa when our beef and bacon cook and our cabbages boil."

"There will be no bonfires," said Boudicca. "You will drive the cattle before you and slaughter and cook elsewhere. For today you can eat fruit and whatever bread and cooked meat is available. When you are well away from here you can light bonfires."

All that day Boudicca labored in the treasury with the household women and the knights. Galga had decided after much ponderous thought that each of his men could carry twelve of the heavy sacks of gold if a harness were made that would hold six sacks on each side of the horse. Cangus was good with hemp and by midafternoon had woven two heavy nets connected together by ropes that could be laid across a horse's back. While one of the knights went for a horse to test the harness, Boudicca went outside to see how Brennius was faring.

When she saw the crowd she pursed her lips and frowned. It was much bigger than it had been in the morning. She found Brennius in the kitchen. The smell of baking bread filled the overheated air and made her ravenous. Small round loaves of freshly baked bread were heaped in piles on the floor and the bakers were busily kneading dough, putting trays of raw loaves out to rise or bustling around the ovens. Brennius saw her and held out a loaf. She broke the loaf and bit hungrily into it. "How many of these do you plan to make?" she said, angry that he had ordered them made. At this rate the crowd wouldn't be out of here in a week.

"By the time mother Luna shows her face," said Brennius,

"we'll have a thousand, which will last us for a day or two what with all the fruit and vegetables and little bits of cooked meat that Einon is getting together for us outside, bless his ancient heart."

"And how many people do you plan to feed?"

"I counted them meself before I come in here and there was less than a thousand, which I figured by holding my thumb before my eye and there not being more than three of em behind my thumb at any one time. I will admit that more than once I forgot what I'd already added up, and once or twice someone spoke to me and threw me off my count and on top of all that the people would not stay still while I counted em. But all in all I figure there's pretty close to a thousand."

"There's more than two thousand inside the palace walls," she said. "And there are more coming all the time. You must take what you have and leave now."

Brennius looked black and his eyes seemed to cross more. "Those that get no bread will not be pleased," he said.

She stamped her foot. "Then give no-one bread. You must have them away from here before dark. Some Rummy is sure to see such a crowd and raise the alarm." She gulped down the last bite of her loaf, gave him a parting glare and went back to the treasury. At times like this she missed Atak sorely. He would have had that crowd on its way by this time.

When she got back to the treasury, Boudicca was glad to find that Cangus' harness worked. All they had to do now, she reflected grimly, was make the other twenty-nine that would get all the gold aboard Galga's horses. To set the example, tired as she was, she had Cangus show her how to weave a net and then sent him off to show the others while she worked. Several times she fell asleep while working and almost toppled from the stool. But each time she would shake her head vigorously and go on working. If she indulged herself the others would also and they would lose another day. She fell asleep again and jerked awake to find the boy Coel standing before her with a man at his side. How long had she been asleep?

"You are Coel's father?" she said to the man. He was a tall wiry man with an intelligent face.

"Yes, my lady." The man bent his knee. He seemed surprised to see his High Queen working like a common servant.

"I'm afraid I am very tired," she said. "Coel tells me you can take all our horses to the Parisies?"

"All of em, majesty?"

She nodded. "King Prasu is near death," she said. "When he dies they will confiscate them if we don't get them out of here."

"It'll take a few months."

"Two months?"

"More like three."

"Can you do it in two and not be seen by the Rummies?"

"If we do naught else."

"I will see that you are well rewarded."

"Thank you, my lady. Will I care for your horses in Parisi?"

"Until we need them. Take them to King Afan. Then send your son to me. I will foster him and he will be a knight."

The man bent his knee again and kissed her hand. "He is a good boy is Coel. Say thank you to Queen Boudicca, boy."

Coel bent his knee and she gave him her hand to kiss. "Britain will need boys like your son," she said. "He is a bright lad." She laid down the half finished net and walked outside with Coel and his father. The evening air would help to awaken her and she must see whether Brennius had got his mob under way. She was relieved to see most of it had disappeared. She waved farewell to Coel and his father and turned to go back into the treasury. The air felt so fresh after being cooped up all day that she decided to linger for just a moment and sat down on the cool grass near the treasury entrance. She was instantly asleep.

When she awoke it was quite dark. For a moment she was disoriented, not knowing where she was. The grass felt damp and her bones stiff. With a cry of anger she struggled to her feet, colliding with a man as she did so. It was Prasu's standard-bearer, under orders never to let her out of his sight whenever she was outside the palace. "Why did you let me sleep?" she muttered. "Has the crowd gone?"

"Yes, my lady."

The air was still and the only sounds were of birds and animals. She went into the treasury and found they were still at work.

"We'll be finished by midnight," said Cangus. "Then we can load up the horses."

"We're not leaving tonight?" said Galga.

"As soon as the horses are loaded."

"My men need rest. And so do I."

"You will have plenty of rest when we reach the Parisies."

Galga glowered. "We can leave at first light and be in the swamps before any Rummies could get here."

She looked at Cangus. "That's true," he said. "Rummies won't come near places like this at night. If they came here it would be nearer noon than nighttime. And we could all use a rest."

She felt guilty, having slept while everyone else worked. Her intuition told her they should leave as soon as they could, but against that must be weighed a sullen and uncooperative Galga, a mistake-prone group of tired knights and her own sense of fairness. "All right," she said. "We will load the horses at first light. Is there any gold left we can't carry?"

"Yes." Cangus showed her what was left.

"Sprinkle it on top of the bronze coins," she said. "The Rummies will think the gold hasn't been touched. When we leave in the morning, I would have you send a rider to King Venutius in Siluria. Ask him to meet me at King Afan's."

At first light Cangus wakened Boudicca. Like her, he and Galga had slept on couches in the great hall. She awakened Habren and Gwenda and went into the bedchamber to bathe. She would not allow herself to look at poor Prasu, but out of the corner of her eye saw that he was still propped up by pillows as if asleep. The servants had put out water, a clean shift and stockings and her traveling clothes: a heavy tartan tunic and cape and leather boots. Habren helped her bathe then combed her hair and fastened it behind her neck with a jewel-studded band of gold. She dressed quickly and hurried back to the hall. Einon had been right. Prasu was beginning to stink.

Most of the knights were outside by this time, washing themselves, eating Brennius' loaves and drinking mead passed around by servants. She stood in the doorway facing the palace gates to make it apparent that she was ready to leave and squinted at the rising sun. As she bit into one of the loaves a line of horses appeared walking toward the treasury. As soon as they were loaded they would be on their way.

To her horror the palace gates crashed open and Roman legionaries rushed in carrying the ram they had used to force the gates. Trembling with dismay, she threw the rest of her loaf on the ground as other legionaries flooded quickly in with drawn swords and crowded the knights back against the palace. The line of horses stampeded and ran toward the stables. When all had quieted and Cangus and Galga and the knights stood around her in a tight group menaced by the swords of two centuries of legionaries, a small group of men on horseback came through the gates and dismounted. Two of them came toward her. One was Marcus Rutilus, the Ninth Legion legate who had been a friend of Sabinus, and the other the Procurator, Decianus Catus.

"You may put up your swords," she said to Rutilus, struggling to keep her voice under control. Why had she not obeyed her intuition and left at midnight? "My knights are unarmed." What she said was not strictly true as most carried concealed daggers, but none carried swords.

Rutilus made a contemptuous gesture with his hand and a centurion ordered his men to stand back and sheath their swords. Cangus came to her side. "We are here to speak with your husband, King Prasu," said Rutilus.

"Do you usually smash down the gates when you visit a Client King of Rome?" she said.

"We take whatever steps are necessary to control illegal assemblies. Where is the mob that was reported here yesterday?"

"Those fleeing to escape slaughter by your troops are doubtless hiding in the swamps," she said. "They came here to be fed and were sent away."

Catus said something in a low voice to Rutilus, and Rutilus started toward her. "I understand your husband is sick," he said. "Take us to him."

She put a hand on his chest and stopped him. "King Prasu is too sick to see anyone," she said.

Rutilus knocked her hand away and would have pushed past her had not Cangus intervened. Before she could say or do anything there was a sudden rush, Rutilus was pushed back against her and the centurion had driven his sword through Cangus' stomach, driving him to the ground. As she watched in horror, the centurion put his foot on Cangus and jerked his sword free. Rutilus and Catus swept by her and she knelt by Cangus' side and placed her hand on his arm.

"My dear good man," she said, tears flowing down her cheeks. Why had he done such a stupid loyal thing? What good had it done?

Cangus put his hand over hers then his eyes glazed and he died.

She got up unsteadily and walked toward the bedchamber, heart filled with anguish at Cangus' useless death, the centurion and some legionaries keeping pace with her. Was this how it was all to end? Should she draw her dagger and sink it into Catus and then die as Cangus had from this brute's bloody sword? No, she would not die a useless death. Duw willing she would die in one of Ingenius' chariots, killing off the last Romans defiling this land. Before she reached the bedchamber door, Catus came out followed by Rutilus.

"How long has he been dead?" said Catus.

"He is dead?" she said.

"He's been dead for several days," said Catus. "He stinks. Why have you not reported it? Why did you lie?"

She stared at him stonily and said nothing.

Catus turned to Rutilus and the centurion with a dramatic sweep of his arm. "You will both attest to the fact," he said, "that Queen Boudicca concealed the death of her husband and lied when interrogated." So the little clerk intended to have her arrested. He turned back to her. "It will not go well for you at your trial if you insist on lying."

Again she stared at him coldly but said nothing.

"It is well known," said Catus, "that you wish to incite your people to rise against Rome. Your many treasonable visits to the unconquered regions are all known to us." Cartimandua, she thought, a cold rage flooding through her. Cartimandua has betrayed Britain. "You have sheltered under the protection of your husband's status," Catus went on. "But that shelter is now removed. All your possessions are confiscated and you and your daughters are under arrest."

Rutilus nodded to the centurion, who formed up his men on either side of her. They marched her to the door, where they waited while servants were sent to bring her horse. The guard parted on one side of her and Gwenda and Habren were thrust next to her. She clasped the weeping Gwenda in her arms and kissed her. "Do not fear, my love," she said. "And do not let these foul Rummies feel that a Briton is afraid of them. Dry your tears, my sweet. We will cry when we are alone."

"Where is your other daughter?" said Catus.

"She is far away from here." Thank God she had left.

"She will be found and brought to trial for treason also. None of you will escape Rome's justice."

Cangus' knights surveyed them in shocked silence as the horses were brought up, but she could see from their eyes they would try to avenge her. She could not permit it. These men were valuable and if she got out of this, as she fully intended to, she would need them.

"Do nothing, my good lords and knights," she said. "I am being taken to Colchester to be put on trial but all is not lost. You must disband and return to your homes." She suddenly wondered whether Catus would inspect the treasury. He was so anxious to watch her humiliation he might forgo it for the present. "And my brother king Galga," she said, "must see that my husband is buried with honor, and that his personal things are properly gathered and disposed of." She looked Galga full in the eyes and mouthed: Take the gold to Afan.

Galga looked as if the events of the morning had bewildered him, but he nodded acknowledgment. She looked at her own knights. Had any got the message? One or two seemed to nod significantly as if they knew what she meant. Duw enlighten them, she prayed. Wake them up and show them what to do.

They were led down to the horses and she quickly mounted, looking stonily across the palace grounds as the legionaries formed up around her.

Chapter 9

Prisoners

The servant dabbed a perfume laden cloth under Atak's armpits, pulled the gold embroidered jewel studded blue shirt over his head then wrapped around him the pleated tartan skirt. After he had deftly pinned the skirt in place with a golden fibula, the servant placed the delicately filigreed leather belt with its jewel studded silver hilted golden sheathed ceremonial dagger around his waist and fastened the oversized jewel encrusted golden buckle that kept him all together. With a gentle practiced push the servant got Atak to sit on the heavily cushioned silk embroidered stool while he pulled on the gold embroidered blue stockings that matched the gold embroidered blue shirt and slid Atak's feet into soft beautifully tooled leather shoes fastened by large golden jewel studded buckles. The servant was about to go under Atak's skirt with the perfumed cloth but changed his mind when Atak growled at him.

"If my lord will let me rake his beard?" said the servant.

"No," said Atak, wrinkling his nose at the perfumed stink that came off his body. "Where is Prince Coilus?"

"I will bring him as soon as he is ready, my lord."

Atak shooed the man out, picked up the bone comb and began absently to comb his beard. Neither Caradawg nor he would be able to stand much more of this. Life in Barwick for the first few months had been enjoyable. Cartimandua and Velocatus had been in Colchester sucking up to Paulinus and he and Caradawg had been free to fish and hunt as soon as Caradawg finished his lessons.

But since an excited Cartimandua returned a few days ago without Velocatus, he and Caradawg had been forced to dress in these stupid clothes and sit in the hall listening to pipes and harps and poets with Rhys and all the other court sycophants. Hunting and fishing had been declared taboo for the winter and weary hours had been spent practicing the manners and dances that Cartimandua wanted displayed when her eagerly anticipated guest, the Roman Governor himself, arrived.

Atak looked forward to meeting Paulinus. He had heard that he was a great general. If he kept his ear open he might learn something of advantage to Boudicca. He missed being with Boudicca. Even with her nagging and impatience, life was never dull. He wondered what Boudicca would say if he showed up one day with Caradawg. What would she think if she saw him dressed up like this? She would break her sides laughing.

The door opened and Caradawg came in, a scowl on his face. He was dressed like Atak and reeked of perfume. "I tried to get it away from him," he said, "and it spilled on me."

"I'll talk to Queen Cartimandua," said Atak. "Maybe we can get out of having that stuff dabbed on us."

"When are we leaving here?"

"You're a hostage and she won't like it if you disappear."

"If you weren't here she'd forget me."

"You may be right," said Atak, "but I'll have to think about it. We're going to meet Paulinus."

"He's a Rummy."

"He's a famous general."

Caradawg shrugged.

Paulinus was a short square man with fierce black eyes, light gray stringy hair and a dark gray stringy beard. His face barely came level with Atak's chest. Like the legates and tribunes who came with him, he wore a heavy military cloak over a white pipe clayed toga that smelled of the urine in which it had been laundered and which in turn was draped over the top of several rumpled tunics. Paulinus shivered as Cartimandua introduced them. "What a shitty climate," he said. "I can't get warm or dry."

"It gets worse in summer," said Atak.

Paulinus looked at Atak contemptuously. "They tell me you had an ala under Plautius," he said. "You stink like a whore. Why are you dressed like that?"

Atak glowered at Cartimandua. He would never wear this stupid outfit again. Paulinus walked over to the roaring firepit and held out his arms to get warm. Cartimandua hurried to his side while his legates gathered around the fire at a respectful distance. They seemed afraid of Paulinus and did not chatter among themselves.

"When did you retire?" said Paulinus.

"I didn't," said Atak.

"You were kicked out?"

"Caligula kicked all his Germans out."

"Is he the one gave you that shitty outfit? It looks like something he'd wear. It even smells like him."

Cartimandua put a gentle hand on Paulinus' shoulder—almost as if she were fond of him, thought Atak. "I gave him that outfit," she said. "All the members of my court must dress in blue."

"On you it looks good," said Paulinus, patting her bottom. "How many years had you left?" he asked Atak.

"One," growled Atak, watching Cartimandua. This man was not a pushover like Scapula and Cartie was having trouble dealing with it. It would do her good.

"So you got no pension and no citizenship." Paulinus cocked his head and looked at Atak as if some thought had just struck him. "You have no rights at all," he said. "You're just like the Britons so don't cross me." He turned back to the fire. "Caligula was a shithead. What have you learned about the Britons?"

"Enough."

"Catus is going to slap levies on all Britons with property to get back the cost of roads and fortifications. He's going to recall all the gold that Claudius handed out. What will they do?"

"I thought those were gifts from Rome?"

Paulinus sneered. "If you thought that you're as stupid as the Britons. How can leeches like Catus get rich if we give everything away? Will the Britons rise?"

"It might be wise to go slowly."

"So they won't rise? I want them to rise. I want a rising and a good slaughter and I want that little bastard Catus to get the blame for it."

Caradawg kicked some dirt in the fire so that smoke billowed out near Paulinus. Paulinus glared at him.

"This is Prince Coilus," said Cartimandua, introducing Caradawg. "He is the son of Queen Boudicca."

"The one Catus had us arrest?" said Paulinus.

"Arrest?" said Atak. Why hadn't Cartimandua told him?

Paulinus looked up at Atak as if sensing his interest. "Catus accused her of treason. Her treasury was cleaned out by the time he went to claim it. Serves the bat-eyed little bastard right. Hope he never gets his money." Paulinus bent down to stare at Caradawg, who stared back unflinchingly. "Your father was a Roman," he said.

"No," said Cartimandua. "His father is my former husband."

"Is he a Roman?"

"Of course not."

"Then he's not the father. Look at that nose. Look at that hair. Look at the build on him. His daddy was a legionary."

Cartimandua stared at Caradawg then gave Atak a frosty look. "Sabinus," she said. "I knew there was something between them, and she so holier than thou. Sabinus was the father."

"When was Queen Boudicca arrested?" said Atak. He put his hand on Caradawg's shoulder and pulled the boy to him.

Paulinus shrugged. "A month ago."

"What will happen to her?"

Paulinus gave him another quick look. "You know her?"

Atak glanced at Cartimandua, whose eyes were on Caradawg. "I used to work for her."

Paulinus laughed and rubbed his hands. "Catus is up to his neck in cow shit. By law he should sell her estates but if he does it will become public record and he'll have to give half to Nero instead of sopping him off with a few denarii. He wants us to keep her locked away until he gets her treasure back. Then he wants her flogged and killed."

Atak winced. "Where is she?"

Paulinus stood in front of Atak and stared up at him. "You want to get her out from that little bastard's clutches?"

Atak glanced again at Cartimandua but said nothing.

Paulinus reached out and pulled Cartimandua to him. She bent to him willingly, but still glared at Caradawg. "I'm thinking of getting married," he said, winking at Atak. "As a wedding present maybe I'll let you put your last year in so you can get a pension and your citizenship." Cartimandua smiled prettily.

So that's why Velocatus didn't come back, thought Atak. He's been put out to pasture while she snags a bigger fish. Caratacus had been right. Cartimandua wanted a Governor as husband so she could become Queen of all Britain. He looked again at Paulinus. The Governor knew he didn't want Boudicca flogged or killed. He's either threatening me or trying to bribe me with this talk of a pension. What is he after?

"Is he really Sabinus' son?" said Cartimandua, glaring at Atak. "Or has she foisted some camp follower's brat on me?"

Atak drew himself up with as much dignity as he could muster. "This is Prince Coilus," he said. "I brought him here myself from Caer Leon."

There was a tense pause while Cartimandua stared at Caradawg. "Where's the food?" said Paulinus. "I'm starving."

After they had eaten, Cartimandua and her ladies left to attend to their needs and Atak watched with wide eyes as Paulinus urinated in the firepit, sending up a huge cloud of steam and a terrible stink. Paulinus had sent his men away with a few jerks of his head and the two of them were by themselves on this side of the fire. "Ah," grunted Paulinus. "It's too cold to go out there. Don't you have to go after all that shitty wine?"

Well why not, thought Atak. He and Caradawg added their streams to that of Paulinus' and made a great black area steaming among the embers. Cartimandua would go berserk if she saw what they were doing.

"Two more of us," said Paulinus, "and we could put this fire out." He stood back, rearranging his clothes. "Catus is a shithead," he said, when Atak was done. "I want that little bastard out of here."

"Can't you send him home?"

Paulinus snarled and shook his head. "I can't touch a Procurator," he said. "What I can do is prove to Nero he's a thief. But I also have to make up my losses. He and Seneca took me for a bundle." He tapped Atak on the chest with a steely forefinger. "Where's the Druids' gold?"

"They keep moving it around."

Paulinus frowned. "That little bastard has men looking all over for it," he said. "If he finds it first, none of us will get a piece. Nero will be lucky to get a piece." He tapped Atak on the chest again. "I need to find the gold before he does," he said. "But first I want to set up a little trap so I can have him arrested and sent back in chains." He rubbed his hands together and grinned a mirthless grin. "Nero will treat him right if I prove he's a thief." He clapped his hands together. "And you're going to help me. You want that British Queen out?"

"Yes," said Atak.

"She's in Longthorpe. I'll have her moved to Colchester and put in a house. You will go to her. Get two things from her, she goes free and you get your citizenship. I want a stash of gold set up. It must be big enough to get attention." He prodded Atak's chest. "My men will inventory it and show it to Catus. When he tells Nero what he's found after taking most of it himself, I'll send back the true inventory and Catus is up to his ears."

"What's the other thing?"

"I want to know where the Druids' gold is."

"If she knew, she wouldn't tell me."

Paulinus grabbed hold of Atak's shirt. "I don't care if she knows or not," he said. "If you want her freed you find out where it is."

Atak looked down at the hand gripping his shirt. "Are you going to marry Cartimandua?" he asked.

Paulinus let go of his shirt. "She's rich isn't she?"

"Richest queen in Britain."

"Where's her treasury?"

"It's better hidden than the Druid's gold."

Paulinus slapped him on the arm. "Get the Druid's gold first," he said. "Then you can find her treasury for me."

"How will I get into see Queen Boudicca?" said Atak. Cartimandua was rapidly approaching and he wanted this business settled before she got within earshot.

"I'll give you a warrant."

"What are you talking about all by yourselves?" said Cartimandua. She glared at Atak and Caradawg. "And why is the fire so dead? Couldn't you call for more logs?" She clapped her hands and a servant came running to tend to the fire. "There's a bad smell over here," she said. "Bring something to kill it."

"It's this outfit you have on him," said Paulinus.

***

Atak whistled when the legate at the Governor's palace told him they had put Boudicca in Ingenius' old house. The Britons were in an ugly mood. He could sense the pressure and hostility in the air like the quiet before a violent thunderstorm. The word of Catus' levy must have got out. These people were ready to rise and here their Arviragus was locked up in an unfortified house in their midst. He wondered how long it would be before the house was attacked.

Both he and Caradawg wore plain shirts and tartan trews. Cartimandua seemed to be straining as hard as she could to please Paulinus and during the few days they had waited for Boudicca to be moved she had paid no attention to them. Having a warrant from Paulinus Atak also had on a Roman sword belt and sword. He showed his warrant to the gate guards and then rode to the side of the house and dismounted. There were guards at the front entrance and dotted around the walls inside. Even so, thought Atak, this place is not defensible. A good sharp attack would get Boudicca out of here. Was Paulinus trying to bait the Britons?

He and Caradawg sat down on a couch in the hall and waited for Boudicca to be brought out. He wondered how she would receive him. He had betrayed her by not going back when she needed him and maybe she would not forgive him. If she rebuffed him he didn't know how he could handle it. He hadn't realized how much her good opinion meant to him. In many ways she was like a daughter. He would have liked a daughter like Boudicca and a son like Caradawg. He shrugged. A family had suddenly become important to him now that Tetra was dead and he was too old to start one? His spirits sank. But when he saw her approaching with her daughters, he knew all was well. She opened her arms as she reached him and he clasped her to him. His eyes watered and he had to blink.

"Dear Atak," she said when she finally released him. Her eyes were wet also. "I knew you would come." She glanced at his Roman sword and he could see the question in her eyes but she simply looked down at Caradawg. "What is Caradawg doing here?"

"Cartimandua caught on," he said. "Paulinus told her his father was a Rummie so I thought I'd better get him out of there."

She patted Caradawg on the head. "He does have a Rummy nose. Have you joined Paulinus? Is that why you wear a Rummy sword?"

"He sent me here to talk to you. I have a warrant from him."

"How did you arrange that?"

"He knew I'd had an ala. We talked like old comrades. It didn't bother him that I'd been with you all these years."

"And you are now with them?"

"No, I'm with you. I've always been with you."

She paused as if to let his words sink in then drew her daughters to her. "You remember Goneril and Gwenda," she said.

Atak bowed and kissed the princesses' hands.

"I only had Gwenda at first," said Boudicca, "but when Ingenius and Goneril came to see me, the guards wouldn't let Goneril go again."

"How did Ingenius get in to see you?"

"He has a safe conduct from Catus. He's supposed to be looking for the Druid's gold. He thought the safe conduct would cover Goneril but it didn't, and Catus wouldn't change it. Ingenius wanted to stay here with us but I wouldn't let him."

"Does Catus come here?"

"He lives here when he's not in London."

"Has Ingenius found the gold?"

"If he knows where it is he didn't tell me."

"Ingenius was showing me how to drive the new chariots in formation," said Goneril, her voice bitter.

"Ingenius is doing many things for me now that I'm locked up," said Boudicca. She stroked Goneril's hand. "You must do some things for me too. I must get Goneril and Gwenda out of here. These retired legionaries take liberties. I spoke to Catus but he just leered. I don't like the way he looks at Gwenda."

"I'll get word to Paulinus right away," said Atak, surprised by the depth of his anger. "I'll have you put somewhere else."

"Thank you," said Boudicca. "What is Paulinus' message?"

Atak kept his voice low and spoke in Celtic. "Paulinus and Catus are enemies," he said. "Paulinus wants to have Catus recalled. He can do it if he proves the man's a thief."

"That shouldn't be difficult," said Boudicca.

"If you help him he will let you go free."

"Doesn't he know I will attack him if I am freed?"

"Paulinus sees no threat here he hasn't seen lots of other places. What he wants is gold. Catus and Seneca cheated him out of a lot of money. He wants it back."

"If he wants it from me he'll be disappointed. The Parisies are holding all mine for swords and arrows and chariots."

"You must get some back." He paused and tried not to sound melodramatic. "Your lives depend on it."

"You mean Catus will kill us? He won't get the chance."

Atak glowered at her. Did she think she was invulnerable? "He's told Paulinus he wants you flogged and killed," he said. It was brutal but it got her attention. "As soon as he finds your treasure he'll have a mock trial and do it."

Boudicca laughed. "Then I'm safe," she said. "He'll never find it." She reached out to pat his leg. "I will be out of here before long," she said. "Guderius is waiting for the word to attack."

"Attacks are dangerous," said Atak. "I would feel better if you gave Paulinus enough gold to trap Catus. We'd all be better off if Catus was out of here."

"I won't argue with that. How much does he need?"

"Half a million?"

She stood up and clapped her hands as if something had just come to her. "Go to Iorwerth," she said. "Tell him to show you the gold we found when we burned the archives. There was at least half a million. When he's shown you the gold, go to Guderius and tell him what you've told me. Then go back to Paulinus and tell him where the gold is."

"There's one more thing," said Atak. "Before he'll let you go, Paulinus wants the Druids' gold. He's afraid Catus will cut him out of his share if he gets to it first."

"I have no idea where it is. You must ask Owain."

Atak shook his head grimly. "Owain won't tell me."

She kissed him and patted his cheek again. "You must not fret," she said. "You'll see me out of this alive, my dear friend. Go back and tell Paulinus that if he wants his cache of gold he must guarantee my freedom. If he wants to hurt Catus badly enough he'll settle for that. Tell him you'll help him look for the Druids' gold later."

Atak grimaced. Why was he always caught in the middle? "I'll do my best," he said. He looked around to find Caradawg.

"I think he went to the latrine," said Goneril. "Here he comes now."

Caradawg came walking toward them, a pleased smile on his face. "I fixed the drain for em," he said to Atak. "They'll be up to their knees in it before long."

Chapter 10

The Trigger

Ingenius stood back and sighed discontentedly as two of his men rolled the chariot out of the long hut, Caradawg riding inside it with a broad grin on his face and the blades on its wheels flashing wickedly. It was a gray cold day, snow still on the ground and the wind damp and bitter, no sign yet of spring flowers.

"What's the matter?" said Atak. He had come to help Ingenius after showing Paulinus' men Boudicca's cache of gold. "That's four hundred you've built. Another hundred and you'll have met your quota." Ingenius gripped Atak's arm. Being together again after a separation of many years had restored most of the easy friendship they had shared in the old days when they both fought with Caratacus. But something had been bothering Ingenius during the weeks they had been together and Atak had not felt able to probe.

"It's Goneril," said Ingenius.

"Princess Goneril?" said Atak, eyebrows climbing.

"It was stupid to let her go with me to see her mother, but she insisted and now she's a prisoner. I keep wondering where she is in my house and if she's in the room I used to sleep in."

"Oh?" said Atak, eyebrows still raised.

"I know what you're thinking," said Ingenius. He smiled

bitterly. "She should be wife to a High King, but even if we win this war there will be few of them left. I have no rank in her eyes, but in the days when I was rich I could have married a Roman girl with blood as good as hers. Catus urged me to."

"You want to marry her?"

Ingenius nodded, looking more downcast than ever.

"Does she want to marry you?"

"To her I must look like soiled merchandise."

"And you wish you were fresh and pure again like she is? Don't we all."

"There are times when she is friendly and close, but there are times when she lets me know she is a princess. Sometimes I think there's hope but other times she makes me feel unclean."

"Sounds like her mother."

"Her mother was like that?"

"Yes," said Atak, remembering the time in Gaul when Boudicca, full of blood lust after killing Romans had tried to get him to make love to her, and the time when he had tried it on his own and she had threatened to kill him. "When she was Goneril's age you never knew where you stood with her."

"Do you think I'd lose her if I asked her?"

"Before you can ask we have to get her and her mother out."

"Guderius would get them out."

"But it would trigger a rising before we're ready."

"Will Paulinus really free them when Catus gets recalled?"

"He said he would if I find the Druid's gold for him. If I don't I'll end up on one of his galleys."

Ingenius looked around warily. "It's on Mona," he said. "At the bottom of Llyn Cerig Bach.[27]"

Atak's mouth fell open. "They just threw it in there?"

"It's fastened to chariots. They threw a lot of other junk on top to hide it."

"Why are you telling me?"

"If it's a question of their lives give Paulinus the gold. The Druids can always get more."

"You didn't tell Catus?"

Ingenius snarled. "I hate Catus worse than Paulinus does," he said. "I told him it's in Cartimandua's treasury."

Atak whistled. "He'll have to get Paulinus and Cartie out of the way before he can look there for it."

"That's why I told him it was there."

Atak put a hand on Ingenius' shoulder. "You know," he said, "Boudicca had to marry a High King like Prasu, but she fell in love with Venutius. He was only a prince with no inheritance and no land but he's been her real husband all along. She'd take that into account if Goneril wanted to marry you."

Ingenius brightened. "You really think so?"

"It would help," said Atak, "if you had another hundred chariots to show her. Cruker's met his quota of swords and lance heads. She wants to attack Paulinus as soon as she gets out."

Ingenius looked at him without speaking.

"If you want to marry Goneril," said Atak. "I'll talk to Boudicca. But it's the chariots that will convince her. Where's Caradawg?" he said, looking out of the door. He felt a sharp prod in his back and turned to see Caradawg holding the point of one of Ingenius' chariot knives against him.

"If I'd been a Rummy," said Caradawg, "you'd be dead."

How had he got in here without me seeing him? "Well you're not a Rummy," he said, grabbing the boy's wrist and sweeping his feet out from under him, "or you'd be dead."

On their way back to the long hut where the chariots were built, two horsemen appeared and dismounted as they approached.

"Brigantes," said Caradawg.

"Paulinus wants to see you," said one of the horsemen to Atak. "He's with Queen Cartimandua."

***

Atak stood by Cartimandua's firepit, hands held out to let the warmth of the fire seep into his bones. Caradawg had run off to seek his old playmates. Hearing the crash of a door flung back on its hinges, he turned to see Paulinus stride toward him accompanied by his legates and several legionaries. Something in the governor's manner warned Atak of danger and he tensed. Paulinus flashed no welcoming smile. "Arrest him," he said, and Atak found a legionary on each side of him.

"Why?" said Atak.

"You're a shithead," said Paulinus. "You let Catus make an ass out of me."

"How?"

"That stash you set up was gold painted lead. It's the stuff that Claudius brought with him to fool the dumb Britons. Catus had collected it to ship back and some Britons stole it when they burned the archive building. The sneaky little bastard wrote a report showing exactly the same amount ours did but said the Romans he got it from—that's my men—must have got the Britons to burn the archives. He also said only an idiot would be fooled into thinking it was real gold. Now Nero thinks my men burned the archives and that I'm an idiot."

"It looked like gold to me," said Atak, pulling on his beard. How could he have been so stupid as not to test Boudicca's coins? Since Claudius' visit, Britons had got in the habit of testing Roman gold coins by biting on them. The imitation ones bent in the mouth and the paint flaked off.

"Thanks to you, Catus is now in solid with Nero and Nero thinks I'm a shithead. Also, I hear the little bat eyed bastard has told Nero he's got a fix on where the Druid's gold is."

"How did he find out?"

"He's got some Briton who scouted it out for him."

"Was his name Ingenius?"

"Yes," said a legate. "That was his name."

"Then he doesn't have a fix on it," said Atak. "Ingenius hates him worse than you do. He told him Cartimandua has it."

"How do you know that?"

"I just came from Ingenius."

Paulinus grabbed Atak's cloak. "Where is it then?" he said, his voice soft.

Atak paused to consider while he looked into the eyes of this fierce little man who held the power of life or death over him. Would the man turn on him if he pressed too hard? He steeled himself. "Are you going to let Queen Boudicca and her daughters go?" he said.

For answer, Paulinus pushed himself away and kicked Atak in the groin so that he doubled up with the sudden unexpected pain. "You fat German pig," said Paulinus, bending down to hiss in Atak's face. "You don't make trades with me." He turned to the centurion at his side. "Take him out and flog him," he said. "When he's through with you," he said to Atak, "you'll tell me where the gold is." He turned on his heel and marched off, his legates scrambling to keep up.

"Come on," said the centurion, jerking his head. The two legionaries shoved Atak forward.

Atak shivered in the biting cold. The legionaries had stripped him naked and bound his hands to an iron ring set in the wall above him. A light sleet fell against his back and the afternoon had turned into dim grayness so that he could barely see the little rivulets of water coursing down Cartimandua's palace wall a few inches from his face. He had witnessed Rummy floggings before and the sheer horror of what was about to happen froze his mind as the sleet froze his body. Why didn't they get it over with? He heard a scuffle to his left and turned with a wild fruitless hope that it was Paulinus come to cancel his order. It was Cartimandua, a look of genuine horror on her face. "Cut him down," she said. "At once."

"Can't do that," said the centurion.

"Then you must wait until I see the governor," she said, and disappeared from view.

"Can't do that either," said the centurion.

"Get on with it," said Atak. "Before I freeze to death." He had forced his mind into utter numbness and his mouth spoke its bravado all by itself.

"This'll soon warm you up," said the centurion and Atak cried out in shock as the metal barbed lash took its first bite out of his flesh. A wave of nausea swept over him and he almost vomited. He was too old for this. This could kill him. Time after time the lash struck. He bit his lip to keep from shouting and felt the blood seep into his mouth. The strokes now were like someone slamming a door in the distance. He could feel them, but the pain had grown so intense the additional blows seemed to add little to his agony. He could feel the flesh hanging in ribbons from his back and the blood congealing on his buttocks and legs. Those black marks trickling down the wall in front of him were splatters of his blood. How many times were they going to lash him? Finally, he lost count and sagged against the ropes holding his hands. He slumped, almost unconscious, and was vaguely aware of being cut down and collapsing on the ground. A voice screamed somewhere and he wondered if it was his own or someone else's. Then he felt a small body scuttle beside him and warm hands and tears on his arm. Then the body was jerked away.

"Caradawg," he mumbled, sinking into the pulsating darkness.

The ride was as agonizing as the flogging. He rode slumped forward, his back too lacerated and sore to allow him to sit upright. His shirt stuck to him in a hundred places and each movement of the horse caused him agony. The flogging had robbed him of his strength and there were times when he would have fallen to the ground had not legionaries reached up to shove him back. In front and behind and on either side legionaries plodded steadily onward. He had no idea where they were going and no one bothered to enlighten him. Once, he asked the centurion about Caradawg, but the man merely shrugged. Caradawg must have been left back at Barwick. He hoped Cartimandua would look out for him.

Day after day they plodded on with few stops for food and drink. At night he was taken from the horse and given a cloak to put over him. The legionaries were always close by but none spoke to him or cracked the usual soldier jokes. He wondered if he was going to his own execution. But why would Paulinus send him all this way to kill him? Besides, Paulinus wanted the gold. At the thought of Paulinus the hatred of Rome that had lain dormant in him sprung to full life again. Who did these people think they were to impose their will on people as intelligent as themselves? Who were they to think they had the right to flog a man to work off their own bad temper? He regretted the times he had cracked jokes with Paulinus as if they were old comrades. The man had simply used him and then had him whipped like a dog. If he ever got the chance he would kill him with his own hands.

Near the end of the fourth day they emerged from the forest into a clearing and he saw in front of them the contours of a low rising hill fort and a large British village. It had just stopped raining and the wattle covered houses shone brightly in the weak afternoon sun. Villagers moved sullenly about, giving the legionaries looks of hatred as they approached. It all looked familiar and he shook his head to clear his addled brain. Where were they? Then he remembered. It was Tas, Prasu's fort. They had come back to Iceni. Why?

They crossed the river over a slippery wooden bridge and climbed up the entry passage and through the gate into the fort. Not a British warrior was in sight and he wondered why the fort had been abandoned. The legionaries stopped in the square before the doors that led into Prasu's palace, and the centurion motioned to Atak to get down. He slid wearily from the horse and leaned against it until his head cleared and his back stopped screaming its litany of pain.

"Go inside," said the centurion.

During the next week, Atak's back slowly began to heal. He managed to convince a sympathetic legionary to wet down his shirt and pull away the fragments that by this time had become embedded. It was a painful process that reopened many of the cuts, but he felt much better after it was over. The centurion allowed him to walk around freely but warned him not to go outside the gate. He ate with the legionaries and slept as they did on the dirt floor near the firepit. There were only twenty of them so they didn't take up much room.

He was in the square one morning, trying to stretch his legs before the rain started again, when he heard the noise. It was a low sighing shuffling noise, quiet but powerful, and he stopped to listen. It came from outside the fort and seemed to be on all sides. The legionaries who watched him heard it also and he joined them as they walked to the gate and climbed up the ladder to the gallery above it. The area that had been cleared around the fort was jammed with Britons. There must be thousands of them. They stretched away on all sides as far as he could see, and many were armed. The noise was the murmur of their voices and the shuffling of their feet. Had they risen without Boudicca? Or had Boudicca been freed? He heard a clatter behind him and turned to see the centurion had climbed up to join them carrying a coil of hempen rope.

"So they're here," said the centurion.

"Were you expecting them?"

"Paulinus put out word for them to come. They're to see a show. One like you just put on for us."

"Someone's to be flogged?"

"That's right."

"Who?"

"You'll see when Paulinus gets here. There's the pole we put up for it." The centurion laid the coil of rope over the rough-hewn rail that ran along the gallery and pointed to a heavy stake driven into the ground on top of a hillock not far from the fort's gate. An iron ring had been fastened near the top of it.

Atak shuddered, not willing to visualize someone being flogged. "Aren't you afraid of that mob?"

The centurion shrugged. "Paulinus will bring cavalry. They'll handle a rag tag like that."

It was cold up on the gallery and Atak shivered in the wind. He pulled his cloak tight around him and winced at the pain caused by the movement. Cold or not he was going to stay up here to see who was to be flogged and what the mob would do about it. As he waited a sick fear began to gnaw at him. Who was important enough for Paulinus to bring here to be flogged? And why in the Icenis' principal village?

At first he wouldn't let himself think about it but the thought kept forcing itself on him until he had to listen to it. Boudicca. Was it to be Boudicca? Catus wanted her flogged and killed. Were they bringing her here to do it? He looked down at the centurion's sword, six inches from his hand. If they brought Boudicca here he would grab it and throw himself on Paulinus.

The noise made by the crowd increased and far to his right he could hear screams and shouts of anger. The crowd surged as if reacting to pressure from its flanks and then he saw the Roman cavalry approaching from the direction of Colchester. It came along at a fast clip, knocking the crowd out of its way, and as more of it came into view he saw it was an entire ala of five hundred Thracians. They must be from the rebuilt Twentieth legion. In the middle of it were two or three covered chariots and a wagon. The crowd scrambled to get out of its way, but many were trampled as the Thracians deliberately made a path for the chariots and wagon to approach the gate and the hillock on which stood the flogging stake. Soon, the cavalry had cleared a great semicircle and stood facing inward, swords in hand and the rumps of their horses pressing the crowd back.

The chariots and the wagon stopped near the gate, and out of one of the chariots stepped Paulinus. He was in full armor and wore a heavy paludamentum. As soon as he was on the ground, giving a cursory glance at the fort and the Romans on its walls, his legates and tribunes also stepped to the ground and clustered behind their Governor. Paulinus waved his arm and Atak felt the bile rise in his throat as Boudicca was handed down from the wagon to stand erect beside it. Dressed in her royal tartans she was every inch a queen, the long red hair of her flowing down her backside to her waist and her nose curled in absolute disdain of the legionaries guarding her. A great angry shout went up from the crowd and it surged forward, jostling the cavalry horses. Atak made an involuntary step forward. Suddenly, two legionaries grasped him and the centurion passed the coil of rope around him as he struggled. It was drawn tight around his arms, sending a wave of agony down his still tender back, then tied around the guardrail.

"You're to watch," said the centurion, "but don't get ideas."

Bound and helpless, a great surge of grief flooded through him and in his agony he roared, tears streaming down his face. How could he have let himself get trapped like this? Two legionaries would never have held him in the past. Was he finally getting too old and weak to fight?

Through his tears he saw Boudicca look up at him. "Fear not, my good Lord Atak," she said, her voice firm and clear as a bell in the sudden stillness that followed his roar. "The people will avenge anything that happens to their queen."

Another great shout came up from the crowd and the Thracians were forced to turn their horses around and plow into the heavy mass of people pressing against them. Here and there Atak saw Thracians pulled from their horses, and others began hacking with their swords until the crowd fell back. Paulinus bared his teeth in a grin of contempt. He showed no fear of the crowd and it grew silent again as he walked to the flogging post on the hillock, a centurion following in his footsteps. He spoke to the centurion, who Atak realized had been brought along to translate the Governor's words, and the centurion faced the crowd.

"Your queen is a queen no more," he shouted. "By Caesar's order there will be no more kings or queens. You are all slaves under Roman law and have no rights save those granted by the Roman Governor."

The crowd said nothing in response but Atak could feel the ominous anger building up around him. Surely Paulinus must recognize the danger? More people crowded up, increasing the pressure. Thracians again hacked with their swords but the crowd did not retreat far.

"Your queen," shouted the centurion, "has broken Roman law by stealing treasure, horses and cattle rightfully belonging to Caesar. The penalty is flogging and death. This sentence will now be carried out."

Gripped on either side by a legionary, Boudicca was marched to the flogging post. The centurion took the cloak from her and tried to rip her shirt down the back but the material was too strong for him. With a contemptuous gesture, Boudicca pulled off the heavy shirt so that nothing protected her but her thin linen tunic. The centurion tore it down the middle so that her back was bare, while a legionary bound her hands together and pulled the rope through the iron ring. He jerked it so that her arms were forced upwards, bringing her body hard against the pole, then tied it around the bottom of the pole. He took the beautiful mass of red hair that cascaded down her bare back and draped it over her shoulder so that it came between her and the pole, leaving her back exposed for the lash.

Paulinus turned on his heel and walked toward the gate as a legionary approached carrying the lash. Atak groaned and sagged forward over the rail as he saw the metal barbs that would wreak such havoc on a woman's flesh. As his weight pushed against the rail it creaked and buckled slightly, and for an insane moment he knew he could wrench it from it fastenings. He straightened up and pulled against the rope that bound him to it. He was ready to exert all his strength against it when he heard a clatter on the ladder and saw Paulinus come up onto the gallery. He stood at Atak's side and gripped the rail looking down at Boudicca. "It's a shame to do that to her," said Paulinus, "but she's as big a shithead as you are. She wouldn't tell us a thing. After she's flogged she will. Or you will."

The legionary holding the lash looked up at Paulinus and the Governor nodded. "How's your back?" he said to Atak as the first blow whistled down and crashed against Boudicca's bare skin. Boudicca's head snapped back and she gave a short sharp cry. Trickles of blood appeared where the metal barbs had dug in.

Atak roared again and tried to pull off the rail with the rope, but a legionary gave him a kick in the groin that brought him to his knees. The rail buckled under the strain but held firm and tears of rage coursed down his cheeks. Five times he heard the lash strike Boudicca. Oblivious to his own pain he doubled over and tried to shut out the awful tearing sounds from below. "Let her go, you bastard," he said to Paulinus. "Let her go."

"Where's the gold?" said Paulinus.

"On Mona. I'll show you on a map."

"Get my maps," said Paulinus to the centurion, who clattered off down the ladder. Paulinus leaned casually over the rail. "Hold it," he said, and Atak struggled to his feet. He couldn't help looking at Boudicca, who sagged limply against the pole, her back streaming blood from a crazy pattern of lacerations. The legionary with the lash stood looking nervously at the cavalry battling at the edge of the crowd. Another Thracian was dragged from his horse to disappear in the melee. Paulinus seemed to enjoy the spectacle, the snarling grin rarely leaving his face. "Cut the shitheads down," he shouted. "Shove em back."

The centurion hurried up the ladder clutching a scroll, and unrolled it on the floor of the gallery. Two legionaries stretched it out and held it while Atak looked down at it. "Loose my arms," he said, "and I'll show you."

"You think I'm stupid? Point with your foot."

Atak tapped the toe of his boot near the western edge of

Mona. "That little island there," he said. "The lake's two miles east of its southern end. The gold's in chariots on the bottom."

"How deep is the lake?"

"Can't be that deep. You can drag with chains to find it."

There was a sudden roar from the crowd and Atak turned to see several of the Thracian horses were down. A vicious sword battle was going on between Britons and the downed Thracians. Paulinus gestured to the centurion to roll up the scroll and took it down the ladder without a further word. Atak saw him pass through the gate beneath and get into his chariot. Trumpets blew a signal. The legionary dropped his lash and hurried with the legates and tribunes to climb aboard the chariots and wagon.

"Wait for us," shouted the centurion, sliding down the ladder followed by the other legionaries on the gallery, but the vehicles were out of reach before they were through the gate. The Thracians gingerly backed away from the crowd and pressed along the road in the direction away from Colchester. As they did, they passed behind the rolling vehicles to form a dense protective shield. With the Thracians flailing vigorously with their swords, the crowd fell back then surged toward the gate of the fort as the last of the Thracians disappeared up the road.

"Close the gate," the centurion shouted. "The bastard left us." The legionaries began to push the heavy wooden gate shut, but before they could get it closed the crowd was upon them, blocking the gate so that it wouldn't close. The legionaries quickly killed the Britons blocking the gate and kept the others at bay with their swords while they tried to shove away the dead bodies that now prevented the gate from closing.

Atak straightened up and exerted all his strength. The heavy rail came away from its supports and he staggered under its weight. Then he swung it around so that its end was aimed at a legionary below and drove it into the man's back. The centurion looked around to take in this new attack and Atak swung the rail's end into the man's face. The centurion fell spread-eagled and Atak drove the rail into the man's chest with all his might, letting out a satisfied roar as he felt bones crunch. Then two legionaries seized the rail and pulled him off the gallery. It seemed a long helpless fall, but as he fell he saw the gate pulled back as the crowd surged in. The bodies beneath him cushioned his fall but the rail cannoned into his head and he lost consciousness.

When he came to, a Briton was sawing at the rope with a knife, and as the rail fell from him he sat up and shook his head to clear it. After all the excitement it seemed strangely quiet, and then Boudicca came through the gate with several women. He staggered over to meet her.

"Well, my dear Atak," she said, the pain showing in her face and voice. He fell to his knees, seized her hand and kissed it as the hot tears flowed. She patted his head with her other hand as if to comfort him. "Now that I am free," she said, and he knew her words were not for him. "It is Paulinus who will feel the lash of British anger."

The shout that went up from the crowd was no longer just rage. The rising had begun.

Chapter 11

The Rising

A week later

"Leave me be," snapped Boudicca, waving away the Druid Mahel and his pot of salve. The painful wounds in her back would heal more quickly if they were left alone. At first she had felt self-conscious arguing with the Kings and Druids who had flocked to Tas with her back completely bare, but the lacerations were a constant goad and she felt no compunction about using her wounds in a good cause. Her flogging and the insulting Roman decree that royals and nobles were to be deprived of all their possessions and lowered to the status of slaves had aroused even lowborn Britons as nothing else could. Kings and Council had unanimously decided to put an end to the occupation at whatever cost. The word to rise had gone out and a mob grew daily bigger outside Tas. Armies were on the move and Owain Longhead would soon arrive to give his blessing.

The Silures, Ordoes and Demetes under King Linus would bring Cruker's swords in their light chariots and cross into Iceni territory through the swamps near Longthorpe. King Afan and his knights with five hundred of Ingenius' new chariots and horses were on their way down from Parisi and would arrive in two or three days. She must not be forced to fight without those chariots. The Belgies and Duroes would come up from the south and be the last to arrive.

Guderius' and Brennius' armies had been hidden in the forests close by and had already built defensive positions. Roman patrols had probed them and been repulsed. The first real test, however, was yet to come. If a significant force attacked before the growing mob could be properly organized and the new chariots were in place, the rising would be over. Could her armies even fight if they were swamped by this huge mob anxious to join in?

From what Atak had said, an uprising would give Paulinus a legal opportunity to massacre the Britons and destroy their will to fight. Now that the rising was in being he could not ignore it for long. He would want to destroy it while it was still mostly an undisciplined mob. A force of several cohorts and cavalry from the Twentieth Legion had already left Verulam and her scouts were shadowing it as it marched leisurely northward. In less than three days it could be upon them. If the Ninth Legion also moved against them, her armies and chariots would have to abandon Tas and flee west through the swamps. Some of the kings already argued for this.

Atak came into the hall, brushing rain from his cloak. "Any word yet on the Ninth?" she asked.

"They haven't moved," he said. "We have signal fires set. We'll know if they move out. I'm more worried about the Twentieth than the Ninth. They will have passed Hertford by now."

She stood up and waved to Habren to bring her cloak. Atak had fixed a light frame for it so that it was held away from her back. "Let's talk to Guderius about that mob."

"We should form a new army with it," said Atak. "And get it off Guderius' back."

"Who would train it and lead it? Would you lead it?"

One look at his face told her he wouldn't. No one in his right mind would lead a mob like that. She felt nervous and irritable. Where were Ingenius and Afan? They could have made it by this time if they had pressed on day and night. And where was Owain when she needed him? And Venutius—where was he? She walked out into the rain, Atak right behind her. Cuneda, the new captain of her guard hurried toward them but she waved him away and stopped. An uncovered horse drawn cart plodded slowly through the gate, the guards walking in with it, and came to a halt in the square. For some reason she felt a wave of dread pass over her. A man got down from the cart and shuffled toward them, head and shoulders bowed as if under a great weight. He was a peasant dressed in old worn clothes and gave her a half-hearted knee when he stopped. The guards stayed by the wagon and from the way they looked at her she knew something was dreadfully wrong.

"You be Queen Boudicca, my lady?" he asked.

"Yes," she said.

"I brought your daughters."

"What!" She clutched her cloak to her and ran awkwardly to the wagon. She grabbed its side and looked in, Atak right beside her. Her knees buckled at what she saw and she would have fallen had not Atak caught her. His sudden grasp sent a wave of pain through her but she barely noticed it. He picked her up bodily, her stomach against his shoulder so that her back would not be hurt and took her into the palace. Dazed, she looked at his face as he put her back on her feet, at the grin of hate that absorbed it. Then Habren came running to them with a scream. "Stop that," she said. Atak led her to a couch and took off her cloak. "Are they both dead?" she said, trying to still the trembling, her voice flat and lifeless.

"I'll bring them in," he said, and went back outside as she sat down. Several knights and kings went out with him.

When he came back in, he carried Goneril in his arms, her long red hair trailing on the ground. Half out of her mind, Boudicca rose and ran to them, picked up the mass of wet hair so it would not trail in the dirt. As she did, Goneril's eyes opened. Her face was filthy and bruised and her clothes were wet, dirty and torn, blood-soaked on the right side from a wound, but she was alive.

Boudicca kissed her forehead and wept. "Oh my darling," she said. "Bring her to my bed." She ran into her bedchamber and hovered mindlessly while Atak laid the girl tenderly on the bed. Her voice sounded like someone else's and her ears rang as if she stood inside a huge resonating cave. "Get my bath filled with hot water," she said to Habren. "And bring Mahel." In her horror she felt a great urge to take Goneril, her beautiful child of love, and flee. Let the mob fight the Romans. She would live only for her darling and make up to her for all she had suffered. But a long suppressed picture of that first Goneril, her childhood friend raped and killed by the legionaries in Boulogne came into her mind, and she screamed with rage. She could never leave until she had avenged this desecration of all she loved.

The burly Cuneda appeared in the bedchamber doorway, tears running down his face. He carried Gwenda, but Boudicca could see with an awful sense of detachment that the girl was dead. What more could possibly happen? Gwenda was horribly bruised, her clothes soaked with water and blood and in tatters, and smeared blood was on her face and legs. "They've been raped," said Cuneda, his mouth working with rage and anguish. "The bastards raped and stabbed them."

A terrible howling noise came from outside the fort. She looked at Atak, startled out of her grief.

"It's the mob," said Atak. "They found out."

Tenderly bathed and put to bed by Boudicca herself, Goneril slowly came to life. Like her sister she had been stabbed, but the wound had missed her vitals and Mahel treated it and bound it up saying it would heal. The eyes that had been fixed and glazed like those of a frightened rabbit regained something of their normal look, and her unnaturally stiff body lost some of its tenseness. But she would not break into the tears that might dissolve the tension nor speak of what had happened. She drank the broth spooned out to her by Boudicca then settled down as if to sleep, but her eyes would not close. After a while, Boudicca kissed her forehead and went out of the darkened room. Maybe if she were left alone she would be able to sleep.

Gwenda, always Habren's and Prasu's favorite, had been taken to her room by Cuneda, and there Habren washed the battered body and dressed it in clean linens. Looking down at the bruised and bloodless face that Prasu had so loved and holding Habren to her to still her tears, Boudicca almost choked on her own remorse. What kind of a mother had she been to let this happen? She should have sent Cuneda to Colchester to smash down their prison and bring them home. She had been too busy arguing with her kings to remember their danger and protect that for which she fought. What use was it to defeat Rome if all she loved was to be lost?

There was a commotion outside and she went blindly into the hall. It was Venutius, dirty and bedraggled from his journey, Owain and Atak right behind him. The shock of seeing him made her dizzy and a great hot surge of grief welled up in her. At last, she could unburden herself on the one who loved her most. Venutius stretched out his arms as he saw her and she ran to him, oblivious of the sudden pain as his hands came against her back and he kissed her. "You must never leave me again," she said, as the tears burst from her in a flood.

He stood back from her, his face radiant with excitement. "Look," he said, showing her the hand that had been crippled when he killed Sabinus. "Elsa healed it," he said. "Now I can be Arviragus again."

It was too much. With all her might she struck him across the face. His head twisted sideways from the force of the blow and he fell against Atak. She could barely see them for the red rage that clouded her vision. They were dark shapes in a red fog.

"We didn't have time to tell them," she heard Atak say, as if from a great distance. Venutius straightened up, a dazed look on his face. Mouth open, he looked at her as a mistakenly beaten child might look, but she could not let go of the rage.

"Tell us what?" said Owain.

"Queen Boudicca's daughters were raped and stabbed in Catus' house. Princess Gwenda is dead."

Venutius fell to his knees at her feet and clutched her to him. She could feel his tears burn through her tunic. She put a hand softly on his head, and now the tears flowed gently and the fog began to clear.

The day after Venutius received his surprising welcome the first wave of chariots showed up with Ingenius himself at its head. Ingenius was shocked into incoherence when he heard what had happened and saw Goneril. He spent the rest of that day with her, while Boudicca, Atak and Venutius went to look over the chariots and decide with Guderius and Brennius where and how they could best be used. When she walked through the gates still numbed by grief for her daughters a great cheer went up from the mob. She waved and smiled, but inwardly quaked at the sight of that unending mass of people crowding around the fort waiting for someone to lead them.

"Guderius can't take any more," said Atak.

"We must make a new army out of them," she said.

"But who can we get to lead it?" said Atak.

Venutius looked at both of them but said nothing.

One of the chariots broke away from the formation to come smartly to a halt in front of them. It seemed heavier than its peers and more beautifully decorated. Even the wicked blades protruding from its wheels had been burnished until they shone like silver. Four powerful Iceni blacks drew it, and the two lead horses had short burnished blades fastened to the straps across their foreheads. The charioteer jumped down and went on one knee before Boudicca and she smiled in surprise. It was Coel, the boy who had got her horses out of Iceni. "This is your chariot, my lady," he said. "And I would be your driver."

"Nay, Coel," she said. "I drive my own chariot. But thank you for bringing it and for getting my horses to King Afan."

Coel looked chagrined as he got to his feet.

"You have not forgotten my promise to your father?" she said.

"You shall join my household as my foster son and be trained as a knight. Then you shall fight for Britain. Now go into the palace and tell the Druid Mahel what I have just told you."

She bent down and kissed the lad on the forehead and patted his behind as he ran off. "Come on," she said. She climbed aboard the chariot and seized the reins as Atak and Venutius got on behind her. Then she headed through the mob, the chariots streaming along behind her. She saw swords, pickaxes and shovels being brandished, and grieved as she thought of what a cohort would do to this ignorant seething mass of people. If it were possible she would send them home, but this was their rising. They were here to be led and she must find leadership for them. They must be kept out of the way of the cohorts and her armies. She must find something for them to burn and loot. Iorwerth the Burner must help.

Once through the mob she raced down the Colchester road toward Guderius. Just as Ingenius had said, the blades shrieked as they gained speed, and she could visualize how frightening this charging body would look and sound to anyone confronting it. Suddenly, she had forgotten all about Venutius and the mob, even about Goneril and Gwenda. This was Britain's answer that she held in her hands. This was Rome's defeat.

***

Boudicca and Venutius knelt together before Owain and the assembled Kings and Council.

"There are no contracts?" said Owain. "No transfers of land or cattle? No dowry? No paraphernalia?" He seemed disappointed.

"Nothing," said Boudicca.

"And the marriage with Queen Cartimandua is terminated?"

"She married Velocatus," said Venutius. "I don't know how much more terminated that could be."

"And bad cess to the both of them," said Brennius. "I hear she's dumping Velocatus for Paulinus now."

"We are both quite free," she said. "And as neither of us know what we have we will not concern ourselves with exchanges."

Owain bent over the table that had been placed at his side and poured wine into two glasses. He handed one to Boudicca and one to Venutius. "You will drink this wine," he said, "as a symbol of the joining together of your blood. And now," as they drank, "in the name of the Three Natures of God and in the presence of these witnesses, I hold above your heads the holy mistletoe. You may kiss each other," he said, "beneath this holy vine."

Venutius' kiss was short and nervous. Owain lowered the mistletoe and reached into a basket that sat on the table. He pulled out a handful of dried corn and flung it over their heads. "I pronounce you man and wife," he said. "May God grant you long life and happiness."

"At last," she said to Venutius, kissing him again, "we are true husband and wife. How often have we both wished for this?"

He clasped her to him. "Nothing else can ever come between us," he said. "Now, would you hear my wedding present to you?"

"What is it?"

"I will lead the mob and make an army out of it. Brennius gave me Iorwerth the Burner and his knights, and Guderius has promised me some seasoned captains."

Speechless, she embraced him. As the Kings and Council members crowded around to offer their felicitations, she saw Cuneda come in with two of his knights and talk to Atak. "What is it?" she asked.

"The Twentieth's not coming," said Cuneda. "They're heading northwest to join up with the Fourteenth at Wroxeter."

Owain frowned. "Where are they all going if not here?"

"Probably Mona," said Atak. "That means we've been given

to the Ninth. We must ride west and look for a good place to fight."

"Fight the Ninth?" said Galga, his mouth dropping open. "Tis one thing to defend against a few centuries from the Twentieth. Tis quite another to meet a full legion in the open field."

"It is a risky venture," said Owain. He looked as alarmed as Galga. "We should at least wait until Linus gets here."

Boudicca bristled. From Galga she expected defeatism but not from an Archdruid. "Will you then send one of your Druids to the Ninth and ask them not to attack until Linus is here?" she said, and Owain looked properly crestfallen. "We will meet the Ninth at a place we choose," she said. "We will break it up with our new chariots and Guderius and Brennius will destroy it. This is our last opportunity to defeat Rome and by Duw we shall not lose it."

"We'll get moving," said Guderius. "What about that mob?"

"Venutius will burn Colchester with it," said Boudicca. "We'll join him after we've destroyed the Ninth. You should know," she said to Owain with a peacemaking smile, "Atak told Paulinus the Council's gold was on Mona."

"Then we must warn Basil," said Owain. "Fortunately, we have it hidden this time where they'll never find it."

Atak smiled as if relieved of a burden. "Good," he said. "I'm glad you took it out of Lynn Cerig Bach."

"What!" Owain slapped his forehead. "Who told you it was there?"

"I told him," said Ingenius. "Who is left on Mona?"

"Basil is heading a synod there to unify the churches," said Owain, a worried look on his face. "Bishop Morfudd and Lord Bodin will be there with their chief priests as well as those from Basil's church."

"Can he get the gold out in time?" asked Atak.

Owain looked grim. "We didn't want Morfudd to know where the gold was," he said. "But there seems little point in her not knowing if the rest of the world knows." He turned to Boudicca.

"I will go to Mona and have it thrown into the ocean. I'm tired of moving it."

"What about a place to fight the Ninth?" said Atak.

"There are places between here and Longthorpe where my chariots can do their work," said Boudicca. "Take Ingenius with you as he knows best how to position them. And send scouts to track Paulinus so we know daily where he is. When we destroy the Ninth he will come back and we must be strong enough to meet him." She turned to Venutius. "And you, my consort," she said, "will come with me. Britain will spare us a few hours together."

Chapter 12

Interlude

They lay naked on the bed together, satiated with love making and barely visible in the soft candlelight. Boudicca's back was still sore but between her grief for Gwenda and Goneril and her joy at Venutius' return she barely noticed it. She ran her fingers down Venutius' ribs and kissed the scars. "Our bodies are not what they were," she said.

"Rome has put its mark on us."

"Did this go deep?" she asked, kissing one near his heart.

"That is not from a Rummy," he said. "I got that from you."

She kissed the scar again, laid her head against his chest and sighed. If the Rummies had not come, what a life she and her hot head could have lived together. But for the Rummies she would not have had to marry poor Fat Prasu.

"Do you remember that dark dark night in Gaul when Cadwallader and me thought Atak's ala was close by?" he said. "And you said it wasn't, because he wouldn't be drinking by himself if it was?"

"Aye," she said, remembering how she had stood there trembling, aching to kiss him even though he was so far beneath her in rank. His hands had come against her stomach as he groped for her in the dark, and she could still feel the place where he'd touched her. She took his hand, placed it over the spot and pressed it to her.

"That's where I got the scar," he said. "That's where you took the heart out of me."

"Because I was right?"

She could feel him shake his head. "Because I touched you. You felt so soft and warm."

"You touched me right here where your hand is."

"Then you remember it too?"

"I shall never forget it, my sweetheart." She picked up his hand. "It looks perfect," she said. "How did Elsa heal it?"

"I don't know. She said the power comes from God and if we empty our minds of hate and learn to love we can all do it. Somehow it made sense, the way she said it."

"Then why couldn't I who love you heal you?"

He kissed her shoulder. "Because you don't love me like her God. Her God wouldn't have belted me one across the face like you did when I showed you my hand."

"And God wouldn't roll in the hay with you either." She kissed him and sat up. "I know Elsa is right," she said. "But I can't love the way she does and won't try. I need all the hate I can get to drive these Rummies off. When they are gone, then I will try to love everyone and everything as she does. Get up and get dressed. I want us to do something."

He grumbled but climbed out of bed and got dressed as she did. She took his hand and led him out into the hall. The fire pits had burned low and only a few candles broke the darkness. A gray shadow by the wall got up, most likely Cuneda, but except for a few sleeping bodies near the fire pits the rest of the hall seemed deserted. She led Venutius to Goneril's room, opened the door and pulled him inside.

Two candles on a chest by the bed filled the room with flickering yellow light. Goneril was hunched up among the pillows, not asleep. She put a hand out as Boudicca and Venutius came to her and Boudicca kissed it. "I feel stronger," said Goneril.

"Perhaps tomorrow you can get up."

Goneril sat up straighter and Boudicca caught the half concealed wince as she did so. That wound must still hurt and she must tell Vallo to keep her in bed a while longer. "I want my fifty chariots," said Goneril. "I want to kill Rummies."

"You shall," said Boudicca. "But first you must get well."

"I am well. I want to avenge Gwenda."

She kissed Goneril's hand again, not willing to argue. "Gwenda will be well and truly avenged," she said. "And you will help us when you are well. Are you pleased that King Venutius is now your stepfather?"

Goneril smiled vaguely at Venutius. Boudicca put Goneril's hand in Venutius' and Venutius kissed it.

"I'm sorry for what happened to you and Gwenda," he said.

"I will find Catus and kill him."

"It was Catus who did it?" said Boudicca.

"It was his men."

Venutius stood up, face aflame. "You will let me kill him."

Boudicca put a hand on his arm and made him sit. Catus would die, and die slowly. She would make sure of that herself. "King Venutius and I have a confession to make to you," she said.

"Oh?"

"Before you were born, while I was still a princess as you are and while King Venutius was still a prince, we fell in love."

"Before you married father?"

"Yes."

Goneril looked at Venutius with new interest.

"I was forced to marry Prasu to keep Iceni in the Alliance. But I have always loved Venutius." There was a pause while she wondered how to say what she had come to say. "Venutius has always been my true husband."

"Why are you telling me this now?"

"Venutius is your father."

Goneril pursed her lips and looked solemnly at Venutius.

What is she thinking? Boudicca wondered. Is she disgusted with me? Will she hate Venutius? Venutius looked steadily back at Goneril, and she was pleased that he didn't flinch under Goneril's stare. "You were not Gwenda's father," said Goneril. "She was not like me."

"No," said Venutius. "She was Prasu's daughter."

Goneril held her hand out to him and he took and kissed it. "I am glad," she said. "I never felt that father was a true Briton. You were Arviragus before mother and defeated the Twentieth Legion. I am pleased that my true father is a great soldier for Britain."

Boudicca leaned over and kissed Goneril, careful not to hurt her. "My darling," she said. "I knew you would understand."

"And now," said Goneril, looking at both of them. "You understand why I must have my chariots. With this much soldier blood in me, I must fight. I will not be denied."

"As soon as you are well," said Boudicca.

"I am well now, but to please you I will stay here two more days. Vallo will bind me so that I stay in one piece." She looked directly at Venutius, who still held her hand. "As your daughter," she said, "I look to you for support in this."

"You have it," said Venutius. "By Duw you have it."

He did not even look at me to see if I approved, thought Boudicca. I will have to watch these two. She stood up. "We must go," she said. "Tomorrow we will be on the march." She stooped over and kissed Goneril again. "I feel better now that you know," she said.

Atak was waiting outside the door, Cuneda and Ingenius at his side. "We found a place," said Atak. "We can hide two hundred chariots in the foothills where they'll have a good run either side of the Ninth. We can bring the rest up behind them."

"How far is it?"

"It will take us half a day. And that's all we have. The Ninth is on its way. Guderius and Brennius are almost there and so are the rest of the chariots. We've sent out scouts but there's no sign of Linus yet."

She bit her lip. Without Linus could they really defeat the Ninth? "Why didn't you tell me right away?"

Atak pulled on his beard.

"He wanted you to get some rest," said Ingenius.

She looked at Venutius. "You must head south with the mob and attack Colchester. There is little there to defend it. I want Catus found and I want Colchester obliterated from the earth to avenge Gwenda and Goneril. Not a stone must be left standing. Iorwerth will know where to start. We'll join you as soon as we've taken care of the Ninth."

"May I say farewell to Goneril?" said Ingenius.

She frowned. Ingenius was spending too much time with Goneril. Atak had mumbled something once about Ingenius being in love with Goneril but she had passed it off as an idle remark. Who that knew Goneril could not love her? Ingenius was so far below Goneril that love between them was unthinkable and Ingenius must know this even if Atak didn't. In any case, Ingenius must be thirty-five now, twice Goneril's age, so there surely couldn't be any danger of Goneril falling in love with him. "Yes you may go in with Habren."

She watched Ingenius set off to find Habren but her mind was already on the coming battle. If only Linus were closer. The first of the two legions she must destroy was on its way and those unseasoned chariots would have to carry most of the burden. Thank God she could trust Venutius to get that mob out of her way. She felt a tug on her sleeve and saw it was the ponderous Galga. Several minor kings and nobles were with him.

"We should all go with Venutius," said Galga. "Without Linus and the Belgies we cannot face a legion. We can burn Colchester and then disappear where they'll never find us. Like you say, there's nothing there to defend it."

"Do your men feel the same way?" she said, looking at their fearful faces.

"Aye," they said, eager to have her agree.

"Then go with Venutius and be part of the mob," she said curtly. "I will have none with me but soldiers." She turned her back on them and went outside.

Chapter 13

Victoria

Despite herself, Boudicca felt an icy chill as she looked down from her vantage point and watched the Ninth Legion prepare to attack the British armies blocking its path. She had harangued her captains and worked herself and them up into a battle fury. Was she to lose it at sight of her enemy? She forced herself to relive that awful shock at seeing Goneril and Gwenda, raped, stabbed and huddled in the peasant's cart like a heap of discarded rags, and ground her teeth in rage until the chill dissipated. At the end of this day not one of those Rummies would be alive.

Atak had found a good site for the battle, one of the few places in Iceni where there were rolling hills and only a scattering of trees. He had wanted her to direct the battle from up here but she had refused. She wanted the heat of her rage down there where it would do the most good. "It won't be that kind of a battle," she had said. "The chariots have one chance to break up the shields so our foot soldiers can get in there man to man. If we get in, Guderius and Brennius know what to do and things will move too fast to change from up here. If we don't get in, the battle's over. I will lead the charge and my Britons will not let a woman shame them."

She had divided the chariots into four groups and carefully

hidden two on each side of the road. Atak and herself would each lead a group directly onto the flanks of the legion and Afan would bring his group in from behind. Ingenius, the quicker thinker, would hold his back in reserve ready to exploit their breakthroughs. She had sent out hand picked Silures to hunt down and eliminate Rummy flank scouts who could have warned the legion, so their attack should be a complete surprise.

Cohort by cohort the legion's maniples of heavy infantry clanked like the workings of some great impersonal machine until a massive shield-encrusted chevron emerged, its point aimed squarely at the center of Guderius' and Brennius' armies. Behind the legion trotted an ala of cavalry, five hundred horse confidently ready to sweep past the infantry and run down the survivors once the legionaries had smashed the British armies apart. Behind the legion's center marched the guard with the sacred aquila and legion standards, and behind them the Rummy general and his staff, a reserve cohort of infantry, the artillery train and baggage carts. Here and there among the steadily marching troops waved the battle standards of individual cohorts and maniples. It was a fearsome array and Boudicca felt again the strange mix of awe and loathing she had experienced so many years ago when she watched the legions maneuver on the beach at Boulogne.

Could she infuse her Britons with enough courage and staying power to break up one of the most powerful fighting machines on earth? Venutius, Linus and she had defeated the Twentieth but they had met and vanquished it one piece at a time. Here was an entire legion to be met all at once and with less Britons than had been mustered against the Twentieth. The ratio had been eight to one against the Twentieth. Against the Ninth, since Linus and his army had not yet appeared, it would be less than four to one. All that she had to tip the balance in her favor were the new chariots with their vicious blades. Surely flesh and blood would quail before a determined charge by these monsters. By Duw, it must and it would. But she wished Venutius was in her chariot with her instead of Cuneda and Giraldus his knight.

The legion was ahead of her now, less than a quarter of a mile from the British armies. She knew how frightening it must be to stand before that terrible wall of impervious shields advancing remorselessly toward them. Before long the first wave of barbed lances would be launched, burying themselves in unprotected bodies and flimsy shields. She couldn't risk a premature break for cover. It was time to move. She motioned to the standard bearers mounted on either side of her to raise Pendragon and the battle standard her father had given her then looked back at her guard and the wedge-shaped mass of chariots behind her. "Keep closed up," she shouted, and the horses snorted as the charioteers waved and gripped their reins. "For God and country," she yelled.

She flicked the reins over the shining rumps before her as the warriors yelled, and the great Iceni blacks burst over the brow of the hill, galloping with all their might down the rough grassy slope, forcing Boudicca and her passengers to hang on for dear life. Looking grimly ahead, feeling at one with the mass of chariots racing behind, she roared with sudden blood lust. The whirling blades around her took up their awful deafening shriek, drowning out the thunderous roar of the wheels and the pounding of hundreds of hooves.

Ahead of her the legion faltered as this new and strange threat appeared on its flanks. As the cavalry wheeled to meet her she could see Atak's chariots pouring down the hills on the other side, a mirror image of her own attack. The legion began to change shape as its maniples hurried to form new walls in her path. Then it changed again as Afan appeared to its rear. Guderius and Brennius sent their men charging at the legion expecting to penetrate the gaps she had not yet made, mouths open in a hubbub she could not hear.

With less than a quarter mile to go the Rummy cavalry came between her and the legion and she screamed with rage, fearing the dense mass of horse would sacrifice itself to blunt the charge. To hit such a mass would destroy half the chariots and bring the battle to an end before it even began. The horsemen were brave and charged head on, lances pointed at the chariots and hoping she knew to frighten them into swerving away from their target. She waved and pointed dead ahead, whipping the blacks into even greater speed. She would not back down even if she crashed into the horses. At the last moment the cavalry parted and roared past on either side, the dust and stones raised by its passing flung insolently into her face.

She opened her mouth in a fixed grin and her eyes narrowed to slits. The wall of shields ahead of her looked like an impenetrable metal barrier. Would the legionaries have the nerve to stand and absorb the awful shock of these racing vehicles with their whistling howling blades that threatened to tear open their stomachs and break all their bones? She could see the cloud of dust raised by Atak's chariots charging at the other side of the legion. If they both hit just behind the two front walls they could break off a full third of the legion then with Afan split apart the other three walls. Ingenius could smash whatever was left. They must break through.

The charging vehicles were a few lengths from the shields and the first wave of lances rose to meet them. Thrown by legionaries standing shoulder to shoulder and six deep, they filled the air like a cloud of angry hissing snakes, so close together it seemed impossible not to be hit and she steeled herself for the sudden terrible impact. Then she was underneath them as they arced down and realized they would hit the chariots behind. There were three knights in each chariot and if the driver was hit one of the others could take over. If a horse was hit, the sheer impetus of the charge would bring it and its chariot crashing against the wall, which now seemed right beneath the forefeet of her own horses. Would the legionaries break?

Even if the men stood their ground they would be knocked aside and ground under the wheels. But it would be better if they broke. If they broke, discipline would break and the integrity of the legion would be lost. "Break," she screamed as she looked into the faces behind the shields and saw the fright there. "Break, you bastards."

Her horses almost on top of them, the legionaries folded back opening up a wide breach in the wall, many dropping their shields in their hurry to escape those wicked blades. She charged through, bending her horses to the left to head the wide wedge of chariots toward the point of the shallow vee that had been broken off, barely conscious of Atak's chariots thundering past her to smash into the back of the line she'd just breached. Wheels, blades and bodies flew through the air as some of the wildly gyrating vehicles crashed into each other and disintegrated. Other chariots had lances embedded in them so they looked like porcupines.

"Keep the speed up," she screamed unheard as she ran down behind the line of legionaries, closing in on them so that they broke and ran or bunched up irregularly, their eyes on those whirling blades threatening disembowelment. Then she broke through again, swinging wildly right to avoid British foot soldiers rushing in to throw lances and fire arrows into the distracted legionaries. A quick glance told her the chariots were still massed behind her, although it seemed she had lost many to the lances. Groups of Rummies were forming up again where Atak had smashed through, but they fell back and scattered as she turned in to widen the gap. By this time the two broken segments of the front line were submerged in Britons, fighting hand to hand as they looked wildly for standards around which to cohere.

Almost blinded by dust she wheeled left and tried to take in the confused scene at the rear of the legion. Afan had broken through but most of his chariots were halted, a tangled mess of wood, iron and struggling horses. His knights had dismounted and were fighting hand to hand helped by the British foot soldiers flooding in through the breaches. There was no sign of Ingenius but it looked as if the rear wall had not been broken. As she charged down toward it, Atak burst through the line to her right and turned to run parallel with her. The heavily guarded aquila and legion standards moved across her front and instinctively she headed to run them down, thinking almost dispassionately that Atak had lost many chariots.

The guards stood their ground. She crashed through and felt hot liquid splash on her as the sacred eagle went down with the guards and with them her leading horses. The guards had driven their swords into the animals, she found herself thinking, as the chariot floor rose beneath her and she flew through the air. She landed on a downed horse, conscious of sharp pain in her shoulder as she slid down its belly, barely missed by the blades of the chariot careening past. Geraldus had been thrown out also, his face smashed to pulp by a ballista bolt. The hot liquid she had felt was his blood: she was covered in it.

The standard bearer holding Pendragon came to her side and was immediately killed by a lance. As he fell from his horse British foot soldiers surrounded her and caught the pennant before it could touch the ground. A legionary came at her with a lance, but Cuneda came up from where he had fallen and chopped the lance before it could reach her as a foot soldier speared the legionary.

"I'll hold Pendragon," said the foot soldier, and Cuneda and three knights who had abandoned their chariot surrounded her, swords drawn. She pushed through them, angry that the chariots were slowing because hers had been wrecked. The pain in her shoulder was excruciating but she waved them on urgently. They must not lose impetus or that last wall would reform.

Rummies pressed toward her, attracted by Pendragon. More Britons fought their way over and she raised her sword to urge them on. With a cheer they pressed the Rummies back, their longer swords at last effective against legionaries no longer protected by their wall of locked shields. Feeling the sword in her hand, the lust to kill almost blinded her to her taboos and her own duties, but she pulled back in time to see Atak's chariot behind her. She screamed and almost fainted from the pain as she felt herself lifted into it. Her shoulder must have been dislocated. The Britons around her cheered again when they saw she was safely on a chariot.

"Get Pendragon," she shouted, and Cuneda shoved the grinning Briton aboard still holding the great pennant. She leaned gasping against the front of the chariot, bucking as it gained speed. "There," she groaned, nodding to the legion's unbroken rear wall now beginning to form into a square. The chariots had slowed too much to break through and stopped, their knights on the ground fighting. "We must break them up."

Atak shook his head grimly. "We've lost momentum and there's not enough of us. We'll have to fight on the ground." He slowed, but as he did there was a sudden turbulence among the rapidly forming legionaries and they broke and scattered as Ingenius smashed through. Unhampered by the cloud of lances that had decimated the other charioteers, Ingenius was able to circle around the Britons at full strength and open up another huge hole. As he charged through, many of the stalled chariots raced to catch up and Boudicca waved Atak to follow. "Head him off," she said. "We must regroup."

Ingenius began a wide curve to his left to attack the legion again but straightened out and slowed his group when he saw Pendragon cracking in the wind and Boudicca coming across his front. It was difficult to get the charioteers to stop. Their blood was up and they were in the foothills before they ground to a halt and Atak was able to bring his chariot alongside that of Ingenius.

"Where's the Rummy cavalry?" said Atak.

"A scout came for them," said Ingenius. "They went north in a hurry. Maybe Linus is coming."

Pray God he is, Boudicca thought, but her eyes were on the battle below. "We must keep out here until we can see where best to hit them," she said. She rubbed her shoulder, glad that the agonizing jarring of the chariot had stopped. The Rummies had broken up into many small pockets so their vaunted tactical organization had been destroyed. Each pocket was surrounded by Britons and it was difficult to tell what numbers were involved but it seemed to her the Rummies were dwindling. The field was littered with bodies but it wasn't possible to tell which were Britons and which Rummies. The two largest pockets contained but a few hundred men, and none of the rest, she figured, had more than a hundred. One of the large pockets had formed around the artillery and baggage carts. Hand to hand without that wall of shields to contend with her Britons were standing up well to the Rummies even though their losses would likely be twice as great.

"They've lost half their men," said Atak. "But so have we. We can't let those two biggest groups reform."

"Let them," she said. "They'll make a better target." She turned to Ingenius to tell him to be ready to charge when she saw the knight crouched at his side. The bundled up red hair and dirty face was no disguise. "Goneril," she shouted, anger sending a wave of pain through her shoulder. "What are you doing here?" She turned to Ingenius, fury in her voice. "Why did you let her come?"

Ingenius crimsoned but said nothing.

"Get off that chariot," she said to Goneril, shaking with anger. How could she put her life in jeopardy like this?

Goneril stood up, blue eyes as icy as she knew her own must be. "I will not," she said. "I will fight with Ingenius."

So she was in love with him, and him so far beneath her. As soon as this battle was over she would be sent to Marius in Caer Leon. She stood glaring at Goneril until Atak put a hand on Boudicca's arm. "Do not shame her in front of the others," he said. She shook his hand off angrily, sending more pain through herself. He was right to defend her daughter, but he knew nothing of royal obligations. When these Rummies were driven off Britain would have to be rebuilt and restocked with royal leaders, and Goneril would marry a High King to help bring it about.

Angry at being distracted she looked back at the battle and saw the two large groups of Rummies had almost come together. "You see your target," she said to Ingenius. "Destroy it." She could not bring herself look at Goneril.

Alone on the hill with Atak, her guard and the scouts, Pendragon now turned over to a mounted standard bearer, she watched Ingenius' chariots thunder toward the battle, the raucous shriek of their wheels frightening even from this distance. Before they reached the battle the two Rummy groups began to form a dense square around their artillery and baggage carts. With their shields locked together in such a mass they would be invulnerable to the foot soldiers. She raised her fists and shook them, oblivious to the pain in her shoulder, as if the energy she expended would lend impetus to the chariots. They must hit and hit fast before the square formed.

A cloud of lances rose to meet the racing vehicles as they approached the new wall of shields being erected. Swirls among the tide of vehicles told of chariots going down, but the impact must have been fearful as the wedge drove itself into the wall. She could not tell whether Ingenius' chariot had survived. The Rummies absorbed the shock and closed around the chariots as they ground to a halt in the middle of the square. Charioteers were on the ground fighting, the foot soldiers flooding into the square through the breach behind them. It was a bloody battle and it was not clear who was winning or losing. Pushed to the back of her mind was a black cloud of horror, a dreadful certainty that Goneril must now be dead. Why had she not made Atak take her off that chariot? Why had she not kissed her before she left, or at least smiled and praised her bravery?

"They're reforming," said Atak.

There was a change in shape among the Rummies. Like some strange living organism the battered square began to spew out the Britons in its midst and flow to one side until it became a column marching quickly back the way it had come. The Britons around them stopped fighting and started dancing and cheering.

"They've given up," said Atak. He slapped his thigh. "They're leaving their wounded and baggage and retreating. By Mercury there isn't a quarter left. You've defeated a legion."

"If there's a quarter left," she said. "Our job is not done. Let's get down there and see how many chariots we have left."

The foot soldiers cheered wildly as she rode through them to find Guderius, but she would not smile at them. The ground was littered with broken chariots and dead and wounded men and horses and she wondered dully when she would come across Goneril's body. "We are not finished," she said to Guderius, who rode to meet them, a triumphant smile on his face. "Get your trumpets to work and your army on the move. We must follow and finish them. I want no Rummy left alive to remember this day."

Guderius' brow blackened. "We have won a great victory," he said. "Our men have fought well and need rest."

"I am not interested in winning great victories," said Boudicca. "Nor in resting. I am interested in costing the Rummies such that they will leave and never set foot on this land again. There is a quarter of a legion marching away from us. It must be caught and destroyed."

Guderius rode off angrily sending scouts for his captains. If he didn't move faster the Rummies would quick march out of his reach. "Hurry," she shouted, and he waved irritably as Brennius came to join them, picking his way delicately among the bodies and waving his sword.

"Was there ever such a victory?" said Brennius. "Finally I have got me an invincible sword. Twas sent to me by King Conaire Mor his very own self. There is not a Rummy left who has challenged it. The bards will sing forever of this great day."

He seemed taken aback when she glowered at him. "Get your men marching," she said. "Before our enemy escapes us."

"Escapes us?" said Brennius, looking toward the retreating Rummies. Then he too trotted off to get his men together.

She motioned Atak to go on. A great sense of weariness descended on her, not helped by her painful shoulder. Why were her generals so ready to give up when complete annihilation was within reach? "Let's see how many chariots we have," she said.

There were many still moving around on the outskirts of the

battle area and they came to her when the trumpeter blew the assembly signal. Her heart lifted when she saw Ingenius. If he had survived then so had Goneril. He was wild-eyed from the excitement of combat and there was blood on his head and shirt. She felt remorse now for the way she had shouted at him. She had jumped to conclusions that perhaps were not warranted. "Where is Goneril?" she said, her voice kinder.

"She took another chariot," said Ingenius. "We lost many knights to the lances." His apparent lack of concern for Goneril's whereabouts reassured her. He did not sound like a man in love or like one who felt his loved one was in danger.

She looked at the chariots assembling around her but couldn't see Goneril. "I don't see her," she said.

"She's there somewhere," said Ingenius. "She has to be. I left her when the Rummies broke off. She has to be there."

"And you? Are you badly hurt?"

"I'm fine," he said, but she noticed his arms and hands trembled. "But is this all the chariots we have left? There is less than fifty here."

"It is enough to make another charge."

Atak put a gentle hand on her good shoulder. "Guderius and Brennius will never catch up with them," he said. "They're two miles away and their cavalry might come back. If we're caught out there with fifty chariots we'll lose them for nothing. You've won a great victory and must be satisfied with that."

She had to admit the truth of what Atak said but she scowled nonetheless. To completely annihilate the Ninth would send a powerful message to Rome. Something less than complete erasure of a legion could be obscured by pretty phrases but nothing could cover up a total loss.

"A lot of these chariots broke their wheels when the blades dug in," said Ingenius. He had squatted down by a damaged chariot and held on to its broken wheel with both hands. She saw again how much his arms trembled as he tried to get control of himself. "We can take wheels off other chariots and get them running again."

Before she could answer, a scout galloped up and slid to a halt. "The Rummies have stopped," he said. "King Linus is on the other side of em."

Thank you God, she thought. When this is over I will lay down my sword and serve You only. "Tell King Guderius and King Brennius," she said. "They must move quickly to surround them. Our chariots are enough to break up that column for Linus."

***

It was dark and cold, and the hills were covered with a thousand campfires. Torches moved around in the valley below as the search for wounded went on. Here and there, especially in the kings' tents, the noise of carousing could be heard as the victory was celebrated. But the butcher's bill had been high and the silence of mourning and exhaustion outweighed the noise of joy. King Afan had been killed in the first chariot charge and uncle Guderius in the last battle. Goneril had not been found. After greeting Linus and his kings and finding that her loved Cruker had also been killed, Boudicca had left the carousing for the quiet of her own tent.

She lay face down on the cot, a cloth gripped between her teeth while the Druid Mahel reset her shoulder. He had given her a soporific of wine mixed with herbs but the pain was excruciating. At last he was finished and Habren covered her up as he rushed out to tend the other British wounded. She was too drained to move and shook her head when Habren offered her wine. Nor would she let Habren remove the cloth from her mouth. With it still between her teeth she lay inert and watched the sharp random pictures of the day's fighting flash through her mind as the pain slowly subsided.

Trapped between the armies of Linus and Boudicca, the remnant of the Ninth had been annihilated as she wished. Only its commander and a few guards had got away, saved by a last charge before the decimated cavalry abandoned the field. Not a legionary was spared. Even the Rummy wounded had been killed on her express orders. Atak and many of the Britons had demurred but she had insisted, her rage cold and calculating. This was no time for *clementia*. The Rummies were masters in the use of *atrocitas* to frighten their opponents into submission, and in this instance she would be a willing pupil of her Roman teachers.

Elimination of the Ninth would send a shock wave through Rome. It would tell its people in unmistakable terms that Britain was not conquered and never would be. She had ordered the battlefield searched for the broken aquila and legion standards. They would be delivered to the Roman Senate. If that didn't get the Senate's attention she didn't know what would.

Dully, she heard Habren mutter as someone entered the tent. It must be Atak coming to report. Slowly, she reached up with her undamaged arm and pulled the cloth from her mouth, surprised to see bloodstains on it, black in the dim candlelight. Through the corner of her eye she could see two dark shadows by her bed. Ingenius must have come with Atak. "Have you found Goneril?" she asked.

The biggest shadow knelt down by her bed. It was Atak. She could sense that he was weeping and her heart shriveled within her because she knew what he was going to say. "Goneril is dead," he said.

She said nothing, letting the quivering shock sink in. She had known Goneril must be dead, but without word there had been hope. She could see her again standing by Ingenius, fiercely angry at her mother's rebuke, and with bitter self contempt she could see herself again, not willing to look at her daughter before she rode away, not willing to praise her for her bravery. Oh God, she thought, if I could but kiss her once and tell her that I love her I would exchange for that all the lives of all the Rummies I have caused to die this day.

"She was killed in her chariot," said Atak. "The horses bolted and went for the hills. We just found her a short while ago."

There was a long pause. Her eyes and throat burned but the tears would not come. Was she past weeping? "Is that Ingenius with you?" she said at last. Her voice was barely a croak.

"It's Caradawg. He got away from Paulinus and found his way back to Caer Leon. He came with Linus."

She stretched out her hand and felt Caradawg touch it. "Where is Ingenius?"

The pause was ominous and she strained to see Atak's face. It was a black shadow. "He killed himself when he found Goneril," he said, and then he bowed his head by her arm and the cot shook with his sobs.

Chapter 14

The Swath

Riding at the head of her army, a passenger in her own repaired chariot, Boudicca saw in the distance the pall of smoke rising above Colchester. Her shoulder was still painful so Atak drove while Caradawg stood by his side gripping the front of the chariot, pride radiating from his face. For Atak's sake the soldiers had made him their mascot. She half wished her own Coilus were there instead, but Coilus must stay with Marius and Dedreth in the mountains. He was all she had left now besides Venutius. Her eyes filled with tears as she thought of Goneril, gone from her angry, without a kiss or a smile from her mother. Ingenius too, who with all his faults had been like an erratic younger brother to her, gone to fulfill a love in the Otherworld that could not have been fulfilled in this.

Behind her chariot rode Linus and the irascible High King Corio, the standard bearers and the minor kings. Behind them rode Cuneda and the combined guards, and the chariots salvaged from the battlefield led by Brennius. Brennius had broken his invincible sword in the last battle and had begged to be given the new chariots. Behind Brennius marched her armies, over twenty thousand strong now that Linus had joined his forces to the remnants of hers. Last of all came the baggage carts, both Roman and British, captured artillery and broken but reparable chariots. Despite the joyous songs of her troops there would be little enough to face Paulinus. The Belgies and Duroes must join before that last battle.

It would soon be dark so she ordered the army to camp when they were within view of the burning city and sent for Brennius. "I want every one of the chariots gone over," she said. "And I want every horse that can be used rounded up. You must work all night. I must have at least two hundred to meet Paulinus."

"Two hundred you shall have," said Brennius. "And they will be invincible because I will make the two pieces of my invincible sword held by Eremon when he whipped the De Danann at Taillte into two hundred pieces and pound a piece into each chariot."

"If it was invincible," said Atak, "how come it broke?"

"Feredach Finn Feactnach warned me," said Brennius, "twas only invincible when held vertically. When I broke it on a Rummy's head it was horizontal. Now its pieces shall always be vertical."

Boudicca looked appealingly at the Parisi workmen who had come with Brennius. "Those chariots must be ready to move by nightfall tomorrow," she said. Oh Ingenius, she thought. Without you or Cruker will I have my chariots ready in time? And will they work if they are?

She left Atak and Caradawg with Brennius and rode on past Grandfather's old palace at Gosbecks where Cunobelinus and her father and mother were buried. With Linus and the guards, she picked her way among the debris and the burned out shells of houses. A terrible stench of burning filled the air, butchered and headless bodies littered the streets, and scores of Britons guarded piles of goods they had looted from the Rummy colonists. As far as she could see, the mob filled the part of Colchester that had already been burnt. It was thickest around Claudius' temple, which still stood, the people cheering wildly and crying 'Victoria!' when they recognized her. Scouts must have brought news of the victory over the Ninth. She stopped near an overturned and headless statue of Claudius, and Venutius, his face and clothes black from the smoke and soot, threaded his horse through to her side and dismounted. The crowd cheered when he went down on one knee and kissed her hand. He wept when she told him of her losses.

She raised him to his feet and kissed him, the crowd cheering again. "Goneril would have loved you as I do," she said. "But it was not to be. I will miss her, and I will miss Ingenius and uncle Guderius and my dear Cruker."

"You have won a greater victory than ever Briton did," he said, his voice loud so that all around could hear. "You are Britain's greatest Arviragus and your unbearable losses will be avenged."

"Where is Catus?" she said.

Venutius scowled. "He took two hundred horse and was half way to London before we reached Colchester."

She shook from the blinding rage that seized her. "Then you must burn London and every place he has been. This time he must not escape." Through a red haze of fury she saw the huge temple of Claudius, still desecrating the Trinoes' holy land. "Why is that temple still standing?" she said.

"It's full of colonists," said Venutius.

"Destroy it."

"Twill not burn, my lady," said a bystander. "And we cannot break down the door. They have it shored from inside."

"We have the Ninth's artillery," she said to Venutius. "Go to our camp and get what you need. Destroy it and all inside."

"There'll be women and children," said Linus.

She stamped her foot in anger and almost struck out at Linus. "I will not be balked," she said. "This rising shall strike such terror in the Rummies hearts they will flee this land forever. Kill every woman and child. Not one wall of that temple must be left standing. The Rummies must know they face annihilation."

Calmer but still trembling she placed a hand on Linus' forearm as Venutius sent men for rams and catapults. "Your heart is good, my brother," she said, "and we shall need its goodness in the years to come. There is evil to be done in stamping out this plague, and by all we have lost my heart is now prepared to do it. But let me be the one to bear its cost. Simply do what I ask and question it not and you will be safe from the judgment of God."

"I would have you too be safe from such judgment," said Linus. He kissed her sadly. "But what you ask shall be done."

***

Near tears, Boudicca sighed as she held Venutius' face close to her breasts. She felt his ardor die and his breathing slowly become normal again. He had been like a wild animal when he came to her in the tent, almost tearing the clothes from her in his passion. The terrible work he had done had inflamed him and she knew his driving lust was a way to blank the pictures from his mind. Unable to erase the images from her own mind she had felt no arousal, content to let him satisfy his need and collapse in her arms. Throughout, she had been conscious of the dull thumps of the ram as the Britons worked on destroying the temple. Cruker's swords had been given to the mob and her conscience screamed that children were being slaughtered, but she hardened her heart, bit her lip and met the scream with pain. This war must be won, even at the cost of Rummy children. The door of the tent was partly open, and through it came the flickering orange light of flames as Colchester burned.

Venutius raised himself with a groan and rolled to one side. She could feel him tremble and stroked his chest to comfort him. "Would you rather Iorwerth led the mob to London?" she said. "It is not soldier's work. I could ask King Corio to go with him and you could go with us."

He kissed her sore shoulder. "Where then are you going if not to burn London?"

"There are two cohorts of the Twentieth still at Verulam," she said. "Our army must move by dark to destroy them before they can head north to reinforce Paulinus."

Venutius raised himself up on one elbow and looked down at her. "By Duw," he said. "You are ruthless far beyond any man. While we bask in contentment at having destroyed a legion, you burn our bridges behind us so we can never make peace and point us at the next threat that must be overcome."

"Those two cohorts could weigh the battle in Paulinus' favor," she said. "He already has the Fourteenth and most of the Twentieth with him. And he will doubtless send for the Second at Exeter. We must destroy Paulinus before he can combine his forces. If we crush Paulinus, the Second will be all the Rummies have left. With such losses they will evacuate Britain."

Venutius bowed his head and frowned. "I don't know whether to be inspired or frightened," he said. "The Ninth cost half your new chariots and men and you would go against almost two full legions with what is left, after destroying two cohorts on the way?"

"Linus has brought ten thousand men and a thousand Silurian chariots. When Salog joins there will be ten thousand more men."

"Silurian chariots will not frighten like the new ones."

"They can get inside the legions once we have broken through. They're good swordsmen. Is there ought of the mob we can use in the army?"

"A few, but I have a better idea if you will hear it."

"I will hear anything from you, my loved one."

"What if I were to go to Cartie and get her to help?"

"To Cartimandua? I would as soon ask the Jews' Satan."

"Think of what you have done and how it must look to her. You have defeated a full legion in the field and have sacked Colchester. By the time I reach her, London will be afire and you will have destroyed the two cohorts and sacked Verulam. That mob is still growing. Hundreds are flocking to it daily. The Rummies are about to be annihilated and if she takes no part she will have little say when Britain is freed. That more than ought else should stick in her craw."

"What would you have her do?"

Venutius swallowed as if something distasteful were in his

mouth. "She can put an army of thirty thousand under you. Against such a combined force Paulinus could not win."

"You really believe she would break her treaties and do that? Atak says she wants to marry Paulinus."

Venutius snorted. "She must know by now it will never happen. She cannot tempt him with her bed and he wants only to find her treasury and make off with it."

"What would be her price if she did decide to fight?"

"You would have to make her queen of all the northern nations."

"She would be more concerned that I would be queen of all the southern nations. She will not do that which gives me more power than she."

"Then give her Iceni so she has more than you. Such a sacrifice would be worth assuring the Rummies' defeat."

"You would have your wife less than Cartimandua?"

"I would have my wife free and let others fight for power. I am tired of war. Once it is won I would like us to go back to the mountains with Coilus and be a family."

She pulled him to her and kissed him. "I too am tired of war. I do love you, my sweet man. Go to her and see what she will do. I would like nothing more than you and me and Coilus."

It was misty the following morning as Boudicca watched Venutius and his guards ride off to see Cartimandua. The night had been full of screams from Colchester, but now the cold mist had mercifully blanketed all sight and sound of the ravaged city. Venutius had barely disappeared into its silver grayness when she had a sudden premonition she would not see him again and called to him. But they had already ridden too far, the noise of hooves and the anguished cry of her heart alike swallowed by the deafening silence of the mist.

Atak appeared at her side and led her gently toward the chariots. "The cohorts are still at Verulam," he said.

"We will wait one more day and work on the chariots, then

we must go to them," she said dully, still aching for Venutius. "We will use the Ninth's siege weapons to break down their fort."

Her heart lifted when she saw the good work done by the Parisi workmen. The first hundred chariots had been gone over and even in the mist she could see they had been brought up to fighting condition. The blades were attached firmly to the wheels and each chariot was coupled to a pair of the surviving Iceni blacks. There were now only two knights for each vehicle, but they were cheerful and confident. "Where are the rest of them?" she asked.

"Well, my lady," said Lucius, who was chief of the Parisies. He began to walk and she and Atak followed him. "That first hundred were the best of the lot. We have a hundred and twenty more, but most is in bad shape, missing wheels and spokes and axles and sides and tongues and all. We divided em into two lots. No offense meant, but my lads couldn't work under your King Brennius. Nice man he is, but he put my men off with his crossed eyes. One of em almost chopped his own hand off he was that put off his stroke." Lucius stopped. "We have one lot here that my lads are working on. These were the worst of the bunch. The other lot is better so I give that to King Brennius and his lads."

She walked down among the orderly rows of damaged chariots and smiled at the workmen busily repairing them. "How many will you have for me by tonight?" she asked.

"Another forty," said Lucius. "I don't know how many your King Brennius will have." He sniffed. "Nor how good they'll be."

The mist had thinned considerably by the time they got to Brennius and his workmen: men drawn from his own army. The chariots had not been laid out in orderly rows, but she was surprised to see that Brennius had already finished twenty of them and had set them to one side. All of his men were crowded around one chariot, but they stood away from it as she approached and Brennius came to greet her.

"We have just finished pounding in the bit of sword that will make this chariot invincible," he said, a great smile lighting up his face. "Come and see what a fine job we are doing and us not even in the business, and see for yourself which is better: the Brennius chariots or the Parisi."

Boudicca, Atak and Lucius inspected the chariot. "That will not do," sneered Lucius, kicking one of the wheel blades with his foot. The blade had merely been fastened on with hempen rope. Lucius pressed down on it and the blade pivoted until it pointed to the ground. "It'll come off if it hits anything," he said.

"Aye, that it will," said Brennius. "Instead of breaking the spoke which breaks the wheel which breaks the chariot which puts its knights on their backsides and its horses upside down, the blade will fall off and the spoke will not break nor the wheel nor the chariot."

"But what good is it?" said Lucius.

"The good of it, my darling man," said Brennius, "is that it shrieks and howls and looks as fearsome as any that is fastened to a spoke with an iron bracket ready to tear the wheel apart when it hits a Rummy. The Rummies will not stop to see how well it is fitted but will jump out of the way as fast for these as they do for yours. And we can put these on so quickly your brains will swim in amazement."

Lucius scowled, but Boudicca stopped him before he could say anything. "King Brennius is right," she said. "Lucius, fix your chariots properly as you see fit. But what you cannot have ready by nightfall I would have Brennius repair in his way. It is fear of them that makes them effective, and the more we have the more fear we will arouse."

Days later, the Belgies and Duroes under King Salog had joined forces and the two cohorts of the Twentieth had been slaughtered to a man along with all the colonists in Verulam. As the flames of Verulam subsided, a courier found his way to a tired Boudicca and handed her his message.

Fort of Queen Cartimandua at Barwick
Dear Wife and Queen:

Cartimandua is sending twenty thousand under Velocatus and he will meet you at Beltane where the road to Wroxeter crosses the Anker. Paulinus crossed over to Mona and killed off some Druids and priests but he didn't get to the gold because word came of your victory over the Ninth. Paulinus is marching south and will be at Wroxeter by Beltane so you will have time to pick a field. I am to be held hostage here until you have agreed with Cartimandua on the boundaries of your future kingdoms. Duw give you a quick and glorious victory that Britain be freed and you once again in my arms. It grieves me that I cannot be with you on this final field, but take care my darling and keep yourself safe for me.

Your loving husband
Venutius.

"Thank God she has come to her senses at last," said Linus after he had read the scroll.

"Owain went to Mona," she said. "I hope he was not among the dead." She was strangely unmoved by the thought. After losing Goneril, Ingenius and Cruker, the possible demise of Owain shrank in significance. She joined in the joy of her kings and captains as their cheers went up at the news of Cartimandua's help. With Velocatus' army coupled to hers Paulinus could be crushed. With the hundred and fifty chariots repaired by the Parisies and the hundred or so patched up by Brennius, she would break Paulinus' wall of shields as she had broken the Ninth's. Once broken, the overwhelming numbers on the British side should make short work of the legionaries. She gave ready approval to a feast well earned and endured as well as she could the fulsome worship of men made maudlin by wine. But she noticed throughout the festivities that Atak seemed preoccupied and wondered what gloomy eventuality he now envisioned.

"What is it that sticks in your craw?" she asked him.

"I don't trust her," he said.

"Let us walk." She had had enough of the carousing in Linus' tent and would welcome the cold night air. She threaded her way through knots of drunken knights and soldiers and responded to their cheers as well as she could. It made her nervous to see her army's guard let down like this, but the men had earned their rest and debauchery and she could not deny them one night of freedom. Well away from the camp, she climbed to the top of a hill and waited for Atak to catch up. Now that the fires in Verulam were almost burnt out the night sky to the southeast glowed lurid from the fires in London. The scouts had reported the city almost totally destroyed and the rising spreading to the west. There would be nothing left for the Rummies to want.

"Nor do I trust her," she said when Atak stood panting at her side, as if he had just then voiced his concern. "I trust not her but the logic of events. If she does not join in this battle then she has lost all standing and I shall be supreme. She will fight not to help me or Britain but to protect herself."

"But suppose Velocatus doesn't show up?"

"We will still be almost three to one against the Rummies," she said, "and we have experience now with our new chariots. But he will show up and fight because she cannot risk being on the wrong side should we win. And by Duw, we shall win." A low rumble in the distance halted her, and she grabbed Atak's arm. "What's that noise?" she said.

He listened with her and she felt the tension rise as the noise got louder. Then he jerked his arm away and started down the hill. "It's cavalry," he said. "An ala at least."

They ran pell mell down the hill, but long before they reached the camp they could hear the yells of Britons running drunkenly before the horsemen and the screams of horses being killed. Atak stood before her like a rock as frightened foot soldiers ran past and then gradually worked their way toward the edge of the camp where the cavalry circled at high speed, keeping the Britons away.

"The chariots," she gasped. "The chariots are in there."

"Look," said Atak, pointing to a group of officers stopped near a bonfire. "By Duw, it's Paulinus." He drew his sword and set off running toward the group, but trumpets blared and the cavalry ceased its circling. With a rapidly diminishing roar it disappeared into the night, Paulinus with it. She ran frantically toward the chariots, hardly noticing the many bodies of Britons she had to avoid. In the dim flickering light of the fires she could see only ruin and chaos. It seemed as if most of the Iceni blacks had been killed and many of the new chariots smashed with axes. She sank down on her knees and wept.

Chapter 15

One Church

The two black robed priests stood one on either side of the door of the meeting room and looked at Owain like hungry crows. He should have dressed their priests in brighter colors as Almedha had suggested. There was also something strange about them. The front of their heads had been shaved from left to right as if they had been interrupted in the middle of a haircut and it reminded him of that day in Corinth when Paul had absent mindedly given a speech in the Forum in such a condition.

He paused to collect himself before giving the signal to open the door and sighed. Inside this room on the ground floor of Owain's palace on Mona, Bodin the Fox along with Basil and Morfudd and their chief priests and priestesses had been meeting for the past several weeks to consider how their churches could be combined into one as Boudicca had demanded. Boudicca would never know nor care, he thought grimly, how much he had had to debase himself to get Bodin and Basil to agree to such a meeting, or how many concessions he had had to make to Morfudd to cajole her into attending it. Even Almedha, no longer so submissive now that she was married, had brought up several doctrinal points on which no compromise could be allowed. Irritated, he shook his head causing the feathers in his hat to rattle. Realizing the noise must be audible from within the room he plucked up his courage and nodded to the priests, who opened the door. He went in, the two priests on his heels.

He had half expected that Bodin would be seated at the head of the table and was surprised to see him sitting in the middle across from Morfudd. He was dressed in a white robe, which Owain acknowledged to himself he had a right to wear as Pencerdd. The robe had a brilliant red cross emblazoned on its front and, as far as he could tell, on its back also. Morfudd wore a tunic of bright yellow edged with black, and her priestesses wore black tunics edged with yellow. Basil, pompous as ever, dressed in his eight color robe and his purple hat, sat at the foot of the table, the position of next highest honor. Basil was plumper and grayer and his nose seemed swollen and inflamed. Several priests and priestesses wearing Basil's gaudy uniforms or black, brown or yellow tunics scrambled to their feet on seeing Owain. All the men, he noticed, had the front of their head shaved. Was this to be part of the church dress?

He smiled austerely and bowed to the room at large while he tried to read the faces around him, his eyes inevitably drawn to his archenemy. Bodin had lost much of the look of a young upstart that had been so offensive in the past. His remaining hair was tinged with gray and there were lines around his eyes and mouth. Maybe marriage had taken some of the fire out of him. But the bright glance was still there and a suggestion of the old swagger as he and Basil stood to bow to Owain.

"My Lord Archdruid," said Bodin, his harsh voice not in the least hostile, "how very pleasant to see you again."

"Yes it is pleasant," said Owain, immediately on his guard. He had not seen Bodin since that day ten years ago when Morfudd had left him to help Bodin establish his infamous church. Why was Bodin being so nice? What was he after? "And to see you again, Basil. I am sure that under your leadership we have arrived at a satisfactory union."

He smiled hesitantly at Morfudd and was taken aback by

her obvious pleasure at seeing him. She had blamed the dead Badwin for stealing the gold that was to have been given to Marius to repay Ingenius. According to Morfudd, Badwin had insisted on taking the gold to Marius himself and had made her wait some miles from Caer Leon while he delivered it. While she submissively waited he had doubtless buried it some place that would now never be known. Owain had not really believed her, nor had he tried to conceal his disbelief, but seeing how fresh and lovely and innocent she looked he wondered had he misjudged her all this time? It had been right by this table that she had let him make love to her so long ago and the sudden memory of it came so freshly to his mind that he involuntarily gasped. It had been wonderful even though she accused him of raping her and he wondered if he would ever be allowed to do it again.

Basil bowed ceremoniously. "As one of the original apostles ordained by the Lord Jesus," said Basil, "I am always here to be of service to those seeking the true Way. We have received word from the brothers in Jerusalem that this-" patting the shaven part of his head-"is now the true tonsure of those following the Apostle, Paul himself. It was the first thing we adopted."

"Ah yes," said Owain, bowing in turn and then going to his chair at the head of the table. He had no intention of cutting his hair in such an undignified way. For the first time he noticed the black haired Regan standing behind Morfudd, her back to the wall, a wicker basket at her feet and a faint smile of contempt on her face. The atmosphere suddenly seemed chillier. He was tired after the long journey. He had arrived only a short while ago, rushed to his chambers to don his Archdruid robe and hat and rushed back downstairs to join the meeting. He sank into his chair with a sigh and a rattle of feathers, his eyes closed as if in prayer while he wished he had had time for a hot bath. Then, his eyes still closed as he adjusted his robe and chain, the vision of a naked Morfudd on the floor of this very room flooded back into his mind. Startled by the vividness of the vision, he opened his eyes and found himself staring right into the eyes of Morfudd.

She smiled at Owain as if nothing had ever come between them and as if he were still her teacher, counselor and-lover? A faint waft of seductive perfume titillated his senses so that he had to find some way to blot out her presence. He apprehensively turned his gaze on Bodin, who also smiled in a very friendly manner so that Owain felt a cold chill. Had these two been plotting together again?

The atmosphere seemed to darken. Around the table sat the most motley collection of priests and priestesses he had ever observed, dressed in every shade and combination of colors imaginable. It looked like an aviary. For a moment he wished he were back with Boudicca and her generals, getting ready to meet the Ninth legion. With Boudicca and her kind, even with the uncouth Atak, he felt a certain aura of reality. With these people he felt like a sleepwalker.

He bestirred himself and said: "I bring news of great importance. The rising that will hopefully eject Rome from these shores has already begun and the armies are gathering around Queen Boudicca to meet the Ninth legion in battle. Paulinus is on his way north and in a very few days Mona itself might be invaded. We must therefore bring this synod, important as it is, to a close. Now, might I ask, my Lord Basil, what besides this remarkable new tonsure has been accomplished in my absence?"

Basil sat back in his chair with his hands folded over his capacious stomach. His fingers twitched nervously and his face had turned gray at Owain's words. He spoke hurriedly as if anxious for the meeting to be over. "With the exception of a few minor details, my Lord Archdruid," he said, "we are one church."

"They are not minor details," said Morfudd. She looked at Owain with mute appeal in her eyes. Was she asking for his help? Would she seduce him again if he didn't provide it?

"Whatever they are they can be resolved," said Basil with a small bow in Morfudd's direction. "We are one mind and one body. All that is required is first your own agreement and then, of course, the agreement of Kings and Council. With their consent we can consider that the agreement reached here commits all of civilized Britain to a single church."

"Except for a point that only the Archdruid can resolve," said Morfudd.

"Just what have you agreed to?" asked Owain. Morfudd lightly touched his arm and he again felt the thrill of that long ago tryst. "And what must yet be resolved?"

The door opened and the arm of Clotenus the steward appeared holding his pole of office. Clotenus tapped the pole on the ground. "Go away," said Owain. "We are busy." The arm and pole disappeared and the door closed.

"On doctrinal matters," said Basil, "we are in agreement that the Three Natures of God shall be uniformly worshipped."

"Good," said Owain. He had made that point very clear.

"Candles and braziers will be used throughout all the churches to waft our prayers heavenwards. Also, at the suggestion of the Druidess Almedha, singing will be part of our liturgy as it is with our brother Jews. It does seem to attract converts. Some walk for miles just to sing."

Owain nodded. "That is certainly agreeable."

"It has also been agreed to drop any mention of healing," said Bodin. "It places unreasonable demands on our priesthood. From now on the word saved will be used in its place. People will be saved after they die and get to go to the Otherworld only if they obey our priests."

"That's very good," said Owain. "Very good indeed. Healing has always been a problem and postponing it to the Otherworld will make it easier for us to gain converts. Now what about discipline?"

"Anyone arguing against the authority and sanctity of the one Holy British church shall be burned as heretic," said Bodin.

Owain frowned, and Basil, whose eyes had never left Owain's face, raised a cautionary hand. "It is not pleasant to burn those who violate God's will," he said, "but Lord Bodin had a revelation from God and it was made plain to him that this was not only our duty but also a way to cleanse the heretics of their sin so that they would be better prepared to enter heaven at some judiciously arrived at time. To burn them is to do them a favor."

Owain looked at Bodin, who nodded grimly. "It was made very plain to me," said Bodin.

"And lastly," said Basil, "we have agreed to adopt the style of dress designed by Morfudd. All priests will wear black robes trimmed with yellow, and black hats. Bishops will wear yellow robes trimmed with black and yellow hats. These should in no way be confused with any Druid colors."

"That is so," said Owain, pleased. He smiled at Morfudd. "The robes are very becoming."

Basil coughed and glanced at Morfudd. "We have agreed to divide Britain into two areas: the northern nations under the Empress Cartimandua and the nations south of her borders. I will be archpriest of the northern nations and Lord Bodin will be archpriest of the southern nations. As Archpriests, each of us will continue to wear our present robes of office. Each of us will have twelve bishops and each bishop will have twelve priests. To become a full priest each man will have to show proficiency at conducting the Love Feast in either Hebrew or Latin so it will sound more mysterious to the Britons."

"And more fearful," added Bodin.

Owain had sensed danger as Basil talked and raised his eyebrows before looking furtively at Morfudd. "And what of Bishop Morfudd?" he said.

"Their idea," said Morfudd, her voice bitter, "is to make me head of the church archives. I would be Chief Deaconess in charge of the scrolls. I would also be responsible for storing and supplying candles, and for baking and supplying all the bread for the love feasts. My priestesses would become deaconesses responsible for keeping the churches and the priests' quarters clean. We would wear brown tunics trimmed in blue so we would not be mistaken for priests."

"That sounds like a very responsible assignment," said

Owain. "Brown and blue go very well together." Much better than Basil's purple and yellow, he thought.

"As you know," said Basil, "it is against the policy of the Jerusalem Council to assign the function of priesthood to women, and at this early stage of our church growth we can't afford to lose their support. Perhaps later we can modify a few things and resolve some of the concerns of our new Deaconess."

"These are the resolvable points you spoke of?"

"Yes," said Basil.

"I believe they're quite resolvable," said Bodin. No matter what the man said, thought Owain, he seemed to say it with a sneer. Maybe it's a congenital defect. "We can't afford to offend Jerusalem by having female priests or Bishops. Certainly not female Archpriests."

So these two are still enemies, thought Owain, relieved. Fearfully, he turned to look at Morfudd, but before he could speak she spoke. "I proposed that Britain be divided into three areas," she said, her voice quite calm. "And that I should be Arch priestess of one of them. Beneath me I would have women bishops and priests just as would these two gentlemen have men bishops and priests. They do not feel such a role for me would be appropriate and I sense that you agree. What is your view, my Lord Archdruid?"

"Well," said Owain, his voice placatory. "They haven't provided a role for me either."

"Forgive me for not mentioning the obvious," said Basil, raising his hands in alarm. "You would be Father of the Holy United British Church. As Archdruid you would, of course, have overall direction of the Church and your advice and counsel would be sought on all matters of importance."

"Such as this?" said Morfudd.

"Such as this."

All eyes turned on Owain and he rattled his feathers in alarm, fearing an outburst from Morfudd. It would take all his oratorical skills to convince her to accept her new role without at the same time destroying any chance of renewing their delicious relationship. "It seems to me, my dear Bishop, I mean Head Deaconess Morfudd, that what Lords Basil and Bodin say about the Jerusalem Council is unfortunately true, as you and I discussed once. They . . . "

Morfudd cut him off with a hand on his arm. "Then you do agree with their position?" She seemed calm and reasonable. The authority of his presence must have melted her resentment. After all, she had been his pupil and he was still her teacher.

"We unfortunately must at this juncture," he said. "As Lord Basil has pointed out, once we are more or less free of the obligation to follow the leading of the Jerusalem Council, we can reappraise our position and make appropriate changes. In the meantime I can think of no-one more qualified than you to be our Head Deaconess."

Morfudd stood and smiled sweetly, although it was obvious to Owain from the way she breathed that she was exerting great control over her features. "I merely wanted to be sure that we were unanimous," she said. "If we are to be one church then we must subordinate our own aspirations to its needs. Now that our Archdruid has spoken, I accept the decisions of this synod without reservation."

"Why, that is wonderful," said Basil.

"It certainly is," said Owain, relieved that the conflict could be so quickly resolved. In spite of all the demands made upon him his diplomatic skills must still be undimmed. Even Boudicca would be impressed by this unity he had achieved.

"We are one united church," said Bodin.

"Feeling sure that you would ratify the decision of your male subordinates," said Morfudd, her smile so sweet and unassuming that Owain wondered if she might let him kiss her later on, "I have asked Regan to supply us with wine of a special and rare vintage so that we all may ask for a blessing on our new church and drink a toast to its continued health and vitality."

"As adviser and counselor to the Archpriests of the Holy

United British Church," said Owain, "I advise and counsel that we take advantage of the Deaconess' offer and drink a toast not only to the church but to this synod, this group of brothers and sisters that has been led to its divinely unified status by the Holy Spirit." He nodded graciously to the priestesses, and was surprised by the apparent anger in their faces. What were they upset about? he wondered. Maybe they didn't like their new uniforms.

Regan opened her basket, placed an array of small cups on the table and filled each with a small helping of the wine she poured from an ornate vessel. The vessel, he noted, was shaped like a coiled serpent beautifully decorated with bright orange, yellow, black and red designs. Such bright colors were most often found on poisonous reptiles. He smiled at Regan's ignorance and how shocked she would be were he to point this out to her. But he was impressed by her efficiency and felt it boded well for the prosperity of the church that he above all had brought into being. Regan could always be helped in choosing colors.

"Those seem like very small portions," said Basil, licking his lips.

"You will find they are quite sufficient," said Regan. "This is a rare wine that will satisfy as nothing else ever will."

"There are not enough cups to go around," said Morfudd, "so we will serve the men first. Then, as is proper and fitting, the women will drink their toast to our church."

"It's a pity we can't all drink together," said Owain, regretting that he would not be able to drink after Morfudd, thus tasting her lips if only by proxy. He lifted the cup that Regan pressed into his hand and tasted it. It truly was nectar of the gods. It had a velvet texture and was smoother than honey. It lit a gentle fire within that slowly spread itself through his entire being. Anxious to consummate the wine's promise he lifted the cup in salute to those around the table. "To the Holy United Church of Britain," he said, and quaffed the liquid in one gulp.

He sat back in his chair and smiled at Morfudd, standing

there so proudly by the table, her breasts rising and falling as if she too were experiencing an ecstasy. His eyes seemed a little out of focus and he blinked them rapidly. There was a black corona around her figure and he could feel within himself the beginning of a release greater than he had ever before experienced. He didn't know what it could be but he knew it was coming and his fingers splayed out and grasped the edge of the table of their own volition as if waiting for it to appear. As it rose and pulsated within him, the corona growing ever darker and the brightness around Morfudd growing ever more brilliant, he was vaguely conscious that Clotenus the steward stood by his side banging his pole on the ground.

"What, what is it?" he asked, his voice slurred and barely audible even to himself.

"Rummies," said Clotenus. "Coming across the straits."

The corona was almost complete, the pressure almost at bursting point. "Go away," he mumbled. "Go away." As if from a great height he could hear Morfudd telling her priestesses to go out and frighten the Romans away. Morfudd mustn't get away from him. He reached out to clutch her and entered her being, rising higher and higher, blacker and blacker, the blackness of eternal night and not a star, not a star.

Chapter 16

Mancetter (Manduessedum:

Place of Chariots)

"Here he comes," said Atak, and Boudicca signaled a halt.

Almost thirty thousand strong since Salog had joined them with his Belgies and Duroes, they had reached the river Anker. In the fields and among the scattered trees were clustered the men and horses of Velocatus' army, easily twenty thousand strong. Above the forested hills to the west, distant smoke rose fitfully into moist skies from the dying fires of Beltane. Heavy clouds moved ponderously overhead, driven by dank winds foretelling imminent rain.

Velocatus, wearing bright mail armor and a polished metal helmet came toward them with his captains and standard-bearer, who carried the blue and gold banner of Cartimandua. All his captains wore armor and helmets, and carried polished bronze shields. The group sparkled even in the gray green light of the approaching storm. To Boudicca they looked like Romans. "They will make fine targets for the ballistae," she said. "I would have them stay well away from us."

Atak pulled on his beard but said nothing. She knew that

joining forces with Velocatus had upset him and she had not been able to shake his suspicions. In spite of Atak's doubts, she felt sure of the coming battle even if Velocatus made no contribution. The Belgies were as fierce fighters as Linus' Silures and would make their presence felt once she had cracked open the Rummy shell with her chariots. The damage done at Verulam had not been as bad as she had first feared. A hundred and fifty chariots had survived and horses for them had been rounded up to replace the ones that had been killed. Atak might feel glum and suspicious but she had a duty to keep her troops inspired and in fighting mettle. She could not let her optimism wane.

Several times in the past few days they had seen Rummy scouts so it was clear that Paulinus knew where they were, and from her own scouts' reports she knew he could not be far ahead. Her scouts told her that Paulinus had ridden to London to assess the damage and, alarmed by the scale of the insurrection and slaughter, had been in too big a hurry to get back to his legions on their way down from Mona to do more than he had done. Scouts sent by Iorwerth also told her Catus had escaped the sacking of London and had fled to Gaul, news that sent her once again into a blinding red rage that had been hard to overcome.

She stepped down from her chariot as Velocatus dismounted, and with Brennius, Linus and Salog at her side held out a hand to greet him. To her surprise he went down on one knee and kissed her hand. "I bring greetings from my wife, Queen Cartimandua," he said, "to the Arviragus of Britain. She told me to obey your commands as if you were she herself."

So they are still married she thought as she raised him up. "Then my cousin is a true friend and queen of Britain," she said. "We have quarreled in the past but now we are united against Rome. Long may our unity last."

"And me?" said Velocatus, his grin crafty. "Am I true friend and king too? There was a time you would not have called me king. Am I now to be called such by you?"

"Serve Britain well in this coming battle," she said, "and I will call you king before Kings and Council."

"You hear that?" said Velocatus, turning to his companions. Her eyes had been drawn to one of Velocatus' kings as they talked. He looked familiar but she couldn't recall where she had seen him before. Suddenly, Brennius jumped as if he too had recognized the man. "By the holy sword of Eremon himself," said Brennius, "dashed into two hundred pieces as it was and buried as it is in the planks of the chariots that will send the Rummies running like a gaggle of geese with their throats cut and their tails on fire, tis the gruesome Grud himself. I thought you long since drowned in the fight that all have proclaimed the greatest fight that ever was, standing up to our necks as we were in six feet of the rushingest water that ever flooded a ford, and I the absolute victor and you the utterly vanquished."

"I were not vanquished," said Grud. He stood before Brennius but would not look him in the eye. "I were thrown off my stroke by your crossed eyes that, by Duw, are crosstier now than they were then. If it had not been for them eyes it would have been a fair fight and you'd be dead."

"We found him four miles down stream," said Velocatus, beaming proudly. "Half drownded but still holding his sword."

"Dead!" roared Brennius. He seized a handful of Grud's mail armor. "It would take more than a decrepit bandy legged weasel faced flea brained excuse for a man such as you to be the death of me, and me ten times the man you ever were in the prime of your misbegotten youth. Give us swords and find us a ford and we'll have at it again and this time you shall not sneak away under water to escape my trusty blade."

For answer, Grud joined his hands together in a double fist and brought them crashing down on Brennius' head, felling him to the ground. The men around them growled and moved forward. "Enough," said Boudicca, pushing Grud away. "I am glad you did not die, but we are here to fight Rummies, not each other."

"It were not a fair fight," said Velocatus. "I said that before and I will say it again. Twere not a fair fight, him with crossed eyes and all. No man can look him in the eye and aim straight."

She scowled. "King Brennius leads the chariots," she said. "If his eyes throw the Rummies off their aim then I will ever thank the good God who crossed them for us. Now, what word have you of Paulinus?" she said, as Linus helped the dazed Brennius to his feet.

"He's across the river," said Atak. She got into the chariot with him and looked where he pointed. Not much more than a mile away she could see a fort on a rise above the river, and through the scrub and trees that dotted the ravine scarred landscape she saw the telltale glint of armor stretching in a line to her left. Here and there clusters of battle standards fluttered like deadly flowers among the undergrowth. The Rummies had the advantage of height. Behind them rose forested foothills and ravines protected each flank. Paulinus had picked a good position.

"Aye," said Velocatus, putting a hand on the side of the chariot. "He's been there all morning waiting for us."

"Why didn't he attack you?" said Atak.

Velocatus shrugged. "He picked himself a good spot. We can't flank him and he knows we have to attack him."

"And that we shall," said Boudicca, "but first we must get him down here. We cannot race our chariots up there." She turned to Velocatus. "King Velocatus," she said, and he smiled as she gave him his title, "I would have you and Linus and Salog join Lord Atak and me. We will go down to the river and take a closer look."

Accompanied by fifty guards, she rode along the east bank of the river to size up the Roman disposition. The river was not a major obstacle and could easily be forded, but there were some marshy areas that would have to be avoided. As they approached the Romans' left flank, the river curved sharply in toward the fort and she found herself less than half a mile from the serried ranks of legionaries. Between the legionaries and the fort, an ala of cavalry waited, and she had seen an ala on the other end. The familiar chill ran down her back as she stared at the solid lines of Romans above her, staring impassively ahead as if they were one merciless mass of metal. Could that line be broken? This was the last test. Pass it and the Rummies are done for. By Duw, we must win this day. "What are the numbers, Atak?" she asked.

"Eight thousand infantry," said Atak. "The Fourteenth's in the center, auxiliaries on their left, what's left of the Twentieth's on their right. Must be two thousand auxiliaries and a thousand horse."

"Then we outnumber them four to one."

"Aye," said Velocatus, "but our men will be tired running up that hill dodging javelins."

"Then we must get the Rummies to come down."

"How?"

"We will put our army across the river out of javelin range while we use the ballistae we got from the Ninth against them. They'll fire back but at some point they'll have to come after us if only to get within javelin range."

"We'll need archers and lancers on each flank," said Atak.

She nodded. "When they charge we'll retreat back across the river. King Velocatus will stay well back with the chariots on his left so they have a good run to get up to speed, and we'll move to their left as we retreat. When there's enough room between the river and the Rummies, Brennius and I will take the chariots against the center and break it open. My chariots will fold the Rummies' right and Brennius their left. After the first breakthrough the chariots will smash up the Rummies as long as they can. My foot soldiers will follow the chariots at the run and get inside the Rummies. The Silurian chariots will pick off pieces of the legions as they're broken off. King Velocatus will act as reserve and attack where the Rummies are weakest."

"By Duw," said Velocatus, rubbing his hands together in glee. "I cannot wait to send my men in through the hole you'll smash with those chariots."

"We'll have to move fast," said Linus. "But the Ninth fell and so will these. You must harangue our troops," he said to Boudicca. "No-one can fire them up as do you."

"I will," she said, her own blood rising at the thought of the Rummies defeated. When they had reached their own troops and Velocatus and his officers had ridden off to form up his army behind Boudicca's, Atak gripped her arm. "What is it?" she snapped, eager to get her own army arrayed.

Atak's face was dark. "I don't like Velocatus behind us," he said.

"Then why didn't you say so in the chariot?"

"What could I say in front of him? I don't like him behind us, I don't trust him as a reserve and I don't like that shiny armor. It identifies him to the Rummies."

"You are saying he is a traitor?"

"I'm saying I don't trust him."

She was so angry she stamped her foot and hissed so that he recoiled from her. "I don't trust the low born son of a bitch either," she shouted. "Nor do I trust that scheming wife of his. But in God's name, what would you have me do? I have put our own troops in front because I can rely on them to attack. If that man fails us we are still over two to one and must defeat Paulinus without him. Whatever happens this day, my great gloomy advisor, we must prevail or you and I and half of Britain will be dead. Now cease your carping and fight as you have never fought before. Turn your gloom into resolve and convey it to these my captains or get off this field and never enter my presence again. What will it be? Will you fight or leave?"

Atak fell on his knees before her and grasped her hands, tears flowing down his cheeks into his beard. "I will say no more," he said. "I will die or live with you."

"Then get on your feet," she said, still furious, "and help me prepare this army."

Velocatus' army was drawn up a mile from the river, the chariots on his left as Boudicca had specified and the baggage carts of both armies behind him. The baggage carts should not have been brought so close to the action but she was not about to quibble. Velocatus himself was prancing up and down before his army with his captains.

She had worked with Brennius and his knights to find the best place for the chariots' run and it seemed clear to all what the tactics would be once the Roman line was broken. The chariots had been divided into two columns, one of which she would lead herself once her foot soldiers had lured the Rummies across the river. Moved by a sudden inspiration she had taken two of the women knights, Tayled and Cwentryth, into her own chariot and made them let down their hair as she had done to make clear their sex. A wide gap separated Velocatus' army from hers, and he was to maintain the same distance as her army moved forward across the river, stopping when she signaled the starting place of the chariot run.

She rode between the two armies with her guards and Pendragon and saw Atak and his Germans with the six ballista carts ensconced in the middle of her own ranks of soldiers. Linus was on the left with the battle standards of the Silures, Ordoes and Demetes, and Salog on the right with the Belgie and Duroc standards. Her heart thrilled at the sight. At the end of this day there would be Roman battle flags and aquilas to nail to the trees as trophies of British prowess. She waved as she rode around to the front rank and Atak waved back, his face still as gloomy as ever. Poor Atak, she thought. I must make it up to him after the fight. But surely he must see I have to work with the tools at hand even if some be rotten. Would he have had me send Velocatus off the field and risk forever alienating the Brigantes? She glanced up at the Rummies standing so securely in their impregnable position. She could trust Atak to do his best to lure the Rummies down but would his ballistae be enough? Would Paulinus rise to the bait? What else could be done?

She stopped in front of her army and looked at the expectant faces, wondering how far her voice would reach across a multitude such as this. "Before we begin this battle," she roared, moved by a sudden inspiration. "This battle that will forever free Britain from the Roman yoke, I want every man in the two front ranks to yield his place to a woman."

There was a shuffling and grumbling but the exchange began and soon the two front ranks were comprised only of women. "Let your hair fly free," she shouted, "as mine flies free." The women unfastened the bands that held their hair above their heads and laughed nervously as they shook it free. Only royal women could wear hair as long as her own but, by God, the womens' hair was long enough to identify their sex, infuriate the Rummies and get them off that hill.

"Let the men of Britain," she said, "as well as our adversaries, look well upon those who lead the way to battle. They are women, and women as all well know are weaker far than men. But weaker though they are in physical strength and prowess yet are they as strong in purpose and in courage. The Rummies will quail before their onslaught because British women will not yield their children and their children's children to be slaves to animals such as those who wait cowering on yonder hill. No more will they yield their bodies to be raped and scourged, nor will they tolerate the further desecration of all that we hold dear as Britons. Are the men on this field content to let their women outdo them in combat? Or will they show the teeth of Britain to this foul invader? Will they savage him as the lion savages the jackal? Will we prevail?"

A deafening shout went up from those before her, and the terrible din of swords beaten against shields, of trumpets blaring and metal tongues clacking. "Then men and women of Britain do your duty," she shouted. "Conquer or die." She stirred her horses into motion and circled back to her chariots, hair flying in the wind, as the army marched forward. Surveying the Roman lines as she rode, she caught a glimpse of Roman officers standing before their men. So Paulinus too was haranguing his troops. She felt the first raindrops wet her forehead and glared at the sky. "Later," she growled. "When this is over."

By the time she reached the head of her chariots Velocatus' army had moved forward to maintain distance between itself and the soldiers now crossing the river. As she waved to Brennius to bring the two chariot columns level, she saw Velocatus was moving too quickly, narrowing the gap that would give her chariots maneuvering room. In the rear of his army she saw the baggage carts moving forward with him and sent a scout to tell him to keep the same pace as the chariots and send back the carts.

Velocatus waved when the scout gave him the message and his army slowed a little, but the baggage carts still rolled forward.

"What's the matter with the man?" she snapped to Cwentryth, but her attention was drawn to the hill beyond the river. Her army had stopped out of javelin range, but before Atak's ballistae could fire their iron bolts the Romans suddenly surged forward and came down toward the Britons almost at a run, their wall of shields forming a great wedge. Her army turned to retreat, but the ranks of women in the forefront had enraged the Romans and they did not escape the javelins, sighing through the air on their mission of death. She gritted her teeth as her warriors broke and ran for the river, following the standards that led them to Boudicca's left. Order was lost in the mad scramble for safety, but the chaos had been foreseen and the soldiers instructed. Once across the river and out of her way the Britons would reassemble around their standards while she and Brennius waited for the Rummies to cross.

She reached the point they had decided upon and signaled a halt. Velocatus' men also halted and she could feel the tenseness behind her grow to the breaking point as the chariots waited for the Romans to get across the river. All behind her became deathly quiet as if her army had become one with the elements and a great human as well as aerial storm were suddenly about to unleash itself in a fury of lightning and thunder. It must be sinking into the minds of all how important was this battle. This was life or death for Britain.

She looked around to encourage her charioteers and was

suddenly filled with foreboding when she saw Velocatus' men spreading out behind, dividing themselves from her with the line of unwieldy baggage carts. Had Atak been right? Was Velocatus about to run from the field? If not, why was he hemming her in like that? She tried to see him among his army, but his bright armor was no longer in sight. Grimly, she sent a scout to order Velocatus to disperse the wagons and gather his men as they had agreed then turned her attention back to the Romans, now across the river and advancing toward her reforming army.

Some of the chariots edged forward and she impatiently waved them back. They must wait until there was maneuvering room behind the Rummies. At last it seemed right and she raised her sword to bring it down with a roar of pent up anger. Yells of rage filled the air as the two columns of heavy chariots rumbled forward, gaining speed until the screams of warriors were joined by the shriek of whirling blades. Her eyes narrowed to slits as she focused on the white faces getting ever larger as she bore down. Barely aware of the cloud of javelins falling around her, hitting her chariot and knocking Tayled from it in a spray of blood, she screamed at the top of her voice. "Break, you Rummy bastards, break." A light rain began to fall, its drops exploding against her face as she rushed through them.

The line before her flattened like wheat before a gale and she felt her chariot jolt and shudder as the blades dug into stomachs and groins, and the wheels chattered over broken bodies. "Keep the speed up," she yelled, knowing that no-one but herself could hear, whipping her horses into a frenzy that matched her own. Vaguely wondering why the myriad weapons thrown or swung at her had not struck, she smashed the line of Rummies again. Broken chariots and dead horses were everywhere, but so were the mounting piles of Roman bodies. When the bloody chariot, its wheels broken by its own blades and its horses dying from many sword thrusts, tipped over on its side throwing her heavily on the ground, knights of her guard surrounded her, hacking away with abandon at the Rummies.

Quickly on her feet and sword in hand she urged her guard forward at a knot of Rummies fighting back to back. Their line smashed, their javelins expended, their wall of shields broken, they were fair game for British swords. But the heavily armored Rummies were not yet beaten. Broken up as they were they still exerted pressure, pushing or being pushed backwards and forwards across the field as one side or the other gained predominance. The slaughter had reached equilibrium. If Velocatus attacked the center the battle would be won, but there was no sign of Velocatus' men. Where were they? A large body with a blood-covered face struggled to join her. It was Atak. "Where is Velocatus?" she shouted.

"He's still behind us," said Atak.

"Get us to him," she said. As she struggled she could feel the pressure around her increase. The Britons were being forced against the Rummies, losing their ability to swing their weapons against the vicious shields and short stabbing swords advancing on them. Through the furious melee of battle she saw the reason for the pressure: an advancing wall of baggage carts, Velocatus' army behind it, a blurred Brigante figure on top of a cart aiming a ballista bolt toward her. With a scream of rage she turned as Atak grabbed her arm, and did not feel the blow that struck her down and sent her hurtling into darkness.

Chapter 17

After the Battle

The rain fell in a steady drenching downpour. Sore and bleeding, Atak sat with his back to a tree, an equally bloody Linus at his side. Remorse and hatred filled his heart: remorse because he had not been able to convince Boudicca that Velocatus planned treachery, and hatred for the cowardly Brigante who had fired the ballista bolt that struck Boudicca down. Seeing their queen fall under such a lethal blow, the British army had disintegrated. He had seen the ballista swiveling on the baggage cart and had not been able to pull her out of the way. If it took years, he would find the man who fired that ballista and tear him apart with his bare hands.

Around them in the forest were scattered the few knights left of Boudicca's guard, keeping watch over their stricken queen. A makeshift tent had been rigged to protect Boudicca while the Druid Vallo tended her wound. Down below, Atak knew, the Roman cavalry was mopping up what was left of the British army, grinning with delight as they ran the fleeing men and women down, spearing them with their lances. Caradawg had been with the baggage carts and by now must be dead. Atak's eyes filled with tears at the thought. Before long, the Roman infantry would be combing the fields and forests looking for Boudicca. Velocatus would help them so he and Cartimandua could gloat over her capture and degradation. "By Duw," he said, clenching his fists, "we had the battle won but for Velocatus. Those chariots broke the Rummies."

"Boudicca must be got out of here," said Linus. "But by Gorry, when she is out, though I am a Christian, I shall kill Velocatus."

Atak nodded, fists still clenched. If Boudicca were found she would be dragged off to Rome to be exhibited, tortured and killed. When night fell, he and Linus and the guards would find horses and take her to Caer Leon where Elsa could heal her. He shook his head in dismay, recalling the terrible wound in Boudicca's back. It would take all that Elsa could wring out of her God to put Boudicca back together.

A distraught Vallo came out from under the tent. "She wants you," he said to Atak, then stumbled over to sit by Linus.

Atak stooped under the cover and knelt by the muddy blanket on which Boudicca lay. Unable to help himself, he burst into tears and bowed his head at the sight of her pale pain-wracked face. The fiery red hair, once so soft and lustrous, was muddied and disheveled. The eyes that had sparkled like ice blue diamonds were clouded and sunk deep within a skull that seemed barely wrapped in transparent bloodless skin. Weakly, she lifted a hand and laid it on his knee.

"You must not weep for me," she said.

He lifted her hand and kissed it.

"I should have listened to you and not put Velocatus to our rear."

"He will die for his treachery."

She smiled feebly. "Nay, it is Cartimandua who has sold Britain."

"Then she too will die."

She shook her head so slightly he could barely detect the movement. "Vallo tells me it was not a death blow but I shall be forever a useless cripple. That is worse than death."

His tears came afresh. "We will get you to Elsa," he said.

"She will heal you."

She looked at him with some of the old fire. "I am past Elsa's aid," she said. "And I little deserve it. I cannot linger here to have the Rummies capture and mock me. Vallo has left me poison. You must give it to me."

He saw the small earthen cup by her shoulder and shuddered as horror flooded his being. "No," he said. "Do not ask that."

He could feel the frail hand within his move, as if she were trying to shake it at him as she had so often in the past. "I am not afraid of death," she said. "You have always been my right arm and you must be so once more. Now hear me." She took a deep breath and gasped with the pain it must have caused her. "You will tell Venutius I died loving him as his true wife and that my last thoughts were of him and Coilus."

"I will."

"He must build more of Ingenius' chariots."

Atak put her hand to his lips again. "Those chariots defeated the Rummies," he said. "If Velocatus had not betrayed us the Rummies would be dead by now. You were truly the victor."

She sighed dreamily. "They called me Victoria but my misjudgment let them down."

"You did not misjudge," said Atak, almost shouting. "You were betrayed."

"Enough," she said. "Charge my brother Marius and his Dedreth to bring up Coilus as a true and proper king, for Britain will need such in the years to come. Have him remember his mother as one whom, though she saw him rarely, loved him well. Tell him of the chariots and how they must be used."

Atak nodded, unable to speak.

"And last of all, my dear dear friend, you must not let the Rummies desecrate my body and hold it up to scorn. I would have you burn it and put the ashes with my father's and grandfather's in the old palace grave at Gosbecks. Do you promise to do that for me?"

"I do," said Atak. He kissed her hand, still blinded by his

tears. If only Elsa were here. She would stop this ebbing tide and bring back the life and glory and spirit that had been Boudicca's so short a time ago.

"Now you must do your last task for me," she said. "Support me while I drink. It is a painless potion."

"I cannot," he wailed.

"You must and shall. I would die by the hand of one I love. You would not have me die by a traitor's hand."

Blindly, he lifted her until she was able to rest against his knees. He winced at the groan of pain that escaped her.

"The cup," she gasped. "The cup."

He held it unsteadily to her lips and she quickly drained it. He threw it from him with a cry of anguish then kissed her forehead.

"I have always loved thee, dear Atak," she said, as he laid her gently down and clasped her hands between his. "Thy counsel has always been that of true friend."

"And I have always loved thee."

She lay still, her hands in his and her breasts barely moving as she breathed, while he screamed inwardly, envisioning the poison doing its deadly work within that loved body. He thought she had gone. Then she opened her eyes briefly and he saw through his tears that they were unfocused. "Goneril is coming," she whispered. "And Ingenius is with her. Tell Elsa that I died loving her Christ."

Atak stumbled out into the relentless rain and squatted under a tree. Linus and Vallo would not look at him. It would soon be dark enough to find horses. The world of the forest seemed to recede from him as he nursed his agony, and all he could see was Boudicca at seventeen, a bronze naked goddess sitting in a boat stripped of her clothes by the Romans who had tried to rape her, the fires of Boulogne bathing her in lurid light as she raised her fists to the heavens and swore eternal enmity against Rome. As she had sworn, they had trembled at her name. Treachery might have taken away her last victory but it could not take away her name. It would be forever Victoria.

It was almost dark when approaching footsteps roused him. He shook off the stupor and stood, brushing the rain from his beard and face. Coming toward him through the trees was a small dark figure, a soldier at his side.

"They thought I was a Rummy's kid," said the figure.

Atak fell on his knees to clutch the boy to him. "Caradawg," he said. Life was not yet over.

"It's time to go," said Linus.

Afterword

There is very little documented history to support this novel and its predecessor *Young Boudicca*, but what there is, in terms of events recorded by Tacitus and Dio Cassius, is not violated. All we know for sure about Boudicca is that in 60-61 a.d., she was the Queen of Iceni, wife to King Prasutagus; that her nation was despoiled upon the death of Prasutagus, her daughters raped and she herself flogged. She gathered together a vast army, defeated the 9th legion, burned Colchester, London and St Albans, met Paulinus and his legions at a place assumed to be Mancetter, was defeated and died.

There is no recorded connection between Boudicca and King Caratacus or between she and Venutius. All we know about Venutius is that he was the on-again off-again husband of Cartimandua, fought with Vellocatus, his man at arms, for her favors and caused a couple of civil wars. Cartimandua comes down to us as a devious and sexy Queen who betrayed Caratacus and was able to inspire the Romans to provide help whenever she needed it. Only a brief glimpse of her has been recorded in the years after Boudicca's last battle: still instigating war between Venutius and Vellocatus, still embroiling the Roman army in her affairs and ultimately losing her kingdoms. Scapula and Veranius both are recorded as dying from mysteriously unexplained causes while governing Britain.

The strange tonsures adopted by the early British Christian priests were modeled on Paul's haircut (as, unfortunately, was that of Simon Magus, the arch heretic) and caused much consternation among Roman priests (whose tonsures were modeled on Peter's circular bald spot) when they arrived in Britain to convert the British. From such sparse ingredients has *Boudicca and the Women at War* been constructed.

According to Tacitus, Boudicca's revolt cost the Romans seventy thousand casualties among their citizens and allies. After the battle, Tacitus reports that two thousand legionaries, eight cohorts (almost five thousand) of auxiliaries and a thousand cavalry were sent to Britain from Germany to make up the Roman losses.

Far from being subdued by the battle at Mancetter (called by the Romans Manduessedum, the field of chariots) the Britons fought on until Rome recognized that the rapacious policies of Catus and Paulinus would never bring peace with such a 'high-spirited' nation. Paulinus was recalled and a new governor, Petronius Turpilianus, was sent over to temporarily stop the war through a policy castigated by Tacitus as 'tame inaction veiled under the honorable name of peace.'

Notes

1 A *lingua franca* common to countries bordering the Mediterranean
2 Chief
3 A nation including most of today's Lancashire and Yorkshire.
4 Maiden Castle in Dorset
5 Near St Albans
6 Doctor
7 London
8 Anglesey
9 Nobility
10 White tower by the Thames, site of the Tower of London
11 taboo
12 A contemporary of Caratacus'
13 Wroxeter
14 Leicester
15 Colchester
16 Pudens and Claudia became Christians and are mentioned in 2Timothy 4:21
17 Palestine, the Holy Land
18 A Harbor in the Bay of Penzance, Cornwall
19 The Zacchaeus of Luke 19
20 Gloucester
21 Mount St Michaels in the Bay of Penzance.
22 Wroxeter
23 Gloucester

24 Tasburgh
25 Midsummer Festival at which trial marriages often commenced, a couple promising to live together for one year and one day and then to marry or part.
26 An armored umbrella formed by shields held above the legionaries' heads.
27 A lake on Mona (Isle of Anglesey)

Bibliography

Aries & Duby Gen Ed., Philippe & Georges, *A History of Private Life Vol I,* Belknap–Harvard University Press, 1987

Arnold, Eberhard, *The Early Christians,* Baker Book House, 1979

Barrow, R. H., *The Romans,* Penguin Books, 1965

Bede, *History of the English Church and People,* Penguin Classics, 1978

Blair, Peter Hunter, *Roman Britain and Early England,* W. W. Norton & Co, 1963

Branigan, Keith, *The Catuvellauni,* Alan Sutton, 1987

Brown & Meier, Raymond E & John P, *Antioch & Rome,* Geoffrey Chapman, 1983

Caesar, Julius, *Gallic War, III & IV,* Black's Readers Service Co, 1957

Capper, D. P., *Moat Defensive* (Isle of Thanet & the Wantsume), Arthur Barker Ltd, No date.

Carr-Gomm, Philip, *The Druid Tradition,* Element Books Ltd, 1991

Couch & Geer, Herbert N & Russel M, *Classical Civilization— Rome,* Prentice Hall, 1952

Cowell, F. R., *Life in Ancient Rome,* Putnam Perigree, 1980

Daniel-Rops, Henri, *Daily Life in the time of Jesus,* Hawthorn Books Inc, 1962

Detsicas, Alec, *The Cantiaci,* Alan Sutton, 1987

Dio, Cassius, *Roman History: Books LVI-LXX,* William Heinemann Ltd, 1982

Dobson M. A., Rev C. C., *Did Our Lord visit Britain?* Covenant Publishing Co. Ltd, 1936

Elder, Isabel Hill, *Celt, Druid and Culdee*, Covenant Publishing Co. Ltd, 1947

Elder, Isabel Hill, *Joseph of Arimathea*, Spectator, Bangor, no date

Ellis, Peter Beresford, *The Celtic Empire*, Constable, 1991

Eusebius, Schaff & Wace Ed., *Church History*, Wm. B. Erdmans Pub Co., 1982

Ferrill, Arthur, *Fall of the Roman Empire—Military Explanation*, Thames & Hudson, 1988

Franklin Ed., Fay, *History's Timeline*, Ward Lock Ltd, 1981

Frend, W. H. C., *Martyrdom & Persecution in Early Church*, Baker Book House, 1981

Frere, Sheppard, *Britannia A History of Rome in Britain*, Sphere Books Cardinal Ed, 1974

Gordon, E. O., *Prehistoric London*, Covenant Publishing Co. Ltd, 1946

Grant, Michael, *Jews in the Roman World*, Dorset Press, 1984

Hadas Ed., Moses, *A History of Rome*, Doubleday Anchor, 1956

Hall & Merrifield, Jenny & Ralph, *Roman London*, HMSO Books, 1986

Hubert, Henri, *Greatness & Decline of the Celts*, Constable, London, 1987

Johnson, Paul, *A History of Christianity*, Atheneum, New York, 1977

Jowett, George F., *The Drama of the Lost Disciples*, Covenant Publishing Co. Ltd, 1966

Kightly & Cyprian, Charles & Michael, *Travellers' Guide to Royal Roads*, Routledge & Kegan Paul, 1985

Klingaman, William K., *The First Century*, Harper Perennial, 1990

Landels, J. G., *Engineering in the Ancient World*, University of California Press, 1978

Lewis, Rev Lionel Smithett, *Joseph of Arimathea at Glastonbury*, James Clarke & Co Ltd, 1964

Markale, Jean, *Women of the Celts*, Inner Traditions, 1986
Matthews, Caitlin, *The Celtic Tradition*, Element Books Ltd, 1989
Meeks, Wayne A., *The First Urban Christians*, Yale University Press, 1983
Piggott, Stuart, *The Druids*, Thames & Hudson, 1985
Ross, Anne, *The Pagan Celts*, Barnes & Noble, 1986
Richmond, I. A., *Roman Britain*, Penguin Books, 1986
Simkins & Embleton, Michael & Ron, *Roman Army: Caesar to Trajan*, Osprey, 1987
Suetonius, *The Twelve Caesars*, Penguin Classics, 1982
Taylor, John W., *The Coming of the Saints*, Covenant Publishing Co. Ltd, 1969
Tacitus, P. Cornelius, *The Agricola & The Germania*, Penguin Classics, 1986
Tacitus, P. Cornelius, *The Annals Books XI—XIV*, Encyclopaedia Britannica, 1952
Tacitus, P. Cornelius, *The Histories Book III*, Encyclopaedia Britannica, 1952
Wardman, Alan, *Religion and Statecraft among the Romans*, Johns Hopkins University Press, 1982
Watkins, Alfred, *The Old Straight Track* (Ancient British Roads), Garnstone Press, 1975
Webster, Graham, *Roman Conquest of Britain*, B. T. Batsford Ltd, 1965
Webster, Graham, *Roman Invasion of Britain*, B. T. Batsford Ltd, 1980
Webster, Graham, *Boudica*, B. T. Batsford Ltd, 1978
Webster, Graham, *Rome against Caratacus*, Dorset Press, 1981
Webster, Graham, *Celtic Religion in Roman Britain*, Barnes & Noble Books, 1986
Wilcox & McBride, Peter & Angus, *Rome's Enemies: Gallic & British Celts*, Osprey, 1987
Wilken, Robert L., *The Christians as the Romans saw them*, Yale University Press, 1984

Wood, Michael, *In Search of the Dark Ages,* Facts on File Publications, 1987

Maps

Gilbert, Martin, *Atlas of British History*, Dorset Press, 1975
Tabula Imperii Romani: Condate-Gleuum-Londinium-Lutetia, Oxford University Press, 1983
Tabula Imperii Romani: Britannia Septentrionalis, Oxford University Press, 1987

Printed in the United Kingdom
by Lightning Source UK Ltd.
105954UKS00001B/42